The Fair Fight

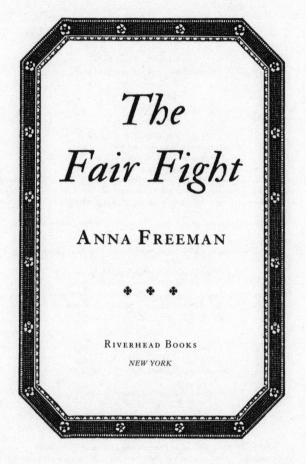

The Fair Fight

ANNA FREEMAN

* * *

RIVERHEAD BOOKS

NEW YORK

Riverhead Books
An imprint of Penguin Random House LLC
375 Hudson Street
New York, New York 10014

The Library of Congress has catalogued the Riverhead hardcover edition as follows:

Freeman, Anna.
The fair fight : a novel / Anna Freeman.—First American edition.
p.   cm.
Originally published: London: Weidenfeld & Nicolson, 2014.
ISBN 978-1-59463-329-4
1. Women boxers—Fiction.   2. Bristol (England)—History—18th century—Fiction.
3. England—Social life and customs—18th century—Fiction.   I. Title.
PR6106.R43F35   2015   2014019046
823'.92—dc23

First Riverhead hardcover edition: April 2015
First Riverhead trade paperback edition: April 2016
Riverhead trade paperback ISBN: 978-1-59463-408-6

Printed in the United States of America
1   3   5   7   9   10   8   6   4   2

Book design by Gretchen Achilles

For Caroline,
and for brave women everywhere

PART I

Ruth

❖ ❖ ❖

Chapter I

❖ ❖ ❖

Some folks call the prize-ring a nursery for vice. Boxing is talked against by all the magistrates and held up as unlawful and wild, even sometimes called unchristian. As I see it, those pious old smatchets are right, but what of it? Prize-fighting is all those things, but more, it's beautiful. The sight of two people—for it's not only men, you know, who take the ring—who've built their skills and their bodies, struggling together with nothing between them, no ball or stick, but only desperate force and the will to live—why, there's the root of all mankind, the stuff of our lives played out. Till you've seen one pug, bare chest steaming in the frosty air, half blinded by his own blood, drop the other to his knees on the frozen turf and turn to roar to the sky, well, if you ain't seen it, you can't know. It brings you to the base of yourself; just the sight brings a bellow to the throat. Prize-fighting is named "the noble sport" by the fancy crowding the ringside, and so it seems to me. Nothing much else in my life has been noble.

I'd like to say that my beginnings were humble, but they weren't beginnings, because I never really left them but for a short while. I was born in a narrow house we called the convent, and I came into the world as fighting and blood-soaked as I mean to leave it, upon a big oaken bed that had carried the weight of a regiment of cullies. Ma used to say I might've had twenty daddies. She meant, by the look of me: my jaw too large, my eyes too small, my nose thin and hooked as a gypsy's. I'd teeth to spare, crowding my chops and hiding one behind the other, too bashful to line up straight. I was a puzzle made of the plainest parts of those twenty daddies, the parts they left behind and went on to give handsome children to their lady wives.

Ma never would answer questions, but she couldn't stop the misses' talking. The story went that when she was young, a fine gent bought the house to set her up as his mistress. He grew tired of her, as cullies do, and had given the place over to her as a means of saying sorry. Dora always thought that the cully who flit was our daddy, but as we grew up and grew so different, it was plain that whichever man had a hand in making Dora, he wasn't likely the same cull who made me. It didn't much signify in a house like ours. In our house a girl's worth could be counted out in pounds, shillings, and pence, and that was all the worth that mattered.

A babe, of course, never can be much counted that way, and as infants Dora and I had always to make ourselves useful or else stay out of sight. It's the same choice children are given the world over: be of service or be gone. We were there to scrub the flags and empty the pots, we were there to fetch the callers to the misses or, if some sailor became more trouble than he'd paid to be, we were there to fetch the bullies to see the cully out. The misses all held the same view of keeping house, however they lived before they came there; they'd do what they must to keep their own fires lit and whatever Ma stirred herself to bid them in the way of housework, and never be fashed to lift a finger more. All the rest fell to Dora and me.

Every so often there'd come a new miss with a desperate look about her, lugging an infant that screamed and spat up into its blanket. Ma was fond of pink-cheeked wretched misses; she'd always take a ruined girl over a hard-faced strumper. Then Dora and I would have a babber to drag about like a doll, or carry up to the garret, if it wouldn't hush. We never could keep any of those infants long enough to love them—we'd come down one day and it'd be gone and none of us would ask where it'd been whipped off to. Sometimes the miss it'd belonged to took it hard and wept. Ma never minded weeping in the kitchen, but if a molly couldn't smile for the cullies she'd be turned out quick as blinking. She might sit at breakfast bawling as though she were the infant herself, if she could dry her eyes and flutter them when once she stepped foot outside the kitchen. I remember a miss who never could stop weeping, and was put out upon her arse for it. I recall standing in the hall, my hands twisting in my apron, as she was hustled from the door, the bully's big hand between her shoulder-blades. I was only five or six, I should think. Her thin back was aquiver with tears, in only the same poor dress she'd come in, for of course Ma kept back the silks. A miss could get along all right if she'd silks of her own, so it was spite as well as greed that drove Ma's hand. I went to the parlour window and watched her struggle down the road with her box, dragging it by one handle and rucking up a wake in the dirt of the street like a skiff at low tide. I pressed my face right up to the glass, to see her as long as I could. I couldn't say what it was about that particular miss that caught my fancy, but I'd think of her sometimes, after that; I liked to imagine that when she'd turned the corner she'd found her baby waiting there and would be mother to it again. Later, when I grew up a little and had a grasp of the trade, I wondered at Ma keeping Dora and me. She kept us and never did hire us out to the cullies whose tastes ran to kiddies, though she threatened to often enough. I suppose, in a woman like our ma, that passed for love.

The convent was so narrow that it looked to have been built in an alley, crushed up against the houses on either side like a drunken crone held up by two fat fellows. Ours was the oldest house on the lane, the houses that had once stood on either side having been burned down, or torn down to make room for the new ones. Because the house couldn't spread out, it reached up; there were five floors, if you counted the cellar, and all the rooms were full, though the bodies in them changed about. My whole life, we never had a spare room for more than a day.

In our house we went to bed when the whole world was rising. I'd lie there and listen to the milkmaid shouting in the lane, and the women calling to those below to look out, as they emptied their pots. I'd fall asleep with the sun pinking the dark behind my eyes. I always thought it the best way to live; in daylight the world was merry and safe. At night it was always better to be up and ready. I'd no choice in it, so it was well that I thought it so fine—Ma would never have stomached me creeping about the house in the daylight, while all the house was abed.

Sleeping all day as we did, we took our breakfast when other folks had dinner, at three or four o'clock. The kitchen table had been built just where it was and took up near the whole room; you'd have had to chop it to firewood to get it out of the door. We sat around it, pressed together on the benches, the misses in their silks, all bare arms and bosoms, and Dora and I always pushed to the ends of the bench, with half our arses hanging off. The bullies would put heavy bars across the front door and come to sit with us, though sometimes they stood, the room being so full. There were chairs at the head and the foot, and the bullies never did sit in them, as the men might expect to in any usual house. Ma sat always at the head of the table. The other chair was for whichever girl she saw fit to reward, whether it be a miss who'd taken good earnings the night before or a newcomer who was proving difficult to turn and so needed softening.

When Dora and I weren't making ourselves useful we'd be huddled in the garret in the bed we shared, or else out upon the street, teasing the pigs; there were always pigs upon our street, let out and brought back in at night. Sometimes we'd be sent to the tavern around the corner, on Frog Lane, which hired out rooms to misses, to fetch home one of the girls. Our mollies were put two to a room at the convent, so one or other of them was always using the rooms at The Hatchet Inn. I preferred that errand over any other. I liked the smells: ale, straw, and smoke. The folks there knew my name and called out, "How d'you fare, little Ruth?" and best of all was the yard, with its roped stage, upon which there had been so many bouts between pugs, or cocks, or dogs, that the boards were patched black with old blood. I always lingered as long as I dared when Ma sent me there.

If you were a caller at the convent on a usual day, you'd think it as fine as any swell's place, with velvet hangings and sconces for candles upon the walls. The front stairs were always lit and the parlour, where the cullies sat, had a brocaded settee and a table with curved legs that looked ready to drop a curtsey. The parlour always had about it an air of waiting: all those breaths of restless old goats, waiting for a miss to have done with his crony and come to fetch him for his turn. None of the family ever would sit in that room, though it was done out so nice. If no sailor was waiting there, and if I thought no one would miss me, I sometimes went in to look at the pictures upon the walls. One was a small painting of a little girl, all done up in mourning dress, her face very serious and drear. The other was a fine picture of trees upon an autumn lane, made all from feathers. Ma had taken them from some likely lad by way of payment. I had a special fancy for the painting of the girl. I'd pose before the glass and with my hands clasped under my chin, as she did. I never could make my eyes like hers, no matter how I turned my head. Her eyes were sweet and mournful; mine were a pig's, too small for my face. Sometimes, I used to imagine the little girl stepping from her frame and strolling off down the autumn lane, perhaps to some place where she needn't look so sad.

The mollies' rooms were hung with as much finery as Ma could arrange, all feathers and cushions and draperies. All of this was for the sake of the cullies—the minute you went up past the first landing or into the kitchen, why, the walls were bare lime-wash and the furnishings as plain as my mug. Ma charged a good rate, three or four shillings a time, so we were never short of misses willing to work. The cullies paid it, because Ma never would stand to see a cull robbed at the convent. There were houses like ours where a fellow had to keep an eye on his coat and boots, never mind his pocket-watch, but Ma wouldn't stomach it and all the neighbourhood knew it.

When I was perhaps ten and Dora twelve or thirteen, one of the misses—a smooth-skinned negress who'd shared a room with Gypsy Jane—was turned out for smiling her slow smile at one of the bullies once too often. Ma never could tolerate anyone else's pleasure if it didn't pay.

Dora and I were in the scullery. I was scraping the porridge pot and Dora was at the sink, trying to stretch half a bucket of water to clean all the dishes so that she needn't go back to the pump. All we heard was a squawk of raised voices, a scuffle, a cry, the slam of the door and then Ma, calling Dora's name. We looked at each other and I felt hot relief that it was my sister's name Ma called, not mine—I didn't know, when Dora swallowed hard and put down the bowl she was wiping, that it would be the last one she'd clean for a good while. I was left there amongst the dirty dishes to finish on my own. From then on, she'd help about as much as any of the girls, which was to say, as little as she could. Dora was to earn and I was left to be young by myself and so must be all the more helpful or all the more invisible.

YOU'D NEVER HAVE GUESSED, to see Dora at table that first breakfast after, how she'd turned her back on me when at last she came to bed, so that she might snivel. She was quiet, but Dora and I were always quiet at table. Her nose was tipped as pink as a mouse's but her eyes were dry. She held herself carefully, as though she'd just discovered she was made like a teacup: breakable and worth good money. When Ma put the first piece of the bacon—a better piece than Dora had ever eaten, I'd suppose—onto the plate in front of her, she looked up in surprise.

Ma nodded and smiled, which was queer to see, her smiles being so stiff from underuse. Ma's smile was not a cheery sight, nor a comfort; it made my belly clench. Dora looked only confused and put to the blush. Her hands darted toward her plate and held the rim as though someone might wrest it from her.

I was so green over that bacon I was near sick. I'd been given plenty of reason to envy Dora; my whole life long, people had been forever stroking her cheek and telling her she was a beauty. I expected to feel ugly, but I wasn't ready to see the best bacon on my sister's plate. It was as thick as my finger and pink as a baby's tongue, spreading out a puddle of juice for Dora to wipe her bread in. The fat looked crisp enough to melt at the edge and inside, thick enough to chew. My own piece was scarcely enough to flavour the bread. Dora and I were used to comparing our portions mutely, sliding our eyes at each other's plates; now she looked at me only once, to be sure that I'd marked how far she was risen. I tried to keep my face still, but she'd seen what she looked for and was smug as a house cat. She didn't look at me again for the rest of the meal. She needn't now, for just as she wasn't to be kept hungry, nor was she to be left to herself. The misses were all fluttering over her and Ma was watching it all like a poultryman over a flock of geese.

"The captain knows how to put a girl through her paces—reckon you're raw this morning, ain't you?" Polly, a thin girl who'd not been in the house more than a month, shot a sly glance at Dora.

Dora nodded, her mouth being as full as she could stuff it. In any case, she wasn't used to being spoken to at table.

"If you thought it sore yesterday, you wait till tonight," Gypsy Jane told her. She sounded glad about it.

Dora's eyes grew wide, and she looked as though she struggled to swallow.

"Ah, don't heed her." Irish Anne patted her hand. "You're born to it. You'll not have trouble."

"I didn't say trouble, I said she'll be tender."

"That'll wear off soon enough. You'll have a cunny like a leather purse before you know it," Maggie said.

Polly, who'd wept every day for a week when first she came, let out a laugh like a dog barking.

"You'll use Jane's room." Ma's voice could lay all the talk to silence.

Gypsy Jane only nodded. She'd not expected anything else.

"And we'll find you a gown. I have something in pink silk just right for a virgin girl," Ma said. "I think we can call you unspoiled awhile longer."

All the misses made a face. Jane leaned over and said, "You'll have to bleed."

"Hush," Ma said, "don't make more of it than it is. It'll scarce be a scratch."

My sister gripped the edge of the table as though she could barely keep her seat. I thought I knew what a stirred-about mixture she felt; she was always a coward about blood, but she was head-over-tail for silk.

I WASN'T CALLED UPSTAIRS to help dress her, and nor was I called to admire her. I knew she was made fine from the cooing of the girls, but I'd not go to look. I didn't lay eyes on her till I passed her sitting with the other misses in the hall, where the cullies might come to look at them. To my eyes, then, she looked a stranger, her mug painted high and her figure pushed into a ruffled gown of palest pink. Her hair was put up and curled about the face, as the other misses wore theirs. The five of them sat like mismatched sisters, in a row of all different shapes and shades, pressed together against the cold. My own dress was plain enough and grown ragged at the hem, but I had sleeves and a flannel shift. She looked very small between Gypsy Jane and Maggie. As I watched, she laughed aloud at something Maggie said, though I didn't think she'd seen me. She wasn't taunting me. If I knew my sister, she was keeping her courage up.

She mightn't have been teasing me then, but it was almost all she did in the days to follow. She still came to sleep in our bed in the garret when at last she'd done, smelling of sour salt and pinching me that I might move, even if I was pressed up against the wall when she did. I didn't know if she came because she liked to, or because Jane was a wasp over her room—there was always that kind of quarrel going on in our house. Dora still came creeping in, and she'd pinch me even if I was pressed up against the wall when she did. At first I'd wake to her nails cruel upon my skin and a whisper, "You've taken all the bed," or "You're snoring, you sow," but at last she gave up the play. She pinched because I was abed and she wasn't, and both of us knew it. Sometimes, when first she began, I'd pinch or slap at her hands and we'd start to scuffle on the bed till Ma called up the stairs that she'd take the skin from our arses if we kept at it. Then we'd freeze, Dora's hair in my fist and her arm about my neck and warily we'd release each other, each of us ready to fly at the other if she made a move to go again. At last I learned that the surest way to madden my sister was to accept her pinch and only burrow deeper into the bed.

Dora always had painted up every chance she got, even when she was too young to do more than make a mess of herself. Ma wasn't one to waste paint on a child who couldn't earn, so Dora had begged from the girls for any pot with a little left inside, or painted her lips with beetroot and her eyebrows with charcoal, as anyone could who had those things about the house. She'd always been in a fever to get me painted up too; I'd had to fight her off sometimes, so desperate was she to put black smudges along my eyebrows. Now she'd her own paints and powders, she never thought of wasting them on my plain mug. Instead she spent as long as she dared in front of the broken piece of looking-glass we had up there, dabbing at her face with a piece of sponge.

When she saw me watching her, she'd remark, "How plain I am. My teeth ain't quite straight."

Her teeth weren't crooked, mine were. She meant, *Look, Ruth, how handsome I am beside you.*

Sometimes she'd say, "Oh, I wish I were prettier. The captain swears home I'm the bonniest creature he's seen in all his travels, but I'm sure he don't mean it."

And she'd sigh as though the cully were a prince, rather than a weather-beaten, gypsy-faced goat.

"You're bonny as a turd stuck with primroses," I'd say, or some other weak retort. She'd only toss her head and smirk.

After a few months of this, Ma finally bid Dora sleep downstairs. I couldn't say what turned her mood; Ma was changeable as a cat.

Dora acted like she'd been granted a high favour, though she might've complained to Ma long ago if she'd really wanted to share Jane's bed.

"You might be fitted to live up here like a scullery maid," she said, tying her clothes into a blanket, "but I'll move down."

"It's down in truth," I said, "to those sheets crusted stiff. I'd not sleep down there if you paid me."

"But no one will pay you, Ruth," she said, and swept to the door, "to sleep or otherwise."

It was sudden as a slap; in that moment, I grew wild to be earning myself. I couldn't bear to be the servant of the house, to be cold and hungry and alone, on top of it all. I knew that ten was too young to be a regular miss, but Ma had said only days before, when I said my shoes had grown holes, that she'd find a cully for me if my feet were so devilish cold. She'd meant it to be a threat, but now it seemed more like a promise.

If I'd had any kind of sense, I'd have asked Ma to find one of those cullies for me, but she was in one of her rages and had been so for days. I couldn't approach her; she was likely as not to take her stick to me before I spoke. If she did hear me out, she was as likely again to find a cully who'd pay to hurt a girl, just for spite at my daring to ask anything of her. If I'd had any kind of patience, I'd have waited for her to grow calm, but at ten years old, patience wasn't a virtue I was blessed with. Instead I waited only till all the girls were painted up and the house opened, when all in the place were occupied with the night's business, and I supposed to be ready to run at anyone's call.

I crept back up to the garret, keeping the door open and one ear cocked to the stairs. I didn't have silks, but in the corner of the clothes press was a dressing gown that had once been Maggie's. It was of silk twill embroidered white-on-white, the opening edged with knitted lace. It was spoiled by a bloodstain to its skirt that wouldn't lift out. I'd tried to lift the stain with salt, but the cloth was so thin it couldn't stand much scrubbing, and in the end I'd left it stained rather than tear it. Ma had given it to Dora, who'd left it behind now that she'd her own, unspoiled things.

I took off my gown and drew the dressing gown on over my shift and stays. The broken bit of looking-glass was too small to see much of myself;

I stood and bent in front of it to glimpse here a shoulder, there the knitted lace about my neck. My shift showed grey where the dressing gown hung on me, but I couldn't go without it; the dressing gown being so big, I'd have showed my chest bare to the nipple the moment I moved. I knelt on the stool so that I might see the skirt with its bloom of dark rust.

I tried to put up my hair as the misses did. I had only two pins, but at last I got it into a kind of knot. I wished I'd any kind of paint at all, but Dora had taken everything. I pinched at my cheeks to pink them and bit at my lip till I tasted blood. Then I went and hesitated at the top of the stairs.

From below came the sounds of boots on the stairs and a breathy laugh. The doors on the second landing opened and closed. Other voices drifted up from the hall. A cully said something I couldn't hear in a complaining tone.

I heard Dora reply, "Come this way, then, if you ain't fond of waiting."

More boots sounded on the flags of the hall. There came the sound of another door opening and closing—the parlour, I thought it. Then all fell quiet.

I crept down the staircase. On the second landing I stopped, to listen for signs that all were occupied. I couldn't hear much, only an uneven creaking that could've meant anything. I'd have to trust. Down I went.

I stopped on the middle stair and looked about the hall below. The front door was half open, and through it I could hear the sound of the bullies talking upon the step. I could smell their pipes, the cheap clay kind they always smoked, sold with the tobacco already inside and thrown away after. There was nobody in the hall. The kitchen door was shut tight; the door to the cellar steps stood open a little way. This was where Dora had taken her cull, most likely; Ma would throttle her if she took a man into the kitchen, which was the one place in the house where the cullies never could go. The parlour door was ajar, and from here there came gentlemen's voices, smooth with good breeding. Here sat the cullies who'd been willing to wait.

My plan was simple; I'd open the parlour door and offer to fetch the gents some rum. If any of them seemed to give me the eye, I'd offer a little more than rum. I didn't feel nervous of finding the words; I'd heard the girls do it more often than I could count. I only thought of how it might be to put coins into Ma's hand and see her queer smile.

By the time I reached the parlour I was nervous as a flea. The breeze from the open front door raised the hairs on my arms, and I suddenly felt how thin and low was the dressing gown. I stood there in the hall like a noddy, unable to decide whether to go forward or back.

As I hovered there, the cellar door opened behind me, and someone screamed. I jumped and span about; Dora stood in the doorway, on the top step. Behind her a young cull's mug peered over her shoulder from the darkness of the cellar steps.

Now I heard the parlour door open and turned to see the gents come out, crying, "What's this? What ho?"

At the same moment, the bullies burst in from the front step and then stood as foolish as I'd been, not being sure who to manhandle out of the house.

Dora stopped her shrieking and began laughing.

"I took you for a ghost," she kept saying, and each time was too fitted to say more.

The young cull behind her pushed out into the hall and looked me over. He was barely grown, eighteen or so, but dressed sober as a monk. I'd noticed him about the place before, and marked him as being like a lad in an old man's costume. His hair was curled and powdered like that of a cull twice his age. He didn't smile to see Dora so merry.

"What the devil?" he said. "What is this child about? Is that blood upon her?"

I didn't like to be called a child.

Dora came forward, still laughing.

"She's playing at having her courses." She tried to touch the skirt, and I pulled it away from her fingers.

Dora's young cully looked stern at this, and the other gents only looked fuddled. One of our bullies stepped up, opened his mouth to speak, and then closed it again.

Dora was still the only one who saw the joke. It was enough for me, mind. I'd only two roads open to me, and I'd sooner have been hanged than run back upstairs, so I took the other and threw myself at her. I got a good hold of her dress with one hand, and with the other I began to beat her anywhere I could reach. She put up her hands to defend herself, still laughing, till I landed a couple of blows in good earnest.

Then she called out, "She's run mad! Take her off me!"

I had time to strike her perhaps twice more before strong hands gripped my neck hard enough that my shoulders came up about my chin like those of a frightened chicken. I let her go. It was Ma's hand that had caught me. I'd rather have had the bullies a hundred times.

Ma struck at my arse and I twisted as far from her stick as I could, which, her grip on me being what it was, wasn't far enough. She couldn't reach my buttocks and instead the blow struck me in the small of my back, which had me shrieking like a hog. It ain't the worst pain, to be struck upon the spine, but it's painful enough.

"Hold still," she said, and drew me back toward her.

By then I thought only of escape, twisting and bucking, heedless of my skirt and my bare legs. I raised myself up and heard Ma's grunt of effort, and then quite as suddenly threw myself toward the flagstone floor. I felt her lose her grip and had one moment of freedom, my hands out to take the force of the stone, when she again found the cloth at my waist, and I stopped with a jerk, like a dog coming to the end of a short rope. Now I was dangling helpless, and Ma still with a stick in her free hand. I put my arms up to cover my head.

"Madam, stay your hand," one of the gents said. I thought it was Dora's dowdy cull.

No blow came. I could hear Ma huffing and snorting, and the gent talking to her very low, though I couldn't make out what he said.

I heard Ma say, "Four shillings," and the cull replied, "Done."

Suddenly she let go of my skirt, and, it being so unexpected, I'd no time to brace myself. I fell onto the flags, hitting my elbows hellishly. Both arms were set to humming.

"Get up," Ma said to me.

I got to my feet as fast as I could, lest she strike me again for being slow.

Dora was watching me with a blank face; my sister was none the wiser than I.

"Go on," Ma said, "into the yard. These gents want to watch you fight."

I started forward before I even heard the words properly. I was still only relieved at being spared a beating. My arms were devilish sore.

Dora must've complained, for behind me I heard Ma say, "She'll not spoil your face. She'll regret it if she does."

It was dark outside, and cold. One of the bullies from the door came out holding up a lamp. A little ring formed around me, of the girls and what callers were about the place. Into this circle Ma pushed Dora, who stumbled and righted herself and looked as though she'd protest, if only she dared. More cullies came out, pulled from the beds of the misses by the promise of amusement, and were now calling, "Oh, good sport!"

"What, are we to have a show? I'll put a shilling on the stocky one!"

That meant me.

I wasn't vexed any longer, and Dora looked only fearful, holding her arms against the cold.

"Come on," one gent called out, "set to!"

I looked at Ma. She nodded at me and raised her stick a little. I squared up to Dora and showed her my fists. She looked only miserable.

"Put your fives up," I said to her, "for I'll have at you whether you do or no."

"I'm changing my bet," one voice called out. "I'll put six shillings on this one. I shall want to see blood for it!"

This perked me up, and I quipped, "Blood is a pound."

All about me laughed, and I felt it as only a ten-year-old, who is suddenly the centre of admiring attention, can. I could hear the betting increase.

"Wait," Ma said now. "Put some pennies in a purse for the girls. Whoever wins shall take it."

"You have taken four shillings for them already, madam," said Dora's young gent, the one who'd sent us out there.

"For their services," Ma said. "Put something in a purse for the girls. They'll fight the harder for it."

I heard coin hit coin as one of the culls passed a hat about. Ma stepped close to Dora and said something in her ear that made her straighten up and let go of her arms, though she still looked miserable as sin.

"Go at it," Ma said, when once the hat was passed.

What could I do then? I stepped to Dora and fibbed her on the cheek as hard as I could. As I did it, I thought, *Now Ma will thrash me, for marking her face.* This thought only made me fight the harder. For Dora, that first blow seemed to clear her head. She'd been playing the nervous princess, but we'd grown up fighting as often as we ate, which was one too much and the other not often enough. We fell to now as though we were alone in the garret, all feet and teeth and fistfuls of hair. I forgot the gents and Ma's stick. I forgot the hat full of coins. I didn't remember that we were in the yard till I had Dora down on her back, one knee upon her chest, and felt my other knee grow wet with mud. My sister's throat was in my hands, her pulse beating hot beneath my palm. Her hands pushed at my face and raked my cheek, but I only pressed my knee into her chest and kept my grip till she choked out, "Enough."

I never got hold of the purse of pennies; Ma kept that, as I could've told you she would. I hardly cared, for my slice of bread was near as thick as Ma's that night, with butter all the way to the edges.

"Don't you grow used to it," she said. "I can't imagine you'll earn so much again."

To Dora she said, "You'll have a good slice too, but it will likely be the last for a while; you look like you've been through a mill."

If anyone else had said so it would've been a jest, for "mill" was a common word for a fight. None of us sitting around that table knew whether to smile; if Ma was punning, it was the first we'd ever heard from her. In the end, none of us laughed, only twitched anxiously about the mouth. Ma's face was stern, and she spoke as though Dora had begun the scrap herself, rather than begged to be spared it. Dora's right eye was pinked, her lip was swelled, and she had a scratch upon her cheek, which later would scab like a string of beads.

I made that slice last as long as I could, keeping each bite small and working my way about the edges to save the middle. Before I had done, Ma said that if I didn't get on and eat my supper she'd have it back from me as being too large, and then I had to eat that soft buttery middle in two hasty bites.

Now, when I think back over it, I'm surprised that Ma treated me, seeing as I'd ruined Dora's looks for a week. She liked to keep us unsteady, so that we never could predict how she'd turn, one minute to the next.

However good it was, that slice lasted only a few bites, and soon I was hungry again and cold upstairs alone. Dora seemed to prefer the company of the other misses, and I was left to do everything about the house, without company to speed the work. So, though I was fearful, I was glad with it when, a few weeks later, Ma called me out from where I was chopping turnips in the kitchen. I found her waiting with two gents in the hall. One of them was the sober young cully who'd set us to milling, the other a yellow-haired, stocky cull of the same age, eighteen or nineteen, with a shiny blue coat and a silver-topped cane.

"Go with these gents, Ruth, and do as they tell you," she said.

The straw-headed gent was goggling at me quite openly.

"She's damned small, Dryer," he said.

"I tell you she will suit," the sober one replied.

"She's as biddable as you please," Ma said, in the special voice she used for gentlemen.

I'd have chosen a thousand times to go off with strange cullies before

I'd talk back to Ma, so I took off my apron with unsteady hands and went to them. Ma nodded.

"She'll do as she's bid," she said. She turned away and began to climb the stairs.

"Come along, then," said the sandy cull. "Ruth, is it? I am Mr Sinclair. This is Mr Dryer—but he tells me you have met before."

I was struck dumb; I could only nod. Why did they take me out of the house? I should've been far easier in myself if Ma had told me to take them upstairs.

Once I was out in the street, the hand of fear closed about my bladder and I thought, *I can't be sure if I'll ever come back again; perhaps she's sold me outright.* All about me was familiar, excepting the backs of the two gents, and it was them I must follow, trailing behind as they strode on with long legs and sure steps. If I'd had more sense about me I might've been calmed by that; they didn't expect me to run from them.

When I saw The Hatchet ahead of us I chided myself to be calm. We were to take a room, then. It was something indeed, to have two cullies to begin. The misses would want to hear it all; they'd crowd about me. I'd have bacon. The sober gent turned at the door to be sure that I followed.

"Hurry up, girl," he said.

I felt my bowels bubble and loose. I'd not expected to be so anxious. I suddenly realised how ragged was my dress and wished Ma had given me silk. *I'll have silk tomorrow,* I told myself. *I'll have silk tomorrow, if I'm brave today.*

I felt as though my head was floating above my body.

The sober gent was talking in the ear of the innkeeper. Mr Sinclair, the yellow-headed one, came toward me and took me by the arm. His fingers were stronger than I'd have thought them.

"We shan't have use for a slow girl. Pick your feet up."

All about me were culls and misses who'd come and gone through the convent rooms. In any usual case I'd have been bidding all the company a good evening, but now I could barely look at them. I was so awash with fear and pride that I didn't know whether I hoped they'd marked me or not. The gent's hand was hot upon my elbow.

He pulled me through the tavern, winding around the people. I stumbled after him, trying not to trip over feet and the legs of stools. It wasn't till he stopped and turned to face the room that I realised that he wasn't taking me to the little stairs that led upstairs to the chambers to hire, nor to any of the back parlours used for the same purpose. We were going toward the back door, where the beaten mud of the yard gave way to the low wooden stage roped round with cord.

Mr Sinclair turned and addressed the whole room. His voice was loud and as honking as a goose.

"Come out now, and watch this little girl go against the butcher's boy!"

"All bets to me," called Mr Dryer.

Then we were pushed outside as the whole tavern tried at once to get out of the doors.

I was more fearful than ever I'd been when I thought I'd have to play the whore. There was a boy waiting up there with his chest bare and his fists bandaged, and they pushed me up beside him. I knew his mug, though not to speak to. He didn't say a word to me, but paced and puffed and put his maulers up, fibbing at the air.

Mr Dryer climbed up beside me.

"You will fight in your shift," he said. "Take your dress off."

It was the first word he'd said to me. I only looked at him, till he put out a hand and twitched at my sleeve impatiently. Then I slowly loosed my dress enough to pull it over my head. The men watching whooped and whistled.

"All bets to me," he called again, and leaned over the ropes to take coins from countless hands.

I stood there, shivering and trying not to look at the crowd about me, till Mr Dryer came back to the middle of the ring.

"Who will second the girl?" he asked above the noise.

I couldn't help but look now. A scattering of hands were up in the crowd. Mr Dryer pointed at one of them, a miss I thought I knew. She came climbing over the ropes and smiled at me. I felt a little better to have a second, even one not very familiar. She came beside me and patted my arm. She looked rough about the face, but kind—looked, in fact, like just the sort of miss I was most used to seeing. She took my dress from my hands and hung it carefully over the ropes at the corner, and then sank to one knee and put the other out before her.

"Come on, then," she said, below the calls of the crowd.

I sat upon her knee, just as a real pug sits upon the knee of his second, just like all the big-name pugs at the fairs. It was that, more than anything, which gave me courage. It made me feel at once that it was more real than any moment I'd lived, and yet, more of a play. I felt a great calm settle over me. I looked at the butcher's boy, now sitting on the knee of his own second, his breath still puffing in and out like a bellows. I thought, *I'll drive that breath out of you, sonny.* I thought it so hard that he seemed to feel it and looked up at me. He stuck his tongue out. I only smiled, the same smile I used to tease Dora.

Mr Dryer called, "Come up to scratch!"

I walked there for the first time. The scratch in The Hatchet, the first I ever put my toe upon, was one of two lines painted white upon the wooden stage. All the lines I'd walk up to after that moment, some made in the earth with a stick, or chalk upon stone, or sometimes only agreed— the scratch shall be here, where the twig points—all of those lines have blurred one into the other in my mind, but my first scratch was a true one. I've always preferred a painted scratch. It can't be argued with, nor scuffed.

I've a very clear memory of that moment, though I see myself in it, which can't be real. It's dusk, not yet dark but falling fast. Two torches burn in holders at The Hatchet's door, lighting the crowd about them strangely. The crowd is a shifting mass of murmurs and hats. The straw-headed gent stands at the front of the crowd, so close to the ropes that he'll take a kick in the eye if he's not quick on his feet. I'm standing at the painted line, my fists bunched but hovering around my waist. My chest is flat, my stays too small, so that my nipples show clear under the flannel shift. My legs are bared shamefully high; my shift is too short. Already my legs are stocky and solid as a sow's. My arms, too, are thick as logs, grown strong from the work of the house. My face is calm, my narrowed eyes fixed on the bobbing, puffing butcher's boy. I'm willing him to die.

That's what I remember. That, and I cut my fist on his teeth. I'd not learned then how to harden the skin and no one had thought to bandage them. His teeth pierced my hand, and from then on each fib I landed left a mark of my own blood upon his chops, like paint upon the door of a plague house.

That night I ate a plate of oysters so juicy they burst in my mouth like berries. The girls asked me to tell them the story of the mill over and again, and each time I told them how I'd thought I was to have two cullies for my first time, they screamed with mirth to think of it.

Chapter 2

✦ ✦ ✦

Mr Dryer came calling for Dora more often, after that, till one evening I found him sitting in the parlour and fetched him a nip of
rum, as I would've any cully, then. He took out his snuffbox and took a
pinch off the back of his hand, tipping his head back with little, fussy sniffs.
Then he dabbed at his nose with a devilish fine wiper. I remember looking
at the needlework about its edge and wishing it were mine. I'd a porridge
on the stove and he didn't seem about to talk of boxing, so I turned to go,
when he stopped me.

"How long must I wait?"

"I couldn't say, sir, but I'd not say long," though I knew Dora liked to
take her time between cullies, to make herself nice again.

"I wish to see her now," he said, as though I could pull my sister from
my pocket.

"I'm sorry, sir." I didn't know what other reply to make.

"Sorry will not serve. What must I pay, to see her now? Tell me and I
will pay it. I do not like to wait."

I ran to fetch Ma. When we came back, Mr Dryer was standing in the
hallway, gazing up the stairs with a look on his mug as though he'd a mind
to run up and pull the other cully off my sister. Ma thought it too, for she
pinched me.

"Fetch Sam in from the door," she said.

I ran to fetch Sam then, excitement like beer brewing in my belly. Any little thing to change the shape of the day was welcome.

Ma was speaking softly to Mr Dryer. He shook his head. He'd grown even more sober, where another man would've grown wild. He brought out his purse. I couldn't hear what was said, but now Ma was the one to shake her head. She put her hand upon his sleeve. He didn't shake it off, but only stopped speaking and looked at it. Ma took it off him. The tone of their whispering grew fiercer. At last Ma said, "Well, I hope it please you, after all this," and turned to Sam, the bully.

"Sam, fetch that fellow out of Dora's room and bid her clean herself. Tell him he can have his pound back if he's not done, or have another girl, whichever he likes."

That cull up there with Dora had paid nothing more than three or four shillings to lie with her and we all of us knew it but Mr Dryer.

Sam shook his head and began climbing the stairs. Mr Dryer said something to Ma and went back into the parlour and shut the door, just as if he were in his own house.

"Sam," Ma called, "tell her be quick, mind."

And that was how Mr Granville Dryer, young as he was, came to be Dora's fancy man. He paid enough that no other cully need visit her. He was promised they never would, though of course they did, especially the black-eyed sea captain—Ma wasn't one to turn away good coin, if she could be sure that Mr Dryer was otherwise occupied. He was occupied often with me.

He came to see my sister perhaps twice a week. Near as often, he came to fetch me to The Hatchet, to have me stand up and mill before a crowd. A few times he took me to fight at other taverns, and twice I went to mill against stout, barefoot women in the fields at Lansdown. I preferred The Hatchet's ring to any other. I always did fight better there.

Sometimes Mr Dryer brought straw-headed Mr Sinclair with him, sometimes another dandyish cull, who Dora declared so handsome that she'd be tempted not to charge him. She'd no opportunity to charge him or otherwise, for he was always with Mr Dryer, and Mr Dryer guarded her as another cully would his wife. He was much the same over me. Whichever of the other two came to fetch me, Mr Dryer was always with them. When the culls in the crowd thrust nips of gin into my hands, Mr Dryer took them from me without a word and passed them to his friends. He let me drink cider, ale, and sometimes wine. When a sailor turned lech on me one day and reached beneath the ropes to stroke my ankle, Mr Dryer took the man aside and spoke to him seriously. I near died when this same rough sailor came afterward to beg my pardon, and said he'd not bother me again. All this and yet Mr Dryer barely ever spoke a word to me unless it was to bid me follow him, or call me to come up to scratch.

After that first bout against the butcher's boy, I went to bed only a little bruised up, but I woke dizzy and sick from the hits to the skull. I thought I'd a fever, I was so bad. My hands were so stiff they'd scarce close, and the skin on my face was grazed, where his knuckles had slid across my sweating cheek. I'd no notion how much pain was to be had from my giving a lad a thrashing, and his half-missed blows upon me. I learned to expect it all soon enough, and I learned that it passed. I never would grow used to the shock of the full-facer—all you feel is speed and weight and surprise, and all the other ills come later—but I learned how fast I could be, when I'd a need to. I found that Mr Dryer would stop a bout if he feared me too injured. That's not to say I wasn't left beat, but there was always talk about this or that pug who'd died, gasping up blood with his last words. Mr Dryer wouldn't let that befall me; he'd guard me as he would his purse.

In a place like The Hatchet, near as important as winning was having bottom; this was the fancy's word for courage so deep it runs close to lunacy. I stood up against anyone they brought me and never backed down even when I knew I'd take a beating. I fought a sailor with only one foot, who grabbed me by my hair and wouldn't leave off, however the crowd screamed "Coward." I fought a lad even littler than I, who looked over at a cull in the crowd—his daddy, I supposed—every time he made a hit on me. I used that to my benefit and fibbed him in the eye the next time he turned his head. I fought girls bigger than Dora, thick-armed washer-women who knocked me off my pins as fast as I'd have done an infant. I fought brats my own size till we were both so weary all we could do was lean against each other at the scratch and hear the crowd cry "Shame." I stood up against grown men, and the fancy who gathered to watch only laughed and cheered. A little girl up against a big swinging cull is as divert-ing as a dog against a bear, and if the puppy gets a bite in, so much the better.

I learned, the first time I was really beat, that it was better to mind what Ma told me and go back to the ring than to try to stay at home in the convent. Once you've stood in front of a woman like Ma, a one-footed sailor looks like a fairy. I begged to be allowed a holiday and she gave me a beat-ing I swear home I can still feel if I close my eyes. The next time I came back so battered I'd have liked to have slept a good week away, I got up and took myself back to The Hatchet as soon as she bid me, with never a whim-per aloud.

In any case, I was happier in the ring than I was at home, whatever the price in bruises and cracked teeth. I had bottom and all the fancy cheered me for it. I'd never in my life been cheered before—no one had ever had cause to celebrate me. The fancy called me Miss Matchet and declared I was match for anyone. They called me a real pug, which I'd never heard a girl called before. When I walked down the street, folks called out to me and begged me to show my arm, or make a fist. It was the happiest time of my life. Soon enough, the culls in The Hatchet knew me so well that not one of them would try to get his hand up my dress anymore, for all the rest would've turned on him before Mr Dryer could get there.

Ma fed Dora and me near as well as she fed herself. She bought me a new dress from the bow-wow shop and had it sewn up short, so that I could mill in it without tripping. She had me pickling my knuckles in brine and brandy. She had me posing in my boxing dress to entertain the visitors. She threatened the misses that she'd set me on them if they didn't mind her.

Mr Dryer, for his part, came and went in our house whenever he pleased. He arranged that Dora should have her own room, and wasn't there a scene over that, with Jane shrieking and Ma slapping her and chasing her out of the house, only to have Sam bring her back again. Ma made Jane a room in the cellar and she wailed over it loud enough, but she stayed there. She was lucky to be in a house like ours and she knew it; her looks were near enough gone.

Mr Dryer had some culls come in and fit up Dora's room with a desk and a glass-fronted cabinet for his books and bottles, till it was more like a gent's study than a molly's bedroom. For me he sent padded mufflers to protect my hands in training and a leather dummy stuffed with straw, which hung from a rope in the yard. The chickens used to peck the straw out of the seams at its bottom end, till at last I hoisted it too high for them to reach. I named that dummy after Ma, and each morning I beat it till it was sorry.

When I was perhaps thirteen, the cullies began asking me to do more than pose for them. Ma took me aside and said that Mr Dryer paid enough each week for my keep that I needn't—indeed, that I mustn't, if I thought it would weaken me for my sport upon the stage. I'd not realised till that moment that Mr Dryer had bought me, as he had Dora. I told Ma that I thought it would be best to keep my strength for the ring, and she let me be. I didn't say so for Mr Dryer's sake, nor for boxing. I said so because by then I'd noticed Tom.

TOM WEBBER WAS a great swinging cull, as big as the bullies and only fifteen. He wasn't what you'd call handsome; he'd a brow so heavy it looked to have been chiselled in stone, and a nose to match. For all that, he didn't look mean. He held himself as though he wished he weren't built so large.

When first he began to appear beside the ring at The Hatchet, I thought nothing much of it, though I noticed him as being so big and his face so young. He would come and stand right beside the ropes, or if not that, then perched upon the rail, as clumsy as a goose on a fence, where he could see all the goings-on in the ring. I'd try not to look at him. When I came out of the ring afterward, whether defeated or victorious, the men all gathered round and pushed cups of cider or wine-and-water into my hands. Now Tom began to make himself part of this circle, edging ever closer. Sometimes he stood right beside me, yet never said a word. I didn't quite like it; he was like a spy. I'd go to the privy, out past the yard, and when I came back his head would be sticking out above the crowd, seeming to scan the place. His eyes would meet mine and he'd seem to settle. Whenever I looked up I felt his eyes upon me. I didn't know what he looked for; he couldn't admire me. I'd been fighting for three years then, and was plain to begin. By the time Tom laid eyes on my mug, I'd had my nose knocked sideways, and my teeth, which were always crowded, well, they weren't so cramped up as they'd used to be. I'd almost no teeth on the top left-hand side, till close to the back. The ones that were left still hid behind one another, as if scared—as well they might be. I wasn't a picture to look at, and I didn't care; my hair was always in a cap, for my idea was only to keep it out of my eyes, not make myself handsome. I no longer wished for silks, but wore hardy cotton gowns, sewn up so that my ankles showed. When I went out past the neighbourhood, where folks didn't know me as Miss Matchet, I drew stares and comments: "Ooh, what did you do for that beating?" and the like. Mine wasn't a mug any young lad would find to make sheep-eyes at. And yet—there he was. I didn't know if he meant to mock me, or if Ma or Mr Dryer had paid him to watch me, or if he was touched in the head. He could've been any or all three. I hated him, and yet I looked for him too.

Then came the day I climbed down from the ring, stretching and sore, the inside of my lips tender and tasting of blood, my knuckles numb with the promise of pain to come. Suddenly it was Tom's hands pushing ale into my own, though now he wouldn't look at me at all. I only took it and held it in my stiff hand. I was scared to drink it—I had wild thoughts of poison. He was confusing me so, I was near as loosely tied in the head as Ma.

Ma by then was grown devilish queer. She'd never been a trusting woman, but now she was suspicious in the wildest ways: accusing the girls of sneaking away to meet cullies when they went to the water-pump, saying they were out to cheat her of her cut. She accused them of pleasuring the bullies for no charge, the same charge she'd thrown at that slow-smiling negress so long ago. If I walked too close behind her she whirled about to face me, as though she thought I'd a mind to push her down the stairs. She peered at the coins handed her, feeling them all over with her fingers, counting them over and again before she believed them fair and put them in her purse. She began always to touch the walls as she went about the house—I thought perhaps she was going blind, but then she sometimes wobbled so upon her pins she could've just as easily been holding the wall to keep steady. I didn't know whether she was took sick; she wasn't a woman you could ask such a thing of. She began to feed scraps of her din-ner to her dog before she'd taste it. Sometimes when her wine was poured she made one or other of us swap cups with her; her eyes then would flame as though she'd foiled a plot to poison her.

Now I looked at the ale Tom gave me in the same way, and felt the bindings of my sense unravel. What did he want from me? I couldn't bear it. I pushed the cup back at him so firmly that it hit his chest and splashed up against him, leaving a brown half-moon stain against his shirt. The folks about us laughed and cried out.

"What's this?"

"Scorned, sonny!"

Hands clapped Tom upon the shoulder so that he jumped a little.

Tom's mug reddened, and he took his cup back. He looked lost as a choirboy in Hell.

I let myself be carried off then, in the crowd of culls clapping me upon the back as though I were a man. I felt a little spark of glad spite that I'd thrust his cup back at him. *There, now,* I thought. *Let him goggle-eye some-one else.*

I went for home not long after. The street was dark, lit only by the lamp hanging over The Hatchet's door and what little light came through the windows of the houses. I stepped out onto the soft grime of the road, and even before I was out of the circle of lamplight he was at my shoulder. I span around fast enough that he had to step back, and he must've known I was ready to plant him one by the look on my mug. He held up a hand, palm out.

"Please," he said. "I only want to walk with you."

I'd never heard his voice before. It was the voice of a farmer, soft and thick as fur. His eyes were like a dog's, though that sounds badly. They were brown, deep and trusting.

"But why?" I said. "What in all the hells would you seek me out for?"

He didn't flicker at my language.

"I'd like to talk to you," he said, "and see you home safe."

I laughed at him and put all the scorn I had into it. It was a whore's laugh.

"I'll be safe enough," I said, "and if I'm not, why, it's nothing I'm not used to."

If he'd continued to look soft I believe I'd have been off then, but he laughed instead.

"Then I hope we'll be robbed, and I'll watch you chase off the foot-pads."

"No one'll rob you when you're with me," I said.

"Then you'll let me walk with you," Tom said, and it wasn't a question.

Tom was from Coalpit Heath. He told me it was a tiny place where all in the village worked in the colliery and black dust covered everything. He might've had the voice of a farmer, but his family were all miners. He said he was grown too big to be any use down a mine, though he'd tried to keep at it. I thought he walked as though he were down there still, hunched over and sorry, keeping his arms close.

He'd been sent to Bristol to look for work on the docks and was lodging with a lady in St Thomas, who'd thought him a negro when first he'd arrived, he said.

"At home we're all black as Turks, with the coal-dust. I never realised how filthy dark I was, till I came here and saw how many colours of skin there are to see." He threw out his arm as though we were still in The Hatchet yard. In The Hatchet, black men, mulattos, Jews, and gypsies were all as welcome as a white man, if they'd coins in their pockets. It was that variety of tavern. Tom's arm wasn't black any longer.

"I scrubbed myself raw," he said, "and the lady I rent from wasn't any too pleased when she saw the state of the bathwater. She made me tip it out and fetch another tub-full from the pump, it was so black. It wasn't fit for a pig to get in after me, she said. The pump's three streets distant. It took me half the day, back and forth with buckets."

I laughed. I still recall how sharp and strange it was when he looked at me. I couldn't help but feel he was mocking me—he must've been—and yet, and yet, there he was, walking beside me and telling me about his home.

As we drew near to the convent, which wasn't far, not far enough, I made him stop. I leaned against a wall. From where I stood I could see the dark bulk of Sam leaning up against the door and the lamplight coming pink through the silk shades at Ma's window. It didn't look like a good Christian home.

"Why d'you stop?" Tom asked.

I didn't know how to answer. He looked awkward and unhappy suddenly, and I thought, *Perhaps he thinks I've stopped so that he'll kiss me and he's looking at my gap-toothed chops and casting his mind about for escape.* I couldn't let him think that.

"I wish you'd go now," I said.

Now he looked even more miserable.

"Have I offended you, Miss Matchet?"

"No," I said, and because he looked so downcast still, "my name's Ruth Downs."

"Oh," he said, "I knew Ruth, but I thought you were Miss Ruth Matchet."

I laughed then, and Tom smiled too, a little ashamedly.

"I suppose I should've guessed it. Miss Matchet from The Hatchet. It's too neat to be true."

I stopped laughing, and then I didn't know what to do.

At last he said, "If you don't want that fellow to mark me, mayn't I just stand here and watch you go in?" He nodded toward the convent door.

My head swam strangely as I walked toward the house. I could feel Tom's eyes upon my back, and I was suddenly conscious of my walk, too wide, too swaggering for a lady. As I reached the door, Sam tipped me a wink, having spied Tom, and was about to speak when behind him the door opened. Ma was standing in the doorway, an unlit lamp in her hand and a look of fury well enough known to me upon her face. She stepped forward, and with her free hand grasped me roughly by the shoulder.

"What's this?" She was loud enough for the whole street to wake. "You, out with young men without my leave? You, who has to save her strength for the ring?" She began to drag me up the step. The fat from the lamp splashed out upon my neck; it was still warm.

If Tom hadn't been across the street I'd have gone mildly enough, as I always did. This one day, mind, I wrested my shoulder from her. We both stumbled. I was burning with the shame.

I screamed out, "I did nothing but talk!"

Ma slapped me across the chops so hard that I staggered to one side. I heard Sam suck in a breath, but he didn't stir to help me. Tom came across the street so fast that I could hear the slops in the gutter splash up around his ankles. We all of us turned to watch him puff up.

"Madam, I'll swear it, I didn't lay a finger on her," he said.

"You may touch her all you like, for four shillings," Ma said over my head, "but none of my girls visits with young fellows just to talk."

Tom fumbled in his pocket.

"I'll give you two shillings now, to talk to her," he said, "and so you shan't beat her. I'd give you four, if I had it."

Ma took the coins from his outstretched hand and peered at them in the half-light. Then she simply stepped back and closed the door, leaving Tom, Sam, and me standing on the step.

Sam shook his head, though what he meant by it I didn't know. I couldn't speak, even to thank Tom. We all three of us stood there like noddies.

At last I said, "I'll give you two shillings back," though I didn't know how I'd manage it.

"You gave me those two," Tom said. "I won, betting on you tonight."

"Oh," I said.

He was standing on the street, just looking at me. His eyes were very dark; I couldn't see what look they held.

At last Sam said, "Ain't you going to kiss the lad a thank-you?"

"She needn't do that," Tom said, so quick it was near all one word.

I was more fuddled in that moment than I'd been my life long.

"Good night, then," I said at last, and I went inside, just so that I could stop thinking about it.

Before I closed the door I heard Sam laugh and I saw Tom's dark shape turn away, his head lowered as it always was.

I couldn't stop thinking about it after all. I couldn't stop thinking about it for days.

WHEN NEXT I FOUGHT, I looked for Tom the moment I took the ring. When I saw him sitting on the rail, I couldn't help but smile at him. He smiled back, and I found myself so flustered it took a hard fib upon the cheek from my opponent to bring me round and have me straight again.

When I came down from the ring that day, I took the ale from his hands, and some of the culls called out, "Oh, she favours you now, lad!" and the like.

Tom and I blushed together.

After that, it was accepted in The Hatchet that Tom would hand my ale to me and not a word more was said about it. When Mr Dryer called out for anyone willing to be my second and bottle-holder, Tom would sometimes raise his hand and I'd feel my belly shift and not be sure if I hoped he'd be chosen or passed over. I knew that if he were too near to me I'd be too flustered to fight well. Mr Dryer never did turn his finger to beckon Tom, so I can't say how well my nerves would've fared. Mr Dryer seemed never to see Tom's raised hand at all. When I came out of the ring, mind, whether victorious or defeated, before long there he was at my side, looking at me again. I couldn't believe he'd choose to do so, and yet I must believe it.

One day he brought me feathers, bright yellow and blue, won from a sailor just off a ship. I kept them in an old cigar box, which I'd hidden up the chimney breast. In a house as loose as ours, it was hard to keep hold of anything as being truly your own, and I guarded that box as if it were filled with jewels—though it held nothing much besides a few broken beads I'd had from one miss or another, and a silver button from a gent's coat that Ma never knew I found. Now I pushed all that to the side and laid the feathers in careful as anything, and stroked them till they were flat. No one had ever given me any kind of present before.

Tom walked with me only a very little way now; I couldn't let Ma catch him again. Every time we parted I felt my belly swoop, unsure if he'd kiss me at last. He never did try. He always stood watching me, his hands in his pockets, till I turned the corner.

Ma never said a word, but she knew too many folks with flapping chops and I could be sure she'd heard enough. Sometimes I thought she was watching me with new eyes, the way she watched the new misses. I'd become an uncertain creature in her mind, and I found I liked it; she couldn't fathom what else I might be doing when her eyes weren't on me, and more than that—someone had thought it worth a whole two shillings just to talk to me. No man had ever paid two shillings for Dora's conversation.

I'd taken to going to The Hatchet even when Mr Dryer didn't come to fetch me. Ma never spoke against that, either; I suppose by then I was earning enough, or she was biding her time. Perhaps she was run mad enough by then that she didn't think of me unless I was in front of her. She was certainly grown forgetful.

One evening I was waiting at the door to the Hatchet yard, watching two lads about to fight upon the stage, stretching themselves and jumping about, when up came a sailor. This was a cull fresh off a boat, all full of ginger and half-soused already. He came over beside me and touched my face, where I'd a bruise or two, as I near always did.

"Ain't you all scuffed up," he said. "How'd you like a little ointment for that?" His face made it clear enough what he meant by that.

"Tom," a cully standing nearby called out, "here's a noddy talking foul to your missus."

"He'd best shut his bonebox," Tom called out, walking toward us, "unless he wants it closed for him."

The sailor called back, "No offence meant, son. Bruise the little bitch yourself, did you? I'll warrant she keeps quiet enough, now."

Tom kept coming through the crowd, which moved aside and, guessing what he was about, turned to watch. He stepped right up to that sailor, smiling, and struck him right in the chops, so hard that the cully's head cracked against the door and bounced right off again. He slumped forward, and everyone about reached out to help him to the floor.

Tom turned to me, and I could see he was anxious then, that I'd be vexed at him playing the knight.

I reached out and touched his big hand, just gently.

"I knew you'd have a good fib on you," I said. "You'd have to, with maulers like that. You should go up in the ring."

Tom shook his head, but he looked pleased enough to piss. "I'd rather watch you," he said. "I should've let you fight for yourself, just now. I didn't mean to take liberties."

"I've been waiting for you to take liberties," I said, just to see him blush.

* * *

AND JUST LIKE THAT, Tom seemed to grow bolder. Nothing much changed that you could see. He never asked me outright, but from that day he'd sometimes say of a stream he'd fished as a boy or the mine his father and brothers still worked, "I'll take you there, when once we're married."

And this without once kissing me, or taking my swollen-up hands.

I sometimes told him, "Ma never will let me marry you, Tommy."

He'd only smile then and say, "She will."

But he knew nothing about it. He was too good to know.

When once I understood that he meant it, the agony of uncertainty was replaced by worse—I began to love him. I told myself I mustn't—I forbade it. That was as much help as forbidding Ma to love money, or Mr Dryer to love boxing. I knew I'd never hold him; as soon as he knew me truly, he'd run, of course he'd run. Oh, he said he'd never known a girl like me; that he thought me brave and liked to see me carry myself so proud and spirited, but that wasn't like to last, that wasn't what lads looked for to marry. Surely, soon, he'd find some other girl, with curling hair and unmarked cheeks, and I'd have to kill them both, or die of it. I thought about this and still I walked beside him. I laughed when he joked. I cast about for him when I took the ring and couldn't be easy till I knew his eyes were on me, and then couldn't be easy for the reason that they were.

Mr Dryer saw all this and said not a word to me. One day, mind, I came downstairs, meaning to go to The Hatchet, when Ma opened the parlour door and bid me step inside.

Mr Dryer was there, sitting neatly upon the overstuffed settee, his hands upon his knee and his back very straight. He looked soberly at me, though he didn't catch my eye. Rather, he looked me over as though considering me for a mill. Beside him, perched on a stool too small for him and scarlet about the mug, sat Tom. He looked about to cry. My belly shrank to see him. He was too good and, though it sounds wrong of me to say it, not sharp enough to be there. Ma and Mr Dryer were like to eat him alive.

Ma stayed at the door so that I had to pass her too close and take in the sweet and rotten scent of her, grown stronger in recent days. She was still made up fine, with her dress cut low and her pearls—which I knew were paste—about her neck. Her face was painted as high as it always was. Below the paint the lumps were beginning then, one cheek pushing outward, her eye drawn out with it near to a slit and the white of it turned ruby. Her look was at its most stern, and even I, who was so well used to it, had to grit my nerve to pass her. I suddenly saw how she must look to Tom. How brave and foolish he'd been to come there.

I sat in the chair Ma pointed out to me, facing Tom and Mr Dryer. She came in, closed the door, and placed herself beside Mr Dryer upon the settee. Now I was facing them, all in a line. First Ma, stern and lumpen, then Mr Dryer, neat and serious, then Tom, all hunched shoulders and sorry eyes.

"Now, Ruth, this young lad"—Ma made the words "young lad" sound like a shabby thing—"has come to ask me for your hand."

I didn't know what I'd expected to hear, but it wasn't that. Tom looked as though he were regretting it. But oh, he'd come to ask for me. How silly he was, how simple! What kind of girl did he think he was asking for?

"Of course," Ma was saying, "he wasn't to know that the choice belongs to Mr Dryer as much as to myself. We've talked it over well, and we're of a mind. He's to have our blessing."

She looked hard at me then, as though I'd gasp in shock or gratitude. I was still a convent girl, mind. As much as she and Mr Dryer might be perched together acting the part of Ma and father, they'd never give me up in so easy and usual a fashion. I didn't feel surprised or thankful. I felt only a sickness start up in the pit of my belly. Tom looked as though he wished himself gone.

"Tom's agreed to the terms. He'll work for me, here in the house. When he's earned back what I've laid out for your keep and the earnings I give up by losing you, then you'll be married. Mr Dryer will keep you on; should you begin losing your fights, Tom will have to make up that loss as well.

Marriage cannot break your bond to Mr Dryer. That will end only when he says so, unless you or Tom can clear your debt of years. Tom understands this."

Tom only looked miserable. How well did he know then what he'd done? He'd gone to ask for my freedom and instead he'd sold himself.

"Don't look so, Ruth," Ma said now. "You're thinking that it will take years for Tom to pay back what I'd lose."

I wasn't; I was thinking only how sorry he looked and how dearly he must wish he'd never met me. My eyes found the child in mourning dress, looking out of her little picture. Her eyes were nothing to Tom's.

"I've considered that," Ma said, "and he may have you now. Jane will move into the garret and you can make yourselves a room together in the cellar. Your married home." Here she laughed. "Tom will begin work tonight and later he'll have what he's come asking for. Now, you've a bout tonight, Mr Dryer tells me, so go and do whatever it is you do to ready yourself. Your husband will stay here and learn the ways of the house."

And so it was that at thirteen or fourteen I was given to Tom in Ma's parlour, and bound together more tightly than we'd ever have been in a church. Mr Dryer said not a word throughout.

As dawn came that morning, we had our first kiss, in the dark of the cellar, on bed linen already clammy from the damp of the air. I whispered to him how sorry I was. I called him a fool.

"I'm your fool now," he said. "I hope you'll not be sorry any longer."

"You're a dear fool," I said, and he kissed me again. His lips were salty, and softer than I'd thought.

We lay still a long time. I with my head on his chest, he with his arm about my shoulders, both of us still fully clothed and on top of the blankets. I'd never been held so by anyone before. The closest I'd come was when Dora would push against my back for warmth in winter. When I was sure Tom was asleep, and just as sure that I'd lie wakeful all the night long, I felt his breath stir against my hair.

"I meant to take you out of here," he whispered. He said it so soft I knew he thought me sleeping. He said it like a private thing.

I thought, *Now it's I who'll have to take us both out of here.* I'd never considered before that such a thing might be done, but in that moment I swore it; Tom mustn't stay in the convent to have the goodness bled from him drop by drop. I'd take him out. I felt the wish to save him and keep him good burn so fiercely in my mind that I'd have found it unbearable then, if I'd known; five years on would find nothing much changed and the damp of the cellar grown deep in our lungs.

Chapter 3

✤ ✤ ✤

I say that nothing much changed, but time never will stand still. Dora was delivered of a boy, the first boy we ever kept—girls Ma had tried sometimes to keep as being useful later, though Dora and I were the only ones to live long. This boy Dora thought Mr Dryer's own son, and so he was kept and named Jack. Mr Dryer certainly thought Jacky his own. He dandled the thing upon his knee and bought it all manner of frills and blankets. Dora looked at it only when Mr Dryer visited; the rest of the time it passed from hand to hand, cooed over by whichever of the misses was bored. Most often it was left to scream itself quiet in the garret. I'd never minded infants one way or the other, but Jacky wasn't what you'd call sweet. He was thin and squirming and yellowish pale. He did nothing but shriek or stare. I left him to the other girls, and when Dora tried to pass him to me, I said, "I thought you'd a mind that this one should live," and she'd let me be.

Even when he grew, he stayed thin and yellow. He was a sidling, spying creature and moved about the place in much the way the rats did; he roamed everywhere, but still you barely saw him, and when you did it was a nasty little shock. When Mr Dryer called and had a mind to see the brat, he'd have to be found and made nice. As the years passed, Mr Dryer's interest seemed only to grow as everyone else's waned. By the time Jacky was four, Mr Dryer had him fibbing at the dummy in the yard, though you could tell, even then, that he'd no talent for it. He'd hit it away all right, but when the dummy swung toward him, Jacky would shriek and jump backward, as if it meant to fib him back. Mr Dryer would cuff him around the ear then, and Jacky would shriek anew. When Mr Dryer wasn't cursing Jacky for his cowardice against a dummy, he was using him as a little footman. He liked Jacky to bring a tray, with rum in two glasses for himself and Dora and a bowl of perfumed water, to wash his goaty face and hands once he'd done with my sister. Anyone else would've jibbed at being treated so, but Jacky panted like a dog and ran to fetch the tray the moment Mr Dryer's boot touched the step.

Tom and I expected to have a babber of our own, but we never did. I couldn't say I was sorry, though Tom, I thought, would've liked to play the daddy. We never talked of it, for what would be the use? I supposed that part of me was broke, along with my teeth and knuckles.

Ma, in this time, had grown so weak that she sat abed all day, shouting for one or another of us from her pillow and only heaving herself up occasionally to stump about the house, leaning upon her stick, peering at the misses through swollen eyes. She did this even when it made her wince and moan, even when it took her an age to climb the stairs. She drooled in great quantities—caused by the mercury treatments for her sickness, but nonetheless ugsome. Her face grew steadily more lumpen, her gait skewed. She brought to mind an old hound with a leg missing. Her suspicions were grown as wild as her mind was grown addled, so that she might accuse Dora of holding coins back and never see that she was quite brazenly wearing Ma's own comb in her hair.

Dora was mistress of the house in all ways that signified. If Ma gave an order my sister didn't like, what then could Ma do to make her biddable? Even the bullies never would go near to Ma's bedside unless sent there by Dora. Slowly, we all felt the changes trickle through the house. At table Ma could no longer stand long enough, nor hold her hand steady enough, to wield the ladle. She only sat, muttering even while she ate. Dora didn't use food the way that Ma had, as punishment or reward. As soon as my sister had served herself, she wasn't fashed who else might have not enough or too much. She swung her ladle with a sloppy, distracted hand. It wasn't just, but it set us all a little freer.

Tom worked the door every night, staying up till dawn to keep the misses safe and the cullies calm. Dora liked to use me as more than just a threat, which was all our ma had ever done. Ma was always happy to take a stick to a girl's head herself, but Dora didn't tend that way. The first time she ordered me to beat a miss, a shivering creature who'd run off still wearing the silks the convent lent her and been dragged back, that first time I looked at her and said, "What shall I have for it?"

"Oh, I don't care," Dora said. "Take the cut she would've kept for herself tonight. It'll teach her to mind."

"Then you'd better take the silks from her back or they really will be spoiled," I said.

In truth, I didn't beat her hard, though you'd not think it to hear her. That shivering girl put six shillings and eight into my hand that night, and it was the most I'd been allowed to keep for myself for years. After that, I played Dora's beating hand whenever she needed. I began to keep back some of the money from my mills. Whereas Ma had been sharp and wary, my sister was too lazy to quarrel with me over it. She'd rule the girls with a fist of iron because she'd Tom and me to do it for her, but she couldn't ask us to watch ourselves.

We needed that money; though Ma hadn't liked to give away a penny, she'd bought the things we needed, our bread and blankets. Dora wouldn't stir herself to see to any of that. I bought what we must have and I saved where I could, and slowly I built a hidden purse, which was only what I should always have had. In my mind, I kept it either to buy my freedom from Mr Dryer or, more likely, to run away with Tom.

Then the day came that Dora took it into her head to have Ma's room for her own. Tom carried Ma upstairs kicking and shrieking, and all the house saw it. Ma lived in the garret then, and all her hold over us was lost. The staircase to the garret was so steep and rickety that Ma could barely manage it; soon enough she never came down at all and her only care was that she be kept well dosed with her medicines. Jacky took to hiding up there with her, and would run for whatever she bid him fetch.

THE YEAR OF 1799, when I turned nineteen, was a hard one even for us in the convent, who never did feel hard times like most. Some folks blamed the war with France and others said the crops had failed. All we really knew was that each day the bread was dearer and yet less like something you'd want to eat. The gents still came to call, but were closer with their purses; the price of living had risen for everyone. You'd only to step outside to see the hunger carved into the people's faces. We had more than most folk about us, but still there were nights when I woke with my belly clenched like a fist. This, despite dipping into my little purse of savings, that's how dear flour was then. It was bitter to be watching it drip away on bread and still to go about hungry. I dipped and it dripped and at last it was gone and we'd nothing but what we could earn by the day, or what Dora gave us. I won't list here half the lengths we went to, to scrape a meal from turnips and barley and sometimes peas. I'll only tell that the urchins on our lane came home with handfuls of nettles for their pot, and seeing this, I went right out after them and gathered my own, coated though they were with muck from the river.

On the last day of August, Tom and I were fencing with wooden bills in the yard. We did this to keep me quick on my pins and had been doing it so long that now we parried and thrust like a country dance laid out, barely ever landing a hit. My husband—I called him so and always had, though we'd never been married before God—was nimble for his size. There was something comic about such a bull-beef cull bobbing on his toes, something comic and beautiful both, to my eyes.

Tom's mug was red, but his breath came evenly and his eyes were fixed on the bill in my hand in a way that would've made me fearful, had we been milling in earnest. He had to lean down to meet my stick with his own, and his huge frame bobbing and bending so, he always put me in mind of a bear.

I thrust toward him and he put out his bill to hit my own away, but as he did, Dora screeched my name from the doorway behind him. Sometimes my sister had a voice on her like a pig at slaughter. Tom half turned in surprise and in so doing thumped me, not upon the bill, but the fingers, just above the second joint. I cursed aloud.

Tom span back to me.

"Bloody damn," he said.

"Never a truer word," I said, and held up my hand. Blood was running down my arm and dripping from my elbow in its soft way.

"Oh, hell, Ruthie."

"No matter," I said, though it stung like the devil.

"Let me see." Tom took my hand. "Oh, it's a nasty one."

"It don't signify."

I held my hand out in front of me so that it shouldn't drip upon our clothes. The drops that fell were straightaway eaten by dust and turned into splashes of black mud.

Dora had grown impatient and come toward us. Now she sighed as though my bleeding were a broken plate.

"Mr Dryer bids me tell you"—she was looking at me as though I were a sorry child made dirty—"that he'll be taking you to mill at the fair tomorrow. He's all hot about it, I couldn't say why. He'll be vexed indeed if you've broken your hand, Ruth. You'd best not have broken it."

"The fair!" Tom said.

"It ain't broken," I told her, "and if I had, I couldn't help it."

"As long as you've not," Dora said. "So, will I tell him you'll do what he asks? He tells me you'd better get ready to put on a good show."

"I don't know what I can do in one night," I said, "but you may tell him I'll stand up for him anywhere he chooses."

"The fair, Ruth," Tom said again.

I smiled at him. I'd not let Dora see my pleasure, but oh, I felt it.

"I told him as much," Dora said. "I said I needn't speak to you at all."

"Indeed you needn't, if it's such labour for you." I looked to the air above her head as if it were of more interest than she might hope to be.

"It ain't so much labour," Dora said, looking again at my arm, which in spite of my holding it out had dripped blood upon my bare and dusty feet, "as it is ugly," and here she smiled at me as though I were a gent, a wide and maddening smile, and swept away, holding her skirts up more than she need.

Now Tom and I looked at each other and laughed aloud. Dora heard us and, thinking we mocked her, called back that we might go and rot.

"The fair," we both said at once, and he took me into his arms, even knowing as he did that his shirt would have to be scrubbed with salt, to lift out the blood.

St James' Fair, held every year for the first two weeks of September, was to us what it was to all good Bristolians: the finest time of the year. Oh, there were always those piss-lickers who called for the fair to be outlawed, but come September, there it was, fine as fivepence. All the autumns of my life I'd walked beneath the bunting there; it was the best time for the misses to find trade, as good as ten ships of hungry sailors come ashore. When we were younger, Dora and I would follow the girls, to find likely lads and help them make the acquaintance of the misses, if they were shy. Always, though, I'd found time to visit the sights of the fair—for what brat wouldn't?—and the greatest of these by far was the boxing booth. Any time that I could beg the penny entrance, I went in there and gawped like a hayseed. The crowds that gathered would have you shaking your head in wonder, if you could find the room to shake it, so close were they packed. The big-name pugs down from the Fives Court in London would come onto that stage in the evening and show such high displays of science as would have you gasping aloud. Sometimes these London pugs would take on a valiant Charlie from the crowd, and he'd only to stay three rounds to win a shilling. He'd not even to win. I'd been aching for years to throw my hat in the ring at the fair and see if I could stay the three rounds. Mr Dryer had forbidden it, though it was Ma who'd told me that sour piece of news. I was only to watch and learn and take that learning to The Hatchet ring, where Mr Dryer could take a lot more from my mill than a shilling. Now he wasn't only allowing it but ordering me there. I could scarce believe it and didn't care the reason.

As low as we lived, and as sinful, we were never in real need; bawdy houses and taverns always will float through the harshest times. This is because those folks as can afford diversion will always want it; the lady boxer may stay afloat, too, for the same reason, while all about her sink and pull at her skirts.

"At least something is left, look."

There was the heel of a loaf in the kitchen. Tom took it up and tore it in two.

I took it from him quick enough. It was as coarse as if it'd been baked with sawdust and nearly as dry. I tipped the last of the milk into a saucer and we took all to the table, to sit and wipe our bread through the milk till it was soft enough that it wouldn't cut our gums to eat it.

The kitchen was dark but still warm enough; the misses would only have been in bed an hour or so and a grumble of red still showed in the grate. Tom's face was in shadow. I could see only his shape and the movement of his jaw, working the bread like a cow.

I'd not slept. Tom had found a cull we trusted to take a turn at the door and we'd carried the rushlight to bed at an uncommon hour, midnight or so. I'd meant to rest and rise fresh, but habit is a strong master. I lay in the dark with my eyes open and my mind ran on by itself, along shadowed roads that led to strange places. Above me the sounds of the convent played out, sounds I knew so well that I could near see it all. I might as well have been up there with them, for all the rest I got. I thought Tom hadn't been much different, though he did sleep, at last. I lay and listened to his deep, satisfied breathing and by then I was so weary and queer that it seemed he did it just to tease me, and I hated him a little.

Now we sat in the dark kitchen with only the sounds our own mouths made upon the bread.

"I've a thrupence kept for gin," Tom said. "Shall we fetch a dram on our way?"

This was my husband asking if I were fearful.

"Lord, yes," I said.

I was fearful and excited both. This was to be the most significant day of my life; as other girls dream of their wedding day, I'd dreamt of this. Of course I needed gin, to harden my hopes and my fists.

The fair always did have something of the dream about it, laid out always the same, a village of wooden booths and bunting, a full month in the making. This year, the year I was to be part of it, it seemed to me that every fair before it had stirred itself up to form this new one, waiting for the crowds to arrive.

The day was horrible warm, the sky low and heavy as damp skirts. My head swam from the strange air and the gin. Every year, since the day we met, we'd been here together, crushed in the crowd at the front of the boxing tent, cheering every blow.

Perhaps for common folk it was a diversion, nothing more, but for a pug the fair was a starting line, the place where a cull could make his name, and the buzz was that this year all the fancy would be on the lookout for the next champion of England. Gentleman Jackson had stepped down as holding the title too long, and finding no man willing to match him. All the fancy would come on the rush to Bristol now, the city which had birthed so many champions of the ring. Jack Slack, Ben Brain, The Tinman—all of them were Bristol boys. Even old Jack Broughton had fought his first bouts at St James' Fair. Jem Belcher, the lad tipped to have a good chance at the championship up in London that year, was called "the Bristol youth," and he'd had his start on the very stage that I was to step onto now. Every hopeful young rough would be out with his fives raised, and every fancy name crowding the ring. Tom had great hopes of watching one of these high-stakes mills, or of picking out beforehand which of the likely lads the fancy might take a shine to and carry up to London. My thoughts were fixed on my own fight and I couldn't see beyond, but I thought I'd feel different when once it was done. I liked to see good science in a mill as much as the fancy—perhaps more, for I could learn from the tricks used and turn them to my own use.

Tom held his head up as we walked, and it gladdened my heart to see him unfurl from his stoop. He bent only a very little, so that he might hold my hand, the difference in our heights being so vast. We both called out and waved to the people we knew: Mrs Dick, who sold hot potatoes from a brazier, Black Lou the piper, and the magician's boy, and many more men and women laying out their wares, tuning up fiddles, or hanging bunting. Two brats followed behind us till Tom turned and waved at them, at which they ran off, shrieking up a racket. I supposed they took him for a giant. The great wheel of the flying coaches stood over all.

The boxing tent was something to see, with its painted front showing pictures of bare-chested millers knocking seven kinds of hell out of each other and plenty of gore done in buckets of scarlet. In years before I'd used to stand before it and set upon any girl I could, to encourage the gents passing in to feel obliged to stop and watch, and perhaps throw me the penny entrance. The fancy like to see a cat-fight before the main attraction, even between children. Now I'd fight on its stage, and not as a Charlie from the crowd. I was both swollen and quaking with the thought of it.

The wooden booth had a window cut into it and here an old woman sat, to take the pennies from the fancy. She barely looked at us but only held out her hand for the money.

"My wife is come to fight," Tom said.

Now the woman goggle-eyed me.

"You'd best come in, dearie," she said, and swung open a door cut so neatly into the wall of the booth that I'd never known it was there. Inside it was done up like a gypsy caravan, or almost like, with a stove and a kettle, a lamp and a pair of stools. Behind her was a pallet bed of rags and quilts. I stepped inside. The ceiling was close enough to reach up and touch, if I'd a mind to do it.

"Your young fellow had best wait out there a time," she said. "He's a bully one, ain't he?"

I looked back at Tom.

"Go on," he said, "I'll be in here," and he gestured into the tent, where the ring and the crowd waited.

"Go on in and wait. I'll not charge you a penny, neither," the old woman said, and laughed aloud.

She turned to look at me, and I saw that beneath the frilled cap and curled white hair she had a pug's nose, broken and never made straight, just as mine was. My gaze went to her hands then, to see if the knuckles pushed up high as mine did, but she had on gloves and I couldn't be sure.

"Now, duck, I'm Mrs Narrow, wife of Mr Narrow, who owns this booth. Now suppose you tell me your name and then we're square."

"Ruth Webber," I said, for I'd long ago taken Tom's name as my own.

"Ruth"—she handed me a pair of padded mufflers—"you'll be what we call a novelty. That is to say, we mean to cheat a bit. Not so much, you know, as to be wicked, just so as the fancy sees a good show."

"I never have cheated before," I said.

"'Cheated,' why, that's a strong word," Mrs Narrow said, though it'd been her word. "This is theatricals. You're to win your fight, Ruthie, but at first you must seem to be about to lose it. Can you do that?"

"Are all the fights at the fair theatricals, then?" I was so disappointed as to be unsure that I wanted to go on stage at all.

"My stars no, all the London boys are fighting to win, ain't they? This is only a piece of play to warm the stage. Your swell fellow said you'd be good enough for this. Is he wrong? There's a good purse in it for you."

"I'm good enough," I said, though what she meant by it I wasn't sure.

"You're to seem to lose, then you'll rally and take the fight. Fall at least

49

once, duckie, and be sure not to knock yourself cold when you do. That would spoil it all."

I was more nervous now, everything about this being new to me. I wished I could just put up my fives and fight. I didn't know how else it was to be done, after all. She sent me out then. There was a crowd as thick as fog. I pushed toward the stage and climbed up upon it so that Tom could find me, and I was right to do it, because he was there in a moment.

"You'll second me, won't you?" I said.

"Let them tell me I mayn't," Tom said.

He'd barely ever seconded me before; Mr Dryer hadn't liked to choose him at The Hatchet before we were married, and since then Tom had worked near every night on the convent door. He looked so gleeful now I had to turn my eyes from his face. It was making me churn inside with nerves. I didn't tell him what Mrs Narrow had said. I wasn't ashamed, or perhaps I was, but that wasn't why I held my tongue. I kept silent because to speak it scared me, and because, if anyone should hear, the whole would be ruined and Mr Dryer would be sorry he'd trusted me. It caused me a little bitterness to think that Mr Dryer had sent me there to play a trick upon the fancy, not to fight in earnest. I wondered how much of the purse I could keep.

I stood at the ropes, looking out at a crowd greater than any I'd stood in front of before. At last I spied Mr Dryer, in a tall hat, talking to another gent. It calmed me to see him, though he didn't look at me. He'd a lady clinging to his arm; his wife, perhaps. Dora wouldn't be glad to see her. I twisted to look for my sister, but she wasn't to be found. She'd sworn to watch me only because she knew I'd rather she didn't; now she'd likely not be fashed to come, just when it would be most fun to have her there. These thoughts kept me from boiling over entirely. That, and Tom, who was silent and steady in my corner, waiting on one knee for me to sit upon the other. I left the ropes and went to him. I blessed him for his silence then. The feel of his thigh beneath my own was more comforting than anything he might've said.

Before too long there came a cull climbing over the ropes and taking his place as second in the other corner, followed by the little man who always squired the fights on the booth. I guessed now that he was Mr Narrow. He wore an ill-fitting wig and rushed about the stage, crying out, "Come forward, and see this valiant miss take on a champion of the ring!"

He gestured that I should stand. My head seemed to come up faster than the rest of me. The betting began. From what I could hear the crowd hadn't much hopes of me, and soon I saw the reason; the cully they sent into the ring was near as big as Tom, and with the meanest mug I ever saw. If I'd not liked the sound of theatricals before, I was glad of it now.

"The more in the hat, the harder they fight!" Mr Narrow called out.

Tom was shifting about nervously; he didn't know about theatricals, and thought me ready for a beating.

"Don't fret," I said, but I didn't explain. I couldn't tell if he heard me.

My eye found Mr Dryer again. He looked to be arguing with the gents he was with, Mr Sinclair and the handsome cull that Dora was so taken with.

"This young miss will stand up against the hardest fellow I have on my booth," cried Mr Narrow.

"Step up," I called to the big cull. "Big as you are, you'll take such hits as make you feel like a little girl!"

Mr Dryer always liked me to call out in this way, and now Mr Narrow looked at me and nodded.

"Then let the same be true of you, though you be more sow than woman," the big cull replied, shrugging off his shirt to hand to his second. This friend of his laughed out loud to hear such high wit.

"Sow I may be," I said, "but I kick like a donkey, as you'll soon tell."

All this was said loud, for the ears of the fancy who crowded the ring. Already I could feel my vision narrowing; I might call out for the crowd, but all I could see was that big hackum, with his thick skull waiting to be broke. I had to keep reminding myself about the theatricals. I hoped he'd know how best to do it.

Mr Narrow waved us to our corners. Mrs Narrow had climbed up beside where Tom knelt. She held a bottle of water to splash upon my face if I should need it. I sat on Tom's knee. His big hand came up and rested on my arm. I knew he was wondering if he should take me out of there, but I knew just as well that he'd not dare, unless I asked him to do it. I just stared at that great lobcock opposite me, sitting on the knee of his own second. He didn't meet my eye but gazed at the air above my head, or perhaps at Tom.

At last, after too long and yet too soon, the betting was done and Mr Narrow called us up to scratch. As soon as I was there I might've been back at The Hatchet. I knew I could take him; I knew it. I forgot again about the theatricals and had to pull myself back—I was going to take him because he was going to let me. First I must seem to lose.

Mr Narrow called out, "Fight!"

We began our dance. I threw a few fast pokes, though not much to hurt. When Tom and I played at fighting in the convent yard, to please the misses or the cullies, he'd move his head when I fibbed him, so as to make the force seem more than it was. This cull did nothing of the sort, but rather looked at me with a scornful eye. This riled me a little, and I threw my fist in earnest. There, he felt that. He shook his head like a bullock and I threw two more, fast as a shuttle. These I pulled back so as not to really hurt, but put enough into them to make them sting. He wasn't scornful now. My hand stung something cruel; the cloth inside the mufflers had ripped the scabs from the cut that Tom had given me the day before.

I threw a few darts with the left and parried with my right forearm, to rest my poor wounded mauler. He threw a few, but slow, and I dodged him rather than block, where I could. As I began to plan our pageantry in my mind—I'd leave myself open now and let him appear to best me—this ass of a man squared up and threw such a clout as to knock me fair backward. He didn't pull it but smashed me right in the ivories. I fell on my rump and didn't feel the pain at first, only the weight and the power. It was as I pulled myself to my feet that I was aware of my lips, my nose, my very teeth aflame. Blood ran down my chin; my lip was split. Mrs Narrow pulled me upright and helped me to the corner, where Tom waited. He'd been arguing with Mrs Narrow, I could see it in their faces, but they'd not quarrel before me. Tom rubbed my shoulders and Mrs Narrow sponged my lip, and gave me a drink of water. Then my thirty seconds was past, and she brought me back to scratch, in the centre of the ring.

I looked at the cull who'd made me taste blood and saw that he was serious—he meant to pound me as much as ever he could, not last out the rounds, not lose for a purse. I saw his eyes, and then again I was driven backward with such a fib to the gills as set my skull to humming. I didn't fall this time, though it was a near thing.

He had me frit now. I'd not had such a mill as this since I was a girl, when it seemed that everyone was bigger and heavier than I. My quick pins were the only skill I'd claim to. I began to dance about him, this way and that. I forgot where I was, the crowd, the tent. I didn't hope that Mr Narrow would stop the fight. I saw only those two great mauling fists.

I was faster than he. He was indeed a bull, thickly muscled but slow to the turn. I danced about him; I struck him where I could. I stopped and guarded till my arm grew numb from taking the fibs upon it. His left made a feint at my stomach and I stopped it with my right elbow, even as his right went for my face. I blocked with my left forearm, but I didn't throw my head back quick enough and he drove my own arm into the bridge of my nose. This was how it went; I parried the blows all right, but so heavy were his maulers that even to block them was to take a pounding of a kind.

I danced so long that soon enough I was flagging. Every hit I landed hurt my hand; the inside of the muffler was wet with my own blood. He began again to close in, throwing his left directly at my face. I blocked him at the wrist and struck him a backhanded blow across the mug with my left, but I was so weak by then that he only took the hit, and dealt me a fib in earnest. I was driven off my legs, and only with difficulty stood.

Again I was brought to sit upon Tom's knee, again I saw my husband's face grown feverish with rage.

He muttered to me, "If you need, Ruth, throw the fight. You drop to your knees, girl."

Mrs Narrow threw him a glare. Tom cursed aloud, though he didn't precisely aim his curse at her.

I began to reply, but my head was too fuddled to think what I meant to say, and in the end I only patted his hand with my soaking muffler, and moved to stand.

Mrs Narrow pressed my arm before she left me at the line. I supposed she meant some comfort by it.

I began again to dance. I felt a new surge of strength, and knew from experience that it was likely to be my last. I had this chance only, and must use it or do as Tom said, and drop the match. As that whoreson closed in once more, no pity in his eyes, I began to mill on the retreat in the style of old Jack Broughton, who'd been dead ten years then and was still called the father of English boxing. I struck one, two, three at his face, all the time stepping backward. The cull followed me and in that way he put his own weight into my blows. The first two fibs were pokes only, but the third caught him neatly on the right side of his jaw, even as he moved toward me.

My wounded hand screamed with the pain of it, but I fibbed his jaw all right, I'll say I did. My stars, but I hoped I broke it. He'd not had an idea it was coming, and his head was driven back like a bladder on a stick. I couldn't have given a fig at that moment for broken fingers; I'll swear home it was one of the most satisfying things I'd ever known to see his face driven sideways, his mouth opening like a noddy's, his breath huffing out an evil wind.

My chest was filled with heat. I meant if I could to see him stove in, to turn him to dogmeat. Quick as anything, before he could come back to his senses, I fibbed him as hard as I knew how with my good left hand. This time a tooth left his mouth to decorate the boards, and I screamed aloud with the wild joy of it. He had blood and spittle coating his chin. His mug was the match of mine for blood, now.

That's as far as I remember, that day. I heard later that directly after that he planted me a good facer and my head hit the boards something devilish when I went down. The scar upon the back of my head, which to this day forms a little bald worm amongst my hair, would seem to prove that tale true. I remember none of it. To me, the fight ended with his tooth flying across the stage, a much more agreeable end than the breaking of my crown.

I was told that I lay there all through the cheers and the declaring of that clotpole as a hero for soaking the sawdust with my blood. He had his arm lifted high and took his cheers, and I, half cold as I must've been, knew nothing of this. By all accounts, when Mrs Narrow came to help me up I wrested myself from her and lurched back up to scratch, as though the mill wasn't done.

It was nothing much that I didn't know what I did, or that I went back to scratch. I'd spent the main of my life at scratch in one way or another, and it must've seemed more natural than a feather bed should've done at that moment, had one appeared. What happened next, mind, was that this brute, seeing me lurching bloody as a butcher's block toward him, came for me quite as though he meant to knock me down again. I was told that when he moved for me, Tom leapt forward and dealt him a facer that turned his nose to smash. It still makes me smile to think of it now. I'm only sorry that I've no recollection of that boy's eyes as his nose came to join him inside his own head, or the sweet sound of my good Tom's mauler turning his bones to powder.

PART 2

George

✦ ✦ ✦

Chapter 4

* * *

I have never considered myself a fighter; call me, instead, a gaming man—a far merrier mode of living, I assure you. The sweat and sawdust of the prize-ring cannot compare to the elegance and high excitement of the gaming houses. If ever the two were to compete for the title of Champion of Amusement, the foppish gaming house would drive the brutish prize-ring to its knees and skip away, its pockets jingling. No, I was never particularly interested in pugilism, but for the pleasure that might be found in placing wagers upon the outcome. Eventually, however, I came to feel differently—although that was in pursuit of the greatest gamble of all.

The stakes were against me right at the start of play; God, in his questionable wisdom, saw fit to give me three elder brothers, all as brutish as gentlemen's sons are wont to be. I, being the youngest, was often the target of their jokes and rough treatment. In retrospect, perhaps John, Charles, and Edward were quite as foul to one another as they were to me, but I took it hard. I was always small for my age and prone to weeping, which infuriated my father and my tutor in equal measure. At ten years old it was decided that I should be sent away to school, to see if the bullying of the schoolyard might succeed in toughening my spirit, where that of my brothers had failed.

I could not believe that my mother had agreed to the plan. I see now that she meant to do me a service by it, but at ten years old I felt only baffled and betrayed. It seemed to me that my brothers had been at fault, but it was I who was to be punished. All the journey to Bristol—which was not above two hours, but felt longer—I sat in the carriage beside my tutor, quivering with the tears I dared not shed in front of him. Especially painful, I recall, was the thought of leaving my favourite dog, Balloo, an old and affectionate hound of my father's.

I thought nothing of where I was to go until we were nearly arrived.

Mr Allen's school was a small private academy for the sons of gentlemen, near to St Michael's church in Bristol. There were twelve scholars residing there when I arrived, and although that number fluctuated over the years, it never varied greatly. The boys comprised two types. The first category, into which I fell, were younger sons of noble stock, who could not expect much by way of inheritance but must nevertheless make their way in the world in a manner befitting the reputation of their family. We were all to be prepared for universities and the respectable professions, such as divinity and law. The other boys were the sons of gentlemen merchants, come to learn book-keeping and the casting of accounts, as well as those arts which might enable them to mix with the quality; as with many private institutions, Mr Allen's school was much preoccupied with the teaching of fencing, dancing, and etiquette. My father had paid enough that I need share my bed with only one other boy.

I was standing beside the narrow window, watching the carriage as it drove out of sight. I was very close to tears. When the chamber door opened I wheeled to face it and felt a bitter disappointment at first sight of Perry, as though I had expected to see my mother arrived to carry me home.

Perry Sinclair was the same age as I, but my opposite in countenance. I was slender and dark, whereas Perry looked exactly as I wished to look myself: fair and of good height, with broad shoulders and strong limbs. He had pink, hearty cheeks and lashes so fair as to be almost white, although at that moment they were darkened by tears. His shoulder was held by Mr Allen, the schoolmaster, in a grip that implied that the boy had been dragged there. As we looked each other over I thought, with a determined kind of dread, that I had better knock him down as soon as ever I could, to get things straight between us.

"Make yourselves nice, boys," the master said, "and come straight down, or you won't have time for tea before chapel."

He shut the door behind him with a neat click, somehow more intimidating than a slam.

We were left to eye each other, both of us awkward in our new coats and moleskin breeches. I struggled with the catch of my trunk and got it open only with the greatest effort; Perry watched me wordlessly.

When we had made ourselves as nice as ten-year-old boys know how to—which is not much beyond a washing of the hands and face—we made our way down the staircase and out into the yard, where several other boys gathered. Their bored and comfortable air declared them seasoned residents of the school. Perry and I were easily the youngest there.

The moment we got down to the yard, I put my scheme into action and tripped him. I did this easily, as we came off the bottom step, in exactly the way my brother John had tripped me countless times at home. Whereas I would tend to fall obediently and perhaps weep, Perry fell only to his knees, from which position he seized my stockinged leg and pulled me down beside him. We set-to upon the ground, the other boys howling with excitement. By the time Mr Allen pulled us apart we had both dirtied our new costumes disgracefully. In the event, Perry and I were so evenly matched— for I was sinewy though I was small, and not afraid to bite—and the fight so soon ended that it served to make us equals.

We were caned straight after chapel. Mr Allen called us into his office and beat us one after the other, both trying not to cry out, both failing and shrieking at the last like piglets. When he had exhausted himself and sent us out, Perry and I wiped each other's tears and compared our welts, each of us sure he had received the worse punishment. I'll wager that there is nothing better able to cement a friendship than the experience of being whipped one boy beside the other. All young bedfellows should suffer it, just for the sake of camaraderie.

I had never had a real friend before. Perry was a younger son, just as I was, though he had only one brother and two younger sisters.

"My sisters are a pestilence," he said, as we paced about the courtyard after dinner. "They are fleas. They do nothing but irritate, until I have to slap at them just for peace and am thrashed for it."

I nodded emphatically. "My brothers will do the same. They torment me until I cannot be calm and then it is I who is called naughty and sent to bed."

We stopped and leant against the wall, but two of the older boys, standing close by, looked at us fiercely until we began to move again.

"I should rather be sent to bed than thrashed. Early to bed is a soft chastisement. You need hardly be afraid of that." Perry put his hands into the pockets of his breeches and assumed an air of great nonchalance.

"You, Sinclair," the master called, "take those hands from your pockets. This is not a dock-yard."

Perry did so, and I did not remark upon it.

"Pish!" I said, instead. "Before I am sent there I have likely been thrashed twice by my brothers' hands. Your nurse never beat you as my brothers have me. They are brutes of the first order."

"I should rather have a brute for a brother than Arthur. He does nothing but study his books. He would not stir if the house was burning."

"I wish my house would burn, with my brothers in it," I said.

"Do not wish for that, bird-wit. Your fortune would be burned up with them."

"Pirates, then. I wish pirates would come up the cliffs and slaughter them all in their beds."

"You will burn eternally for saying that, you know, George." Perry sounded perfectly peaceful about the notion.

"Do not you wish the same for Arthur? You lie if you say you do not."

"I never think of it."

"You lie, then."

"Upon my honour, I do not think of it. If he were to disappear, I suppose I would be glad. But I would rather be a pirate myself, than take Arthur's place."

"Oh, yes, let's. Let's be pirates together and never go home but to show our chests of gold."

"I will be captain," Perry said.

I replied by pushing him, hard. I had not yet learnt how to express a gentlemanly objection. I pushed him and we fell to fighting and had to be pulled apart.

On that occasion, Mr Allen fetched not a cane but a measuring rod of birch-wood.

"Hold still, Sinclair," he said to Perry, and when my friend could not stop his hand from shaking, he whipped my own palm first. I believe I shrieked at the very first blow—the burning buzz of a wasp sting across my palm. I could see nothing but my own tears. Again and again he whipped, and each time I squealed aloud.

"Remember this, young Mr Bowden, when next you are inclined to behave like a savage," he finally said, and sent me out.

I looked over at Perry as I left, but he would not look at me; he was holding his hand by the wrist to still it.

"Now, you quaking pudding," I heard Mr Allen say to him, as the door swung to behind me. Perry's shriek was quite audible through the wood.

There was a wooden pew set outside Mr Allen's door for boys to tremble upon, and it was there I seated myself, to examine what injury had been done me. My palm was striped with lines of white where the cane had struck and a hellish purple between. At the edge of my hand, where the rod had bitten repeatedly, I had begun to bleed. I was weeping when at last Perry emerged, still clutching his inflamed hand by the wrist, his eyes rather dazed.

We compared our injuries. Perry's hand was not bleeding.

"Now, look, George, and don't cry any longer," Perry said, digging his nails into his injured palm until he, too, sprung bright red.

"Don't, Perry!"

"Hush and give me your hand," he said. "There. Now we are blood brothers. I will never let any harm befall you, and you must defend me likewise. Loyalty until death."

I found this thrilling and dried my tears at once.

"Like soldiers," I said.

"More than soldiers," said Perry, but I could not think what that meant.

When Perry and I were not fighting each other, we were laying bets. We had no money, for the younger boys were not allowed to carry coins lest it encourage vice; Perry and I bet our possessions instead. I would lay my pen against his handkerchief, or my pocketknife against his bag of marbles. Our things passed between us in this way so often that sometimes we forgot who owned what. We had a wager for everything: whether there would be pease-porridge or milk gruel for supper, or the number of times the parson would clear his throat while he read the lesson; these were contests as exciting to us as the result of a race.

The school kept its boys very close. We were always within its walls unless we were walking to church, and we did not see much of the city even then. We were less worldly than we might have been had we been kept at home; we had no society outside of the other boys and no feminine company at all. In these circumstances, who can be surprised that Perry and I grew to be more, perhaps, than soldiers? We studied, slept, bathed, and dressed side by side. As we grew and our bodies made their own demands, it was the most natural thing in the world that Perry and I should relieve ourselves together. It was not unusual in that school—I might go so far as to say that it was commonplace. All growing boys sin, unless they are Christ himself. For Perry and myself, we began so young that we did not consider the nature of the sin until the sin itself had formed our nature. Until, that is, it was too late for real repentance. One cannot repent what one does not wish to alter.

In the winter Perry's family lived at Bristol, in a house at Queen Square.

His father intended that Perry live at home with them in the winters and attend school as a day-boy; we were in terror, as winter approached, that we should be parted. We were sure that Mr Allen would place another boy as my bedfellow, and once that happened, how were we to come together again? I can only imagine how earnestly Perry must have entreated his father to allow him to remain a boarder. He was joined in his persuasions by Mr Allen, who did not like to see the loss of the boarder's fee, it being so much dearer than that for a day-boy. At the last, it was agreed that Perry stay on and be released into the care of his family only each Friday tea-time and each Sunday, to attend St Mary Redcliffe with his family, rather than St Michael's, beside me. Sometimes, at Mrs Sinclair's express wish, I was allowed to accompany him and partake of the most sumptuous teas—at least, they seemed so, next to the fare we were accustomed to at school.

In the summer, Perry's home was at Aubyn Hall, near the town of Keynsham, only five miles from Bristol. My own home was considerably farther and in the opposite direction, near to the town of Bridgwater. I greatly envied Perry that; his family home was perfectly placed between Bristol and Bath, so as to allow for amusements in either city within two hour's ride.

During the summer, I visited Aubyn Hall and stayed as long as the Sinclairs, and my parents, would allow. I did not find Perry's sisters, Charlotte and Louisa, an annoyance. I delighted in the way they followed us about, or glanced at me and giggled. How much did I envy Perry's home, with those sweet sisters and his elder brother only noticeable as a quiet presence upon the settee, a book open upon his knee.

My mother was pleased at my acquaintance with the Sinclairs. They were a very well regarded family.

I was obliged, of course, to visit my own home also. I found it difficult. All my new and joyful independence would fall away and I would become as shrinking and weak as I had been before I went to school. It was not just John, Charles, and Edward, though they were as thuggish as ever they had been. It was my mother, who would every time be shocked, and, it seemed to me, appalled, by how much I had grown.

"You are not my baby any longer, George," she would say, as though I had done it on purpose to vex her. "You are quite changed. I would hardly have known you."

I did not wish to be her baby, but I should have liked to climb onto her lap. Instead I let her fuss and fret, and order that I have my hair cut.

I always returned to school with relief. I was only really comfortable there, and with Perry.

THE YEAR WE WERE BOTH FIFTEEN, a grievous blow was dealt my friend. We were at school, practising fencing together in the yard. I was quicker on my feet, being so much the lighter. I was driving him backward when Mr Allen came into the courtyard and called out Perry's name. I stopped immediately and Perry took the opportunity to jab me hard in the stomach. His rapier had a stop upon it, so I was not injured, but it winded me enough that I bent over. It was from this position that I heard Mr Allen give the news that Perry's siblings were all taken by smallpox and gravely ill. Before I could straighten up, Perry had sunk to his knees upon the ground. I shuffled to his side and pressed his hand to my cheek. We knelt, I wheezing and Perry weeping, while Mr Allen hovered over us, looking uncharacteristically doubtful as to how to proceed.

Only Perry's younger sister, Miss Charlotte, survived, and she was left scarred. When the pox descended, Mr and Mrs Sinclair had been from home, visiting near relations, and so were saved. As soon as the house was declared safe, Perry's parents returned to bury their children and wished him home. A manservant was dispatched to fetch him.

What a strange, mixed burden for my friend to bear. He had lost two siblings in one swoop, and yet as the only remaining son, he could suddenly expect to be lord of a great estate. He would not speak much, only said that he was not sure that he wanted to go from school. We both wept I know, though we took care to do it privately. Perry, I suppose, wept for his brother and his pretty sister, but I—well, I wept secretly and selfishly, and cursed the fates on my own account that I should be parted from him.

My new bedfellow was a fifteen-year-old merchant's son by the name of Granville Dryer. When first he was shown into my room my heart sank to see him. He was very thin and pale, with the most serious expression imaginable—the very opposite of the sturdy and smiling boy he came to replace. *No fun shall be had here,* I thought.

Granville was not of good stock, being the son of a merchant made rich by trade. Bristol was built on trade, of course, but in the case of the Dryers the wealth was so newly acquired that the family still had the scent of bread-and-dripping dinners hanging about them. His mother dressed like a maid got into the clothes-press of her mistress: a muddle of lace and bright silks. Her son, by contrast, looked quite the little Puritan, with his plain buckles upon his shoes and his unadorned coat. Here I mean plainly cut, not unadorned in the modern, natural style—the tailor's scissors had been guided by the word "serviceable" rather than "fashionable." This grieved me for two reasons: I didn't like to go about with him, dressed as he was, and it was only by his own perverse nature that he wore it. His mother bewailed it at every visit, brushing at his coat as though she could wipe the austerity from it.

"Why will you not wear the frock coat I sent you?" she would scold.

Granville would only stand and wait for her temper to run its short course. When later I glimpsed the lamented frock coat, I better understood his disinclination. It looked like the kind of gold-braided thing one's father would have worn and thought himself the dandy.

At night, listening to Granville's quiet breathing, I ached for Perry, his warm bulk and familiar snores. I missed everything about him; I would have given anything to be scratched by Perry's overlong toenails, or to have to wrest back the blankets that he had stolen.

✦ ✦ ✦

PRIZE-FIGHTING WAS the only subject which could move Granville Dryer to animation. He had persuaded his father and Mr Allen to allow him a subscription to *Felix Farley's Bristol Journal*, from which he carefully cut the sporting pages. These he would peruse in whatever leisure time was afforded us, which did not make for merry company. I could inspire the cove to converse only by asking him about the pugs he admired, at which point he would begin an enthusiastic sermon scarcely less dull than his silence. I thought him the most tedious creature imaginable. I was wrong, however—Granville Dryer was up to his eyes in vice, quite as deeply as Perry and me. He merely had an unattractive coat upon his back to hide it.

One morning, Granville and I sat idly in the garden, upon one of the few benches placed there, trying to eke what warmth there was to be had from the weak March sunshine. The benches were exclusively the province of us older boys, and I still enjoyed the novelty, having so recently been one of those obliged to always sit upon the wall, which was not allowed and likely to land a boy a whipping. Granville, having arrived at the school at the advanced age of fifteen, could not appreciate what privilege we enjoyed. Now he was seated as straight-backed as if he were at church, his sporting pages open upon his knee and his gaze as intent as if he had not read their contents a thousand times before. I was lazily observing a game of shuttlecocks being played only a few feet away by two of the younger boys. They were hopeless players, each spending more time running after the cock than hitting it. When one of the hapless creatures managed to hit the thing straight into Granville's lap he leapt as though stung. I laughed aloud, so rarely had I seen his discomposure rattled. Granville's glare swung between myself, so evidently enjoying his moment of indignity, and the urchin who'd placed him there. It settled on the boy. The bantling looked ready to soil his breeches at having those sobering eyes light upon him.

"What do you mean by throwing this thing at me?" Granville asked.

"Please, sir, it was his fault," the boy replied, pointing at his fellow.

The other boy gaped at the injustice done him.

"You scaly gull! You hit it so skewed I could not help it!"

"Well, now," Granville said, "suppose we can find a means by which we decide which one of you whelps is to blame. George? Are you agreed?"

"Certainly," I replied, without the faintest notion of what he meant. I was desperate for any kind of lark.

"Then let us have you brats set-to." Granville stood and moved purposefully toward the boys. "The loser shall bear the consequence."

They shrank back, and it was clear enough by their faces that they expected him to strike them. Instead he drew a line in the hard mud with the toe of his boot. Then he moved forward perhaps two feet, obliging the first boy to leap out of his path, and drew another.

"What are you about, Dryer?" I called.

"Providing you some sport, Bowden," he replied. "This shall be scratch. To your lines, gentlemen."

By this time the boys had understood what was coming.

The smaller of the two said, "Please, sir, I don't want to fight."

"What, even though this jackanapes threw the blame upon you? And you"—Granville turned to the other—"this boy called you a scaly gull. If that is not enough to spur on your fists, think you both upon this: either you stand up against each other or my dear friend George Bowden and I will whip you until you wish you had."

Here Granville winked at me. I was delighted with this new side to him and thrust myself up from the bench, crying, "By Jove, yes!"

The two boys shuffled themselves up to their lines.

"I'll lay sixpence on the smaller one," I said, for I had thought he had showed spirit in shouting out the "scaly gull" comment with such vim. We were allowed to have coins by then, being considered to be of a responsible age.

"Done," Granville said.

By now we had summoned a smallish crowd and a few more bets were placed by other boys.

Granville called out, "Set-to!"

In truth, the bout was a damp one. Neither boy was particularly eager to strike his fellow, but in the end my coin proved well placed. My little squeaker got Granville's boy in a fairly respectable neck vice from which the other could only pummel his back and legs with ineffectual fists.

Granville was shouting out all the while, "Strike the backs of his knees! Bring your arm around, you clunch!"

The fight lasted no more than a few moments; one of the servants spied our play from the window, and before any real hits were made, Mr Allen was striding across the yard and pulling the boys apart by their ears.

"You young gentlemen"—he turned to Granville and me—"should be putting a stop to this kind of mischief."

"Yes, sir," we chorused.

Mr Allen dragged the two young pugs off to have their posteriors thrashed. Granville's lad, the larger, looked at us as though we might plead his cause. The other only looked at the ground.

"You owe me a sixpence," I said to Granville, "short as that was."

Granville reached into his pocket. He had only fourpence and a piece of biscuit wrapped in a scrap of paper. I accepted it as being good enough.

"Next time, I shan't accept a wager from you until I have seen the coin."

"Next time, we'll have them fight in one of the bedchambers, shall we?" he replied. "With a sentry at the door?"

In that moment he became, if not such an agreeable companion as Perry had been, at least a satisfactory one.

It was Granville who instigated our surreptitious excursions—something that Perry and I had never thought to do. We escaped not, as one might have thought, at night—we were too thoroughly locked in to the place for that—but in the one hour's leisure time we were granted after dinner. The way out was simple: over the wall behind the washhouse and into a narrow alley stinking of fish and waste, from which we were free to roam the city of Bristol for the best part of a glorious, liberated hour.

It was during these free hours that I discovered Granville's other prevailing vice—the boy, staid as he looked, was absolutely gripped by the pursuit of skirt. Granville, even at the tender age of fifteen, spent every spare penny he could find on the strolling mollies of the docks. As green as I sound by it, this was another activity that I had not thought to try. I had been used to Perry and had never thought to look elsewhere, but in the face of Granville's experience, I found there was the same hot shame and joy in the rough hands of a trollop as there had been in my friend's soft pink palm.

"They are all clapped to the eyes," Granville said, "but you need not fear their hands. It is the only worthwhile advice my father ever gave me."

I SPENT THAT SUMMER at Aubyn Hall. I was anxious all the journey. How would Perry receive me, after so long apart? Would things be altered between us? Perhaps I, myself, had been changed by having known the touch of a woman. I could not be sure.

In the event, as I should have guessed, it was Perry who was changed. His merry ways had quite left him. He did not speak of his pain at losing his brother and sister, but I saw it in his sudden silences, his gritted jaw.

The anxiety, which had felt like a bird trapped in my chest, was only stilled in the dark, when we clasped hands and swore fidelity once more. We slept in the same bed, as we had at school. No one thought to tell us we might not.

For her part, Miss Charlotte Sinclair was grown as quiet as Arthur had used to be. I was so deprived of feminine company that even in her melancholy I found her a pleasure to the eye, and when she could be persuaded to speak, to the ear. She was scarred about the face but was handsome despite it. Poor Miss Sinclair's scars were a constant reminder of Perry's good fortune in being at school when the pox descended. I thanked God for sparing him.

However much Perry and I might have wished our friendship to remain the same, it could not, because we were not. We were no longer equals in situation and standing; Perry was never a boy inclined to humility, and despite his grief, he could not help now but make me feel it. We no longer talked of being pirates. Instead Perry made fierce, expansive plans, and I was only to assist him in them. I was still a schoolboy, bending over to receive stripes across my buttocks, while Perry was brought wine and bowed to.

PERRY MIGHT BE BOWED TO by servants, but he was not caressed by painted ladies. Back at school that autumn, Granville and I were relentless in our pursuit of funds for this purpose. We challenged the younger boys to place wagers on anything we could conceive, in order to relieve them of their property, so that we might pawn it. We wrote letters home plaintively telling of lost purses, and we pawned what few items of value we had of our own: on my part, a pen from my father and a particularly good handkerchief my mother had given me; on Granville's, that gold-braided frock coat at last found some use at the pawnbroker's.

One day our wanders took us past the yard of The Hatchet Inn, where a prize-fighting ring could be glimpsed over the fence of the yard.

Granville stopped to look upon it, empty as it was, and urgently insisted that we go inside. I followed him, quailing a little at walking through the company of dockers and sailors.

Once in the yard, Granville pushed himself up to the ropes and took up a handful of the sawdust and held it to his nose.

"What does it smell of?" I asked him.

"Action," he said. He held it out to me, and I dutifully bent my nose to it. The scent of action was remarkably similar to that of old sawdust.

* * *

THAT WINTER PERRY'S FAMILY came to Queen Square, on the very day
that school was to close for the Christmas holidays. I was delighted; I had
long hoped my two friends might meet. The Sinclairs very generously offered both Granville and me a room for the night, and so it was arranged.

The meeting was not an immediate success. Granville's costume looked
even more austere in the Sinclairs' elegant drawing room, and his manners
could not be said to compensate. He greeted Mr Sinclair with a bow so
small that he might have had an iron rod down the back of his coat. Toward Mrs Sinclair he did a little better, taking her hand and bending from
the waist, but he could not meet her eyes. I could see her looking him over
with a gentle expression of surprise. Perhaps his strange manner was due to
intimidation at their rank; perhaps he thought he was maintaining his own
dignity in refusing to fawn upon them. He did himself no favour by it and
only appeared utterly charmless. Mr and Mrs Sinclair were gracious
enough, but I thought they were surprised at me for choosing such a companion, and my ears burned to know it.

Perry himself was less than delighted; at the first opportunity, he pulled
me aside and whispered, "By God, George, what do we want with this
queer creature?"

"He is not so strange at school," was all the reply I had. I felt as humiliated as if Granville had forced me into his ugly coat and it had been I be-
having so ungraciously to my hosts.

"What do I care if he is the Prince of Wales at school? What do you
mean by bringing him? Are you so attached to him that you cannot bear to
be parted? Have you shared a bed so long?"

I would have laughed, but for the pain on my old friend's face.

"Good God, no!" I cried instead, loud enough that Granville, who was
looking out of a window at the pleasant square, looked over at us. He must
have suspected we were speaking of him.

"Then do you bring him so that I will not ask you to share mine? Are you grown changed?" I could see my friend bracing himself against my answer, even while his fingers plucked at my sleeve.

I leant toward him just a little.

"If we were not watched now, I would kiss all this lunacy from you," I said.

We rarely spoke so explicitly. His fingers stilled upon my arm; his eyes grew soft.

"I swear on your eyes, George, I only ever want you willingly."

"I will give you my eyes, if you want them," I said, to make him smile, "and you can wear them on a chain, like a watch. I give you my word, Perry, I brought him because I thought you would find him a merry companion. He is more of a rogue than he appears. We have the wildest larks when we escape school. I only wish you could be there."

For a moment, Perry struggled visibly with the notion of Granville and I having wild larks without him. Then he conquered himself.

"Well, then, let us escape the house and see what amusement there is to be found," he said.

We set out and simply strolled about, looking at everything there was to see: the quays thick with the masts of ships, the loads being pulled on sledges by sweating men, the women with trays of goods upon their heads, calling out their wares. We were all of us giddy with liberation.

I was eager for Granville to show his roguish side and was not long disappointed. We had taken a pint of ale and a pie in a chophouse and were filling our pipes. Granville excused himself and stood. Perry and I watched, bemused, as he stepped over to a crowd of rough sailors gathered about one of the long tables. We could not hear what was said, but we saw Granville's stiff bow and the surprise upon the faces of the coves he spoke to. Their expressions quickly turned to amusement, however, and one fellow, a dark-skinned cove in a captain's hat, slapped Granville's thin back hard enough that he bent under the blow. He came back to Perry and me as straight-faced as ever he was, but there was a gleam in his eye.

"What do you think of this? That old captain has given me the direction to an easy house, where he says we might expect a fine welcome."

We had never done more than visit the strollers of the docks, never had them do more than lay hands upon us. I cried out my agreement and turned to Perry. He nodded and smiled, but when the conversation turned and we began the business of finishing up our pipes, I thought he looked a little sickly. I realised then that Perry might never have had a hand upon him but mine and his own. I smiled as fondly as though I were his elder, not a boy almost as green as he was.

THE HOUSE WAS ON PIPE LANE, not far from The Hatchet, where Granville so enjoyed the sawdust. It was a narrow, shabby-looking place with a great brute standing at its door. Granville ascended the step quite as if he meant to walk past the cove without a word; he found his way blocked by an arm as big around as my waist.

"Ho, sir," Granville said, "is this not an open house?"

The brute considered this. At last he said, "At this hour of the day it ain't. And 'specially not to squeakers like you."

"Is my money not as good as the next man's?"

"It is if you have it," the brute replied.

Granville slapped his pocket so that the purse clinked.

"Well, sir?" he said.

"That don't change the hour, now, does it? All that does is show where I'm to reach to lift your purse." The brute laughed, and, I must admit, Perry and I could not help but smile.

Granville was not at all perturbed.

"If you would be so good," he said, "as to enquire whether the ladies should like an early visitor? If the answer is in the negative, we will disturb you no longer."

"You ain't got it in you to disturb me," the brute said, but he tired of his teasing and did then leave his post and disappear inside. We heard the scraping of bolts within as he secured the door. An inordinately long time passed, or so it seemed to me.

At length the bolts slid back and the brute appeared.

"There's three of the misses will see you, for a little extra coin."

In the event, there were four mollies waiting inside, in the company of an old bawd with the skewed and lumpen countenance that suggests that curse of Venus, the dread syphilis. The girls were handsome and looked clean enough—especially standing as they were beside that old crone—but one in particular I thought exceptional. She was not neat in her figure; her bosom spilled from her corset, her skirts swung about as she walked forward to greet us. Her face, too, was spilling over: full lips, heavy eyelids, rounded cheeks painted up high. What gripped me, however, was the look in her eyes—never had I seen such a lewd and worldly expression in a face so young. She was an angel, fallen as low as an angel could fall. She was beauty, made dirt. I was seized with an ache upon the sight of her. Granville's face grew still in a peculiarly rapt expression I could feel mirrored in some measure upon my own countenance. Perry, by contrast, looked only frightened.

"I will have this girl for company," Granville told the old bawd.

"And I," I said. "I will wait my turn and visit her likewise."

The young whore shot me a hot glance when I spoke.

"George"—Granville had something like passion in his voice—"I should prefer you to take another. I must have this one to myself."

"Must you?" the bawd said then. "How long shall you want her? Dora don't come cheap, young sir, but she's worth twice what I'll charge you nonetheless. You've never in your dreams been pleased like it."

I thought to protest; he was being absurd. Granville, however, was emptying his pockets.

"That'll not buy you more than ten minutes, lad," the bawd said.

"Make it ten minutes longer and I shall put the coins into your hand this moment," Granville said.

"You'll do that whatever I say," the bawd replied. "You're hot as Old Nick himself. But you'll have your extra ten minutes, just for the brazen cheek of you."

"Thank you, good woman." Granville poured his pennies into her palm. He took my hand and pressed it.

"George," he said, "take another one. I beg you, oblige me."

I thought him ridiculous, but the negro girl had by then caught my eye and was winking and smiling. I was beginning to feel nervous and thought she looked kind enough to guide me through the deed. Perry's hand was seized by a busty, freckled creature, and although he looked back at me, wide-eyed, he let her lead him. Anxious as I felt, it was nonetheless amusing to see his hesitating ascent behind her upon the stairs.

AFTERWARD I WAS PUFFED UP with pride, despite the event being less momentous than I had hoped. I came downstairs to find Perry waiting in the hall with the blackest look upon his face. He would not answer my enquiries as to his experience, nor what was the matter. I was forced to stand there, my thighs aching, with Perry burning with silent fury beside me.

Girls began to appear from the recesses of the house and came to take their seats on the bench in the hall.

Seeing us, they called out, "You're young enough to go again, lads. I'll show you what my sister there couldn't."

"Hie, Sally, what d'you do to the boy? He's sour as a crab."

"Did she bite you, dearheart?" one said, coming toward Perry. "You'd do better with me, look," and she held back her lips to show the pink gums laid bare of teeth.

Perry muttered, "In a moment I shall strike them."

"You do that, dearheart," the toothless whore said, returning to her seat, "and Sam, on the door there, will have your mouth the match of mine."

Granville took an age to reappear. When he did, he was so pleased with himself as to scarcely notice the strained mood.

"Now we will go to The Hatchet," he said, as though he were expedition leader, "and finally see a prize-fight."

"I do not care for prize-fights," said Perry, who had never seen one.

"You will care for the rum," I said.

My friend ignored me, but his face lost some of its sullenness and he followed behind us like a lamb.

THAT NIGHT WAS MORE PLEASURABLE for my companions than it was for me. Perry pronounced the rum as fine as any he had ever tasted, though it was likely the cheapest that the innkeeper thought he could get away with selling. Perry addressed this observation exclusively to Granville and he kept up the game all the evening. He would not reply to any of my own remarks. When I put my hand upon his arm to lead him out to the yard and the boxing ring, he removed his arm from my touch and said, "You stink of bitch."

He followed Granville out, without looking to see if I would follow.

When once the bout began, Perry cried out at each hit as enthusiastically as did Granville, and when our man won he slung his arm around Granville's neck. I had placed my shilling upon the same cove, but Perry said not a word to me. My winnings were little compensation.

Granville affected not to notice Perry's coldness toward me, but I could see his pleasure at being made favourite. For my part, I had never known jealousy like it—I thought I might at any moment cast up my supper. I had never been anything but the first object of Perry's heart. I was so low over it that I was afforded only the meanest kind of satisfaction to see Granville trying to carry Perry's weight about his shoulders as the bigger boy grew progressively more soused. We stayed so late—I, most reluctantly—that we had to hire a linkboy to walk ahead of us with a light, so that we should not be robbed by footpads. We made slow progress, Perry wanting to stop at every chophouse and having to be coaxed onward by Granville, bent almost double under his arm. They veered wildly across the roads, for Granville was not strong enough to counter Perry's floundering progress. I walked behind them, cursing them for their slowness but too bloody-minded to assist.

I was angry and drunk enough when I finally got into bed that I almost wept, but then the spinning of the chamber took my attention and I fell into a sickly slumber.

I woke to find Perry climbing in beside me and laying his head on my chest. I was relieved, but so sick from the liquor that just the movement of him was enough to send my stomach pitching. I wrapped my arms about him as though he was a life-raft upon the ocean of my nausea, and at last we slept again.

THAT WAS MY LAST YEAR OF SCHOOLING. The next year, for want of any better idea, I took a place at Oxford, studying law, which did not suit me. I wished, rather, to find a young lady of fortune and make her my wife, so that I need not be a lawyer at all. My motivations were not entirely mercenary. I hoped for love, as all young men do, but I did not mean to lose sight of the practicalities. I had a devil of a time. I was invited to dinners and parties by families acquainted with my own, but if ever I seemed to be forging a particular friendship with a young lady, I found the invitations died away like autumn leaves. I had not solidified my prospects; those watchful mothers had grander ideas than a fourth son, not yet finished with his studies.

My own mother spared barely a thought for me, now that my eldest brother, John, was to be married. She talked endlessly of the wedding and the couple's future happiness.

Well might they be happy, I thought, *with an estate to inherit.*

I was sure that my mother could have assisted me in finding a suitable bride, had she cared to.

When, on a visit home, I raised the subject, she said only, "Study hard, George, and see that you become an asset to a marriage, rather than an encumbrance."

My brother, Charles, having overheard, took the first opportunity to whisper to me, "Do you look to marry, George? Would you give up your games of backgammon with Perry Sinclair?"

I affected not to know what he meant, but I was made uncomfortable by it. Charles had the acquaintance of many of my old school fellows, and it was not the first such comment to drop from his lips.

WHEN PERRY'S LETTER ARRIVED at my Oxford lodgings, bearing the sad news of the loss of his parents, I barely vacillated. The morning saw me with my trunk lashed to the roof of the mail coach, on my way to my friend's side, my studies abandoned. I had learnt all I thought likely, and I knew I should not make a good lawyer—I hoped instead to be a good friend. Let my brother whisper what he would, I knew where I belonged.

In a strange stroke of fate it had been Granville who had seen my friend saved. Yet again Perry had been in Bristol, this time visiting Granville, when sickness found the Hall. Miss Sinclair, I understood, had been left to nurse her parents and see them laid to rest, with only the company of those servants too loyal to flee; it made an unsettling picture. During the first weeks I spent at the Hall, Miss Sinclair kept to her chamber and was said to be too grieved to receive company.

Perry felt the loss of his parents keenly. I had always known him to be passionate; my friend loved with a fierceness that I rarely felt burn in my own breast. Now he plunged into darkness and drank rum as though it were wine. His eyes acquired a deep sadness that looked incongruous in his youthful face. He took no interest in the affairs of the great Sinclair estate, now left entirely in his hands. It was curious to be in that great house and know Perry to have sole charge of it; I kept expecting to meet Mr Sinclair around every corner. No one would ever again tell my friend what he might or might not do, and while I lived under his roof the same freedom was mine. What little discipline I had learnt was free to fall away entirely, and if I was to have reason to mourn the loss of it, well, that would come later.

Chapter 5

❖ ❖ ❖

U pon my honour, Perry's pain was my own; yet I envied him. In my darker moments, I felt that I should have made no ceremony of forcing my father and all three of my brothers over a cliff-edge, to be in Perry's place, with a fortune of my own and a grand, ancient Hall to govern. I tried to conceal my envy; I was ashamed, indeed, to carry such ugly sentiments, and spent many hours attempting to lift him from his melancholy, with good wine, gaming, and jest.

When at last Miss Sinclair began to venture into our company, I thought her pleased to have me there. She was as melancholy as could be expected; she barely spoke, and when she did, she seemed often at a loss for words. Like her brother, she was blessed with fair hair and even features; pox-marked as she was, she would have been handsome, had not her eyes grown so dull. Even before her bereavement she had never been much in society and had not learnt the art of pleasant conversation, as most young ladies did. Mrs Sinclair, God rest her soul, had kept the young Miss Sinclair rather too close, through grief at losing her other children.

The months passed, and I grew comfortable by Perry's side, and by Miss Sinclair's. Perry daily drank himself into a stupor and wept; I held him, smoothed his hair, and often felt I might weep myself, to hear him. I provided him a listening ear and ensured that he took some nourishment besides rum-and-water. I acted as his walking-cane and, once he had fallen into slumber, spent the remainder of the evening conversing with Miss Sinclair. Her sadness may have been the equal of Perry's, but it took a quieter shape. She spent many hours staring out across the gardens, or into the fire. She grew thin, in body and spirit.

One morning, at perhaps ten o'clock, Miss Sinclair and I sat at the breakfast table, I making light remarks, she hollow-eyed and near silent.

Perry slept on upstairs—for it was becoming increasingly difficult to rouse him at any civilised hour, and I could not bear to see him wake before he had to. For a moment upon waking he would seem his old self, and then the grief would come over him, like the game one plays with babies, passing a hand before the face: happiness to misery. It was terrible to watch.

That morning Miss Sinclair would take only a little bread and butter. Only I made any use of the good spread of hot rolls and plum cake.

I was contemplating the best way to cheer her, when the butler, Fisher, entered and informed us that the estate steward, one Mr Tyne, was anxious for an audience with Perry.

Miss Sinclair's face, always pale, now seemed almost green. She laid down her knife and looked at me beseechingly. I shrugged a little.

"Mr Sinclair is indisposed," I said. "You know that well enough, Fisher. Why did you not say so to Mr Tyne?"

"I beg your pardon, sir. Mr Tyne was adamant that if Mr Sinclair was not available, he must ask for permission to speak with yourself."

Now Miss Sinclair regarded me with an expression of great hope. I sighed and put down my cake. Then I changed my mind and picked it up again.

"Tell him I will be pleased to give him an audience when I have had done with my breakfast," I said, and was rewarded by Miss Sinclair's sigh of gratitude.

"Now, do try to eat," I told her, and was further rewarded by her sweet obedience.

Mr Tyne seemed a passionate cove, for all that he looked like a gentleman-farmer. He stood in front of Perry's desk, where I had thought it best to receive him, and twitched as though he wished to pace about.

"I'd like to know, sir, who it is I'm to report to now. I'm used to reporting to Mr Sinclair every week, and here it's three months gone by."

"I suppose," I said, "you must report to the younger Mr Sinclair."

"Well, indeed I'd like to, sir, but he won't see me. There are matters I must have settled."

"Such as?" I enquired. The cove was obviously desperate to tell me.

"Such as the collecting of the rents, sir. I've collected them in, sir, just as I always do, but Mr Sinclair was always used to tallying the amounts and checking them off in his ledger, sir. And there's another thing."

"Yes?"

"Yes, sir. It is the household accounts, sir. Mr Fisher was always to bring them to Mr Sinclair, but not being able to do so, there were bills owing. I took the liberty of settling them, sir, from the rents—"

"Excellent, excellent."

"Yes, sir. But the bills were higher than what they have been accustomed to be, sir, and I must have approval for it. The wine bill was near double what it was. And I must know, sir, that it's all been for the family's use and that none of the servants have taken advantage of poor Mr Sinclair's passing, God rest his soul, to pilfer the wine cellar."

"I am afraid it is all too likely that young Mr Sinclair has made use of it all himself, as vast as the quantities may seem, Tyne."

"Yes, sir. But if you could just look over the numbers, sir? And perhaps, the servants' wages?"

And so it was that quite by accident, I became Perry's agent in the running of the Aubyn estate. I was making myself of use—indeed, was of more use than I had been in my life before. I found great satisfaction in the sensation, and in being able to respond at last to the letters my mother had been sending. She had been furious to hear that I had given up my studies, and my new position went some way toward mollifying her.

Granville, all this time, was busy making himself rich, a skill inherited from his merchant bloodline. Such an instinct did he possess that when Granville Dryer put his coin to a venture, other gentlemen rushed to do the same. At only twenty-three he was invited to join the Merchant Venturers, the influential Bristol society of gentlemen. His costume remained as Spartan as ever it had.

With a genius of trade as an intimate friend, it made the plainest sense to follow him in investments, though the only money I had to play with was Perry's. I had only the most meagre personal allowance from my father. We would sit at table and Perry would drain the wine flask, while Granville and I ironed out the details of ships and stocks. The machinations of trade and investment were simple enough to follow, after my training in the dry codes of law.

I made sure Perry was informed of every investment I made. He would always clasp my hands and say, "You care for me so well, George," but if I brought the matter up again, to tell him some new detail that had arisen, more often than not he would have forgotten entirely what had gone before.

For my services, Perry granted me a share of the profits I garnered him, though I had a devil of a time obtaining his permission for it. Not through his being a miser, but because he refused to discuss anything but gaming, hunting, and liquor. More often than not, his response was to say, "Take what you like, my dear friend. Take it all. I would see you happy."

At last I persuaded him to agree that I should take a half-share. Perhaps that seems a rather hefty portion, but, I reasoned, without my services the entire estate would have crumbled.

I took my share, more often than not, to the gaming tables. Perry joined me at every opportunity, and gave himself over to the bottle, as I did to the baize. I could not stop myself playing until every last shilling had rolled away.

We went often to Bath and occasionally to Bristol, where Granville kept lodgings. Granville had kept up his obsession with the sweet-faced whore. He visited her as often as another man sees his wife, and spent as much of his fortune in so doing, I didn't doubt. Perry and I never did visit that house again in the capacity of customers, but we accompanied Granville there in pursuit of his other hobby—a young lady-pug. We were always ready to see her set-to, for there was something in it for each of us: Perry had his drink, Granville his pugilism, and I, of course, took the greatest pleasure in placing a wager upon the outcome.

BESIDES MY OWN COMPANY, and what she saw of her brother, Miss Sinclair had very little society. When once her aunt and cousin called, she begged illness and would not come downstairs. I said nothing of it, but I wished she would show herself and perhaps be made merry.

I came to look forward to our mornings together. Because Perry rarely rose in time for breakfast, Miss Sinclair and I were usually alone, an intimate experience for the unmarried. I would lie abed when first I woke, and try to compose little witticisms to cheer her.

One afternoon found all three of us at dinner. Perry was with us and was at his best, as he often was before he sank too deeply into his cups. At such moments it pained and delighted me to see him; I mourned the merry boy that he had been almost as deeply as he mourned his parents.

He was talking excitedly, making expansive plans to stock the woods with pheasants.

"We shall have thousands of the creatures. Arrange it, George. Thousands! We shan't need beaters, they will be so thick upon the ground. I want every pheasant in the county under my trees."

"Then," I said, "we will be the only coves in the county with a bird to shoot at."

"We will," Perry said. "Every huntsman in Somerset and Wiltshire will be pounding at our door. We shall hold daily hunting parties, and you and I will be crowned with feathers, George."

Seeing Miss Sinclair's look, I was moved to say, "You need not fear, Miss Sinclair; the gentlemen shall not bring their wives unless you wish it."

Her expression was strange, and I was not sure whether I had reassured or humiliated her.

In an attempt to soothe her, I took the liberty of cutting her orange into small pieces and dressing it with sugar. My mother was fond of having her orange prepared thusly.

Miss Sinclair thanked me sweetly, not quite daring to meet my eye. A blush spread across her cheeks and down her neck, making the scars even more apparent, white against pink.

I thought, *Oh, ho, Bowden, you have an admirer here.*

I could not help but feel a little thrill. I had been so little in the company of young ladies.

I saw Perry mark her look, and I saw, too, his old jealousy rouse itself. For the rest of the meal I was careful not to pay Miss Sinclair any further special attentions.

I WAS OBLIGED TO ATTEND my brother John's wedding, a week or so later. When, as I had known he would, my brother Charles made a comment about my finding a place at Aubyn—"Old habits die hard, do not they, George?"—I replied that he was as ignorant as he was ugly, and that I had been spending the bulk of my time with Miss, rather than Mister, Sinclair. He laughed aloud to hear it, and clapped me upon the back. He called me a rogue. It was a new, and not unpleasant, sensation.

I had not been back at Aubyn a week before I received a letter from my mother.

Charles tells me that you seek to attach yourself to Miss Sinclair.
It would be a desirable match for you, George. I should be delighted
if your wishes were to be realised. I confess myself rather relieved
that it is love that has drawn you there rather than a dearth
of ambition. Perhaps you will return to your studies after you
are settled.

I almost wished that it were true. She had never been so pleased with me before.

THAT VERY EVENING Perry and I repaired to a gaming house in Bath—one of those places the newspapers liked to call a "modern hell." There was nothing so very hellish about them, except the smoke—though it was pipe-smoke, rather than brimstone. That night we patronised Mr Wiltshire's Rooms, though we were as likely to go to a half-dozen such as that one. They were all alike: an abundance of good upholstery and grand chandeliers bearing twenty or so candles apiece. A pretty enough setting in which to lose one's fortune, and many had done exactly that, and gone home thousands of pounds the poorer.

I played at hazard that night and at some ungodly hour there came a moment when I found myself gaming against a Mr Dewsbury of Stroud. This elderly bachelor was familiar to all the patrons of the gaming houses, and Perry and I had made his acquaintance with interest. It was well known that Mr Dewsbury had a bosom companion, Sir Samuel, and that neither gentleman had married, each having found the company of ladies to be wanting, in comparison to that of his friend. Although they were occasionally the objects of gentle ridicule, they were not without the respect of their fellows. One could not help but admire them, for Mr Dewsbury and Sir Samuel were both first-rate gaming men. I had once watched as they shook hands upon a wager of twenty thousand pounds, over the matter of whose ship would come in first to the Bristol docks. It seemed they were both waiting for ships to arrive, in which they had some interest. Both ships were late, perhaps lost at sea, and instead of wringing their hands, they laid down a sum well over the value of both ships combined and made the wait into a race of the greatest suspense. Should I have been in their position, I would not have hesitated to do the same.

That night, Mr Dewsbury was losing heavily but would not quit the table. I, who had started with nothing more than fifteen guineas, had been blessed from the outset. The coins on the table had almost entirely begun in his pocket, but surely and steadily crept to my side. At last, he had nothing more to bet.

"Well, sir," I said, "do you give over now and go home to your pipe and your porter, never to play again?"

"I could do that, certainly," Mr Dewsbury said, "or perhaps I should make one more attempt to win back what you have so neatly taken, eh, sir?" He looked not at all concerned.

"Upon my word, if you wish to play, I should never deny you the opportunity," I said. "If you have a purse in reserve about your person, pray reveal it and let us commence."

"I have no hidden purse, Mr Bowden, sir," Mr Dewsbury said. "No, I mean to write you out a bond. Will you take a promissory note by my hand?"

"I will, of course," I said, "from such a gentleman as you. How much do you wish to wager, good sir?"

"I shall write you out a bond," he said now, "for the deeds to the house I have lately built at Clifton."

At this, the coves idly watching our play grew attentive. It is these moments of high drama that keep one going back to the gaming houses. Without a word spoken—no one would wish to break our concentration—other fellows picked up the atmosphere, as a hound does a rabbit's scent, and soon a crowd had gathered.

"A house," I said, "at Clifton. How much would you say such a thing is worth, sir?"

"I would say, perhaps the sum you have on the table before you."

At this, the company laughed. I did not, however. For just a moment, I pictured myself declining politely, scooping my profit into a velvet sack and hiring a linkboy to guard my homeward passage. It would not have been sporting, and besides, if I won I should have several thousand pounds and a house at Clifton to keep it in.

"Very well," I said, "the winner is to take all."

I held out the leather pot, in which rested two ivory dice.

My feeling when the dice favoured me cannot quite be described. My mind seemed to split into two: one part could not believe it and was afraid to smile lest it turn out an illusion, whereas the other part of me seemed to say, yes, of course, I knew it all along. This second self was almost rendered bored by the sudden acquisition of wealth. It was he who drove me back again and again to the gaming table. He was never satisfied.

The gentlemen watching clapped and whistled my victory, and called out to ask Mr Dewsbury, did he really mean to see me go home with everything?

"Indeed no," Mr Dewsbury said. He did not look so composed now. The skin beneath his left eye jerked as his nerves danced. "No, now that we have begun, Mr Bowden must see me to my end."

Then, of course, a dozen voices enquired, whatever would he wager next?

"Why, my home, of course," he replied, "my country seat. It is worth everything Mr Bowden has and more besides."

I pushed the profit I had so recently taken back onto the table without a thought in my head. I believe I was afraid to think at all.

Mr Dewsbury cast; the watching gentlemen let out a soft, collective sigh. The dice had not favoured me this time.

IT WAS DAWN when we went to bed. I lay awake, Perry breathing loudly in my ear and the hounds by the hearth slumbering nearly as noisily. I could not stop thinking of how close I had come to making my fortune. I had made it and pushed it back, to be taken from me by the next roll of the dice. I could have bought racehorses; I could have driven a phaeton. I could have married some pretty wife and founded a dynasty, with a solid Bristol town house to leave to my eldest boy—I should not like to be parted from Perry, but to be my own man! Perhaps I should have had a country house built near to Aubyn. My younger sons would have had to find their own way, as I had done. I should have taught them to play hazard.

These thoughts had trudged through my mind so many times that they had worn their own groove, but now they had been made more lively by having had them so close. Who knew but that my chance might have been and gone, and I let it slip away?

I pushed my brow against Perry's warm back, to still the thoughts. At last sleep overcame me and wove its own picture of a town house, an obedient family, and a smiling wife with needlework in her lap; a wife so good and sweet that I should not care that her face was marked with the ghosts of smallpox. In my dream I sat at my own table and Miss Sinclair poured my coffee, not because she need—there was the vague form of a butler behind me—but because she wished to. It was so vivid that when I awoke I was surprised to find Perry, still sound asleep, sweating brandy into his nightcap.

I FOUND, upon going downstairs, that it was already the dinner hour. Miss Sinclair was dining alone and seemed quietly pleased to see me appear. I wanted very much to say something pleasant, but I was grievously affected by the excesses of the night before and could only stumble myself into my seat and call for coffee in a piteous tone.

I could not shake the last tendrils of my dream. Could it mean that in my most secret heart, I loved her? I could not tell. I felt only nauseated and bleary.

She cut her meat into tiny pieces. I found I watched her, even as I had to hold my head up on my chin. She sipped at her cup of wine slowly, and where a drop marked her lip she removed it with the very tip of her pink tongue. She kept her eyes lowered, like a painting of humility personified.

She looked up and found my eyes upon her. She blushed, and it lit her from within, making the pattern of her scars stand out like a Chinese lantern.

"You must excuse me, I am unwell," I said, and fled, to lie on my own cool, rarely used bed, to let my head pound and my stomach swoop as it liked.

I COULD NOT DENY that I felt drawn to her. I told myself that this was only because she reminded me so of Perry, that I lacked the company of merrier ladies, and was flattered by her attention. It felt like an age since anyone had admired me, let alone in that becoming and unworldly way.

I called for a bracer of rum and talked to myself sternly. I reminded myself that Perry would certainly object to my forming an attachment to his sister—could I bear to cause my friend a moment's pain, after all he had suffered already?

It was at that moment, however, that the sense of the thing burst upon me. For some time I had feared that I had before me two choices: find an heiress to be my wife and be separated from Perry more than I would like, or stay beside him, accepting my lot as companion and agent, never to own an estate of my own or gain the full respect of my family. I had been considering the matter from the wrong angle; I had omitted the enormous advantage of an attachment to Miss Sinclair. You will see that I am not so calculating that I had ever thought of it before this moment. I knew from my work as Perry's agent that, through some long-ago dispute amongst cousins, the Aubyn estate had a broken entail. The last will of Mr Sinclair stated that if Perry did not produce children, the estate was to fall into the hands of Miss Charlotte Sinclair's first-born son or, should she fail to be delivered of a male heir, into the care of her husband, to be kept in trust for her daughters. If I felt affection for Miss Sinclair, if Perry could be made to agree, why should I not be that husband? I need never be away from Perry for a moment, safe in the knowledge that even if, God forbid, I should lose him, my place and my home would be secure. My mother was right: it would be a desirable match; the difficulty would lie in convincing my old friend Perry of it.

I BEGAN THAT EVENING, when Perry and I retired to a country tavern that kept late hours. I felt somewhat fragile, but the very air of the establishment soothed me, with its scent of roasting meat and the low tones of the conversations of gentlemen.

When the boy had put the platter down in front of us, and Perry had begun to tear at it—he occasionally abandoned his manners when there were only the two of us—I felt brave enough to test the water.

"I have had several letters of late, from my mother. She is after me to marry."

Perry snorted in derision.

"Well, quite," I said, "but she will not let the matter alone."

Perry looked at me, the grease upon his face shining in the lamplight, the chop in his hand.

"Has she lost her wits? You cannot afford to keep a horse unless I stable it for you. How does she propose you keep a wife?"

This was true; my gaming debts were grown to embarrassing proportions. Furthermore, I could not think how I had expected my mother's wishes to carry any weight with Perry; we had always done exactly as we liked.

"She does not say," I said. Then, because a bloody-minded part of me would not lie down so quietly, "Although, I must say, I do sometimes feel . . ."

"What? What the deuce do you feel?"

"You know very well, as you must feel it yourself."

"Oh, fie," Perry said. "Nonsense! Nothing could be more proper than your working as my agent, in my investments. They could hardly have hoped for better when they sent you to school, dunderhead that you are."

"I? I was never caned for failing to locate Portugal on the globe. But I am not speaking of that."

"What, then? You cannot mean that you are afraid? This is the modern day, George. No man of good breeding will ever face the gallows for a companionship such as ours. It is not as though we were picking up boys at the madge houses."

"No, not that. I meant, sometimes I think I should like to have a son."

"A son would not be worth the price paid to acquire him, old fellow." Perry began again to eat. His hair, which I had recently persuaded him to cut in short curls, flopped over his brow in a fetching tangle. I reached out and tidied it. Perry sat still for me, the chop poised in his hand.

"I do not know that I would mind so much," I said.

Perry laid the bone down and wiped his fingers upon the tablecloth.

"Let us not dance about any longer, George. If you wish to leave me, you must do it yourself and be damned. Do not look for my blessing in it."

I laughed as carelessly as I could.

"Upon my honour, I shall never leave you," I said. Then, very low, "They shall rip my fingers from your cold hand or bury me with you. Do not you understand?"

"No," Perry said, "I do not. I am not sure you understand yourself."

"Perhaps I do not," I said. I could not bear to go on any longer. "I wish I could learn to hold my tongue."

"Hold it now, then." Perry turned back to his plate.

WE DROVE HOME and sat up into the small hours, drinking brandy before the fire in Perry's library and placing wagers on foolish things. We had a book in which we wrote them down. *I, George Bowden, wager one guinea against Peregrine Sinclair's finding where I have hidden his snuffbox tonight. Or, I, Peregrine Sinclair, wager two pounds that George Bowden cannot ride the new colt ten minutes without use of the reins.*

We had been writing in this book for years, and I liked to look back through past wagers as a history of our friendship. When we grew tired of thinking of foolish bets, we burned kindling in the fire, placing wagers on whose twig would turn to ash the quickest. I remember I won a few pounds in all, to add to my profits from the gaming house.

At length Perry grew sleepy, as was his way when he was deep in his cups. I sat, swirling the tawny liquor around the glass and thinking of the innocent, slumbering in a chamber above us. I imagined how it might be to have leisure, night by night, to decide which door I chose: the brother or the sister Sinclair. I thought of all this as I sat by the fire, and I thought of it again, later, while Perry made his stifled sounds, closer to whimpers than pleasure.

"Upon my word, George," he said at last, against my neck, "I could not bear to have you leave. I should rather come to the gallows than see you marry. I should hang myself if you did."

"My dear friend, no one is talking of leaving," I said, stroking the golden down that grew upon his shoulders. "I was rambling."

That night I crept from Perry's bed and into my own cool sheets across the hall.

I would like to say that I let the idea drop, but I found I must try for it, even to fail. It was no harm I would do Perry by it, and certainly I would do no harm to Miss Sinclair; I wished only to secure my own future. If I lost all, at least I would have played for it. It had always been my philosophy that one must play, or be a loser two-fold.

WHEN I ARRIVED at the breakfast table, I found that my old friend had roused himself, and would have noticed in so doing that I had left his bed and slept elsewhere. His very presence was a rebuke.

Even with the air of one wounded, Perry looked far fresher than I felt. He did not mention the matter—Miss Sinclair was with us, and the servants besides. Though unaccustomed to the breakfast table, he devoured every dish placed before him, chewing doggedly and refusing to meet my eye.

Miss Sinclair, beside him, was equally quiet and cut all her plate of bread and honey into exceedingly small pieces—almost crumbs—before she began to eat. To see the two Sinclairs together at that moment was a strange sensation; their eyes were so exactly the same shade of blue. They looked almost violet that morning, where the light from the windows caught them.

I thought, *Now I really must play for it.*

As soon as something is denied me, I feel I must have it. I could not help it—I did desire her on her own account. She was so pure that I could not believe that she had ever had an unwholesome thought. When I saw an object so unsullied and clean, something roused in me and I was driven to spoil it. As a child in winter I would run about the garden paths, scuffing up the new snow before my brothers could reach it. I did not intend to spoil Miss Sinclair in any lasting fashion, only in the ordinary way that a man does a girl-bride.

I ate my own victuals and escaped to the library, where I spent an industrious morning on Perry's business concerns.

AFTER DINNER, Miss Sinclair, Perry, and I sat beside the library fire, Perry wielding the decanter with a generous wrist. At length he fell asleep in his chair. He looked even younger than his three-and-twenty years—too young, indeed, to be nodding off by the hearth like an elderly bachelor.

My eye fell upon Miss Sinclair. Her hair seemed to glow where the light of the fire streamed around the fire-screen she had placed to protect her face from the heat. She was working on a cushion cover with silk, embroidering a little scene. Her slim fingers moved deftly, although her eyes seemed dreaming. I found myself mesmerised by the sight of her. I confess that I had taken more liquor than perhaps I should.

I turned my seat a little so that Perry was obscured from my view by the chair's high back: the actions of a guilty man.

"What is it you work upon, Miss Sinclair?" I asked.

She looked up and smiled at me so prettily that I heaved myself out of my seat, as clumsy as the liquor had made me, and came to sit closer to her.

"They are a series of seat-covers," she said, "or I mean them to be a series, for I have only completed one. It is in my dressing room at present."

"And what is the picture upon it?" I enquired, leaning a little closer to see. My eyes were not as clear as they might have been that night.

"The first picture is called 'The Meeting,'" she said. "It shows a young maid and a gentleman meeting in a country lane. This one"—here she began to blush once more—"will be called 'The Courtship,' which name explains itself."

"Does it, indeed? It may explain its meaning, but not its image. Pray, how will you depict courtship, Miss Charlotte Sinclair?"

Miss Sinclair seemed unsure of the manner of my teasing. She bit at her lip before she replied, "I think to show the gentleman sitting close to the maid and offering her a flower."

"A very fair picture," I said, and I stood and walked—a little unsteadily, I own—to the vase upon the table, from which I fetched a bloom. I went to her and stood, twirling its stem in my hand.

"Shall I sit close to you, to offer it?" I said.

Miss Sinclair did not speak, though her eyes met mine before she bowed her head. She seemed distressed, though she had no grounds for it.

I was a little annoyed, if the truth be told. Here was a very good piece of flirtation, but the young lady was too unworldly to understand how to respond. I left her side so that I should not disturb her further, and resumed my earlier seat, opposite Perry's slumbering form.

At length I considered that it was her very innocence that I found most appealing, and my heart softened. I should not wish her adept at flirtation; if any man were to instruct her in the art, I should be that man.

I called across softly, "The third and fourth cushions in this series—pray, tell me their names."

Still she did not look up, though her posture seemed to stiffen. At last, when I thought she had determined not to speak, she said, "Can you not guess them?"

"I can," I said, "but I should like to hear their names from your own lips. I greatly dislike being mistaken."

She looked at me at last, a little defiantly.

"Well, then," she said, "they are to be called 'The Engagement' and 'The Wedding.'"

"I look forward to seeing them," I said. "I should take great pleasure in having you show me courtship, engagement, and marriage."

I let my face grow tender, and though she turned her eyes back to her work, I thought her confusion a more pleasant one.

THE WEEKS PASSED. I could not think how to manage it, but neither could I let the notion go. The more I longed to achieve it, the more I seemed to long for Miss Sinclair herself. Even her skin I had begun to think delightful; she wore that veil of scars as gracefully as any lady might hope to do. I fancied I could see her own, unsullied face floating beneath. I found myself both more eager and more reluctant to visit Perry's room at night. Perry spent much of his time in the company of his horses. He would go out to the stables and talk to them as he had used to talk to me. He never said a word about my hours spent with his sister; he was sodden drunk so much of the day I could not be sure how much he saw. Even so, his face acquired a morose expression that put me in mind of Balloo, the bloodhound I had loved as a boy. It pained me to see it, of course, but not enough that I would fold my hand while the game progressed. Though it shames me to admit it, if Perry did not call for brandy, much of the time I did it for him.

"You must not deny yourself what little pleasure there is in life," I said.

ONE DAY, as Perry lay on his back upon the drawing room sofa, Miss Sinclair and I walked under the trees beside the stream. There, shielded from view of the house, though not the view of her maid, I at last stole victory in the form of a kiss. She was everything I had hoped, hesitant and soft. It was a herculean effort to release her and walk back across the damp lawns. I had no choice in the matter, her dumpy little maid waiting behind us as she was. I wondered briefly what she would do if I pulled her mistress down upon the leaves, but not in any great seriousness.

The frustration was unbearable; why should I not marry Miss Sinclair? I wanted to wail like a child. Perry's own possessive nature drove me to duplicity. I only wished to remain by his side forever and know myself secure, with the love of a good wife, as any decent gentleman should. I knew that Perry found his sister a burden. What gentleman, lord of his own estate, wishes a spinster sister thrust upon him? Surely, somehow, I could bring him to see the advantages in the scheme.

Miss Sinclair told me that she was afraid of horses.

"This we must change," I said, "for you have never in your life felt so free as you will upon horseback."

I bought her a steady chestnut mare. I had never done such a thing for anyone. I could have taken that money to the gaming houses, but instead I handed it to a horse-dealer and did not even try to double it upon the tables beforehand.

We did not have a chance to ride.

IT WAS LATE. Perry went out to visit his most beloved mare, Fleet, and discovered that the poor beast I had so recently purchased was in agony with a colic. He sent the stable boy on the run to fetch me, and when I reached the stable I found a sorry scene indeed.

The horse was standing, but she clearly wished to roll. Only Perry and the groom, one at either side of her head, prevented her from doing so. In the lantern light I could see her eyes showing the white. I pressed my ear against her side, though her coat was filthy—she must have rolled before Perry came upon her. My ear was met with silence, where there should have been a symphony.

"Colic," I said.

"Of course it is colic," Perry said. "Now will you help us? We must get her into the yard and walk her."

We could have left it to the menservants, but Perry was tenderhearted over horses and would not like to leave her. I agreed to do my part.

She was a devil to get moving. Her legs seemed to buckle at every step, and she threw her head about, once knocking the groom a blow in the nose that had the cove swearing.

Once she felt the night air upon her she moved a little easier, though she still tried to lie down every moment. All that night we walked about the yard, while the poor thing stumbled between us, foaming at the mouth, eyes rolling pitifully. We kept cheerful, but I could not help thinking what none of us would admit; we could not help her. It was likely that she had twisted her guts when she rolled, and all we were doing was forcing the poor creature to go on until she dropped from pain and exhaustion. By the small hours it was plain to see that she was lost, and I gave her up and went to my bed, though Perry refused to go to his. It was dawn when he dragged in. He came into my bed, taking up my arm and pulling it over him.

"She had to be shot," was all that he said.

WE ALL SLEPT LATE and rose in time for dinner. Miss Sinclair was too distraught to appear.

"You should not have bought her the creature, George," Perry said. He was more exhausted than I was used to seeing him; even Perry could not shake off the effects of such a night. "Although lately I am wary of your judgement as to what one should, or should not, do."

"I have not the strength for one of your fits this morning, old friend. Please, let us be peaceful," I said. I waved away the proffered wine and bid Fisher fetch me coffee. My head ached abominably.

"My sister is in fits, not I. She need not make such a display of grief; she did not have the creature long enough even to ride her."

"Sometimes it is those we never ride we feel most for," I said, driven to it.

"One never can be sure when we might find ourselves suffering, old fellow," Perry said. He put his chin on one hand as though he were too tired even to hold up his head. "In such a case we can only hope someone will be merciful enough to shoot us."

I would not rise, nor stop eating.

"I would do the same for you, George. I hope you would do the same for me."

"You hope I would shoot you, Perry?"

"I hope you would bring a quick end to that which caused me pain."

WE WERE ALL THREE OF US stretched thin as catgut and one of us was bound to break. As any good player will, I withdrew from the game to plan my next move. I began to avoid Miss Sinclair's company and pay attention to Perry's pleasure, though it scarcely made him less ill-tempered. He often shook my hand from his shoulder or turned from me at night.

I had expected that the day would dawn when Perry's jealousy came forward in earnest. What I had not expected was that Miss Sinclair would be the first to show her hand.

Some nights later, Perry and I came home from a brief but satisfactory visit to a local tavern specialising in cock-fights. We were in high humour—there had been much of our old intimacy, smiles and glances exchanged in which, without a word, we understood each other's meaning. Perry had consented to accompany me homeward early enough that we both remained coherent and merry. If we were to grow dishevelled and slurring, that night we would do it beside the library fire.

It was the most natural thing in the world that I should suggest fetching our little book of wagers, that we might make commonplace events into a game alongside the brandy and pipes.

The book itself was beside Perry's bed, where we had lately been reading it out loud to each other as a means of recalling our long history. It had been my idea, as an instrument to draw us closer together and repair the rift that had come between us, and it had been uncommonly successful.

Several times we had been brought to helpless laughter as we recalled our old and foolish bets.

Now, as I toddled off to find the thing, Perry took my hand and squeezed it, the most intimate gesture we allowed ourselves before the servants. Of course servants know everything that happens in a big house, but decorum still dictates.

"Off you go, dear fellow!" he shouted, no doubt doing my ear, which was not at all far from his lips, some little injury. Perry never could modulate his tone.

I had just come out of Perry's room, having retrieved the battered old volume, when Miss Sinclair appeared before me so unexpectedly that I felt my heart turn over in my breast. She was standing at the top of the stairs that led down to the half-landing, perfectly lit by the candle in her hand, as though she held it solely so that it might gleam golden in her hair. I had never before seen her with her hair down about her shoulders, and I could not help but imagine how she might look if everything else she applied for decency's sake were stripped away. Her cheeks were so flushed that the scars stood out upon them like flecks of white paint; her breast heaved at the sight of me. I had known that she desired me, but I had never expected her to lose control of herself so absolutely.

"I came to find you," she said.

"I am flattered that you thought of me." It was a fairly poor response, I knew.

"I always think of you," she said. "I am not sure that you think of me any longer. Won't you show me that you do?"

She placed the candle in the alcove and advanced a few steps, then stood on her toes and tilted her face to my kiss. I could not deny her what she looked for. Her lips were as soft as ever, her breath as sweet, but I did not feel the rush of desire I would have expected; I had imagined that she would need coaxing. I found I did not quite like to be approached so brazenly. I pushed her away and held her so that I might look at her. Her eyes were in shadow.

"I wish you would take me away from here," she whispered. "Please, George. We must get away."

At that moment I spied, over her shoulder, the top of Perry's blond head, followed by the rest of him as he ascended the stairs to reach us. I had never known him to move so quietly. Miss Sinclair, evidently, had not registered his approach. I let go of her with all haste, so quickly that she reeled a little.

"I'm far too busy, far too busy just now," I said, meeting my friend's eye above his sister's head. My look said, *You see how I am fixed here. She has come to bother me, not the other way about.*

"Too busy for what?" Perry said, very loud, almost into his sister's ear.

She jumped, as anyone would just then, and her eyes grew wide and implored me to rescue her. Her slim hand crept to her throat.

"Miss Sinclair was hoping I might take her driving one morning soon," I said.

"She will be driven somewhere, if she doesn't go to bed," Perry replied.

Miss Sinclair turned and fled past him without looking again at either of us. I was left alone to face her brother's glare.

"Have you madness in the family?" I said.

"What?" Perry looked as though he should like to throttle me.

"Your sister was ready to drop down raving," I said. "I have seen kitchen mops kept in better care than her hair."

"The only madness here is the lunacy you will drive me to," Perry said.

I went to the library alone and sat, leafing through the book of our friendship, remembering how it had been when Perry and I were equals in our future expectations, and that future an age away.

At last, when I began to feel my eyes closing, I heard the door open and looked up to find Perry standing before me. He gripped a decanter of golden liquid in one hand. I could not see a glass.

"I am come to tell you," he said, swaying the slightest bit, "that you are to cease your teasing of me. I'll be hanged if I'll stand for it, George."

I nearly affected not to know what he meant, but something in his eye warned me not to.

"What have you determined you will do, if I do not?" I asked him. *I might as well know the stakes,* I thought.

"What will I do? I will shoot you. I would shoot us both tomorrow before you part us, George. I have said so many times, and never yet lied to you."

He had said so many times, indeed. I was heartily sick of hearing it. There was something about the way he said it this time, however, that showed me that I would be a fool to discount his words. He looked like a man polishing his musket.

THE NEXT MORNING I AWOKE with a weary kind of dread pressing upon me. I was made even more nervous to find Perry already at the breakfast table and Miss Sinclair entirely absent. Perry was working his way through a plate of kidneys, looking as fresh as the morning dew, and when I entered he looked up and smiled quite as though we had never been at odds.

"By heaven, you need not cringe so, George," he said, by way of good morning.

I tried to look steady, and sat, and gestured for coffee.

"You are in good humour this morning, Perry. Glad I am to see it."

"It is a good morning, is it not? Listen, George, I wonder if you'd be good enough to assist me." He leant forward, the piece of kidney upon his fork dripping gravy onto the cloth.

"Of course, old friend. I am at your service, as ever." I am not ashamed to admit that I expected some repetition of the threats of the night before, veiled in jest.

"I wondered if you might go over to Ashton, to look at a horse I've a mind to buy."

The relief was such that I said, "Certainly, I shall!" far louder than I intended.

"Then you shall have my gratitude," Perry said. "You have shown your aptitude for the choosing of horses."

I would not rise to it.

"You may put your faith in me, sir. As always."

"As always," Perry said, but there was a challenge in his eye.

I RODE OUT WITH A SMILE upon my lips and rode back with my mouth framing curses. The fellow at Ashton had said only to me, "I must say I'm surprised to see you, sir. I told Mr Sinclair I'd not have any beasts worth seeing till Tuesday next."

I turned poor Blackbird around without a moment's rest, though I'd ridden two hours to get there and must ride the same to get home.

My imagination grew wilder with every hoofbeat—what was the dastard planning for me? Perry had schemed to keep me away and he had not even troubled that I should not know it. Would I arrive back to find Miss Sinclair locked away, or the doors barred against me? He wouldn't stoop so low as to harm her, surely? He wouldn't fulfill his old threat to harm himself?

My threadbare nerves wore out before I reached Aubyn, and a kind of exhaustion set in. I should not have cared a jot if I never saw another Sinclair again.

Upon riding into the yard, however, my feelings turned again; there was a strange chaise there. Perry had a visitor. I should have liked to come upon Perry by surprise, but nothing could ever be kept secret at a house like Aubyn. At that very moment, the butler would be announcing my arrival. So desperate was I to gain what little element of surprise I could over my friend that I went straight to the library in my greatcoat, my boots still fouled with mud.

I came upon a footman in the hall and ran past him, though he called out to me. Up the stairs I went, to burst, unannounced, into the library.

There was Perry upon the settee close beside a young gentleman with hair cut into a waxed brutus crop, both of them as guilty as cracksmen. Before them was a decanter of wine, almost emptied, and two half-drunk tumblers. They were both of them very pink about the face. There was a perfume I did not recognise in the air, belonging to the young fellow, no doubt. Perry held a snuffbox in one hand and seemed to have been about to offer it when I came upon them. For a moment, I could not take in the scene, so full had I been with conspiracies and murder. Here was the simplest betrayal of all: Perry had repaid me, like for like. I could not speak for a moment, but only stood and huffed at them like a sweating horse.

"Ah, George, this is Mr Prince. Mr Prince, George Bowden."

I put up my hand to smooth my hair and found it disordered. Perry would never usually miss an opportunity to mock me. Mr Prince stood and came toward me, with a smile as heartbreaking as his name would suggest. His coat was exquisitely tailored, his cravat perfectly arranged. His handshake was a firm one. God alone knew where Perry had found him; the cove was as fine a dandy as I had ever seen. I could not tell if he knew what nest of vipers he came to make his home amongst. If he was aware of his situation, he was unruffled by it.

"A great pleasure to meet you, Mr Bowden." He gave me a bow and I am sure I returned it.

"Come in, George, for the love of God." Perry seemed to be enjoying himself damnably.

I refused to turn and run; I went over to the fire and stood before it to warm my hands and gather my thoughts. Mr Prince's footsteps behind me returned to the settee. I heard the sigh of the upholstery as he regained his seat and the glug of the wine being poured. I heard Perry ring the bell for the servant.

Damn his eyes, I thought. *What does he mean by it?* Was I truly to be usurped, or was this a punishment only, meant to return some of the pain I had inflicted upon him? I could do nothing but compose my face and behave in a manner gentle enough to rival Mr Prince's. I turned and walked to a winged chair opposite the two of them. I could feel the flesh of my jaw twitch.

The footman appeared, and Perry called for more wine and another glass for me. I took off my greatcoat as gracefully as I could, and the footman took it from me with not a quiver of surprise that I should have worn it upstairs. Mr Prince made some pleasant enquiry about the comfort of my ride and I replied, in as merry a voice as I could muster, that it had been tolerably pleasant.

"Then let us continue the pleasantries"—Perry clapped his hands— "and invite Mr Prince to dine. I expect no small enjoyment this evening. Do not you, George?"

"I am sure we shall all be very merry," I said.

"I am positive that you are right, my old friend." Perry fixed me with a gaze already glassy with wine. "You are always right, in both thought and deed."

At that moment, I could have taken my boot to his face.

THE DINNER HOUR found us arranged around the table thusly: Perry seated beside Mr Prince and opposite me, and Mr Prince facing Miss Sinclair. I had thought at first that she would not come down. The three of us were waiting for her at least a quarter of an hour before she deigned to descend. I could see Mr Prince regarding her with an expression of faint surprise; he had expected someone livelier.

The broiled mackerel was brought. Perry barely glanced at the dish before he called for more wine. He took the decanter from the butler's hand and insisted on pouring a generous dose for each of us, even Miss Sinclair, who quivered in silent protest.

Mr Prince said, "You must find great joy in the gardens here, Miss Sinclair. What I have seen appears charming."

I could not look at her. I caught Perry's eye purely by mistake; his look was a black one. For a moment, the full extent of his displeasure showed hellfire in his eyes, and then he snuffed it out and turned his eyes to his sister.

"I should think all places have their own charms," was all Miss Sinclair said. Her voice was so soft as to be barely audible.

"You have no basis for comparison." Perry drained his glass and waved for more. "My sister is entirely unworldly, Mr Prince."

"An admirable quality in a young lady."

"Perhaps you are right. And yet a little knowledge of the ways of the world might be considered prudent. My dear sister would not, I daresay, be able to determine the attentions of a true gentleman from those of a rogue playing at chivalry."

"You speak of your duty of protection, I think," Mr Prince said.

"I do," Perry replied.

"It is a man's duty to protect and guide the fairer sex," Mr Prince said, "and of course you must feel the need for vigilance. But I cannot think that any harm could befall Miss Sinclair under such watchful patronage as yours."

"I do hope not," said Perry, who could not have told you the whereabouts of his sister for days at a time. "I am fearful passionate on the subject. I should not hesitate to run a fellow through with my sword, should I detect a hint of trespass."

"You begin to sound like Macbeth," I said, "seeing shadows where there are none. Can we not be tranquil?"

"And you, I suppose, become Banquo?" Perry said. "But you are right, my old friend. Tranquillity is my dearest wish; I would sacrifice almost all I own to gain it. The bloodiest wars are fought to bring peace."

I grew tired after that, and drained my own glass.

Dinner progressed; Perry grew more loquacious and less subtle the more wine he quaffed. Miss Sinclair barely ate and did not speak. I, too, grew sullen and did not attempt any longer to interrupt Perry's sermonising. Mr Prince responded to Perry's inanities with smiles, but I thought he began to have the look of someone soothing a troublesome invalid. I recognised myself in his manner, if I am truthful. I was spitefully glad; he could hardly admire Perry now. Whatever chance of revenge my friend had engineered was spilled with the wine that spread a yellow stain about his place, like the bed linen of an incontinent. When Miss Sinclair withdrew, I thought she would have picked up her skirts and bolted like a horse, had convention permitted. I had never before wished to be a lady.

The brandy was produced, our pipes lit. The gentle protests of Mr Prince were entirely ignored as Perry served him a portion of the brandy hefty enough to set any man reeling. He helped himself to the same. He seemed to forget entirely to serve me; I helped myself to a modest amount.

"I have had the blue room made ready for you," Perry said, placing one hand upon Mr Prince's shoulder. Mr Prince did not drop his smile, but I thought it acquired an edge.

"You are most kind, but I think I will be obliged to return home this night. I have much to attend to in the morning."

"Oh, I am most disappointed." Perry did not remove his hand. "Can we not persuade you?"

Mr Prince shifted slightly so that Perry's hand fell back to his side.

"Regretfully, no," he said.

I could have laughed aloud.

Perry must have sensed my mirth, for now he looked at me as though he wished I might fall down dead upon the spot. He shrugged, drained his glass, and seemed to forget us both in favour of the bottle, pouring liquor only for himself and staring past me into the fire. His lips moved slightly, as though he muttered or cursed beneath his breath.

I was left in the unpleasant position of making conversation with the cuckoo in our nest.

"Are you fond of gaming, Mr Prince?" I tried.

"I confess I try to avoid it, Mr Bowden. Not, you know, through any piety on my part, but rather I fear my own weakness. Lead me not into temptation."

"Ha!" Perry said.

Mr Prince ignored him. "Perhaps it is why I went into law," he said instead. "In law, you know, the way is clearly set out and all we must do is follow."

"I studied law for a time," I said. "I never had any aptitude for it."

"You could not follow the law if it led you on a rope," Perry said.

Perry rang the bell for the butler and ordered more brandy to be brought. He was gathering himself for some undignified outburst; it hung in the room like fog.

"Well." Mr Prince rose and bowed. "I think I must take my leave of you gentlemen. Thank you so much for your company. Do bid farewell to Miss Sinclair on my behalf."

Perry roused himself enough to make a polite good night, at least.

In my own mind, a thought had raised its disloyal head.

"I will accompany you out," I said.

Perry looked up, but his look was a bleary one and he did not protest, nor offer to accompany us.

We walked out to the yard.

I said, "I confess I had a motive for coming out, Mr Prince."

Mr Prince nodded as though to say "Of course."

"It is a theoretical question, I suppose. I was wondering what it might take to alter the agreed inheritance of an estate. If the beneficiary should displease the family in some grievous manner."

"By marrying someone of whom the family could not approve, for instance?"

"Exactly so. Can the instructions of a will be ignored, in such a circumstance?"

"Do not think me too bold, sir," Mr Prince said, "but I think I know your meaning. Mr Sinclair and I have begun the process this evening, in fact. In the case of an elopement or other grave injury to the family's reputation, the entailment can very easily revert to the nearest male Sinclair—a cousin, I believe."

"Ah," I said.

"These things are better halted before they begin, of course," he said.

"Yes, indeed," was all I could muster.

Mr Prince climbed up onto the seat of the chaise.

"A pleasure meeting you, Mr Bowden. If I may make a general observation, it is a fact often overlooked that an elopement or similar rash act can be quite as detrimental to the fortunes of a young gentleman as to a young lady. All in such a case must be cautious."

"Of course, very wise," I said. The cove was looking at me with something akin to pity.

"Well, good night," he said.

"Good night, go well," I replied, and watched him drive that pretty little chaise out of the yard, taking a good portion of my hopes with him.

Chapter 6

✦ ✦ ✦

I did not return to Perry's company that night. I contemplated my future in earnest; it was not an enjoyable experience. I began seated at the window, then moved myself to the chair beside the fire. Then I found I could not sit and paced about the room. Then I sat once more, only to leap up again and begin my restless walk anew.

Perry had seen all that I was about and he had trumped me. I had to admit defeat. Oh, I knew that I could go to Miss Sinclair and beg her to run to Gretna Green. I could have her Mrs Bowden within three or four days. If I were to do that, we should be poor as church mice with only my allowance to live on and no home besides. I had lost or spent every penny I had made from Perry's investments. No, I did not love Miss Sinclair enough to live with her in poverty, and without Perry's companionship.

I had set my heart on Miss Sinclair largely because she was Perry's sister. Perry and I had been side by side since we were boys of ten years old. He might have been a drunkard, and a jealous man besides, but he was mine as much as I was his. We were bound by blood, more than soldiers. Who else on earth cared for me as Perry did?

* * *

THE FOLLOWING DAY, coward that I was, I avoided both Sinclairs until
the dinner hour, when I knew that Granville was to join us. I hoped that
his company would provide a mitigating influence.

I made a great effort to appear in good spirits at table and talked amia-
bly to Granville and Perry of boxing and business. I barely spoke to Miss
Sinclair. I tried not to smile when she caught my eye, and was relieved to
note that although I felt a tug at the loss of her, it was not an unbearable one.
In contrast, when I imagined Perry lost to me—even while he glowered at
me from beneath those pale lashes—I knew I should feel a worse pain. He
was as a part of myself. No lady could hope to fill the void if he were gone.

Perry, of course, had no idea that I had resolved to cleave to him. He
was not in good humour and grew even more sauced than was his habit.
He ate but little and pressed the wine upon Granville and myself with an
insistence that left little room for refusal.

Granville could not have been blind to Perry's mood. For his part, he
tried to lighten the atmosphere by telling Miss Sinclair of a ship he had
invested in, lately returned with a good profit from the sugar islands.

"Only imagine where the ship has been," he said. "The birds there have
the brightest feathers, though I have heard tell that their song is not as
sweet as the birds one finds in England."

Miss Sinclair flushed to be spoken to. She seemed about to reply, when
Perry growled, "What good is a song sweetly sung, when its words are
falsehoods?" He fixed me with his eye and seemed to believe himself the
lord of subtlety.

"There are some birds who can speak words, are there not?" I said,
addressing Granville. "Parrots, of course, and I believe some others."

"I have seen a parrot," Miss Sinclair said quietly, "at St James' Fair,
when I was a girl. We fed him peanuts."

"And did he speak?" Granville asked her kindly.

I could feel Perry readying to say something and studiously avoided his gaze.

"He said, 'Barrel of rum,'" Miss Sinclair said, "and 'Ho there, my beauty.'"

"He would not say so to you now," Perry said. "Likely he would mistake your countenance for a bag of peanuts and peck you to death."

He laughed and drained his glass. Then the humour of the thing struck him anew and he very nearly choked. I am sure I was not the only diner who felt sorry for an instant that he did not.

Miss Sinclair started a little and bowed her head, but she did not cry. I appealed silently to Granville. He only stared back at me, shocked by my own ungallant silence. Of course, he could not understand why I held my tongue. At last he determined to pretend that Perry had not spoken.

He turned instead to Miss Sinclair and said, "Your parrot sounds a fine fellow. I have a book at home, with the most wonderful engravings of exotic birds. I shall bring it for you, perhaps, the next time I come to dine."

Miss Sinclair managed to thank him, and we ate the rest of the course in near silence. She did not look up again for the rest of the meal, and even when she stood she bid us stay seated with lowered eyes.

Miss Sinclair having withdrawn, we took a glass of rum. Perry, clodhanded, overfilled our glasses so that we could not lift them gracefully to our mouths without a spillage.

With Miss Sinclair absent, the mood in the dining room grew pleasanter and the subjects returned to those that gentlemen most enjoy: business, boxing, and gaming. I took care to reply admiringly to every observation Perry offered, until at last he grew soft enough to announce, "There is nothing that can so much set me at my ease as the company and conversation of gentlemen."

Granville and I nodded and harrumphed in the affirmative.

"It is a curious thing," Perry continued, "that in this day and age, when so many advancements are being made, we should still find ourselves plagued by the company of females."

"Ho, sir," said Granville, "here I must disagree. A lady may not be a gentleman's equal in conversation, but she is not designed to be. I myself take great pleasure in the simplicity and innocence of the feminine mind."

"Simplicity?" Perry said. "I could not describe any lady of my acquaintance so. They all scheme to catch a husband and take over every inch of his home. When they have done so on their own behalf, they scheme on behalf of others of their sex."

"Ah," Granville said, "here we find the crux of the matter; to you, sir, a lady seems to do you harm by seeking to attach herself, and to me she bestows the greatest favour."

"Even with your sweet mistress," I said, "do you wish to marry?"

"I do," Granville said, "and as soon as I find a young lady sensible enough, I shall."

"If good sense is your ambition, you may be searching long," Perry said. "I advise you get a dog and be satisfied. A dog, you know, is always loyal."

He bent to scratch the ears of the hound sprawled beside his chair. He graced me with another glower; evidently, all this talk of marriage was rekindling his own ideas of my betrayal.

Soon enough we retired to the library and settled to a game of cards just as we had as boys at school, with only objects admissible as wagers; a gentleman could not hazard a guinea, but was welcome to lay down a pen, or a watch.

We played so long, and drank so heartily, that there came a time when Perry had been stripped of possessions and his pocket emptied. Granville had taken it all, and good use might he put it to, having so few handsome things ever about him. At last he said that Perry might have a chance to win it all back, if he would only put up his chestnut mare as a stake against them all.

"Wager Fleet?" Perry said. "I cannot, good sir."

"What, are you so fond of the beast, then?" Granville said. "I am surprised at you. Can it be that there is one female creature for whom you profess an attachment?"

"Pish," I said. "He cannot wager his horse because he does not own her. I won the animal from him yesterday and only allow Perry to ride her out of charity. I have owned every horse in his stable at one time or another, but he drives them just the same."

Perry snorted. "Charity, my eye. There is no charity in it. When George wins a horse of mine, I continue to shoulder the cost of it and stable his own mount besides. Do not you forget that."

"Be that as it may," I said, "it seems you are lost, Perry. Granville has stripped you bare, unless you wish to pillage the rest of the house?"

"That will not do," Granville said, "unless Perry has a mare in his dressing room. I am interested in giving you one chance, to win back all you have lost. Surely you have something of good value you can hazard. I will take any good horse you can vouch for. You have a stable full of the creatures, do you not?"

Here Perry's expression grew thoughtful. After so much liquor, his eyes, usually so clear, sat in pools of moisture, like winkles from a barrel.

"I do have one thing of great worth to lay before you," he said.

"Pray, fetch it out," Granville said.

"I do not need to fetch it, for I hold it here," Perry pounded a fist against his breast.

"By Jove, Perry," I said, "do not tell us you mean your honour as a gentleman or some such intangible? Surely you are not brought so low?"

"No," said Granville. "I believe it will be the secret to eternal youth. Come, sir, tell us that you are many thousands of years old, and give me the recipe for your potion."

"Dash it all, I mean no such thing," Perry said, "though it is an intangible, perhaps. I mean to wager the hand of my sister, Charlotte. Upon my honour, Granville, if you best me this time, you shall call me brother."

"Ridiculous!" Granville said.

Perry did not reply, but fixed me with a slightly unfocussed eye. I looked back at him, though my own vision swam a little.

"Ridiculous, sir? How so?" I said, my eyes upon Perry's. "She will make you a good wife." I had taken so much rum that I felt nothing: neither relief nor pain. We might indeed have been discussing Fleet.

"The hand of Miss Sinclair? How could you promise such a thing? Only she could bestow it, and she has never showed the least sign of wishing it."

"My sister will do as she is bid," Perry said. "She must marry someone, and you seem to me as good a gentleman as any. Perhaps a better man than I, or Mr Bowden, might hope to be."

"This is most unorthodox, sir," Granville said. "I cannot accept."

Perry leant close enough to Granville that he was forced to move back, or feel Perry's damp breath upon his face.

"You must accept," he said, putting his strong hand upon Granville's smaller one, "I insist upon it. It is an advantageous match for you, this you must concede. She is far above you in station, if not as handsome as she was. She will have a dowry, of course. You will find me willing to negotiate terms."

"She is a very pleasing young lady"—Granville turned his head to the side as Perry leant closer still—"but I could never think to impose myself upon her in such a way."

"Damn it, man, you will take her!" Perry cried, far too near to Granville's face.

Granville stood, as dignified as could be. He brought out a handkerchief and wiped his cheek. I put a hand upon Perry's arm, but he behaved as though I were not there, even when I pulled at him.

"Come, dear Mr Dryer," Perry said. "You do not need to play for her. She is yours. You said you wish to marry, and now you shall."

Granville was carefully placing all the objects he had gained back upon the table. I hastily fumbled in my pocket and withdrew the silver visiting-card holder I had taken from him earlier. I held it out and he accepted it from me with grave courtesy. Perry slumped back into his seat and informed Granville and me that we might both go to the devil.

I saw Granville to the door and into the hall beyond. As the valet fetched his overcoat, I said, "He will doubtless be ashamed on the morrow." I was not at all sure if I spoke truthfully.

"Tell me, George," Granville said, "I have had her acquaintance for years and yet I could not call myself familiar with Miss Sinclair. Do you find her to be foolish or overly fond of frivolities?"

It was only in that moment that a pain set itself about my heart.

"On the contrary"—each word dropped heavy from my lips—"she has a most retiring nature."

"Then, please, offer my apologies to Perry for departing so abruptly. Tell him I shall call on him tomorrow and if he should be remorseful, he may recant his offer himself."

With that, he bid me good night. I stood in the hallway until the butler came to enquire if I needed anything. I waved him off and slowly made my way back to the library. Once there, I found that Perry had swept everything off the table and was drinking straight from the decanter.

I SPENT AN UNHAPPY BREAKFAST and did not speak at table. Miss Sinclair, always quiet, would not break the silence but only looked at me sometimes with a questioning gaze. I ate quickly and spent the rest of the day at Perry's desk, staring blankly at the list of accounts. Perry, when he finally rose, said nothing of the matter to me, and I did not tell him that we might later expect Granville.

Perry spent the morning by the library fire, gazing into the flames with an intense expression, as though trying to divine the secret of their heat. He was in an ill-humour, and long before the dinner hour the strong liquors had been begun. He did not proffer the decanter, and nor did I express a wish to join him.

When the butler announced Mr Dryer's presence, Perry looked up in surprise and then turned triumphant eyes to me.

"You misjudge me," I said. "I advised him to accept." I walked from the room.

I heard Granville admitted to the library and Perry's loud voice, although I could not make out what was said. I returned to my chamber, surprising the chambermaid sweeping the grate. I sent her from the room and sat upon the bed, feeling like a foolish coward and unable to think of where I should go, or, if I should return, how it might be gracefully done. Before long, the dilemma was solved for me by the arrival of the butler, saying that Perry had asked that I join himself and Granville, if I so pleased. Here was my test. I went down immediately, pausing only to smooth my hair. Outside the library door, I paused again to affix a smile to my face.

I opened the door and cried out, "Well, am I to offer my congratulations?"

Granville came toward me and took my hand.

"Not yet, perhaps, but soon. That is my hope, at least."

"I am sure you will be accepted, old friend." The sincerity in my voice surprised even me. "She would be a fool to reject you. She will not, indeed."

Behind Granville, Perry looked at me with something of his old warmth.

"Let us call for spiced rum," he said. "It is your particular favourite, is it not, George?"

"We should call for whatever Granville wishes," I said. "It is his celebration."

"It is celebration enough to have the company of my two oldest friends," Granville said.

"I'll drink to that." Perry pulled the bell for the butler. "For God's sake, George, come in and sit down!"

He patted the seat beside him, and I went to him. I was experiencing an ache about my throat. My old friend wished only to be the first object of my heart. I had regained Perry's trust, by proving myself low and untrustworthy to his sister.

Dinner was a strange event. Perry was merrier than I had seen him for years. I did not speak much to Miss Sinclair, but nor did I need to; Granville and Perry quite dominated the conversation. Although Granville did not speak to Miss Sinclair, I saw him smile upon her, and I began to feel that perhaps I was doing her a service. God knew the man was rich enough to give her anything she desired—if he could be persuaded to spend any of it.

When dinner was over and Miss Sinclair withdrew, Perry took Granville off to the library for port and pipes, and bid me go to her.

"Wait long enough that Granville and I can discuss a few minor details, and then send her up to me," he said, as though I were a footman. "If you feel obliged to make her any apology, George, now is the moment for it."

He took my hand and pressed it. When he turned to go, I felt suddenly bereft. I wanted to cling to him; I wanted him to cradle my head against his chest.

In the event, I could not make Miss Sinclair the apology I owed her. Though I knew that I could never satisfy her wishes, though I knew that I would make her an inconstant husband, still it was a difficult prospect, to go into the drawing room that night. I spent the ten minutes in the hall, knowing myself to be about to discharge a very unpleasant duty indeed.

When, too soon, the time came, I only managed it by refusing to meet her eye, and so denied myself the last opportunity I would have to look upon her as Miss Sinclair, who loved me. The next morning, I left Aubyn and stayed away until Miss Sinclair and Granville were safely married. After that, of course, everything was different.

PART 3

Charlotte

✦ ✦ ✦

Chapter 7

✣ ✣ ✣

It is easy enough, in looking back on our lives, to say here is where the road took a turn, and here, and here. At the moment we are turning, it feels not at all like it; revolution may be upon us and we will be fretting over the breadth of our noses, or wondering whether the missing hairpins have been stolen by the chambermaid.

I was twelve when my brother and sister, Arthur and Louisa, were taken by pox. Miss Gale, our governess, said, "It is always the good ones are lost to us soonest."

She spooned me soup, for my hands were still bandaged. They were bandaged not because they were blistered, although they were, but because I could not help but scratch. My fingers were wrapped tight enough that they ached. The rest of me they bandaged more gently. I was left helpless as an infant, in the bed I had used to share with Louisa, though they had taken her pillow. I had a fear of allowing my limbs to stray toward Louisa's side of the bed.

"It is always the good ones are lost to us soonest. You must be as good as you can, Miss Charlotte," Miss Gale said, as she brushed my hair that was still bright, though the rest of me was made plain. She said the two things together so often that it seemed to me that she must wish me dead.

Louisa had always been good, where I was naughty. She was so good that I had used to hate her for it. She was gone and still I envied that she was mourned more than I thought I would have been. And yet if I could have had the chance again, I would never pull her hair or jog her arm as she sewed so that she pricked her finger. But perhaps it was too late for me to be good.

My brother Perry had been safe at school when the pox found us; he had never been good.

He was brought home from school as soon as the doctor declared the house safe. He arrived back full of curses and secret kicks below the table. He was furious to be at home, to find himself the eldest child. Perry and I had always tormented each other, and grief did not serve to bring us together.

We ate dinner at our parents' table, but we still breakfasted in the back parlour. Perry took up a spoonful of his flommery and tipped the spoon so that it slowly slid back into the bowl. He smirked at me.

"Eat your breakfast, Master Perry," Miss Gale said.

"Shall I eat it, Charlotte? Or shall I dip my face into it to be the match of you?" This was said quietly, so that Miss Gale should not hear.

"If I am flommery, you are bacon," I said, for his face tended to flush, which I knew well enough he was ashamed of. I stuck my tongue out at him, and that she saw, and scolded me for it.

Perry waited until she had done and whispered, "Were you showing me the only part of you left unpoxed?"

Perry had a host of new insults to call me, though which of them he had dreamt up and which he had learnt at school I could not guess. He called me cribbage-faced and corny-faced. He called me chicken-breasted and crowdy.

I set out to vex him. When he borrowed a book from our papa, I took it and hid it just to watch him hunting. When he found it—for it was only underneath one of the cushions—he looked at me triumphantly. *Very well*, I thought, and when he received a letter from his schoolfriend, George

Bowden—a letter that he read intently and held to his breast—I seized the first opportunity to cast it into the fire. I took the poker and pushed it under the coals so that he should not see it.

"I know you have it, you dumb-glutton scut," he said. His eyes darted about the room as if he did not like to search in front of me but could not help but look.

"It is you who is the dumb-glutton," I said, but he only laughed and shook his head.

My ignorance of the meaning of the words and Perry's laughter brought me to rage. I reached out to pinch or slap and he skipped away, making retching sounds within his throat and laughing still. I leapt upon him and began to pull his hair.

"Get it off me," he cried. "A beast! A scutty monster!"

Then he grew tired of our play and pushed me roughly onto the floor. I landed on the base of my spine and the jolt of pain surprised me into tears.

Miss Gale chose that moment to enter and looked at us sadly. She was leaving us for a new place and could not bring herself much to anger anymore.

Perry reached out his hand to help me up, and I took it.

"We were dancing, until Lottie tripped on her gown," he said.

I stood and wiped my face.

She sighed. "You must learn to be graceful, Miss Charlotte. A good posture can do wonders for a plain girl."

Once she would have made me wear a wooden busk and walk about, trying not to breathe, until my shoulders ached from holding them so stiff. Now she only sighed again and walked from the room.

Perry said, "Your hand feels like a bag of lead-shot."

He held his own hand out from his body as though he had soiled it by helping me stand.

I tried to slap him, but he skipped backward. At the last, I showed him my back and walked off, though I had nowhere to go and nothing at all to do.

"What nice posture you have," Perry said, as I reached the door. "I have quite forgotten that you have skin like a toad."

"I need not strike you," I said. "Your cheek is as red as a smacked bottom already."

I skipped out of the room quickly, so as to keep the last word.

I went to the little parlour, where I had begun to sit often, always alone. I was stitching a little scene, trees over water, which was meant to be the stream that ran through the Aubyn estate. When Perry came to ask if I would play at cards with him—for we did play together, as often as we antagonised each other—I only poked my tongue out at him again, and would not agree to be friends. He called me a scut once more.

Once the door closed behind him, I found myself pulling out the blue silks from the embroidered river and threading my needle with red. A river of blood. *Perhaps,* I thought, *I will sew scenes of all the biblical plagues.* I imagined showing Mama the one called "Death of the First-Born." Then I had to stick myself with the needle until real blood sprang to my finger. I pressed it to the red silk. I sat and sewed blood into the river.

"Dumb-glutton," I whispered to myself. "Scut."

I knew I could not really embroider the biblical plagues, or at least that I should not. Instead I drew them with soft pencil and burned them in the hearth. I used good, heavy paper meant for painting with water-colours—far too expensive and nice to burn. It burned so fast and so brightly that the moment it had turned to soft ash I wished only to burn more. I found scraps trimmed from my paintings, and upon these I wrote terrible things. I wrote "Perry will die," and "I will never be married." Then I burned them.

I walked about the gardens, as slowly as a young lady should. When I was out of sight of the house, I picked flowers that I knew I should not touch without permission. I sat on the grass, took off my gloves, and crushed them until my ugly fingers were stained green. When I found beetles upon them—shiny brown beetles, like seeds with legs—I crushed those too. I buried them all in the flower bed. I stood over my beetle-and-flower grave and whispered, "Dumb-glutton scut," for a prayer. I thought, with a savage satisfaction, that God would punish me.

On my way back into the house, I went to the bush that I knew to affect Perry badly, and I took a handful of its flowers to shake upon his pillow. I was not sure that anything would come of it, but in the morning Perry was not at breakfast. Upon visiting his room—although I had not permission to do so—I found that his face had swollen like pudding. He could scarce open his eyes, so puffy had they grown, and they streamed as though he wept.

Miss Gale, who sat beside him, sent me from the room the moment I opened the door. Perry was kept indoors, complaining, and having his fingers slapped when he rubbed at his eyes.

I walked about the garden, feeling great waves of remorse, and then of satisfaction. I had never exacted such perfect revenge before, but perhaps it had been too much—I must be kinder to Perry—but oh, who was made ugly now!

At last the remorse came out the victor. I went to sit beside Perry's bed and read to him from his favourite books. He never knew that it was I who had sent him there.

MISS GALE WEPT WHEN SHE LEFT to go to her new family, and pressed me to her flat bosom. I thought her tears a sham. If I had known how dreary it would be to be a young lady, I might have wept myself.

The maid I was given was barely older than I was and even quieter than I had been taught to be. Her name was Mary, and she looked like a dairymaid in a book, fair and pink and soft. She was so shy when first she came that she could not look me in the eye, but only whispered, "Yes, miss," to her shoes.

Perry, recovered by then, thought it a great joke.

"Look what Mama has sent you," he said, very low, when first he saw Mary. "Look how perfect her skin. In the usual case, it is the maid who must aspire to be like the mistress."

I hated having her about me. Not because her cheek was smooth but because I had grown used to being alone. Whereas a nurse or a governess will leave her charge whenever the fancy takes her, a lady's maid is employed to be company. Mary's company meant that I must be sweet again. I could not draw pictures of terrible things. I could not whisper "scut" under my breath. I could not pick at the scars upon my arms until they bled.

I tried sending her away to tidy my things and walked about the gardens by myself. Mama, who could not bear to have me about her, actually moved herself enough to send for me. Her face, always pale, was almost grey. I remembered, when I was very young, looking at her as we sat at the tea-table and thinking that my mama was the most handsome lady in all the world; now she looked as though she were covered in a fine layer of dust.

"Charlotte," she said, "must you pain me so? Do you seek to hurt me?"

"No, Mama," I said.

"Perhaps you think I have not provided you all I should."

"No, Mama."

"It is no doubt hard for you to be here and kept so quietly. Next year, perhaps, I will take you into society. Shall you like that?" Mama's gloved hand moved as though she meant to stroke my cheek, but at the last she let it drop without touching me.

"Yes, Mama." I had no clear notion of what society would be like, beyond the drawing room tea-parties Mama had held before the pox came.

"Then you must endeavour to be a lady in all the ways left to you, or you won't be fit to be seen. You must practise your singing and your drawing. You must think more upon your dress. And you must have a maid, Charlotte. You cannot any longer go walking alone."

+ + +

AND SO I GREW UP, and to look at me you would have thought I grew as quiet and still as Miss Gale had hoped. Mama developed very sensitive nerves; she grew fitful and often kept to her bed. We still went to Bristol in the winter, and then Papa's sister, Mrs Rayleigh, and my young lady cousins would call upon us. They thought me a very poor creature, to live so dull and left with such a face.

"Charlotte's hair is so fair, it is almost a waste," I heard my aunt say, once.

I found myself as quiet as my maid in their company. They were full of shrill laughter and whispers about their gentlemen acquaintance.

I had my hair pinned up and my gowns made over, but I never did make a debut into society in the way that most young ladies did. It was not that I never thought of such things as balls or gentlemen, only that I could not imagine myself amongst them. The only young gentlemen I knew were Perry's schoolfriends, and though they were polite enough, I could not imagine that they would have singled me out at a ball. They would have talked to a girl with an unmarked complexion and something charming to say. I never found that I could think of anything much to say in company. All the same, I felt safe at the house at Queen Square. Mama and Papa had been there when the pox came and had been saved from harm. Louisa, Arthur, and I had never cried out in fever in that house as we had at Aubyn.

When we were children we had used to go there in the first week of September every year. The house would be full of the bustle of maids and, as if in response, the city of Bristol would be full of the bustle of the fair. Even from so far away as Queen Square we could hear the noise of it; the docks behind the house were full of a great many ships, and all of them gay with flags. The Square would be alive with the cries of barrow-men and flowergirls, who were not usually permitted to flock there in any great number. This alone was exciting and lasted the whole fortnight long. If we minded all she said, after the first two days had passed—when Miss Gale said there were too many horse-dealers at the fair "to allow for decency"—we might go to the fair itself, and that was best of all.

Louisa was afraid of the fair, and Miss Gale behaved as though she were chaperoning us through a den of beasts, which was perhaps why I loved it.

"Don't look, Miss Charlotte, Miss Louisa," she would say, as we passed a group of rough sailors passing about a bottle, their arms about one another's necks, or a pair of dancing ladies, lifting their skirts to show their ankles turning. Since Miss Gale would put her hand to her own eyes, I was left free to peek. How powerful a draw is prohibition! I should never have been tempted to gaze at a soldier relieving himself against a tree unless I had been told that I must not.

As to the other diversions of the fair, express petitions were required for each entertainment that we wished to sample, and we could not hope to be always successful. It was easy enough to beg for a sugared apple, or the penny entrance to see the tumblers, for Papa would give Miss Gale a generous enough sum for the purpose. But let us try to argue for the giants and dwarfs, or the fortune-tellers, and she would cry, "Oh, goodness, no! What heathenish foolery. Not fit for gentle children."

Arthur and Perry, of course, were allowed to do as they would. They might even be permitted to leave us and wander off in complete liberty, if only they promised to be back at the carriage at the appointed hour. How envious I was to see them ride upon the round-about, waving their hats, as the urchin boys turned the wheel ever faster.

Once Arthur and Louisa were lost, we did not go to the fair at all, but only watched what we could see of the flutter and fuss of it from the windows of the house. My duty then was to be companion to Mama, though she did not often wish me with her, and Mary's duty was to be companion to me, though I wished for her company even less.

Once my aunt wrote to invite me to stay with them, but Mama, though she did not like to have me about her much, would not be parted from me either. She wrote back and told them that I was frail and that my health was poor. I know this only because I overheard Papa disagreeing with her over it.

"Charlotte is a young lady, Lenora. She must be allowed to go out into the world."

"Don't ask me, Charles!" Mama said, and I could hear by her breathing that she was readying herself for a fit.

Papa did not press her, and I stayed as dull as I was used to being. I was glad and sorry, both at once.

PERRY AND I TORMENTED each other as much as ever we had. I had very little acquaintance; our teasing of each other, along with reading, drawing, and embroidery, were amongst my favourite diversions.

When Mama gave me the task of ordering our dinner from Cook, so that I might learn the running of a household, my first thought was to order all those dishes that Perry disliked.

I sat opposite him and watched his expression sour as he saw the oysters come out. He could not very well refuse to be served, but neither did he eat them, and pushed them about on his plate. I watched my brother glancing at Papa from the corner of his eye, to see if he would be commanded to eat.

"Why, Perry," I said, "do not you like what I have ordered?"

This earned me a disapproving glance from Mama, for it was not polite of me to speak without first being spoken to. I did not mind; it was wholly worth inciting her displeasure for the dawn of realisation on my brother's face.

"You will eat what you are served," Papa said, before Perry could reply.

He had no choice then, and it was the greatest pleasure to watch him shudder as he swallowed. When the second course arrived, Perry watched me like a cat at a mouse-hole, so that it was difficult to keep my expression smooth. When he saw the sweetbreads and asparagus uncovered, I could not help but smile.

"Ah, excellent," Papa said, and I smiled all the wider.

"A fair choice, Lottie," Mama said.

"Thank you, Mama. You are as good a teacher as any young lady could wish," I replied, in my sweetest tones.

Perry looked at me with a resentful respect, and I knew well that I had only driven him on to greater lengths. It was a competitive sport of the lowest kind.

After dinner, he began by seating himself beside me on the sofa. I was knitting white lace from very fine thread, which I had lately learnt to do. Papa was already gone to his library, but Mama was with us, looking over a fashion paper sent to her by my aunt.

Perry leant in close to whisper, "Now, what would you say if I were to lose my dinner in your lap?"

I only smiled. He would do no such thing, of course.

Perry reached into his pocket and drew out a bundle, wrapped in a handkerchief, stained brown and sodden enough to drip.

"Here is my dinner," he whispered.

He moved his hand as if to toss it into my lap. I was wearing pink muslin and could not help but jerk in my seat. He did not throw it, however, only laughed quietly.

"Oh, don't tease," I said.

Perry smirked and opened his hand; the gravy-soaked bundle dropped directly into my workbox, on top of the white thread-lace I had already sewn over countless, painstaking hours. The handkerchief unfurled to show a mess of sweetbreads. A single piece of lamb's liver rolled out and dropped into a corner of the workbox.

Perry leapt to his feet before I could scream and cried out, "A superb idea, Lottie. Mama, Lottie and I would so enjoy it if you would play for us. Dear Lottie will sing."

He skipped over to Mama's side and took her hand beseechingly.

Mama agreed, and all I could do was flip the lid of the workbox closed and go to stand beside her at the spinet. Perry called out the names of his favourite songs and we played and sang for him, while all the time the juices of chicken gizzards and lamb's liver were staining my hard work brown. I would have to throw it all away and begin again.

When I went to bed that night I left that foul bundle under Perry's pillow, but it was little consolation. Ever after my workbox was to smell queer and rotten, no matter how often I sprinkled it with rosewater.

When I was almost seventeen, the pox came again. Pox will do that, you know; it sweeps through the country like a tide. Perry was in Bristol, staying with an old schoolfriend. Bristol had once again proved a safe place for my brother, even outside of Queen Square.

I knew it was coming. I felt it, creeping through the house. Every day I went, unbidden, to Mama's side, and one morning I found what I looked for. What I had not expected was that it would find Papa first.

He lay on the carpet beside the fireplace in Mama's parlour, which I must cross to reach her bedroom. It was awful to see him upon the floor, where Mama's little dog sometimes slept. His face was as flushed as Perry's was wont to be, and his eyes half closed. I ran to him and knelt at his side. My hand hovered over his forehead; I did not think I had ever touched his face before. At last I touched him. His face was burning and slick with sweat.

His eyes did not open, but he said, "Fisher, I should like to get up."

"It is Charlotte, Papa," I said.

He did not reply.

I tried to get him up alone but could not; he flopped wherever I did not hold him and was heavier than I would have believed. I rang the bell for a footman, but it was Mary who came. All the footmen were gone.

"Mary, help me get him up," I said.

She stood and bit her lip. She looked as though she would cry.

"Listen," I said, "you help me now and I will let you go home. I promise you. Only help me get him into bed."

Still she only shook and twitched about on her legs until I was ready to strike her.

Then we heard Mama's voice calling out Papa's name. She was confined to bed, big with child. I had been hoping, that summer, that she would be delivered of a girl.

"Go to her," I told Mary.

She went, and I rang the bell again. This time Fisher came, and he, at least, did not hesitate to come to my side.

"We must get him up," I said.

Before we could begin, Mary came back.

"Mrs Sinclair is not ill," she said. "She asks, will we put Mr Sinclair somewhere clear of her."

There was a day-bed only feet from Papa's head. Fisher and I lifted him and laid him there, though I felt my arms strain under his weight. I drew the curtains to keep the light from Papa's face.

"I will go and see to Mama now."

I straightened up and put my hands to my back. Mary jiggled about in that same, useless way.

"Go home, Mary," I said, "and do not come back. I have no use for you. Run home and tell your mama what a coward you are."

Her chin began to shake. I walked away so that I need not see her weep. I hoped she would take pox.

Within days, we were only five in the house. Mama and Papa, both struck down with pox, myself, Fisher, and Cook. Even the boot boy had fled.

I TASKED COOK TO SET OUT cold collations for me, which I ate only when I grew so faint that I must, and broths for the invalids, which Fisher brought upstairs. Cook need never come out of the kitchens; it was only with these conditions that I prevailed upon her to stay. I could not dress myself properly without a maid and did not care. I wore my gowns buttoned only as high as I could reach and an Indian shawl to cover the gap at my back.

Mama's anxieties were made the worse with fever.

"Be careful, Charlotte! Be careful," she moaned.

I told her that the pox does not strike the same body twice. I told her to look upon my scarred face as proof that this illness did not signify certain death. I did not speak of Louisa and Arthur. I burned endless pastilles to clear the air, though the scent of them brought back memories of my own sickness so vividly that my throat ached.

I went back and forth between Mama in the bed-chamber and Papa in the parlour. I sponged their faces and tried to stop them scratching open the pustules. I tried to burst those that came inside their nostrils, to ease their breathing. I remembered how I had felt my very innards seething. I felt the pox rising on their palms, as hard as if there were pellets embedded beneath the skin.

In places my own skin had those pellets still, scattered amongst the soft, pitted scars, as hard as they had been when they rose during my fever. I sat beside Mama and Papa and never had a thought for myself, but as soon as I was alone for a moment my hands stole to my arms to press and squeeze at those little lumps beneath my sleeves. I had picked at my scabs when I was still recovering and had my fingers slapped for it; now my fingers went creeping again to the old, hard lumps. In my bed at night I could not stop myself picking at them with my nails, as frenzied as if I were gripped by a terrible itch. When I drew my own blood I felt only glad of it; I wanted never to stop until all my skin was lifted from my body. When the lump was opened and a waxy white kernel squeezed from its inside, I felt only a dull kind of satisfaction at ridding my arm of that old, congealed sickness. I might have continued to claw myself until I was slippery with blood, if my parents had not needed me.

Papa's decanter was on the sideboard. I dosed them both with brandy, and later I dosed myself. Mama always took a nip of brandy for her nerves. I had never taken strong drink before, and the extraordinary heat of it caused me to choke in surprise. It was not long, however, before the world softened and warmed. I slept better, that night. I had dreams of Louisa, alive and running away from me across the gardens.

The doctor came, but would not even ascend the stairs to see them.

"You might keep them cool, but there is little else to do for them, Miss Sinclair," he said, his eyes shifting over my own scarred countenance as though afraid to settle. "I have told Mr and Mrs Sinclair many times how strongly I favour variolation against infection, but they would not hear of it."

"Mama feared it," I said.

"It would have been considerably less fearful than this sad outcome," he said, as if he knew them lost already.

The next morning, Papa opened his eyes and I thought he seemed to know me, but instead he called out for his land steward, Mr Tyne.

"What is it, Papa?" I asked him. "Can I take a message to Mr Tyne for you?"

Papa closed his eyes.

"He will not have the sense," he said, and very soon afterward slept. He would not wake again.

Of our papa's last words, my brother said only that Mr Tyne need not have sense, as he, Perry, would have the managing of the estate. I did not find I cared. My pain at the loss of Mama is perhaps best left unspoken, though she had not always liked me. My brother could not suffer me to be near to him, so little control could I keep over myself.

Chapter 8

❖ ❖ ❖

There is a good reason that the first stage of mourning is described as deep. I could not pull myself up from it long enough to care for myself, only sat in my chamber, dosing myself with brandy from Papa's decanter.

My aunt came and stayed some weeks, and grew exasperated at last with how dull I was grown. When she left, she tried to persuade me to accompany her, but only a very little refusal was enough to silence her.

"Then you must come to us when you are out of mourning," she said. "We must find you a match, Lottie, for you would not wish to live forever on Perry's charity. You must ask him to let you come to us. I am sure he will agree."

That was my situation; I was to live on Perry's charity. If I wished to do such a common thing as pay a visit to my aunt, his was the permission I must have.

Mary did not return, but another maid appeared to bring food and see to my fire. If she had not, I should have sat there until I froze or starved. My aunt left her, I think, when she went home.

I spent long hours sitting at my window looking out at the yard, where the servants walked about at their tasks as though the world went on. Sometimes I went to Mama's dressing room and stood amongst her things. This I did to torture myself. I would stand there until I felt my knees begin to fail under the weight of grief. Then I would return to my room. I did not like to weep in Mama's room; I knew she would not like to see me cry.

I went to Papa's library and liberated another decanter—of rum, this time. When that one was gone, I sent for wine. I clawed at my arms until I had turned the lumps to pits. Then I took to removing my stockings and began the same treatment upon my legs. My fingernails were as rimed with blood as a butcher's. That, and the taking of strong drink, was all that could rouse me to move.

I DID NOT KNOW what Perry did while I sat in the window. It was spring before I began to look about me again, and I found that we had company.

Mr George Bowden was an old schoolfriend of my brother's and had long been a visitor at our house and a favourite of everyone's. Every summer, Louisa and I had been used to follow him about, laughing and teasing him. Louisa did so because she declared that she loved him and meant, someday, to marry him, and I because I could see that it infuriated Perry. My brother had always been jealous over his toys or his pony. He was incensed at having to share the attentions of his friend with his two younger sisters.

It was Louisa I thought of, once I came downstairs and found Mr Bowden at our table and living in a chamber opposite Perry's. Perhaps he had been there all the winter, I did not know.

On one of the first occasions that we all three sat at table, Mr Bowden gestured for wine and addressed me with "Shall I have the pleasure?"

Perry, who had only moments before been trying to bring me to smile by recounting a joke, immediately grew as sour as if he'd swallowed a lemon.

It was a dull kind of habit, more than anything, which drew my response.

"Oh, Mr Bowden, how kind."

Ever after that, I watched my brother, whenever Mr Bowden spoke to me. Perry clearly considered that his friend had come to comfort him alone and begrudged sharing even a drop of that solace with his sister.

Teasing Perry was better than any tonic. When Perry remarked, upon seeing Mr Bowden hand me an orange sprinkled with sugar, "Sweet dressing cannot mask a sour nature," he looked so vexed that I could not help myself simpering at Mr Bowden and then feeling ashamed at making myself so cheap.

It could not be denied that Mr Bowden was handsome. He had lively brown eyes and wore silk stockings even on ordinary days. He had a beauty-mark grown naturally upon his cheek, exactly where one might choose to paint it. His hair he cut in short curls and left off hair powder, which I thought daring. Beyond appearance, however, I found him lacking. He was too shallow to love, a pretty picture hanging upon a blank wall.

Mr Bowden's presence, and the mild weather, turned my grief from a frozen weight to an ache behind my eyes. I began to leave off drinking liquor in the daytime, unless I awoke feeling very melancholy. Perhaps because Mr Bowden stirred in me not love but an awareness of the existence of handsome gentlemen, I found I grieved for my own lost face, though I knew I was ungrateful to God. I left off clawing at my scars and in penance began to massage my limbs with a liniment of juniper and hawthorn.

I never refused Mr Bowden's invitations to go walking or driving. I could not have passed over the opportunity to see Perry's expression drop. I did find that once we were away from Perry's company, Mr Bowden began to seem tiresome. That is not to say that I did not sometimes find him flattering; he said that mourning colours became me, making my hair and eyes brighter by comparison. He called my pox-marks stars upon a daylight sky. He said that when I came out of mourning he would be sorely tempted to run my brother through with his sword, just to see my fair hair falling against my black cloak. That little witticism made me laugh aloud in surprise.

The day came, however, that we were walking in the parkland together when the breeze sprang up cold. He drew me into the trees for shelter and there put his hands tight around my waist and looked close into my face. I could not believe he should wish to do such a thing. I was so astonished that all his flattery had led to something of substance, that I did not stop him when he put his lips to mine. His lips were warm and drier than I had thought they would be.

I could not help but be pleased, but on whose account was the pleasure? Was it only that I knew how furious Perry would be to know it? Was it for the sake of my own vanity, that a gentleman should wish to kiss me? Could it be that without knowing it, I loved Mr Bowden? I drank a jug of wine, just in order that I might not think of it, and stayed in my room until the morning.

I awoke with the expected headache from the wine, but beneath this I was filled with a determined joy. Why should I not have whatever happiness was available to me? I found, that morning, that I was glad to see Mr Bowden, for his own sake. Perry was still abed; I accepted Mr Bowden's invitation to go riding simply because riding would be a pleasure.

I had never been taught to ride. Mr Bowden sat me upon his own horse, Blackbird, and led her about the park. He did not laugh when I grew nervous and clutched at the pommel, only slowed the pace until I grew calm.

Finally I rode her alone, with Mr Bowden beside me on one of Perry's horses, and the sun warm on my face. He did not ask me to go above a walk. The smell of the grass, horse, and leather combined to make the sweetest perfume. I loved the freedom, the slight fear that I would fall, the feel of the animal beneath my legs. We sang as we rode and I did not care that my voice screeched.

One morning I came down to find him waiting at the bottom of the stairs, looking up at me with an expression of great excitement.

"Come with me," he said, and held out his hand.

I took it, conscious all the time of the lumpen skin beneath my glove.

"Where are we going? What about breakfast?" I said.

"Breakfast be hanged." He led me to the door.

"It is raining," I said, but he only held his coat above my head.

"Come, be quick." His eyes were laughing beneath the coat.

I laughed with him, and together we ran to the stables. The groom looked surprised and a little disapproving to see us arrive so, which made us laugh the more.

"Now look," he said, and pointed to a horse I had not seen before, holding her elegant head above the half-door of her box.

"Oh, how lovely," I said.

She was the dearest chestnut mare, with docile eyes and a shining mane.

"She is yours," he said, leading me toward her.

"No," I said, "not mine. She cannot be."

"She is, indeed. This is the first of the gifts I mean to give to you: a loyal friend and the freedom to ride. Do not you be afraid. I will teach you all you need to know."

"Oh, Mr Bowden," I said, for I still could not feel steady calling him George. "I do not know what to say."

"Only tell me you are pleased with her."

"I adore her above all things." I put my hand to that velvet nose, and she dipped her head to me.

"Not all things, surely?"

"Yes, I do. And I promise you I shall, always."

He took my hand and turned me so that I might face him. "Do not you make that promise. Perhaps, instead, there will be a different promise you might make, in time. In the meantime, you may love her. Her name is Locket, for she carries precious things safely."

Lying in bed at night, I took out that moment in the stables and looked it over. He had as good as asked me to marry him. He had, surely. I knew, as though I had decided it long before, that if he asked me, I would accept. I could not expect better, scarred and hidden away as I was. I could not pretend to find him unattractive. To be the wife of a handsome fop was far more appealing than to be a spinster thrown on Perry's charity.

Even without those thoughts to unsettle me, I could scarce sleep, so eager was I to go out and stroke Locket's soft nose. I had meant it when I said that I loved her. I almost loved Mr Bowden, for giving her to me.

The weather was poor, and I could not ride for the first few days after she came, but each morning I was there, gazing into her soft eyes. I sent for the dressmaker and gave her one of my walking gowns to make over into a riding habit. I ordered a hat with a feather. I ordered black, but because it had been three full months since poor Mama and Papa were lost, I had blue and grey ribbons put around its brim.

Perry was in a dark humour, stamping about the house, cursing at the servants. When I passed him in the hall one night on my way to bed, both of us with candles in hand, he reached out and gripped my arm at the elbow.

"Let me go," I whispered. I felt, instinctively, that I should not raise my voice; the battle between us had always been a private thing.

"You let go of George!" Perry's whisper was almost as loud as his speaking voice. "You have always bothered at him. You leave him alone, Charlotte."

"He comes to find me," I said. "Why should he not? Did you think he would be satisfied to be always with you? Of course he seeks feminine company. You are not enough for him."

I had meant not enough of a companion, but I saw something in Perry's face—wincing pain, and shame, and fear—that made me stop. I felt my mouth drop open like a simpleton. I closed it quickly.

"You leave him be," Perry said again, his fingers digging into my arm. "I will find some way to be rid of you, otherwise. You can go to our aunt. You can go into a nunnery. I warn you, Charlotte. Do not cross me."

The words were on the tip of my tongue: *Can you really think he loves you? You are as foolish as Louisa was; he has as good as asked me to marry him—*

But Perry had about him a quality I could not name, and I found it frightened me. I wrested my arm from his grasp and hurried up the stairs, the flame of my candle jumping as I ran.

* * *

I AVOIDED PERRY all the next day. I took breakfast in my room, and as soon as I was dressed, I went to the stables.

The groom smiled to see me hurrying in from the rain. He had lost his disapproval in the face of my devotion. He gave me a soft brush for Locket's coat. I brushed her as he showed me, good firm strokes. I meant to look after her.

"It does my heart good to see you smiling, Miss Sinclair," he said.

"Who could see Locket and not smile?" I replied.

"She's a pretty little beast, right enough," he said. "You deserve a bit of happiness, if you'll excuse my saying it."

I nodded. While I was with Locket I felt that I, and all the world, could be as good and simple as she. The moment the groom went about his business, I planned to fling my arms about her neck like a child.

"Mrs Sinclair was quite the horsewoman when she were young," he said, then.

"Mama never rode," I said.

Locket, seeing that my attention turned from her, pushed her nose into my hand. I rewarded her with a flurry of caresses.

"Oh, she did when she were young, Miss Sinclair. I'd not lie to you. She followed the hounds a fair few times, as well."

After that I longed to ride even more.

THAT EVENING THE GENTLEMEN stayed locked in the library, in a cloud of cigar smoke that drifted through the halls. I ate alone and retired to sit in my window seat and pray that the night be clear and the morning fine.

The yard looked changed at night, a spread of shadows; the line of the pump blending into the black wall of the stable, the top of the gate become a shelf for the darkening sky. The rain was easing into a fine drizzle. I opened the window by myself; I did not like to have the maid spoil the deep quiet of my chamber just then, and I found I enjoyed the effort of it, turning the key and heaving the rope that pulled the sash. I let go too fast and the rope ran against my palm with a strange and shocking heat.

The night air was chillier than I had expected. It came straight through my shawl and made me aware of my skin, all over. I leant into it a little, just so that my face was where the glass had been. I smelt wet straw and clean earth.

At that moment, I saw Perry picking his way across the cobbles, taking care not to slip. He was bareheaded, and his hair showed bright in the swinging lantern light. His step tilted and lurched as the wine unbalanced him. He walked directly to the stables and I heard, quite clearly, the wood-on-wood of the bar being lifted and the open and close of the door.

A great dread started up in the pit of my stomach. Perry had always known how best to hurt me, and he was not one to let a chance go past. If I loved Locket, she could not be safe.

I sat for a moment, caught between fear and action, and then I moved so quickly that I hit my elbow against the window coving. I went from the room and down the stairs. The hall was empty. I went toward the music room, where French windows opened onto the garden. I could hurry around that way, and through the gate to the stable yard.

The music room was empty, the hearth dark. The only light came from the windows, but there was moon enough that I could make out the tables and chairs that I must not collide with. The dark and the quiet made the queer urgency in my breast all the sharper. I went quickly to the French windows; this time, however, I found them locked for the night.

Back into the lamp-lit hall I went, my heart fluttering. I slipped to the yard door, usually the province of servants, the way lined with boots. Boots waiting to be polished, with mud still upon them, boots made ready and shining. Boots I thought were Papa's, waiting for feet that would never more fill them.

I opened the door and went out, into the wet of the night.

I could not think of the last time I had been outdoors in darkness, perhaps not for years, returning from church at Christmas. The yard was vast and strange, and I was afraid to step quickly, the cobbles slipped so beneath my shoes.

A light came from the stables, the swinging here-and-gone of a lantern. The drizzle speckled my face, damped my sleeve where it emerged from my shawl.

Before I could reach the stable, the door swung wide and the yard was suddenly filled with figures; the one holding a lantern was a servant, and the face he illuminated as he held the light aloft was my brother's. Then came the groom, holding a horse's bridle. I knew it was Locket, even before the light showed her eyes rolled to the white and the foam at her lip.

"Oh," I cried out. "What have you done to her?"

"Go you inside, Charlotte," my brother replied.

I moved toward him, perhaps to rush at him, but my feet slipped like an ice-skater's, and I stilled myself.

"What have you done?" I cried again.

"Don't be a fool; it was I who found her. It is colic; she must be walked. Go inside. I won't tell you again."

"Don't you be afeared, Miss Sinclair," the groom said. His voice was tense with the effort of holding Locket's tossing head. He pulled her onward, and slowly she began to walk. Behind them, I saw another dark form at the stable door. I was sure that it was Mr Bowden.

"Please," I said to him, "save her."

It was Perry who answered, "Go you inside, or you will need saving on your own account."

My maid had appeared at the kitchen door and was calling to me. I let her lead me back inside, for I could not think what else to do. I stood in my bedroom while she pulled me about, my arms from their sleeves, my hair from its pins, all the time feeling I might grow wild, slap at her and run from the room. At last, as soon as I was out of my gown, I sent her to fetch brandy, for the shock. I could not bear to think of Locket, if I might not be allowed to help her. I dosed myself so well, indeed, that I did not wake when they shot her.

I COULD DO NOTHING to ease that pain but continue to take brandy. It was days before I came out of my chamber. I had never even sat upon her back. Though I had known her only four days, I felt the grief as though I had been her mistress my life long.

Mr Bowden took my hand and whispered, "I will find you another horse as sweet," but he did not.

After this he did not come down to take breakfast with me any longer. I returned to sitting alone. The weight of the liquor and my pox-marked skin kept me sitting in place, and let fate take me where it would.

I had often felt great annoyance toward Perry, but never as pure a hatred as I felt then. It was so powerful that I could not hold it still.

Who knows that I might not have kept there, frozen by the balance of hatred and sorrow, if Perry had not tipped me out of the scale one afternoon?

I was walking down to dine and met my brother in the hall. I had not expected that the gentlemen would dine with me. Perry had about him an air that suggested that he had been waiting for me. He stood at the bottom step, so that I had no choice but to pass close to him, and waited until I had completely descended the stairs before he spoke.

"I am master of this house" was what he said, "and you will obey me."

I did not stop, nor reply. What reply was there to such a statement? Perry put a strong hand on my arm to stop me.

"You think me more monstrous than I am, Charlotte, but know you this: I will have the mastery of you. If your horse had not died, I would have sold her. You are willing to see me left heartbroken; I will see you left with nothing, I swear it before God. Leave George be, or we shall all be miserable. I will never allow you to be otherwise."

✦ ✦ ✦

I HAD NEVER THOUGHT of escape in any real sense. I had never executed any kind of plot beyond the shaking of pollen onto Perry's pillow. I must, however, do something. I could not live with him any longer; I could not bear to go to my aunt.

I did not know how to plan such a thing. All I could think was, *I shall have to try to seduce Mr Bowden.* Mr Bowden, I thought, seemed still the only chance I had. Perry left me no other course—he had driven me into a corner.

We dined in an atmosphere of the greatest tension. Mr Bowden seemed always to be avoiding my eye; I was trying, for the first time, to catch his gaze.

When I spoke to him, to say something silly, such as, "How do you like the soup, Mr Bowden?" he replied, "Very fine, I'm sure," without ever lifting his eyes from his spoon. The only gaze I attracted was Perry's malignant one.

Perry watched us both—I would turn my head from trying to engage Mr Bowden's attention just in time to see my brother's eyes slide away from me. Mr Bowden's bent head looked just as my own must often have appeared, studiously avoiding the company, whilst still sitting in it.

After dinner the gentlemen did not come to join me in the drawing room. I stood at the window and watched them ride away into the evening. The hoofbeats faded. Oh, how I wished I could just call for a horse and go. There was nowhere at all that a lady in my position might ride off to. She would need someone to take her in; she would need money of her own.

I did not call for my maidservant to put me to bed. I could not sleep, I knew without trying. Instead I went to Mama's room, where I had not been in weeks. I felt a dull shock upon seeing that Perry had ordered the furniture to be covered in dust-sheets. I felt as though she had been buried for a second time. It made me only the more determined.

I stole into Perry's library and poured half a bottle of brandy into my water-glass. I needed to be bold, that night. I was still determined that Mr Bowden must be persuaded to love me again. I went swiftly back to my chamber, carrying the water-glass concealed inside my wrap, in case I should come upon a servant.

At long last, when full dark was come and the water-glass almost empty, I heard the gentlemen return. I could tell from the clumsy thud of their boots and the boisterous sound of their voices that they were pretty well soused.

"Off you go, dear fellow!" I heard Perry call.

Surely he meant Mr Bowden. He would never address a servant in such terms, even whilst drunk. It was an odd good night to make, but my brother was not a conventional man, and sure enough, the footsteps thudded off in two directions—Perry's heavy tread toward the library and Mr Bowden's softer footstep upon the stairs.

I hesitated for only a moment, and then pulled the pins from my hair, letting it tumble down about my shoulders. It could still be called handsome; let me use it, this once. I threw a shawl about my shoulders, then took it off, then picked it up and put it about me again. My dressing glass showed me, not the pale wraith I had imagined myself to be but a wild-eyed young lady with burning cheeks and a mass of dishevelled fair hair that needed a brush taken to it. No matter, no matter, I could not wait. I hurried out onto the landing. I paused and listened for Mr Bowden's steps, like a fawn with ears pricked. *There!* I wheeled about. He was indeed going toward his own room.

I hurried down the landing. The halls had never seemed so long. Down the little stair I went to the half-landing, up the other, to the gentlemen's corridor. No sooner had I ascended the top step than Mr Bowden was in front of me, coming from the other direction with one half of his collar sticking up and a tattered book clutched to his chest. He looked as shocked to see me as if I had indeed been a wraith. We looked at each other for a long moment. I had not planned what I would say to him, when once I found him.

"What's this?" he said.

I walked toward him, but he did not reach for me. I came very close. He did not reach out, but neither did he step back. He stood very still, as though I were a wild animal he did not want to frighten away.

"I came to find you," I said. I did not feel bashful in the slightest; I felt bold.

"I am flattered that you thought of me," he said quietly.

He put a hand to his hair to smooth it, but it seemed to stick to his palm and he only succeeded in leaving it ruffled.

"I always think of you," I said. "I am not sure that you think of me any longer. Won't you show me that you do?"

He shook his head, not in the negative, but rather as if in wonder that I should say such a thing.

I stood on tiptoe and leant toward him—he had no choice then but to put out his hand to steady me, and having put his hand upon my waist, it was a very little matter to lean further forward still, until our lips met. He returned my kiss, the edge of the book jabbing my ribs. *I am shameless,* I thought. *I am loose.* The thought was an exciting one, and I kissed him more ardently for it.

Mr Bowden pushed me from him gently and held me by the shoulder, at arm's length, to look at me.

"I wish you would take me away from here." I tried to make my eyes soft, but one lid kept twitching. My heart was beating in my throat. I wished to get away so very badly. "Please, George." I could not help it. "We must get away."

I was not alluring, I was panicking. He dropped his hand so quickly I might have been a hot coal.

"I'm far too busy," he said, "far too busy just now."

"Too busy for what?" boomed Perry's voice, behind me.

I jerked with the shock of it, like a wooden tumbling man strung on sticks.

+ + +

I WAS HUMILIATED, and yet I thought I might still catch him. His kiss had been passionate enough that I thought he must desire me. I sat at the looking-glass. Was mine truly a face Mr Bowden could love? I examined every inch of it, the pits and bumps of my skin. When I grew weary of that, I practised agreeing to marry Mr Bowden. I thought, *If ever I am given the chance, it will be best done simply.* Clasped hands, modest posture, a whispered assent.

As unexpected as it was, I very soon had that chance. Of course, it was not Mr Bowden but Granville who was to be the recipient of all that rehearsal. And it is not to be expected that he appreciated it overmuch.

Chapter 9

❖ ❖ ❖

Granville, or Mr Dryer, as I then called him, was a schoolfriend of Mr Bowden's. He came to dinner perhaps once a week and said little. He was tall and, though young, was very proper. His hair he kept powdered and curled above the ears, and he wore a very plain coat. He sometimes drove an old gig pulled by one horse.

When we found ourselves seated near each other he would talk to me, with grave courtesy, of the beauty of the garden, or the cooling weather. I answered him as best I could, being always awkward in the company of gentlemen, even such staid, stiff-mannered young gentlemen as Mr Dryer. He might have been a little flat, but he was never rude. When Mr Bowden had teased me to sing (only, I knew, to hear me protest and make me blush), Mr Dryer said gravely that he should prefer that I sit and be easy amongst them. When he said this, I did not know whether to be relieved or insulted.

Mr Bowden said immediately, "Oh, yes, do sit and be easy by me," patting the seat next to his on the sofa.

I could only shake my head and laugh, and note how black was Perry's look. All thoughts of Mr Dryer were driven from my mind.

Mr Dryer never occasioned ill-feeling in me—but he kindled no curiosity, either. If he was anything to me then, it was an inconvenience; his presence meant that Mr Bowden would be less inclined to tease me into intimate conversation and I could not indulge myself in my little pleasure of antagonising my brother. A visit from Mr Dryer signified an evening devoted to talk of business and boxing, and very little else. I paid him only as much attention as I need, for politeness' sake. I did not consider him handsome, because I did not consider him.

One evening we were all four of us at dinner: Perry, Mr Bowden, Mr Dryer, and I. The gentlemen talked of a mill they had bought, or perhaps were selling. It was very dull.

Once Mr Bowden poked at the quail upon his plate as though he were examining it. He had once told me that he did not think much of shooting quail for sport. They were too slow to be much fun, he said, and called them "an inferior chicken."

Now I said, "How does your quail compare to chicken, Mr Bowden?"

"Oh, very poorly," he replied, with a serious face.

"What are you saying? The flavour is far superior," Perry said. "Now, can we cease this incessant talk of buying mills? I wish to hear of the other kind of mill. Granville, how does your boxing miss fare?"

Mr Dryer spoke to me kindly enough, about exotic birds. I replied as best I could, though conversation has never been a talent of mine. Perry was singularly unpleasant, but I would not rise to it in company. Instead I bowed my head as though his tired old insults had stung me, and he only made himself look brutish.

I WITHDREW ALONE, as I must, being the only lady, and waited for the gentlemen to join me in the drawing room. I ordered a decanter of ratafia and took up my embroidery, but the time passed very dull. I sat as near to the fire as I could get in that large and lonely room and hoped that the business of the mill would be finished with along with the brandy.

At length, when I had begun to grow sleepy and think of my bed, the door opened and Mr Bowden came in, quite alone. This was entirely unexpected. All ideas of sleep flew away, and I could not help but think,

Heavens, I believe he may declare himself. He has begged leave of the gentlemen to come in here—but he stood just inside the door. He would not meet my eye.

"Your brother asks that you go to him in his library," he said. He nudged at the carpet's fringe with one high-polished riding boot.

My heart slowed mid-leap.

He would not look up, even as I walked past him to the door. He only moved back so that I should not pass too near and turned his face to the window, though it was dark outside. Even his reflection in the window glass seemed to be avoiding my eye. My face reflected beside his was a pale and patchy moon.

I hesitated in the doorway. From where I stood, I could smell the perfume on his coat. If he would only have turned to look at me, I believe perhaps I would have spoken—but he did not. I walked up the stairs to Perry's library with fear pulling upon me as though I had swallowed lead-shot.

Mr Dryer came out of the library just as I reached the door. He bowed to me without a word. I peeped up at him and saw that he, too, seemed to avoid my eye.

I knocked and was bid enter. I felt very strange. My fear receded, all my sensations as changed and muffled as Mama's room, where familiar things were buried under dust-sheets.

My brother was standing at the mantel, winding the clock, as our papa used to do. I had never before seen him so exactly in Papa's place, and I did not like it. He turned and walked to the desk, waving his hand at the chair opposite his. I sat gingerly, as though I might fall.

Perry sat opposite me, in Papa's polished mahogany chair.

"Charlotte," he said, "you cannot stay here any longer. I have warned you that I will not keep you. You must be married, and as quickly as can be arranged."

This was so unexpected that I did not have a response. I stared at him, my mind quite empty.

"Mr Dryer is an excellent man," he said. "He will make a good husband for you. I only hope you will learn to be a good wife to him. Go now and let him make his offer."

I could neither move nor speak. I only looked at Perry. His face was as serious as I had ever seen it.

"Go," he said. "Why do you stare so? What is wrong with you?"

"Mr Dryer? I have scarce ever spoken to him. I have never thought of it."

"Mr Dryer has thought of you, and that is all that matters. He is just the man you need, Charlotte. He will keep you sensible."

"And if I have other thoughts? What then?"

One of my hands found the lump upon the other that I never had been able to claw free and began to squeeze at it through the cloth of my glove.

"If they are thoughts of Mr Bowden, then you must know that they are impossible," Perry said.

I felt my eyes narrow.

"Give up the notion, Charlotte. He was never in any seriousness. You cannot really have imagined that he might love you. He has agreed, nay, offered, to step back for Mr Dryer. You must forget it entirely. You are to go to Granville."

"And if I will not?"

"Then you will go somewhere less pleasant. Why would I keep you here? If you had never begun this game, I would have provided for you for the rest of your life."

"It is not a life anyone would wish for, to be always alone." *If it was a game, then Bowden played as eagerly as I did,* I thought, but did not say.

"Then let you take comfort in Mr Dryer's company. I told you that you would hurt me if you persisted, and that knowledge did not give you a moment's pause. Do you expect me to care for your feelings, when you have not cared for mine?" Perry looked at me as though he pitied me. It was unbearable.

"Your feelings are unnatural," I said.

"What does it matter, when George shares them? You will never know love such as I have. You could not possibly understand."

My instinct was to leap at him like a cat, but instead I found myself weeping. I did not consider whether or not I might accept Mr Dryer, if the choice were really mine. I did not weep for the loss of Mr Bowden, but for the absolute impotence of my position. I was defeated, and I did not know how to fight him.

My tears were entirely out of character and made Perry furious. He commanded me to go down and accept Mr Dryer. He told me that I should be grateful to find a man who would have me, ugly as I was. He reminded me that Mr Bowden had given me up without complaint and that I would not find him weeping over the loss of my poxed countenance. This made me cry the harder. Eventually he called a maid to help me to my room, and, wresting myself from her touch, I ran upstairs. I crawled into bed in my evening gown and indulged myself in a fit of despair almost as violent as I had when Mama passed on.

I closed the curtains around my bed, forming a box of cloth in which to cry myself into sickness. I consented to be undressed only because it was painful to lie for so long in stays. Not a soul on earth cared for me at all. I told my maid of this whenever her timid face peeped around the curtain. *Better I had died than to live so,* I whispered. *Better I had followed Mama.* When she begged me not to hurt myself and pulled my hand from my skin, I slapped her with the one she left free. It was not a hard slap; I was lying down and weak besides, but it was enough to stop her trying that trick again. I lay there, breathing my own stale air and refusing to eat anything but milk-porridge, for three long and wearisome days.

I rose on the fourth day, through boredom as much as anything else. I was as unhappy as I had ever been, but it was wasted pain. No one but my maid had been near to my chamber in all that time. I had asked her each morning whether Mr Bowden had visited, or sent word; he had not. Though I would not see him, Mr Dryer had called twice, with a strengthening draught, a basket of chestnuts, and his hopes that I would recover swiftly. My brother sent several messages to say that if I would stop my "fit of nerves," I could join him for wine, or to play at cards. I would not, of course. I could not have borne to be near him.

I came to an acceptance then. I would give Perry his victory in exchange for my escape. Mr Dryer's rule of me could not be worse than my brother's. My standing in society, even as the wife of a merchant tradesman, would be higher than that of a spinster sister.

My maid I had bring paint and powder, though Mama would have disapproved. I spent many hours learning its application and its shortcomings; nothing could hide my scars entirely, short of a veil. I had been a fool to think that Mr Bowden would look at a poxed maid and see a wife. He had been playing at flirtation, just as I had. I was indeed lucky that Mr Dryer would condescend to take me.

I did not see George Bowden again until after my wedding, and then, of course, everything was different.

Thus it was that I became Mrs Dryer. Granville had not a title, nor an estate like Aubyn, but he was a man on the rise, or so everyone said, and I might expect to grow richer every year. Besides this, I was mistress of my own home at eighteen, and my brother had no dominion over me any longer. Many ladies were not so fortunate.

I insisted that the wedding be small.

"I should not like a fuss," I said.

"Certainly we shall not have a fuss," Mr Dryer agreed, and his hand reached out, hesitated, and then patted my own gloved hand.

I had been afraid that Perry would insist that I invite my aunt and cousins, but he did not so much as mention it. Although he consented to play the part of witness, he did it with such ill-humour one would never have imagined that he had ordered me to accept Mr Dryer's hand.

We were married at the church in Corston, Mr Dryer's village—our village, I must now call it. Only Mr Dryer, Perry, Mr Dryer's housekeeper, and I were present. Mr Dryer's parents had both passed on, and I did not wish anyone else there. I would not have had Perry present if I could have arranged it.

I wore Mama's pale grey silk and carried a nosegay of white peonies, tied around with a strip of blue muslin. I watched the flowers bob with the movement of the carriage and tried not to notice that the villagers came to their gates to see us pass by and whisper what a shame it was that we were wedding so quietly.

I felt so nervous as to be sick, and Mr Dryer did not look much better. He kept glancing at me with an anxious look upon his face; I believe he was afraid I would change my mind, or perhaps he was changing his own. In any case, neither of us spoke up to call it off, and the ceremony was as quick and as quiet as our journey to the church had been. The housekeeper, whose name was Mrs Bell, wept silently for the majority of the service. She was a big woman, but built on a grand scale rather than plump. She looked hard to the touch: raw-pink skin stretched tight over thick arms and a stubborn jaw. She had dressed herself in a plain black dress, more suited to a funeral than a wedding. No doubt she had no other respectable gown. She had been Mr Dryer's nurse as a boy, and he claimed to be fond of her, though he barely spoke to her at the ceremony. She held a lace-edged handkerchief to her eyes and her solid shoulders shook; I could not tell if she cried from joy or grief. We were the least merry wedding party that ever there was.

"Now we can find ourselves a drink," Perry said, the moment the ceremony was behind us.

"Yes! Let us do that. Perry, will you come back with us to The Ridings, or must we sit in some low tavern?" Mr Dryer—Granville, as I must now call him—clapped his hands. He looked if not happy, then at least relieved.

"I can wait out the journey," my brother said.

We were then getting into the carriage. Perry climbed in first, though I was the bride. Granville handed me inside and then climbed in himself. Mrs Bell made to come inside with us, but before she laid a hand on the door, Perry had leant forward and swung it closed. I did not know if he noticed her there or not. Her face was so startled as to be comic, but then she turned her head and our eyes met. She did not look like the kind of woman it would be wise to laugh at.

"Mrs Bell is still outside," I said. I hoped she could hear me, but the glass was up.

"This is a wedding carriage," Perry said. "Surely the servants ride in front."

Granville said nothing, only jiggled his foot where his legs crossed. Mrs Bell had the same idea as my brother and disappeared around the front of the carriage.

Granville had returned to glancing at me. I did not know where to look. *He is my husband,* I kept thinking. *My husband.* The thought did not feel like a real one. I watched his gloved hands where they rested on his cane. The fingers were very short for such a tall man. When he had taken his glove off to join hands with me during the wedding, I had noticed that his hands had hair upon the backs of them. *I wonder how much hair is on the rest of him,* I thought, and my stomach lurched with the queerness of it.

So I HAD MY FIRST SIGHT of my new home with my brother as well as my husband beside me. It was not far from Aubyn Hall—an hour's ride would see me returned to my brother's side, if ever I should wish such a thing. It was a rambling house that looked as though it had been added to and improved over the years by gentlemen with differing ideas about design; here was a gabled roof, here a set of Palladian windows, here a square turret. It was named The Ridings and was newly acquired, though some parts of it were a good hundred years old. It had lately been the home of some country squire or other, who had fallen on hard times and had been forced to sell it all.

"I got it for a handsome price," my new husband said, "the gentleman needing to make a fast sale. He sold me the entire estate, all that was left of it."

I cringed a little at his vulgarity.

What was left of the estate was not much, it transpired. The first I saw of my new home was the gatehouse, a pretty little cottage, like a manor in miniature. It was empty and in need of some repair. After that, though I would have expected that we enter the park, the road wound on and on past fields full of crops.

"The fellow sold all the gardens before he sold the house," Granville said.

"Dunderhead that he was," Perry said, "for he must have taken a loss on the estate. A manor house is not worth half so much without grounds, surely."

"I told you I got a pretty price for it," Granville said.

I only thought, *But we are left without gardens. Where will I walk?*

PERRY AND GRANVILLE disappeared together the moment we were arrived.

"Mrs Bell will show you about, my dear," Granville said, and added, as he left, "Order us a good dinner. We must have a wedding feast, even if we are only three at table."

"Good man," Perry said, and they left me standing in the dark hall, with the forbidding boulder of my new housekeeper.

I had not expected the house to be so dark and old-fashioned. I followed Mrs Bell's skirts about with a stone in my stomach. The bunch of keys at her waist chimed with each step. Mama had used to hold the keys to the household at Aubyn Hall. The housekeeper came to her each day to request use of them.

"Which rooms would you like to be shown to first, madam?"

I did not know if anyone would pay me wedding visits, but if they were to, where could I seat them, in a house like that? I was already imagining my aunt walking into the gloomy, wood-panelled hall. There was a stuffed fish mounted upon the wall, and beside it, a sword that looked as though it had been there since the house was built. She would pity me. Oh, dear Lord, she would come in and pity me.

"I should like to see my parlour, or whichever room I shall use for receiving company," I said.

"I've not yet had instructions from Mr Dryer as to that, but perhaps he'll say the drawing room."

Oh, but it was a gloomy chamber. The windows were good, large and clean, but the light served only to show the dark wainscoting and the heavy furniture. There was barely a soft spot in the whole of the room, and what there was, a pair of mahogany chairs done out in brocaded silk, was so lumbering and old-fashioned it was not to be borne. Dark oil paintings of bewigged and serious men looked down upon me. No lady would be pleased to visit me in such an apartment. My tea things would appear ridiculous and out of place, delicate as they were. I said as much to Mrs Bell.

"This furniture came along with the house when it was bought, madam. You may come to like it, in time."

"But Mr Dryer cannot mean to keep it so," I said. "I am sure we should have our own things. We should have a pretty place to sit, at the very least."

"I hope he may say you're right, madam." Mrs Bell looked at me with exactly the expression I was afraid of seeing on my aunt's face. Already I was pitied, by a servant.

I waited only until we met at table to raise the question of the decoration. I had forgotten, in my dismay over the house, that Granville had instructed me to order the dinner. It did not signify, for the food arrived regardless, chosen by the cook or by Mrs Bell. Granville made no mention of it, but only ate his jugged hare with a serious face. I could not tell if he approved or not. He must have thought I had chosen it—which I never would, I should have preferred a bird—but he did not compliment or insult my choice. Perry only cared for the wine. I watched my brother waving for his glass to be refilled and my hands itched to do the same. I forced myself to sip at my own glass slowly.

Mrs Bell waited upon us. She proffered the dish of jugged hare to Granville and watched him as though she were still his nursemaid. When he took only a small portion, she stayed beside him and shook the dish very slightly, as a prompt that he should take more. He obliged her.

"What do you think of your new home, Charlotte?" Perry said.

He asked only because he knew I would not like it. If it had been a pretty or elegant house, he would not have said a word.

"It is of good size," I said, "and the rooms are pleasantly proportioned. It will look very well, when once it is finished."

Granville wiped his fingers and folded his hands before him on the table.

"What about this house is unfinished?" he said. His tone was quietly injured.

"It is so old. I should like to decorate."

"You have your dressing room," he said. "You may do with it just as you like, as long as you are not too free with my fortune."

"I just hoped," I said, my mouth dry with dismay, "to have a pretty chamber in which to receive visitors."

"You may use any chamber you like, Miss—Charlotte." Granville laid down his fork. He looked somewhat sad. "I wish you to be happy. But you must know I am not inclined to live like a fine gentleman."

Perry was nodding approvingly. "You are become a merchant's wife. You will grow used to it, in time."

Granville looked at him sternly and then turned to me with a softer expression. "I do hope you will be happy here. I cannot imagine that your lady friends will find my drawing room so very distasteful."

"Charlotte has no lady friends," Perry said.

Mrs Bell's face was perfectly still. She stood just inside the door, her eyes upon her hands, folded neatly in front of her.

Granville smiled upon me. "It is very becoming to a lady to live quietly.

And I am sure any acquaintance you may make locally will have humble enough expectations."

This was his wedding speech to me.

MRS BELL INFORMED ME that my husband had employed a larger staff than he had ever had before, though it numbered only eight: one maid, one maid-of-all-work, one scullery maid, one footboy, an elderly manservant, the groom, the cook, and Mrs Bell herself.

I understood that my maid, Lucy, was a new addition for my particular comfort—Mrs Bell told me of the appointing of Lucy as though she suspected I would lead Granville into financial ruin by the hiring of a maid to help me with my dress. In fact, Lucy was not fit for more than sweeping grates and lighting candles—she was more chambermaid than hairdresser. It signified nothing; there was no one to see me. When, soon after my wedding, my aunt wrote to ask when a visit might be convenient, I replied saying only that, my health being weak, the doctor had advised that I keep from company for a time. She did not write again to persuade me.

AND SO I GREW USED to my married life and found it as dull as the expectations of a spinster. I spent a long while on the decorating of my dressing room: sewing curtains, covering a pretty pair of chairs that Perry allowed me to take from Aubyn Hall, and doing my best to create some not displeasing pictures made from shells. For the walls, Granville allowed me a paper in green and blue, and I had to be satisfied.

I found that my husband could not be riled in the same way that I had taunted Perry. Nothing seemed to disturb him but the wasting of money, and he would not give me a penny to waste, though he always spoke to me kindly. He seemed always anxious that I might be unhappy, but made no move toward increasing my happiness. Besides this, he seemed not to know what to do with me, once he had me. Whenever he was at home, he would send a servant to say, "Mr Dryer hopes that you will condescend to join him in the drawing room," but when I went to him we would make conversation as stiff as strangers, or else be silent. When he came to bed at night it was hard to say which of us felt the queerer. Always, as he took his marital right, he would whisper, "Are you quite comfortable?" as a means of asking permission. I never demurred, though I was not comfortable in the least, and I suspected that he was no better. After he had done and moved away from me, I would lie, feeling his presence as clearly as if we were still touching. I might lie awake all night, until my body ached with stillness and my mind ached also, my thoughts swelling in the darkness, pushing at the edges of my skull. Sometimes he would surprise me by slipping from the bed and creeping from the room, taking great care to be silent. I would realise then that my husband had been as sleepless as I.

He asked me often, in the first months of our marriage, if I should like to go anywhere for diversion. He offered to take me for drives, or perhaps a picnic. I declined every invitation. I might have liked to be taken to a play, or to see the Assembly Rooms at Bath, but Granville did not offer that, and I did not ask. I felt as dull and bruised as I had when first I lost Mama and Papa. I kept to my dressing room and sewed.

Granville liked me to be with him at dinner, so I was many times in company with Mr Bowden, across Perry's dining table or our own. I was careful to address Mr Bowden as though he had never kissed me beside the stream. I tried not to look at him overlong; his beauty had come to seem vexing.

Our union was not blessed with child, or else none that I could safely deliver. Granville took the news of these losses quietly and afterward would avoid me for a day or two. I came to understand that my husband was not comfortable with the expression of feeling. He need not have worried, for I did not allow myself to weep over it. I worked upon my embroidery. I drank as much wine as I thought I could without being the subject of servants' talk. I walked up and down the drive, sometimes with Granville quiet beside me. I went with him to church.

If I thought I was safely alone for the evening, I would order brandy to be brought, though I never could ask for as much of it as I should have liked. Sometimes, once I had the taste for it, I would pace about in quivering frustration. I could not bear to be always alert and feeling. I envied my brother his freedom to make himself gross. I envied him, and I feared it on my own account, for no one sensible would truly wish to be like Perry. Sometimes, even after scolding myself, I would give in and call for more. I kept waiting for Granville to query the wine bill, but he never spoke a word to me. I supposed that Perry was so often at our table that a little more could make no difference.

I did not any longer scratch at myself. I spent many hours painting Pear's Almond Bloom onto my cheeks, my neck, my breast, even when only the servants were there to see me. Granville never quarrelled with this expense either; it was my one true extravagance.

There was nowhere much to walk. Although we had the furniture and stuffed fish of the previous occupant, we had not his land. All the house could call its own was a kitchen garden, a paddock and stable, and the long driveway leading down to the gatekeeper's gatehouse. I often walked down the driveway to the vacant gatehouse, where I peeped through the dusty glass and imagined the rooms filled with firelight and life. It had six windows and, I thought, looking in as best I could, two rooms downstairs.

Granville spoke once of having the gatehouse made habitable and of buying back the fields, to make them gardens once again. He never did, and never again mentioned the subject, though I often hoped he would. It was a mark of how apathetic I had grown that I never once brought the subject up.

In September of 1799, two years after we were married, I finally asked for something once more; I begged Granville to take me to the fair at Bristol.

Chapter 10

❖ ❖ ❖

The day had begun strangely; the weather was close and uncomfortable. Once again I believed myself in a delicate condition, though I had told no one, not even Granville. If I were to lose this child as I had the others, I thought I should bear it better if I bore it alone.

I hated to be so warm. The long sleeves that I would not put aside held my arms in a sweltering grip; the paint applied to my brow instantly became paste and every escaped hair from my cap stuck in it like flies.

I came downstairs and found my husband and brother already seated at the breakfast table. I was too leaden with the closeness of the day to feel surprise. Only the immense amount of food laid out made my head swim.

I had grown used, in those days, to taking my breakfast alone. Granville rose before dawn and was gone before I woke. I did not know what arrangements he made to break his fast, or whether he took anything at all. For myself, I was in the habit of ordering only a warm roll or muffin and a cup of chocolate. The breakfast room faced the little bit of lawn we had left and was not so dreary as most of the house.

My husband and brother stopped speaking as I entered, turned to face me, inclined their heads in greeting, and turned back to begin again where they had left off. Neither spoke to me, nor offered an explanation for their presence.

Perry was drinking ale, having no care for the gentleman's fashion for coffee. He was eating potted beef, and before he had done with it was already reaching out for the plate of tongue. Between mouthfuls he took up a crumpled handkerchief from beside his plate and mopped his brow. His hair looked even fairer than usual, atop his flushed face.

Granville's own face was quite composed, not a drop of moisture upon it. His hair was as neat as ever it was, though he had recently left off from hair powder. He still wore his hair curled above the ears and secured at the nape of his neck with a velvet bow. Papa had worn his hair in the same style. Granville was eating kippers, pulling them apart methodically and looking gravely at them as he did so, as though performing an anatomical experiment.

Mrs Bell poured me a cup of chocolate, which that morning was made too bitter. I did not ask for sugar.

The gentlemen were talking of boxing, as was their wont. I understood almost nothing of it and often found that those pieces of conversation I did follow, I wished I had not. That morning I attended only when Perry, whose habit was to address a person seated next to him as though they were on the other side of a large room, called across to Granville,

"We must leave in plenty of time, you know. We shall have a deuce of a time getting to the fairground. Half the county turns out for it. There will be coaches at a standstill half the way to Bristol."

My heart had risen into my throat and I did not hear Granville's reply. It was September already, then. Perhaps, that day, in Bristol, two little girls would hold hands and beg their nurse to take them to see the conjurer.

I must have made a sound without my meaning to, for suddenly both Granville and Perry turned to look at me.

"What is it, Charlotte?" Perry said.

"I should like to go to the fair," I said, and although I had not meant to say it, I knew that it was true.

"Piffle," Perry said. "It is too rough for you. We are going there to see the pugilists. You would be scandalised."

This only made me the more determined.

Granville laid down his knife neatly and waved him quiet. Perry looked affronted.

"Why do you want to go, Lottie? I cannot recall the last time you asked to be taken anywhere," Granville said.

"I cannot say why, but I wish it very much. I used to go as a child. I should like to go."

Granville was silent for a moment, looking at me gravely, as though we discussed a terribly serious matter. At last he nodded.

"If you wish it, I will take you."

"Thank you," I said, very low.

I glanced sideways at Perry to see how he would respond.

"By God, Granville, what the deuce are you thinking of?" he said.

I was very careful not to smile.

My husband ignored him and turned to me. "Go quickly, then, and change your gown."

If I had been given more time to think and grow anxious, if I had not been so set on vexing my brother, perhaps I would have changed my mind. Besides church, occasional dinners at Aubyn Hall, and walking about the fields and lanes of the neighbourhood, I had not been anywhere for almost two years.

My dressing room was waiting for me, with my tambour hoop pulled out in readiness for a morning's needlework. I was partway through a cushion-cover, upon which I was stitching a maid riding upon a donkey. I had meant that day to fill in the shades of her gown in blue, and the gold of her straw bonnet. I had taken out the correct silks; they lay neatly beside the hoop. The novel I was reading, *Paul and Virginia*, lay upon the writing desk, marked where I had left it with a piece of ribbon. Here was the shape of my day as I had expected to spend it, dull but comfortable, and now I was to abandon it and go out into the world.

I had Lucy fetch out my promenade gown of grey twill and my black half-boots. As I ordered this, I could hear Mama's voice in my ear, chiding me for making myself so dull.

When Lucy had done, I bid her send Mrs Bell to me to dress my hair. Her face brightened, and her mouth opened a little when I said this—I called for Mrs Bell to dress my hair only on Sundays, for church—but her curiosity came too late and she was obliged to curtsey and go out.

Mrs Bell, having served at table, knew perfectly well where I was to go. Her face was harried; she thought herself above hairdressing.

I had my hair dressed in an Indian knot—Mrs Bell's swollen fingers could not manage more complicated hairdressing—and my face framed with hot-tong curls. When once her fingers came close to my mouth to catch up a stray lock, I saw it in the glass and their proximity to my lip rose up a sudden urge to bite her. I did not, of course. I let her draw her sausage fingers away to safety and pinched myself upon the leg instead.

While Mrs Bell pinned and tonged, I worked at the paint upon my face. I did this partly because the movement of my head as I did so caused her to sigh and tut. There was not much use in it; I could do nothing to make my face any more pleasing to look at. I could only try to fix the paint against the heat with rice powder. When once I had done, I was careful not to look at my face again. The paint acted as a shield; when once it was applied, I might never have had a face at all.

Mrs Bell seemed to scrutinise me, which I disliked intensely. Then she said,

"You look very respectable, madam," and dropped one of her bobbing half-curtseys.

"You may go, Mrs Bell."

I took care not to let my feelings cross my face. She called me respectable because no one could truthfully call me handsome; she offered this opinion unsolicited on purpose to vex me. She knew very well that I hated to have my appearance remarked upon. I should indeed have bitten her.

Granville and Perry were waiting in the yard. I could hear the chink-chink of the horses moving in the traces and voices—Perry's loud and impatient, Granville's calm and somehow toneless—drifting through the side-door, which was left open. I had Henry, the footboy, put iron pattens over my boots against the mud. I had not worn pattens for a long while, and it felt strange to be raised off the ground so. If the weather was inclement, I usually chose to stay indoors. I stood wobbling while Henry secured the straps about my half-boots. I kept one hand upon the wall for balance and stared at the tiled floor, worn grey stone, a smearing of dirt about the door, where booted feet had come in and out.

Beside the door, the barometer's needle hovered between *variable* and *rain*. I ordered that Henry fetch me a cloak. It was foolishness to be stepping out so, into uncertain weather.

At last I stepped outside, a little unsteady on the hoops of the pattens, and clinked my way across the cobbles. Perry and Granville were standing beside the carriage, Perry in a coat of deepest blue, which, to give him his due, suited him perfectly. Granville was quite the match of me for dullness, with his coat and breeches of brown upon brown. He turned and smiled at me as I came into the yard, and it was this, more than anything, that broke the seal around my feelings. My husband smiled upon me so infrequently, I began to be nervous.

"Come, Lottie," he called to me, as if I were a skittish dog, and I tottered toward him as though I were one. I took his arm as being something solid to cling to. He patted my gloved hand, and the smile grew tired and fell from his face.

"Henry, step up on the box. You are to accompany us; we may need you," Granville said.

Henry looked surprised, but only bowed and stepped up to sit beside Stephens, at the reins.

My husband turned to me. "We are ready to set off; we wait only for Mr Bowden. Should you like to sit in the carriage? He will not be long, but I should not like you to grow weary before we are begun."

I nodded and allowed him to hand me inside, but as soon as I was settled on the brocade seats I wished myself out of them. I was too confined within the carriage, with Granville and Perry standing so before the open door and the air so close about my face. I had not realised that we would be in the company of Mr Bowden. The day seemed heavier than ever.

Mr Bowden rode into the yard, his horse a-sweat from the cruel pace, and the dust, meeting the moist air, puffing halfheartedly about its hooves. I saw this through the glass, over the backs and the quiet heads of our own horses harnessed to the traces. I saw Mr Bowden dismount and Henry jump down to take his exhausted horse.

The gentlemen, who had moved forward to halloo and bow at Mr Bowden, now returned to the open carriage door. Mr Bowden, seeing me, stopped and offered me a full view of his good teeth.

"Mrs Dryer," he said, and stepped up inside, bending almost double so that he could remain standing as he took my hands in his own. The enclosed space meant that he leant over me and brought his face close to mine.

"What an unexpected pleasure," he said. "The fair will be the gayer for your company."

"How do you do, Mr Bowden," I said, and then, because he seemed to be waiting for more, "I do hope the rain will hold off."

Mr Bowden held my hands still. One of his fingers twitched against my gloved palm; I could not tell if he were trying to stroke it or if he twitched in revulsion at feeling the ridges of scars there. My husband and brother climbed into the carriage behind him.

"The rain may do as it pleases," he said. "I am determined to be happy today."

"I'm so glad," I said. I could not think what other reply to make.

BRISTOL WAS NOT MORE THAN seven miles from The Ridings, but the journey seemed the longer, for my having kept so close to the house for so long. I looked out of the carriage window and remembered what it was, to look upon sights I had not seen a hundred times. Even the ordinary fields and farms seemed fascinating, and were gone too quick from view.

We could smell the city before we reached it. The city of Bristol has a particular scent—a stink, I suppose you could call it—of the docks and the slow brown river. It travelled right through me, to the back of my throat, so that I felt I could taste the very cobbles, the congested water of the industrial quays. It was not a pretty smell, but it was the smell of my childhood. Queen Square was very grand and clean, with a tree-lined park in its centre, but it had the quays at its back. Though one could take a turn about the lawns with a parasol and talk to pleasant ladies in pretty hats, the scent of the river was everywhere. Now it seemed the essence of home, though Mama would have been appalled to hear me say that. She spent her life bringing in flowers and burning scented oils to rid the house of the creeping odour of the river Avon.

I had forgotten what a crowd the fair drew. The city seemed filled with it, the streets thronged with holiday-makers and a great many grand carriages. We drove along Thomas Street and across the bridge, the quayside dense with the masts of ships and all made gay with bunting and flags.

Every type of person had turned out, gentry, soldiers, and paupers alike. I had forgotten, too, how many black faces were to be found at the quay; I had been so much shut up in the country I had begun to forget that there were any faces other than white and people other than country gentlemen, servants, and farmers. I could not stop looking at all the people; they seemed both terrible and wonderful, like an animal show at which the fences were too thin.

As soon as we stepped down from the carriage, the heavy air turned into mizzle. Immediately I feared for the paint upon my face; why had I not thought to wear a veil? I put up the hood of my cloak, but this was little help, unless I kept my head bowed.

Granville bid Stephens wait for us. Henry, he had step down and follow us. Henry jigged up and down in excitement; he was still only a boy, not much older than fourteen. Stephens, seated upon the box, looked hard at him and he brought himself under control, though his rain-speckled face was flushed.

"Remember you're in livery," I heard Stephens tell him quietly. "Conduct yourself properly."

Perry and Mr Bowden walked ahead, and Granville and I followed. Henry trailed in the rear, no doubt looking about him wildly now that the groom's eyes were not upon him.

The fairground was more closely packed than the roads, and built like a village of wooden booths and huts. I held on to Granville's arm and let him guide me, watching my feet in their pattens, my skirt swinging with my steps. Shoulders I did not know touched mine as people went by us. One woman passed before me so close that her unwashed hair brushed my mouth and I could not move back, so close was I to my husband on my other side. I could hear music playing in three or four places at once and smell roasting meat. When I did look up, bunching the hood around my face with my free hand, all I could see was the crowd, and above them, the peaked roofs of the huts and the bunting against the darkening sky.

It was a little like walking through a forest. Here and there the crowd thinned and I saw some piece of the fair—a woman holding a goose aloft to have its fat stomach poked by a thoughtful cook, the painted front of a gypsy caravan—and then the crowd closed up once more and we were lost in the limbs and faces and tall, damp hats. I did not remember the fair like this; in my memory, it was bright and joyous.

"Well, Lottie," Granville said, "what is it you wish to see? The learned pig, perhaps? Or would you like to see the wild beasts?"

"The flying coaches," Mr Bowden said. "I am sure Mrs Dryer would enjoy being whirled through the air by the hand of a couple of ragamuffin boys."

Perry thought this the most amusing comment of the day.

I did not reply. I thought perhaps I should like to see a learned pig. I was on the verge of asking to be taken there when Granville spoke.

"Well, my dear, Henry shall take you to see any sight you wish. Make me a pretty good-bye, now."

"May I not stay with you?"

I had not expected that Granville would leave me. I did not like to be left in a crowd of strangers, with only a boy for chaperone. Henry was looking about himself eagerly, standing on his toes to peer over the heads of the crowds about us, his mouth slightly open. His damp hair fell into his eyes and he shook his head like a bull. He had forgotten he was in livery, after all; I could not trust him to be sensible.

"We are going to the boxing booth, Lottie, it will be rough indeed." Granville spoke quite as soft as I, though the tone of his voice was not.

"I shall not mind it," I said.

"You must go with Henry; I cannot take you to the boxing booth."

I felt my breathing grow ragged and my hands and face begin to tingle.

"Please," I whispered, "I cannot be left here."

I no longer wished to see the learned pig. I wished I was at home.

"Well, Charlotte," Granville said, "you have chosen to be carried home again. Henry will take you to the carriage. Stephens can come back for us."

"Please," I said again, "I thought I might stay with you." My face was quite abuzz now with tingling. My cheeks were filled with bees. My breast ached, and I was sure my spark of a child woke up and swam about, sickening me. I could hear my own breath.

"Charlotte"—Granville spoke slowly—"I brought Henry to accompany you. He will take you to see any sight you wish, but you cannot come with me. It is too rough, you would be shocked indeed."

"You must not leave me," I said. "Indeed, you must not. I will be ill if you do. I will not let you leave me." I would not let go his arm.

Granville was silent for a moment. Perry and Mr Bowden had gone ahead and now came back to seek us out.

"What's the delay, Dryer?" my brother called.

Granville sighed. "This is a madness," he said. "If you find it distressing, you must have Henry take you back to the coach. I warn you, Charlotte, I will not have a scene. You must remain composed or I shall be very displeased."

"I will not displease you," I said. "I give you my word."

"I do not want your word, Lottie, I want proof. Let your actions speak"—Granville began to lead me off—"and for goodness sake, loose your hold on my arm. I have said I shall not shake you off. You need not grip me so."

The interior of the boxing tent was thick with people. Granville kept a tight hold of me, and together we followed my brother and Mr Bowden as they pushed us a path through the crowd. At length I was able to see the stage, on which there was a square of ropes, strung upon poles. We had not long to wait before two figures ascended there and faced each other with fists raised. This I had expected; that one of them might be a lady boxer, I had never in my life imagined. She made an indecent figure; her flannel petticoats had been pinned up, and above her boots she was wholly naked to the knee. Her stays had been loosed. I could not stop staring at her. Her assailant was a great brute of a man; surely, surely, they could not really be meant to fight?

I turned to ask Granville if there were not some mistake, but he was conferring urgently with Mr Bowden.

"I shall see the day saved," Mr Bowden said, and left us, working his way through the press of bodies. I watched him go; I thought perhaps he meant to talk to someone about the cruelty of setting a girl against such a brute, but he went, instead, to the side of a cheap-looking woman in a gown of the brightest pink. She seemed to know him; she touched his arm and tapped him with her fan. She smiled at him so flirtatiously that I looked away, embarrassed.

No one came to the girl's rescue. The fight began, though I could scarce believe it even as I watched.

The ogre bore down upon her with his fists. I gasped as she ducked away, narrowly avoiding the blow, my own head jerking in sympathy with hers. She was a stout enough girl, but the man assaulting her was built uncommonly large. With her jerky, frightened neck, she looked enough like a goose that I found my mouth twitched as though I wished to laugh.

She hit out at him, once, twice, again, again. I held my breath. When at last he hit her in earnest my heart beat so hard it seemed as though I felt the blow.

She fell back, as anyone would, and when she stood I saw that her lip having swollen and split, the white handkerchief around her neck had been spoiled by fat drops of claret red.

An old lady with a dirty apron came to lead her away. I put my hands to my eyes in a kind of relief. I had not thought it would be over so soon.

When I looked up once more, I saw that she had been led not away but back to face him. She stood with her head high and her eye fixed upon his, like the engraving of Joan of Arc in Papa's book. Her own fist looked to be bleeding beneath the strange, bulky gloves she wore upon her hands; thick trickles ran from beneath the padding to streak her arm. As they began again and she hit out against him, blood sprayed across his cheek. Where her hand met his face, an imprint of her glove remained, set in scarlet.

Again she hit out—so fast!—and once more her padded hand left its red seal on his huge cheek. The ogre seemed scarcely to feel it, her size being so incomparable to his own. She seemed to be dancing, toward him, away. He turned as clumsy as a drunken bear, his great head swinging to follow her.

She was a scandal. I thought, *She is barely a woman at all.*

Her face was fierce with concentration. She looked not at all ashamed to have so many sets of eyes upon her. She paid no attention to the blood, though she was so spattered and streaked that I could not have said from when it all sprang. She seemed hardly to notice the crowd at all, though they shrieked and bellowed unbearably.

My husband had forgotten me; all of the men were captivated by the action on the stage. My husband seemed to have a great many things to say to my brother, though I could not hear what he said. The noise of the crowd was very great.

I was jostled from all sides and most especially from behind, as the greedy congregation pushed ever closer to the ring. The gentleman beside me, a stranger, was forced to be always knocking his elbow against my arm. He apologised so many times that I almost ceased to hear him. He could not help it; he was jostled in his turn. Packed so close as we were, a foul mist steamed from a hundred coats and cloaks. I put my hands upon my stomach to protect my child.

In the ring the combatants began to circle each other. Sweat ran into the girl's eyes, and she wiped the back of her glove across them, leaving a crimson streak. If she slowed her dancing, she would have not the smallest chance against him.

Granville seemed not at all disturbed. My husband came so often to the boxing that perhaps the fate of one small girl held little interest. He barely noticed my own discomfort until I was quite pushed against him. Then he was forced to pay attention and drew me in between himself and Perry, to shield me as best they could from the crowd. He pulled at my arm to bid me move. I did not know where he was taking me; I did not know that I wanted to leave sight of the girl. I kept tight hold of my skirts and turned my head to see the stage. The moment I was safely between them I turned my full attention back to the dreadful scene before us.

Above my head, my brother said, "Fifty guineas I have laid on this one, Dryer!"

My husband replied. I was not sure, for he spoke more softly than Perry, but I thought he said, "The end is certain."

I thought he meant by this that the giant would kill her; I began to believe that he would.

Perry was shouting at the fighters, adding his own calls to those of the rough crowd. I was thankful that Granville did not call out, though he had a feverish pleasure in his eye that I was unused to seeing.

The girl's right hand was surely lamed as well as bloody; she held it strangely and seemed to be favouring the left. Her blows were meeting their mark but looked to be so little felt that the force driving them could not have amounted to much. The hulk in the ring accepted her strikes upon him as though they were kisses. At last he hit her so suddenly, so brutally, that I heard myself scream aloud. My heart knocked in my breast like a bird flying into a window.

She fell. Her arms jerked as her knees buckled, and then she was gone from view, collapsed behind the crowd. I found I was breathing rather too quickly. My face was tingling once more. Granville turned to look at me, and I summoned a kind of smile for him. It did not feel true upon my lips, but it satisfied him enough that he turned his attention back toward the stage.

At last I saw her stand, leaning on the arm of the old woman. I couldn't imagine how she managed it. The old woman led her not out of the ring but into the corner, where a man waited on one knee. The girl sat upon his other knee as a kind of stool and drank from a bottle the old woman offered her. She allowed the old woman to wipe the blood from her face. Her shoulders slumped. On the other side of the ring the brutish fellow balanced upon the knee of one of his fellows. He looked ridiculous there, like a giant child upon his papa's lap.

Soon enough, a ridiculous man in an ill-fitting wig entered the ring to call out, "Time!"

The old woman took the girl's arm, and she rose and allowed herself to be led back toward the waiting brute.

I did not scream, only closed my eyes. In that moment, all the thrill was gone; I was near to begging Granville to take me from that place. My tongue was kept still only by the knowledge that it was not to be Granville but Henry who would lead me out. Henry was near enough a child; he could not keep me steady. I held my husband's arm like a blind woman. Granville did not appear to notice my distress. Perhaps he took my silence for enjoyment.

I could not understand why the old woman kept leading her back to be beaten. I could not imagine what had driven her to stand up there, to show her legs and to be made foul with blood. I could not fathom it. I thought perhaps I could not stand it.

I opened my eyes in time to see the beast on the stage swing his gloved hand, a monstrous thing like a boiled ham, and seem about to strike her once more. She danced back, and he followed her. Her hands moved in the air too fast to see; one moment she had swung out her lamed right hand and struck at his arm, the next she had given him such a blow that his face was driven to the side, his ruddy cheeks wobbling with the force of it. A startled breath was forced out of him, his lips seeming to fly forward from the bones of his face.

The crowd roared, I screamed, and on the stage the lady boxer shouted with us. Before her opponent could regain his senses, she had struck him upon the other cheek, sending his head to the other side. This time a tooth soared out of his mouth, trailing an arc of blood and spittle. I did not see it land.

I could not tell anymore how much of the screaming came from my own mouth. I was borne up on the swell of it, I was the sound. We were all howling together, the poor and the quality, the boxing girl and the beast inside my breast. If she was a madwoman, then we were all of us with her, and I had never felt such savage elation, nor known that it existed.

I was dancing with excitement; I could not help myself. The floor of the tent was even fouler than the fairground proper. I moved my feet just a little, but being in pattens and the mud being what it was, I stumbled. Granville was obliged to steady me. As I raised my head, the brute recovered enough to raise his hand once more, and this time sent it crashing into the side of that young girl's head.

"Oh!" I cried. "Oh, she will be killed!"

Mr Bowden laughed and said, "I believe she will!" as though this were an act in a play.

The girl had fallen, I was sure of it. I could not see her. The vast back of her persecutor obscured my view. I fancied he was leaning over her.

I buried my face in my husband's shoulder, careless of the paint from my brow marking his coat. I felt sick at it all; I did not want to see.

"Steady," Granville muttered. "See it through, steady now."

The crowd screamed. Something had happened, but what?

"He has her now!" someone shouted. I could not see. I could not raise my head.

The crowd was louder than ever, a rabid yammering. I felt I might at any moment begin to howl again myself; my throat felt thick with cries unleashed. I did not know what kind of cries they were; indeed I believed I might begin to laugh. He had her now. Had I been asked, I could not have said whether I wished to see her saved or slain. *She will be killed,* I thought, *she will be killed.* The idea tormented and thrilled me in equal measure. I kept my eyes shut against Granville's shoulder. I had seen hangings that had affected me less.

"God be damned!" Granville shouted. He thrust me away. I staggered a little on my pattens and clutched at his arm. He let me hold it, but I had never seen my husband's face so enraged. He was not angry with me; his eyes were fixed upon the ring.

I turned my head to see the girl in the arms of the old woman, who seemed bowed under her weight. The man who had so gallantly given her his knee held her hand. Her head hung on her neck, now flopped forward, now rolling back as the old woman tried to rouse her. I thought perhaps she was dead after all.

The crowd about us was thinning a little. I had ceased to notice how close we were until they began to move away. Now I felt how stifling was the air in that place.

The man by the side of the girl placed her hand carefully back in her lap. It lay there as though the padded glove were empty. He said something to the old woman, and she replied, nodding. Then he rose and strode toward the old man in the ill-fitting wig, standing by the ropes. The younger man's face was quite frightening to see.

The ogre, perhaps murderer, was on the other side of the ring, shaking the hands that were held up to him from the crowd, though what there was to admire in a great beast beating a young girl, I could not have said. He seemed pleased enough with his work and shook their hands.

At last the old woman roused the girl enough to help her to a stand. She was unsteady upon her feet but was alive, at least. She took the old woman's arm and allowed herself to be helped away a few paces, but then, against all sense, shook the old woman's hand from her and staggered back toward the centre of the ring, fists raised.

The ogre, seeing this, left off his handshaking and moved toward her.

"What's this?" cried Perry. "Will you go another round?"

"Narrow will suffer for this," Granville said. I did not know what he meant.

The girl stood, swaying at the line. Her hands were bare and held before her chest. Blood ran steadily from her elbow in such a constant trickle that it formed a string like a piece of crimson wool. The ogre progressed toward her, and to my dismay, I saw him raise his own hands.

"For shame," someone cried.

The next moment the man who had given the poor girl his knee had moved across the stage with a speed one would not usually credit to such a big fellow. He took us all by surprise, including the murderous brute, now knocked upon his seat so smartly that the crowd was silent for a moment. The heavy sound as he hit the boards boomed out through the tent. I seemed to feel it. Blood began immediately to gush from his nose, and with it the sound returned, as the remaining crowd shrieked and called and cheered. The surprise of it made me scream, not in exhilaration this time, but shock. It was terrible that it should happen so, outside of the rules in this way. It seemed real. The murderer—I could not help but think of him as such, although he had not killed her—got to his feet and the two men began to grapple in a manner that was more fearful than if they had come to blows.

Every man present seemed to run toward the stage. Granville's hand closed upon my elbow and we joined the rush, he holding me up so that I should not fall. I stumbled with every step. If I had not been moving forward, I should have fallen.

Upon the stage, a great many men had jumped over the ropes and now pulled the two men apart. The murderer's face was purple. Blood trickled from his mouth and nose. I was savagely glad to see it.

Granville kept pulling me forward. He was relentless, not at all the polite gentleman I was used to. He pushed men aside with his shoulder, only calling out, "Excuse me," when once we had passed.

At last we reached the stage, where Perry and Mr Bowden stood. Granville pushed me toward them, said, "Bowden, take care of my wife," and climbed up onto the stage.

"Gladly," Mr Bowden said. "Would that more such tasks were given me."

He took my hand and pulled it into the crook of his arm. He drew me close, so that I was between himself and Perry, and put his hand on top of mine to keep it there. We were pressed so tight by the crowd that I could feel the heat of him all down my left side. Perry glanced once at me and then turned back to the stage. Henry appeared beside us, his eyes wide.

I did not protest. I allowed Mr Bowden to keep me there, and I watched as my staid husband's breeches scrambled under the ropes like a boy's. Granville stood and brushed himself off, then walked purposefully toward the gallant young man and began to talk into his ear. The young man breathed heavily and seemed to be arguing with my husband. Soon enough, he shook Granville's hand from his shoulder and strode away to where the old woman, I now saw, stood with the dazed girl leaning heavily upon her. He gathered the bruised and shaken girl into his arms as gentle as any nurse would cradle her babe and was gone, only shooting one black glance at the purple-faced murderer. Granville stood somewhat awkwardly and watched him leave. The rageful expression had left him, and he looked only sober and dishevelled. Even as I watched, he came back to himself and began dusting off his coat.

My heart was pounding. I put my free hand to my face and my glove came away white with paint and powder, but I could do nothing to help it.

My face was level with the feet of men upon the stage. I could see blood, soaking its way into the sawdust. I wondered where the tooth had fallen.

The murderer was being led away by many pairs of hands, clapping him on the back and calling out rough things I did not understand.

Mr Bowden's friend, the plump lady in the gown of violently pink silk, now climbed into the ring. Her bosom was about to fall from her bodice. She put her hand on my husband's arm and said something I could not hear, but he shook her from him and came back to the ropes beside us. She tossed her head and glared at his back.

Granville looked upon us for a moment and then climbed down to us.

"Ah, well, Webber's manners are coarse," he said to Perry, "but I can excuse him."

"What, are you so inconstant?" Mr Bowden said. He still held my hand in his arm. "Is your head turned by one well-placed fib?"

"After all this time, I do believe he is the man I have been looking for," Granville said, "and consider: his wife being beaten before a crowd, we should make allowance for a little discourtesy."

"Discourtesy cannot explain his choice"—Perry began to laugh— "imagine being her husband. She is more ruffian than half the fellows in the city. Imagine waking to that bruised countenance!"

Granville did not laugh.

I wished very much then to interrupt the gentlemen, but they gave me no opportunity. All the time they talked, I thought, *That lady boxer is the gallant man's wife.* And, of course, for what man would a lady boxer marry but another boxer? But still, it seemed very strange. I somehow would not have expected her to marry at all. I imagined them together, how rough and queer would be their home.

Granville turned to me. His eyes moved over my face, and I immediately felt how damp were my cheeks.

"I am going to speak with some rude characters now. You must go with Henry, Lottie. It is your choice entire whether you wish to see the sights of the fair. If you would rather go home, Henry will take you to the coach. Stephens can return for us."

I dropped my eyes. I knew I must look a scarecrow indeed. I pulled my hand from the crook of Mr Bowden's arm. He tried for a moment to keep hold of it, but I would not have it, even if my glove were pulled off. I was miserable indeed. What man would want a wife with paint running from her ruined face to follow him about, as introductions were made? I said I should go home, and knew, by the way that Granville agreed so thankfully, that I should not have come at all. It was all I could do to make a polite response to the gentlemen's bows.

I allowed Henry to lead me back through the crowd, out into the mizzle. The air was cooler and the sky a blank grey. The crowds were thick as ever. I found I could keep myself steady by watching my half-boots in their pattens and Henry's boots beside them. At last we reached the waiting carriage and I allowed Henry to hand me back inside.

"Are you sorry you ain't seen more of the fair, madam?" he asked me. "The weather's been sorely against us."

I shook my head and closed the carriage door. He meant he wished he had seen more of the fair himself, as any boy of his age would. I could not remember now what it was I had wanted to see. What was there to compare to the near-death of a girl on a stage?

All the journey homeward, I felt strange, bubbling with something that was not quite fear, nor yet excitement. I kept feeling that she must soon enough die and then deciding that no, it was impossible. But how many blows can one female skull absorb? I determined that when Granville came home I would be bold enough to ask if he knew how the lady boxer fared. How came it that my husband should be acquainted with such a man as a boxer, even a gallant one? The air grew cold, quite uncomfortably so. I did not close the window, but only sat, feeling my cheeks grow numb and the rain collecting in my hair. I knew what a mess I was making of myself.

I had confirmation, by the expression of Mrs Bell when she helped me off with my cloak, that I looked quite as dishevelled as I imagined. I was struggling to keep from weeping by then; my belly felt restless and unhappy. I was sure that my baby was weeping inside me. I had a sharp and gnawing pain. I begged to be led to a sofa, and there I collapsed for a good while. It was only after Mrs Bell had chided me into drinking a bowl of broth that my stomach calmed and I realised that the baby and I were both ravenously hungry.

When once I got upstairs to the looking-glass, I saw it all. The white paint had indeed run and collected in the pits of my scars. It had dripped down my neck and spoiled the collar of my grey gown. The heat of the room after the chill air brought a flush to my face and made the queer texture of my skin plainer than ever. I washed myself clean without looking at myself again.

My embroidery and my novel were still just as I had left them, and this seemed surprising, as though they should have been changed by the sights I had seen. I did not pick them up but went to the window-seat and sought peace there, just as I had at a different window, in the winter of my mourning. I did not feel as I had then, numb and still; now I seemed churning with every conceivable emotion. So tangled were my thoughts and feelings that I could not discern where each began, like a badly kept basket of embroidery silks. The very neatness of my own silks laid out beside my chair seemed unbearable. I stood up and pushed them together into a pile, as I had been taught I must not, blue blending with gold.

I took my dinner on a tray that night and did not, after all, come down when I heard the gentlemen return. My brother's voice came through the floorboards quite as clearly as if I had never left home. There was a city full of people not so very far away, all of them living different lives, and all of them as real as I. I had never before understood how many different paths there were to take in this life. It was as if at that moment I looked up and realised that for years I had had my eyes on my lap.

I was not entirely comfortable with this new view of things. Have you ever half frozen your feet and then held them before a fire, to watch the blue skin blush and grow pink? The flesh screams as it wakes; it is painful to go so quick from death to life.

I sat before my tambour hoop, but I did not sew. I only sipped at a glass of wine. I thought of crowds and mud, maidens and monsters. I thought of split lips, flying teeth, and red blood on white linen.

PART 4

George

* * *

Chapter 11

* * *

After Miss Sinclair accepted Granville's stiffly gloved hand in marriage, I avoided Aubyn Hall and fell into a low mood. I could not be sure that Perry would welcome me back, even with the sacrifice I had made. He had accepted my proposal that I absent myself while the wedding preparations went on with a vehemence painful to hear. I had lost Miss Sinclair entirely, her company at breakfast and her readiness to hear any little thing it might please me to say. I had ensured that visits to Granville's house—one of the few places I felt at home—would now become far less comfortable. I took myself to Bristol and found cheap and dreary lodgings above a print shop, where I could be as miserable as I chose. I avoided Granville's haunts, The Hatchet and The Assize Court Inn, but still I came everywhere upon his acquaintance and was obliged to give out the happy news of my friend's impending union to a lady of good family.

If I shunned Granville's preferred retreats, I turned ever more often to my own, and spent most evenings in the gaming houses. The hells of Bristol were not as grand as those of Bath, but my depressed spirits found succour in the vulgar, shabby atmosphere of those Thomas Street back parlours. As if God favoured a sinner, I found myself winning more often than I had been used to doing. In those places of questionable reputation, it was not wise to win too heavily, lest one become a target for enterprising rogues. It was this fear that stayed my hand where common sense never could, and drove me up from the tables before I sent my finances too dramatically in either direction. One night, with my purse moderately full, it dawned on me that I had before me an opportunity long wished for and the funds available to procure it; I took myself to visit Granville's sweet, kept creature. Here was one of my friend's pleasures I did not recoil from. I knew well enough that he covered all of her expenses and did so in the expectation that she should be his alone. I knew that he would be incensed to think of me wending my way there, with traitorous intentions. But Granville now had Charlotte—whom I must learn to call "Mrs Dryer." I did not feel more than the faintest stirrings of guilt. I bought a jug of wine to take to her, in case it should make me more welcome.

I had been to that house often enough over the years that the cove on the door knew me, and only dealt me the laziest glare as I went by. The mollies sitting about the hallway all straightened up as I entered and tried to arrange themselves becomingly, but I had no eyes for any of them. I strode in as though I were master of the place; my instinct said that surety was the key to success.

"Tell your mistress that I am arrived," I said. By then the old bawd was grown too old to act as mistress of the house, and Granville's young lady had the running of the place.

"Will she be glad to hear it, then?" one of them asked, brazen-faced.

"I will wait," I said.

The girl went up the stairs and knocked upon a door. She was bid enter and disappeared for a moment, then came back out and descended again, smirking at me.

"You ain't expected," she said.

I did not have to decide what course to take, for just then the door she had knocked at opened and Dora herself stood there, looking down at us all in the hall. She was wearing a gown the exact yellow of new butter. It was cut very low, and her plump and creamy skin seemed ready to spill over at any moment.

"My stars," she said, "I'd not have expected you, come all alone. Do you bring a message from Mr Dryer, or do you come on your own account?"

"Whatever I come for, it is not to shout from the bottom of the stairs," I said.

She laughed and said, "Then you'd best climb them," and disappeared back into her chamber.

I climbed the stairs with all the dignity I had at my disposal. My heart was beating very hard. She had left the door open. I stood in the doorway and looked into her chamber, where I had never been and where Granville had so many times closed the door upon me.

She had seated herself upon a velvet settee, her skirts spread out about her. The room was arranged curiously; half done out with a glass-fronted bookcase and gentleman's writing desk, the remainder filled with all manner of delicate tables and lamps. The walls were hung with draperies in shades of blue and green. The air was perfumed, floral and hot.

"What do you have in the jug?" she asked me. Her voice was blurred about the edges with the accent of Bristol.

"Wine."

"Then bring yourself inside, Mr Dryer's friend, and fetch us two of the glasses you see in the cabinet, there."

I came inside and closed the door behind me. I could have objected to being ordered about in this manner, but instead I fetched out the glasses and poured the wine like a footman. It occurred to me as I did so to bow to her, to complete the picture. She rewarded me with a delighted laugh.

I had noticed, by then, the closed door to the left of her. The closed door, with the soft bed I imagined lay beyond it. She saw me looking, and laughed again.

"Sit beside me, hasty sir. Tell me your name. I've seen you so many times and never yet learned it."

I did not know how close I should sit. I thought, *Better to err on the side of caution,* and sat beside her at a modest distance, as I would if she had been a lady.

"My name is Bowden," I said. "George Bowden."

"And shall I call you George?"

"If you wish it, you may."

"Well, now, I'd certainly wish it, if we're to be familiar with one another—so tell me, Mr George Bowden, do you come on Mr Dryer's business, or your own?"

"I come with entirely selfish motives, I must confess."

Her face grew stern.

"And would Mr Dryer be glad to know you're here, on selfish business, and with wine?"

"I should think he would not," I said.

"Would he call you a sneaking sly-boots and throw you off?"

"He might," I admitted.

"Yet here you are. Do you care for me so much, then?" Her voice grew soft once more.

"I do."

"Yes?"

"For years, I have thought of it. Ever since I saw you, I have thought of it. I have always regretted that he, that Mr Dryer—"

"That he laid claim first?"

"Yes."

"And would you have laid claim, as grand as he's done? Would you have cared for me, these years past? Watched over me, paid my expenses?"

"I like to think I would have." I knew that I would not.

Perhaps she knew I did not mean it, for she turned hard again, as fast as a flea-jump.

"Then answer me this, Mr George Bowden, false friend: would Mr Dryer throw me off with you? Has your passion for me allowed you to think on that?"

"I had not thought."

"You'd not, indeed. Why should I risk all I have, all my security, for your passion?"

"I must apologise."

"What do you apologise for, Mr George Bowden?"

"I suppose, for my presumption."

"In coming here?"

"Yes, I suppose I must."

"Do you not offer me what you said you would've, had you been before Mr Dryer, all those years ago? If you're that hot to lift me off him, you'll be needing to better what he gives me."

"What does he give you?"

She leant in and whispered, her breath warm and wet against my ear. The sum was great enough that I would have laid down with Granville myself for it.

"I cannot match it," I said. I had always known that Granville was wealthy but had never seen him willing to spend it—here was a place he had poured his coin.

"Then, you'll come back to visit with me when you've made your fortune. A young dandy gentleman like yourself must have expectations."

"Why should you wish me to? You are cared for handsomely, as you say yourself."

She put a hand upon my knee. "Perhaps, Mr George Bowden, you ain't the only one thought of it."

"You flatter me."

"Do I need to? Have you seen your own face? You're a beauty," and she laughed again.

I grew bold and pulled out my purse.

"I have this."

She took it and weighed it in her hand. I was not sure at that moment what it held, perhaps twenty guineas.

"What's this to get you?"

"Perhaps nothing."

"Do you swear to silence?"

"I will give you my word."

"Then give me your hand with it." She stood and offered her hand to me. I took it—it was as soft as any lady's.

Perry paid his footmen less than twenty guineas a year. I could have bought any of the girls in the hallway for four shillings and kept her an hour for six. I did not think any of that then, and nor, when I did think of it later, did I feel cheated. I only wished to be a rich man.

The bed was as soft as I had imagined it.

I MIGHT HAVE THOUGHT, before I went there, that one visit would be sufficient to avenge the bitterness growing in my heart and satiate my youth's ambition. It was not—my hunger for Dora was awoken as my affection for Charlotte Sinclair went quietly to sleep. I walked the streets burning for her. I was empty without her in my arms. She told me, when I left her the next morning, that I must not return to her unless I could match what Granville provided.

"For I'd be lost then," she said, "and I'll not lose for you, however pretty your eyes."

I felt even more bereft than I had before I went to her, as if in giving myself something, I had only found one more thing to lose.

I WENT HOME to Aubyn Hall the moment that Granville and Miss Sinclair were wed.

Perry received me quietly, and as though I had been gone no more than a day. My old friend did not look well; his eyes were bloodshot and exhausted.

I had hoped that with his sister gone from the Hall, Perry would return to more tranquil spirits. Instead he grew ever more peevish and took to the sauce at an hour ever earlier than the last. He began to sleep in his chair before the library fire. His appetite declined for anything but liquor. He would not eat, and developed a propensity for cursing at me when he was in his cups and calling me every kind of devil. Invitations to respectable social occasions had dried up—Perry and I were alone. My evenings were spent with a companion often too sozzled to speak and who, when he was coherent, was one moment calling me his beloved or his brother and the next wishing loudly that I might fry, or hang, or be otherwise damned. I was as low as I had been in Bristol; lower, because I had no hopes of there being anywhere else I might turn. Aubyn Hall was become something big and empty, full of shadows, echoes, and ghosts. Miss Sinclair's quiet presence had done more to warm the place than I had ever understood. I was too low to reply to my mother's letters. I almost wondered if I should not have preferred poverty with a wife to the half-life I was left with.

When I could persuade Perry to return with me to our old haunts, as often as not I would regret his company, when he became too sauced to walk or showed himself ungentlemanly in one way or another. The worst of it occurred in the card room of the Sydney Hotel, when Perry refused to trouble himself to fetch a pot, but wet his seat and sat in it, still calling for more rum. When the footman there fetched the proprietor, Perry called him a damnable hog-grubber and said that he was entitled to a little puddle, when he came by the side of such a player as I, "rash with the coin and unskilled besides." I was a little worse for drink myself, and took umbrage at this insult, at which Perry tried to strike me. Leaning forward in his chair, his swing unbalanced him and he fell from his seat. Perry, upon the floor, made to spit upon my boots but sadly soiled those of the proprietor instead. This, combined with the full extent of his accident being revealed, resulted in our being asked to leave and not return until we had learnt temperance. Two beefy coves came to assist Perry on his way out—he had refused to leave gracefully, I am sorry to report—and he, wresting his arms from their grip, promptly fell again, and hurt his brow against the corner of an occasional table which stood in the hall. The two roughs hefted him to his feet again, and this time Perry clung to them. By the time they gained the street, he was declaring them both fine fellows, and attempting to persuade them to accompany us elsewhere for a drink.

One night I was out alone and thought to pay a visit to the same establishment. The place was open all night and would serve any kind of food or drink a gentleman cared to call for, as long as his coin held out upon the table. Thus, I reasoned, I might remove the necessity of finding myself lodgings and return to Aubyn in the morning, refreshed a little by a holiday from Perry's company.

The bewigged cove posted at the door knew me well enough, so I inclined my head to him. He, however, instead of bowing in return, gave a dry butler's cough.

"I do apologise, sir, but the premises are closed to the public this evening."

"Don't be absurd, man," I replied. "I have this minute seen Sir Edwin walk inside."

"I must apologise, sir, but the rooms are closed. I cannot admit you."

"This is absurd," I said again.

"I can only apologise," the dastard repeated.

I chose then not to make a public scene, but went instead to Brown's, a dim and vault-like cellar where the doorman was less particular and, more important, where Perry had not yet disgraced himself too badly. I was very depressed in my spirits; Perry's presence hung about me even when he himself was safely snoring at home. We were bound, yet again—his reputation was fated to become mine.

As far as I could see, Granville did not know what prize he had in the new Mrs Dryer. He was more interested in his ragged lady boxer and his whore-mistress than in his wife, and fixated on the London fancy. He had lately visited London to see some display of pugilism or other, and thought himself slighted by the treatment he found there.

"They call Bristol a city without nobility," he complained, "though they will all flock here to find a champion prize-fighter. I have married a Sinclair. I am joined in marriage to a family of the first-rank."

"Were you not made welcome, then?" I asked.

"Welcome is not the question," he replied. "At a prize-ring, social standing counts for less than in other spheres of society, you know. And yet—the London gentry have not the same respect for the self-made man as you find elsewhere."

I thought, but did not say, *You will never be of the first-rank, no matter how many Sinclairs you join to. Blood cannot be traded in a coffee shop.* I could just imagine the London aristocracy, coming upon Granville in his unfashionable coat and overdressed hair. It was a wonder he had not been chased off. Perhaps he had been—he would never confess to such a thing.

Perry and I dined with the new-married Dryers often—Granville had then bought a country estate furnished exactly as badly as one would imagine. Mrs Dryer was almost as withdrawn after her marriage as she had been following the bereavements she had suffered. It pained me to see it. When once she did speak of a wish to ride out, I felt she spoke to me.

"Cannot you ride here?" I asked her.

"We have not enough horses," she said, "even if I were not still a little afraid of them."

"Not enough?" Granville said. "How many horses do we need?"

"I suppose, a servant's horse, so that I might have a chaperone." Mrs Dryer spoke so low she might have been addressing someone concealed beneath the tablecloth.

Granville snorted. "A fine expense, stabling a horse for the pleasure of the footman. If you truly wish it, I shall take you riding myself, whenever I can find the time for it."

I suspected he would not find the time very often, and later I found a moment alone with him, in order to raise the subject.

"You do not need to concern yourself with my wife, George," he said. "The days of your concern for her ended the morning I married her. I am convinced that I must keep her close—and this conversation only serves to reinforce that conviction."

I knew then that Perry had spoken to him.

❖ ❖ ❖

IF THIS PUT ME in an ill-temper, it was made the worse by my receiving one of my mother's infrequent letters, detailing the achievements of my brothers and bewailing my own lack of ambition. My accursed brother Edward—who had gone into the church, despite being as ungodly as I— had married and produced her a grandson. She spared me nothing in expressing her shame at my not taking the trouble to visit the creature.

How you can bear to be situated within five miles of your brother and remain such a stranger is sadly bewildering. I have no doubt but that you could benefit by taking Edward as your example. You cannot live as a parasite upon your friend for the whole of your life, George. You must make your own way. Let you take Edward as your model and lift the yoke of anxiety from around your mother's shoulders.

Having such breakfast reading as this—alone, of course, for Perry could not be shifted—was an insalubrious start to the day. My throat burned with the injustice of it. My mother knew well enough that I was Perry's agent and she had the gall to call me parasite. I could have strangled her with the yoke she spoke of. I was spitting rage.

Quite why this letter made me determined to visit Dora I could not have said, except that I felt a great dudgeon against the whole world. One of my friends was sleeping upstairs in his own fumes, yet was rich as a lord, and the other, richer still, had the only two females I had ever cared for as his own. I had nothing, I was named parasite! I had to go somewhere.

Mrs Sinclair's dressing room had been shut up, dust-sheeted and sombre. I never could understand why Perry had not handed all his mother's belongings to his sister, but he remained adamant that nothing should be touched. I could not even be sure that the maids went in to clean. I thought I would not leave it all to rot; it was a little matter to steal in and liberate an evening gown of handsome teal silk from the press. I wrapped it carefully in paper to keep it clean upon the road, and carried it before me on the saddle, tied on so that I should not lose it.

I tipped the boy at The Hatchet to hold Blackbird, and took a nip of rum for courage. Then I presented myself at the bawdy house.

She took an age to see me. I sat in the little parlour and allowed Granville's lady pugilist to bring me rum-and-water. She had a bruise upon her chin as though she had dipped her face in wine. The rum was of good quality; the whole place looked nicer than it had when first we came there. Granville's money was everywhere: in the silk-covered settee, the papered walls, the abundance of candles. I tried not to consider this, but sat, sipping my rum, the package containing the gown upon my knee, trying not to twitch with impatience.

When finally I was summoned up the lamp-lit staircase, I was ready to burst with it. I felt as young and foolish as I had when I had come there as a schoolboy.

Dora was wearing a silken undress gown and was perfect enough to make my throat catch. She had painted a little heart upon her cheek. Her smile was like a hand, pulling me inside.

"Handsome Mr Bowden, what pleasure," she said.

"The pleasure is all mine, truly."

She laughed at the ardour in my voice.

"What do you have for me, Mr George Bowden?"

"It is nothing much." I walked closer to her and laid the package in her lap. My hand itched to touch her cheek.

"If it's nothing much, you shouldn't have fashed yourself to bring it." She pulled the string from about the package and opened the paper.

On her lap, against the ivory of her skirt, the teal silk suddenly looked a little dull. Dora's smile dulled a little in response.

"What's this?"

"A gown . . . it is very good silk."

"It's devilish old-fashioned." She shook it out. "The waist's as low as my ma wore."

"You could have it made over," I said.

She put it aside without looking at it further.

"Perhaps I will," she said, "but what drove you all the way here with such a dry gift, Mr George Bowden? I bid you visit me when you could offer what Mr Dryer does. He's no sense of fashion, I'd warrant, but even he'd not bring me someone else's old gown to make over."

"I am sorry you do not like it."

She stood. Her face came up to my shoulder. She raised her soft hand and stroked my cheek.

"You're lovely to look at," she said, "but handsome won't pay, Mr George Bowden. I've said as much before."

"What can I offer you?" I said, somewhat wildly. "I can never rival Granville! If I could better it, I would do it in a moment."

I turned my back upon her. I felt almost as though I might weep. Behind me, I heard her take her seat once more.

"There are some things he won't give me," she said.

"Tell me"—I turned and knelt at her feet—"tell me what I can give you that he will not."

"You'll think me dreaming."

"Never." I took her hand and pressed it to my lips.

"I've a wish to be a lady," she said, "with a staff of servants and a carriage. I'm afraid of growing old here, Mr George Bowden. I think to escape this life, before I turn into my ma."

"I cannot offer you that either."

"Maybe so. And likely if you could, I'd not be the lady you'd choose."

"If I had any choice, I would make you my first object, I give you my word."

"You'd have to give me better than your word, George"—she had never before called me by my Christian name alone—"and there lies the trouble."

"If I make my fortune, Dora"—she had not given me permission but I spoke her name heedless and tasted the sound of it upon my lips—"I will come back for you and make you a lady."

"And we'd flit off to somewhere my name ain't known? I look to be a lady, not a whore raised-up."

"We would go as far as we could," I said, thinking of Granville and Perry.

She let me kiss her for a promise but nothing more. She said she would keep the gown and have it made over as being suitable for a lady, until I could come back for her.

Chapter 12

✣ ✣ ✣

O f course, I could not come back for her, and nor was I sure that I wished to. It was only the old draw of the impossible that made me long for her. The next time I did lay my eyes, if not my hands, upon her, was many months later, at St James' Fair.

Granville had dragged us there to see his little milling molly set-to upon a real stage. He was full of pomp over it, insufferably pleased with himself for having got her there. Of course, I went along only for the gaming, and Perry for the entertainment. My own amusement was greatly increased by the addition of Mrs Dryer to the party. God alone knew what Granville was thinking in bringing her to such a place—his face every moment showed that he regretted his choice. There was quite a press in the boxing booth, and she cowered and clung to him, as many young ladies would in such environs. Granville being the man he was, his chivalry would not extend to his missing a moment of the blood-sport.

Perry whispered to me that his sister had quite demanded to be brought, and I could not help but wonder if she had meant to be close to me by it. I was idly turning over the idea of taking her off for a walk about the fair, but I did not like to miss the betting or the lark. Granville had his little hard-headed miss set up against the most enormous brute of a man and was refusing to see the joke of it.

"By God, man! Look at his fists! They are the size of her skull. He shall twist it off her neck in a moment," Perry said.

"You have no appreciation of the use that speed may be put to in cases such as this, Perry. It is not all weight and thuggery. There is science here that you have no knowledge of." Granville's voice was impossibly smug for a man whose bout was yet to be fought.

"I have eyes, you fool," Perry said.

I laughed. "It is a lamb against a lion," I said.

"It is more!" Perry cried. "It is a babe against a blacksmith! It is the most ridiculous thing. I thought you were fond of this chit. You mean to slay her."

Granville looked affronted and replied, "Do not you forget David and Goliath."

Perry and I laughed the harder.

"Well might you quote the Bible. You will need God on your side in this case," I said.

Mrs Dryer, all this time, was watching the stage. She was not listening to our talk, but only clinging to Granville's arm as though she grew there. She paid no attention, therefore, when Granville's eyes grew wide and dismay crossed his face. He caught my eye and gestured with his head to the other side of the ring. There, craning above the crowd to find us, in the most violent shade of pink and with all her creamy wares displayed to best advantage, was Dora.

"Here's fun." I tapped Perry on one broad shoulder and directed his attention to where she stood. His face broke into a smile.

"Oh, ho!" He looked from Granville to Mrs Dryer. "I'd say you have a matter of moments, sir, before you lose the day on and off the stage!"

I thought that a piece of high humour. Granville did not see the merriment.

"George," he said, looking more ruffled than I had seen him in a good while, "you must take care of this matter. You know you must."

I allowed myself another smile at his expense, and then I delivered him from his misery.

"Rest easy, old friend. I shall see the day saved."

Granville's eyes closed for a moment in relief. Then he turned his head and looked only at the ring.

I wove my way toward her. She saw my approach and ceased her craning, leaning instead against the wooden platform on which I predicted that her sister was to be utterly pounded.

"Mr George Bowden. You're bold, ain't you? Right beneath Mr Dryer's nose."

She hit me with her closed fan, a gentle tap against my chest.

I drew her into the crowd by her elbow. Even this was as soft as I remembered her lips to be.

"He is with his wife," I said.

"Oh, my days, swear home he ain't!" This delighted her in some way. She tried then to look, but I had drawn her too far away.

"I didn't mark her; I've got to get a peek. What's she wearing?"

"I don't know, I'm sure. Some gown or other. Sweet mistress, you must know, Mr Dryer sent me himself to warn you that you must not speak to him."

"Well, he needn't think I would. But I might be allowed a look."

"Will you not look at me?"

"I look at you whenever I get the chance, handsome George Bowden." She turned back to me and laid a hand upon my arm.

"I hope you might do more, by day's end."

She laughed. "Grown rich, are you?"

"I have a good sum riding on the outcome of this bout."

"Who here doesn't?"

"Only those too cowardly to lay their coin," I said. "Will you forgive me for betting against your sister?"

Dora's eyes widened, and then she laughed in earnest.

"Oh, you ain't to make your fortune this day! Oh, Mr Bowden, you're lucky you've a handsome face, for you haven't a brain in your head."

"What? What can you mean?"

Dora leant toward me. Her breath was hot against my ear. The scent of her brought back a vivid image of her on that other day, lying on her back, arms thrown above her head.

"Change your bet," she whispered. "My sister can't lose. Mr Dryer swears it's all fixed."

I could not for a moment absorb the meaning of her words, so close did she stand to me, but once I did, I believe I stumbled away from her with barely a word. Rage throbbed at my temples. Granville, who already had everything I never would, was prepared to profit from me and turn me into a fool. He would take all I had left and his conscience allowed him. Dastard! Blackguard! Oh, I should take my sword to him.

I could not return to their merry little group. Even Perry, as much Granville's fool as I was, I could not bear to lay eyes on at that moment. Rage condensed into spiteful determination as I reached the side of the ring, where the girl's opponent rested. It was the work of a moment to tap his shoulder and beckon him to lean down over the ropes, so that I might speak into his ear.

"I know this bout is fixed," I said, very low.

The cove pulled back so that he could see my face. He shrugged, as though to say he could not help it.

"I have here a bond for thirty pounds. It is yours if you lose control of yourself today and forget to allow yourself beaten. I know it is more than they are paying you."

The cove grew very still. Then he said, in a quiet rush, "Give it to that lady, there, in the feathered hat. If it be right, I shan't lose," and he straightened up and turned away from me.

I HAD PUT EVERYTHING ELSE I had upon the outcome of the fight and even borrowed a little extra from Perry. The odds had not been high, but as the result was a sure one and as I had laid out a healthy sum, the returns were substantial, even with the thirty-pound loss. Of course, the greatest prize was Granville's shaken arrogance.

My old friend being what he was, however, he was never brought down for long. He had moved in a moment onto his next project, before the molly's blood had soaked into the sawdust. He was determined to see the beefy fellow from the bawdy house door turned into a champion of England, and himself drawn to the bosom of the London fancy at last. Whether or not Granville felt himself beaten, victory was still mine, and I had the profit to prove it.

I had seen similar sums put into my hand as the result of a wager before, but always in the context of a gaming house, where I would habitually put it back onto the baize. I determined that I would not do that this time, though the little voice in my ear whispered that I was missing my opportunity to double it. Granville might have had many of the things I wished for, but he did not spend his wealth as I would have if it were mine—I went out and purchased something I had longed for ever since I first set eyes on one: a phaeton.

It was a beautiful one-horse machine, built for speed, of glossy deep red wood, with brass trim polished high and a black leather seat. The wheels were so large and slim that to drive it was to fly above the ground. The hood retracted back on smooth hinges, so that the wind whipped about my head as I went. The whole cost me close to two hundred pounds, but I did not regret it for an instant. It was the most beautiful thing I had ever owned, and Blackbird looked the picture of elegance harnessed to its traces.

When I brought it home, Perry said, "Ah, perfectly suited to you, George. A ridiculous, dandyish thing," but he rode with me all the day, tooling about the park and grounds at a fine pace, whooping as we took the corners, until Blackbird trembled with exertion and our voices grew hoarse. It was the most exhilarating thing imaginable. Perry did not even miss his bottle until well after his usual hour.

I took Dora out in it at my earliest opportunity. I would not leave it in the street, but sent a boy to fetch her. She did not even scold me for coming when she saw what I drove, only laughed aloud and went to fix her hair firmly enough that the wind should not ruin it. I took her out to the long, empty roads of Clifton, and we sped through all those half-built streets of deserted mansions and crescents, both of us cock-a-hoop with the speed and danger of it.

When at last we stopped upon the downs, to admire the view and refresh ourselves—I had brought a bottle of ale with a good cork in it and held it between my feet all the time we drove, no small feat—I felt like a king. Dora did not even stop me from caressing her.

She was different that day from how I was used to seeing her. The wind had pinked her cheeks, and despite her care, her hair was escaping its pins to make a golden halo about her head where the sunlight caught it.

I did not tell her that I owed the acquisition of the phaeton to her sister's injury, nor the part I had played in that sad event. I was surprised, indeed, at the bitterness in her voice when she spoke of Granville now.

"He ain't even asked how she does," she said. "He ain't spared a thought for her. Tom's training's all he thinks of now."

"It will surely be to your sister's great advantage if her husband becomes champion," I said.

"Will it? Can you be so sure that he'll keep by her? Granville talks of carrying Tom off to London and having him play the gent. He's full of ideas of balls and the like, and showing him off like a pet. He wants to take him about to all the quality places and have the other gents look him over. Can you see my sister at a ball? They'd not let her through the door."

It was an incongruous image. "Perhaps not," I said. "I never realised you were so attached to your sister. I dislike my own brothers so heartily, I never think of others being fond of their own siblings."

"Sometimes I could strangle her. Sometimes I've tried it. Even so, I'd not want to see harm done her. Tom never married her, you know. She ain't his wife in law. He can walk off and never think of her again, just as Granville could to me; just as any of you could," and she would not let me kiss her again.

At last I snapped the reins to begin Blackbird moving and let the wind blow the bitterness out of her mouth.

"COME, SIR," PERRY SAID. "If you are so sure of your man, let this stake be the match of none we've ever made! A championship of England deserves a kingly wager."

Perry, Granville, and I were sitting beside the fire in Granville's austere library, drinking a particularly fine brandy. Granville would not replace the ancient bookcases, but he filled them with first-class literature in good bindings. He would not lay out his coin for more comfortable chairs, but the decanter was filled with liquor of the highest quality. If sometimes I found it frustrating, I believe that day, with a crystal glass of first-rate nectar in my hand, I found it almost endearing.

"Very well, what say you to a plantation I have lately bought? I am expecting the deeds any day," Granville replied.

Perry looked to me and then directed my gaze to my snuffbox, which was on the table before him. I picked it up and proffered it; my friend's fingers shuffled about inside it for an unnecessarily long time before he was satisfied with his pinch. I have always thought it bad manners to let one's fingers stay too long in another man's snuffbox.

"Now you begin to interest me. Tell me more," Perry said, when once he had taken his pinch and completed the necessary ritual of head tip and handkerchief.

"It is a small island in the West Indies, growing sugar," Granville said, declining my snuffbox with a wave. "There is a house, I understand, fit for a gentleman. A steward watches over the place currently and seems a steady enough cove. The profits are excellent, or I should never have bought it."

"A house fit for a gentleman? I cannot imagine you in foreign climes, Granville," I said. The picture was an entertaining one.

"I am not much tempted to visit, I confess. I bought the place at a good price and mean only to sell it on."

"As I will, when I win it," Perry said.

"Touché." Granville nodded.

"What is the name of the island?" I asked. "Perry was quite the geographer at school. No doubt he can tell us of its longitude and latitude."

"I am afraid I can't recall just now. It is named after some saint or other, I believe."

"George mocks me," Perry said. "I was repeatedly thrashed at school for failing in just such a task. So, jester, what shall I stake against Granville's plantation? You are the master of my investments; what have I to equal it?"

"You have shares in any number of ventures," I said.

"Shares? Shares are not kingly," Granville said.

"Well, then, perhaps the house at Queen Square," I said. I had long thought Perry should unload the thing; it was grown sadly unfashionable as an address.

"I am not sure it's worth the plantation," Granville said, after a moment. "However, I have a purpose it could suit. I accept."

Hands being shaken, the two turned to me.

"Well, George," Perry said, "will you wager your precious phaeton?"

"Perhaps I might. What would you stake against it?"

"I?" Perry looked outraged.

"I dare not bet against Granville this time," I said. "My gut warns me that it would be most unwise."

"You are wiser than you appear, Bowden." Granville raised his glass to me.

"Your instincts are notoriously fallible," Perry said, but he would not lay a stake against me, and he was in an ill-humour for the rest of the evening.

I WAS TRUTHFUL when I said that my instincts spoke in Granville's favour this time. It was partly the cunning the cove had shown over the set-to at the fair; I did not believe he could fix such a fight as an English championship, but I was forced to give him credit for ambition and ruthlessness I had not guessed he possessed. If Granville was determined to make his man champion, I was determined to lay all I could on his having the outcome he wished for.

In the name of keeping hold of my funds, I ceased visiting the gaming houses. I ceased my pursuit of Dora. If I made my fortune, I would be at leisure to pursue her in earnest, if I so chose. I knew myself sufficiently well to hazard that if I had the funds easily at hand to buy her, I might no longer wish to do so. I did not know what path I might find myself taking if I were free and independent; I had never been so before.

Perry seemed glad that I was content to stay at home with him. I spent all my days working hard at his investments, although I had a devil of a time eliciting any assistance from Granville; he was endlessly caught up in his schemes for his pug. I was happy enough feeling my way through the world of trade as best I could; I had learnt enough by then that I did not think I would ruin us and I wished Granville success in his training as heartily as I wished to make profit from investment. Every profit I took I squirreled away, like a wife skimming the housekeeping money. I used the bank at Corn Street instead of a purse concealed up the chimney breast, but the principle was much the same. I had never shown thrift before, and this was my first experience of the satisfaction to be found in watching my hoard grow slowly. I was amazed at my own patience and discipline in letting it sit there. If I had not meant to lay it all on Tom Webber's fight— which would be the greatest gamble I had ever made—I should not have been able to bear it.

Meanwhile, Perry was coming to seem like an old man wearing a young man's face as disguise. When we went out shooting, he walked slowly and missed near every shot. He fell asleep at an hour ever earlier than the last. He still wished me in his bed, but now he desired nothing more than that I hold him. He began to be beset by night-fears. He would wake screaming and sweating and have to be soothed like a babe. When, as occasionally happened, I wished to be intimate with him once more, though he was very obliging, he could not raise himself. He was very downcast then and would not take comfort, though when I put my hand to his cheek he took it from his face and held it. He would not meet my eyes.

"You know what devils plague me, George," he said, and held his other hand out for me to observe. It trembled with a strange palsy.

I took it and pressed it together with his other hand, keeping both those dear hands in both of mine. They seemed to hum with shakes held still. At last our eyes met.

"I cannot fight it, George. I do not wish to fight it." He had a curious expression: a mixture of defiance, shame, and sorrow. I did not like to see it; I preferred him roaring and cursing. Perhaps I even preferred him soiling himself in the armchairs of gaming houses. I kissed him, unmindful of the sticky film that coated our unwashed mouths.

"Do not you fight it, then," I said.

For a moment his lip trembled, and I wondered if he wished I had bid him have strength. Then he turned from me and pulled the bell to call for rum.

I began to see him as a babe in truth, and was astonished at what a proficient nurse I became. I kept my eye upon him, and it was I who called for him to be bathed—the butler and a footman together helping him into the brass tub—I who sat beside him and kept him merry in the water. It was I who watched what he would eat and when. I began to learn his habits as I had not before. He would not rise for breakfast, but when he did wake, he would take a glass of Granville's recommended tonic: a glass of rum with the yolk of a raw egg stirred into it. If I could catch him in the early afternoon, after he had softened himself with brandy but before he fell asleep, he could often be prevailed upon to eat, sometimes in great quantities. Thus we began dining at an hour ever earlier, whilst gentlemen of fashion were elsewhere dining later and later. He grew disinterested in meat and developed a taste for pasties, and bread with butter and salt, which I ordered we keep a good supply of, even while the price of wheat rose.

I did all these things and gladly, even as I poured my remaining energies into the financial arena. I cared for him with all my waking day, yet somewhere below my attachment to my friend, I wondered if I would do those things when once I had made my fortune on Tom Webber's victory. Would I flee my duty? Would I, with choice laid out before me, choose this life, watching Perry dwindle? The thought would not be still, and its stirring in my breast caused me to kiss him ever more tenderly.

THE LONDON FANCY had decreed that Granville must bring Webber to London, to the Fives Court. There he was to be set against the beefiest coves that London had to offer, and when once Webber had bested them— as I felt sure he must do—then he would be declared a fit contender for the championship of England, and be allowed to try for the greatest prize of all.

Granville came to bid us farewell, and I assured him that I would arrive in London in good time for the final bout. I was bound and determined to go—I should not miss the championship bout for the world. Perry refused to consider the journey on his own behalf, and I decided not to press him. Granville, too, seemed relieved. I knew well enough that he was afraid that Perry would humiliate himself; it was a reasonable enough fear to harbour, in all honesty. Granville was visibly anxious that the London fancy should welcome him—I had a few doubts in that quarter, but held my peace.

I went, once, to visit Mrs Charlotte Dryer, to ask after Granville's progress and enjoy a little feminine company. I was struck by how changed she seemed. She was not the shy, blushing creature I was accustomed to. She met my eye. She seemed more awake, somehow. She looked at me as though she were appraising the cut of my coat. She was wearing a gown, I saw, cut in the new style, of draped white muslin, very flowing and cut low across the shoulders. I thought it very becoming, and told her so. She barely dropped her gaze when she thanked me. Her shoulders were dimpled with scars, but very white. I had never seen her shoulders before, I realised then.

"Shall we take tea?" she said, "or should you like something more interesting?"

I could not tell if this were flirtation. Miss Sinclair—Mrs Dryer—had always been either blushing or brazen: one extreme to the other.

"I will take tea, if you will be good enough to serve me," I said.

"Then will you think me rude, if I take wine?" she asked.

I immediately said that if she wished for wine I would join her, and the bell was duly rung.

"Now, you must tell me all that you have been doing," she said.

I could scarcely think of a thing to tell her, suitable for a lady's ear. In the end, we discussed music and so passed an hour pleasantly enough. Mrs Dryer drank more wine than I had ever seen a lady take. She grew pink about the face, but remained perfectly steady—steadier, indeed, than I did myself. I left her feeling very queer, as though someone had picked up my thoughts and shaken them like a box of sand, so that they settled in a new way.

I WAS STILL RAISING all the funds I could in preparation for the fight. I had recently had an epiphany regarding profit; I took half of the profits made on any investment and returned to Perry's coffers the capital, as I always had. However, in the matter of a sale, the profits were less clear. I was thinking then about land; Perry had inherited vast tracts of land, much of which was tenanted and brought in good rents. However, there were swathes of it that were turned over to woodland, and these brought us nothing but a place to hunt birds. We never walked half the wood Perry owned, not anywhere close to half. I sold just a few acres of the furthermost edge, where likely neither of us had ever been. Since Perry received no income from the woods and had paid nothing for them, having inherited them, I reasoned the whole price could truthfully be called profit. Half the money paid was then my own—and all of it was to be laid on Tom Webber's victory. My bank balance climbed steadily; it was almost as thrilling as watching coins mount up on my side of the baize.

I readied myself to leave Perry and go to London. I was both eager to go and anxious about abandoning him.

"Will you be well, old friend?" I put my hand on his arm.

We were sitting together on the settee. I had wrapped him in a rug; he had begun to get very cold in the evenings and seemed unable to get warm. I would ride out in the morning.

"I will be exactly as well as I am now, George. I wish you would stop talking about it."

"I only wish to put my mind at rest. I hate to leave you."

"No one is forcing you to London."

"I go for Granville."

"You go for gambling! I wish you would not pretend to higher motives. You would not notice if Granville was in London or India, if only your bet came good. You would not even notice if I was here when you came home, if your win was enough."

"You do me an injustice."

"Perhaps I will not be here," he said, in the mournful voice I had come to loathe. "Then we shall see where your heart is. You will go straight back out to the tables."

Although I protested and stroked him into placidity, a small piece of my heart thought, *Why don't you make haste to suicide, since you threaten it so often?*

As TRAVEL-WORN as I was by the time I arrived in London and found my lodgings, I was determined nonetheless to have some merriment. I had been starved lately of entertainment. Perry was not hanging about my neck, and I could trust that his reputation had likewise been left behind. I went, therefore, to the Fives Court, to find Granville and his hulking protégé.

What a place it was, galleries and boxes and a ceiling as high as a good-sized church. The roped stage and the scent peculiar to the noble art, of fear-sweat and masculinity, were all that marked it out as the palace of pugilism; otherwise it could have been a theatre or perhaps even an opera house. It was a great distance removed from The Hatchet Inn. It was The Hatchet I thought of when I stepped inside that thronging hall, however; The Hatchet, and Granville as a young lad, smelling the sawdust. I wished for a moment that I had been with him when first he laid eyes on the Fives Court. I could imagine him perfectly, the subtle sparkle that was all one could see of Granville overwhelmed.

The place was fairly full and I perceived, now that I took the time to look about me, that here was another sign that I was back in the world of prize-fighting; gentlemen were seated together with pugilists and common men, almost as though all were equal. I say almost, because of course the obligatory forelock-tugging and deference went on, but with a remarkable air of holiday about it.

The Fives Court being so large and well populated, it took me some time to spy Granville, even with the hulking presence of Webber beside him. In that hallowed hall of pugilism, there were more coves built on Webber's grand scale than in any place I had ever been, so that he was less of a landmark than usual. And Granville! As I approached, I was astonished to see that the cove had cut his hair into short curls and had topped it with a tall hat that was very nearly fashionable. His coat, whilst as sombre as ever, was nicely made and double-breasted, with a fur collar that shone like the coat of a racehorse. When I hailed him, somewhat tentatively, as if it might not be he—though I knew it must be, for by then I had clearly identified Webber—he turned, and I saw that he had even found a cravat that did not entirely shame him. He looked like a glossy little blackbird instead of a dusty crow. It was quite a sight. Webber, too, was made nicer than I was used to seeing him, though Granville's dull taste was evident in every stitch the cove wore. The plain costume was fitting, however, in a man of his station. He looked like a young clerk, if ever one had lived that had been built so large.

Granville seemed not the least surprised to see me.

"Ah, George," he said, as though he had been expecting me every moment.

Webber stood so that I might have his seat—for there was not an abundance of chairs in that place—and Granville sent him to procure some porter for the three of us, saying, "And some kind of victuals, for George will be hungry."

Webber bowed and went off like an amiable hound.

"He is a marvel, George," Granville said, turning to watch his progress through the crowd. As he went, I saw him stopped repeatedly by coves wanting to shake him by the hand.

"He is certainly popular," I said.

"He is the darling of the fancy. I have to be constantly on my guard against vanity. Other sponsors treat their fellows like gentlemen, you know. I think it a very great mistake. Let him break his servitude with victory only, that's my thought upon the matter. If I allow him his head now, he will grow wild; I have seen it happen."

"You are wise, I am sure," I said.

Granville was more loquacious and at ease than I had seen him for years. I noticed a fair amount of hat-tipping and bowing exchanged between my friend and the gentlemen that passed by our seats, and concluded that Granville's new costume and his promising pupil had done much to secure him the acceptance he had been after.

Webber found us again, accompanied by a boy bearing a tray of much-welcomed sustenance. Once the lad had divested himself of his burden, he made it his business to find a stool for Webber and, once found, presented it to him with a decided air of hero-worship. Webber, for his part, took the stool with only quiet thanks, and smiled as the lad saluted and ran off. The stool was only a little three-legged thing and the cove looked precarious sitting upon it, large as he was, but I thought that Granville was right: there was an air of humility about him that was pleasing to see.

"Have you been having much success, Webber?" I asked him.

He answered so slowly it was as though he had not spoken to me countless times over the years, at the door of an easy house.

"I'm doing as best I can, sir. My luck holds to now."

"Not luck," Granville said. "It is hard training and perseverance that smiles upon you. You shall see soon enough, George. He will fight this very evening, for the pleasure of all assembled. For which reason, Webber, you should not eat anything more," and he took the bread from the cove's hand and laid it back upon the plate.

"You are a hard master," I said.

"Not I! I have given Webber everything in my power to assist him. I paid an enormous sum to free Mendoza from prison, that he might teach Webber science."

"Mendoza? The Jew?"

"The former champion of all England, George. The father of boxing science."

"Turned criminal, you say?"

Granville waved a hand. "Debtor, only."

"Ha, I hope you take heed, Tom," I said, to Webber. "England's championship will not gain you a fortune. You will rot in debtor's prison, unless Mr Dryer keeps by you."

"Pay no attention to this dunderhead, Webber," Granville said. "Mendoza managed his finances badly. It is of no consequence—he managed his fists. It is all he need know."

"And which has he taught you, Webber," I asked, "finance or fisticuffs?"

Webber looked at his own fists, laid out on the table like ham shanks.

"He's shown me about science, sir."

"Excellent news. I look forward to meeting the fellow. Is he here?"

"Gone back to prison, sir." The cove sounded ashamed.

I could not help but laugh. "More bad debts, then? You should have given him something for his pockets, Granville. Will you spring him once more?"

"It is not in my power to do so," Granville said. "Mr Mendoza has been held on charges of forgery. Tom learnt a good deal while he had the chance, and I feel sure it will be enough. He has a natural aptitude for the ring."

Webber's neck had turned red, though whether through shame or pride I could not have said.

"That's the spirit," I said. "I care nothing for famous names. I only wish to see Webber raise his arm in victory. I am laying almost everything I own upon it."

Granville looked as though he were a maiden I had kissed; his eyes softened and shone.

"From a man as fond of chance as you, George, that is the highest praise. Your confidence will be rewarded, and we shall be all of us rich."

"You are rich as a lord already."

"A man can always be made richer."

"Amen," I said, and raised my glass.

Soon enough came Webber's time upon the stage. It was a tense moment—Webber had bested so many of London's heavyweights that the fancy had all agreed: he need only win this last fight in order to qualify as a contender for the championship. If he could only be victorious now, he would go on to the greatest match of all. If he failed . . . but of course, I would not think of that.

By then the fancy were all arrived and the room was packed so close that we were all mopping our brows. Had I not been by Granville's side, I might not have secured a view.

Webber's bare-chested appearance in the ring brought resounding cheers from the majority of throats. The fellow was in peak condition and soon set about proving it by knocking seven kinds of hell from the beefy cove they set him against. Webber drew back his fist and repeatedly pounded it into that clunch's skull. With each hit made, my heart soared ever higher. The meaty thud of each fib landing was like a coin chinking into a pile of its fellows. Webber would indeed make me rich; I could have kissed him.

PART 5

Ruth

❖ ❖ ❖

Chapter 13

✦ ✦ ✦

I came to in our own bed in the cellar, where the sagging mattress rose up on either side of me so high as to keep me trapped. I'd woken in the same way so many times that for a moment I didn't know what mill had sent me there. When I did recall the fair and the bout that was never theatricals at all, well, then I moaned aloud. The sound brought Tom's mug, appearing over the wall of mattress.

"How d'you fare, my Ruthie?"

I couldn't answer. Just the moaning had been pain enough; my lips were stuck together, swollen and stiff, my ribs moved sharp as knives with each breath. When once these pains started up, all the rest wanted to join; each piece of me woke and began bawling. My hand was especially piercing in its cries. I tried to flex it and was rewarded by such torment that I jerked in a spasm, which set off my ribs. In moving, I also had the first tidings of the wound to the back of my head. I was a sorry creature.

"Don't move so," Tom said, and, sitting upon the bed, caused the ditch I was in to level out.

My ribs shattered into a hundred hot pieces in my breast. A shriek rose within me but was trapped by my swollen lips and became a dog's whine.

Tom looked intently into my face.

"You ain't dying." He didn't sound as sure of it as I expected he meant to.

He coaxed me into parting my lips, and with a dropper he fed me some of Ma's medicine. This, too, was so familiar after a pounding that I fell into it as I would Tom's arms, and the pain on my chest became a shifting crimson shape that settled at last behind my eyes and sent me into sleep.

THE NEXT TIME I WOKE I was alone. I needn't look to know it. Tom's warmth was gone; my skin felt clammy as a frog's. The sharpness of the pangs had faded off into a banging stiffness. I lay and gingerly began to count my ailments. The inside of my lips were shredded raw and tasted of copper and meat; three of my teeth were loosed. I could barely breathe; I'd a notion that blood might be pooling in my throat, though I knew enough to tell that it was more likely that the swelling of my nose and lips meant I couldn't draw enough air. My ribs burned. My hand was so painful that in flexing it I couldn't tell if it moved or not. My neck was stiff, and even raising my head a very little was like taking a fib to the back of the head.

More to me than these injuries was a leaden feeling in my belly, in the knowledge that I'd angered Mr Dryer. I couldn't fathom what had happened. I was meant to take the fight; how then did I come to be here, so broken? I felt a creeping dread that would have become a flapping fit, if only I could've moved much.

I began to feel I must sit up. I had to know what state I was left in, I had to find Tom, I had to know what had happened at the fair. Slowly, ever so slowly, I began to raise myself. I found I could push myself up with my left arm without too much misery, excepting my ribs and head. I managed, in a poor and unsteady way, to get myself up onto my left elbow. Just doing this was enough for me to have to close my eyes and rest. Then I shuffled myself up just enough that I was half sitting, propped against the bedstead with the metal rail tucked under the base of my skull. Here I rested again. The room was as empty as I'd thought it, just the damp-streaked walls and our few things. There was only a very little light from the high window: morning or dusk, I couldn't tell. It could've been midday, if the day were cloudy. It could've been any time at all but night. If it were light out, the house would be asleep—but if the house were asleep, then where was Tom?

Now I saw that my hand had been put into splints, lashed into a kind of frame. It was become a paddle for beating carpets, though that was a joke; I'd not be beating anything with it for a good while. Seeing it so sorry for itself brought tears to my throat in a hot lump. We'd be hungry now, Tom and I. Hungry or thrown upon Dora's charity, which might be worse. It was in this pitiful condition, propped up, swollen, and about to weep, that I heard Tom's boots upon the stairs.

I struggled, then, to swallow my tears. I'd not wept for years, and I was damned if I'd do it in front of Tom. Blinking, I found that my left eye was swelled up too. I'd not cry. I'd not cry. Here came Tom's boots. I knew his step so well: slow and uneasy with its own weight.

Before the handle turned, there came Mr Dryer's voice.

"Oh, Webber?"

"Yes, sir," said my husband, and up the stairs went his boots.

What was this about? I felt myself grow fearful again. Time went by. I couldn't stay sitting up, yet the thought of lying down again made the panic grow wings to beat against my breast. At last the metal rail behind my head was too much. I slid back down to my mattress trough and lay like a chicken with its feet tied. Still Tom didn't come and didn't come. Though I thought I wouldn't, my body decided the matter and I slept again.

I dreamt that our ma came, and stood over me, and clucked her tongue like she was sorry. Then I blinked and she was Dora, still clucking, pushing a spoon of gin between my puffed-up lips. My throat seized and I tried to tell her, *Stop, I'm like to drown,* but in trying to speak I swallowed, and the gin went down. The fire of it got lost amongst the heat from my sorry ribs. Then Dora was gone, and I was waking again.

I woke to the sound of the door closing and my husband's feet again tramping up the stairs. The affinity of this moment with the other made me feel devilish queer; dreams were tangled in with the sounds of boots and pain, and I couldn't have told you how long I'd slept, nor be sure I'd slept at all. I tried then to call out, but my voice wouldn't obey me and I only lay and heard his boots disappear upstairs.

It was as I tested the stiffness of my body that I knew some time must've passed; the quality of the aches was settled, as though the pain had made itself a home in my limbs and meant to stay a good while. When I began again to sit up, I found my throat foully bitter and knew I'd been dosed as I slept. I'd no idea if it'd been by Tom's hand, or if my dream of Dora had been a true one. Though it'd been gin, not Ma's medicine, that she'd spooned me in the dream—and she'd never in her life been fashed to nurse anyone.

When I sat up I found that my head felt muffled, and putting up my left hand to it, I found the back of it set in plaster and the whole wound around with bandage. The scent of the vinegar came to my notice then, as a sting in my nostrils.

I missed my husband. I was thirsty as the devil. I began to get up, of course I did. I'd never been one to lie abed.

I knew well enough then that my ribs had been broke, for each movement gave me a sharp reminder. Even drawing in breath was a lesson in suffering. If rising from the bed was painful enough, getting into my gown turned out a terrible business. I left off stays, for that seemed too difficult with only one hand to pull the laces, but pulled my gown on over my shift. My poor right hand I pushed through the sleeve first, working the cloth over the splints with the other, to prevent it getting stuck. Then, before I could think better of it, I raised the whole, to pull it over my head. Raising my arms like that was pure wretchedness, and there was a moment, with my head inside and my arms trapped in the sleeves, when I felt that the effort of forcing my head out would be more than I could bear; I had to rest for a moment, half in and half out of it, my head inside and my arms at a painful angle, before I could draw enough courage to force it on. I was glad then to be alone, with no one to see how foolish I must've looked, though I suppose it never would've been the ordeal it was, with other hands to help me. The bit of crocheted lace I'd sewed to the neck raked my tender mouth, and I pulled the gown too hard, snagging the bandage on my head. When finally my head popped through the neck of the gown I jarred myself hard enough that I cried out. I lay for a moment, sideways across the bed, and whispered the most terrible curses I knew. I knew some curses too. I knew words that could send you straight to Hell, I shouldn't wonder.

Next I'd to pull on my boots, and this was worst of all, having only my left hand to grip with. I should've done it slow, I knew, but by then a kind of fever had gripped me, and I pulled at the laces and leather impatiently, sweating with the torment of it. Again I jarred myself when my foot slid in, but by then I was almost glad. I was in a rage: with Tom for not being there, with myself for my own weakness, with Mr Dryer, with the shit-sack who'd beaten me so. I wanted to spit and kick. I was glad to cause myself pain, there being no one else to hurt.

I found a shuffling step that didn't bump my ribs too badly and made my creeping way across the floor and then, slowly, up the stairs. The light at the top, dim as it was, made my eyes blink and water. It being daytime, there was no one much about in the hall or parlour, but clear as anything I could hear thuds and footsteps in the kitchen. I opened the door. The room was empty save Dora's rat of a son, Jacky, standing at the open back door. It was from the yard that the thumps came.

Jacky, being the sly-boots he was, stood half behind the door frame and tilted his head to peer out. He was jiggling about on his feet and had his fists clenched by his sides. I could see quite clearly past him—my husband was bare to the waist, mufflers upon his hands, beating the dummy so hard that it was leaking its straw, and clouds of dust and chaff billowed about his head.

My heart filled with a great tenderness to see him. I'd never seen him set-to in quite that way. He trained with me often enough, but he was always set upon furthering my fight. Here he was pounding that dummy like a warrior, and oh, my days, he looked fine doing it. He was powerful as a dray horse. He was rippling and rage.

I was shuffling painfully forward all this time. When I reached Jacky, he looked sulkish and drew his head back so that I might pass him. As I came out into the dust and daylight, I spied Mr Dryer, leaning against the wall to the left of me, watching my husband sweat and mill.

Tom caught sight of me then, and his hands stopped in midair. He wobbled on his feet, he stopped so sudden. The cloud of dust about him came down, glittering in the light, and stuck to his shoulders and chest.

"Ruthie." He came to me and took me gently by the elbows as though I might fall. "You shouldn't be out of bed."

There was dust in his eyelashes.

"You beat that dummy near as bad as I'm beat." It came out in a whisper. I was so dry.

"Come," he said, "let's get you inside. You need to sit. Oh, you shouldn't be up."

He turned me gently, and I let him. Jacky's head had appeared at the edge of the door again, and as we turned I saw it disappear. Tom stood, holding my elbow.

"By your leave, I'll take my wife inside, sir," he said.

I looked at Tom, but his eyes were on Mr Dryer. Slowly I turned my head.

Mr Dryer nodded. "Yes, Tom, take Mrs Webber inside and return to me. We are not done, you know."

Mr Dryer's eyes went to me. He didn't look angry. That was my first thought.

"I am going to make your husband champion of all England," was all he said to me. He didn't ask about my injuries. He only declared this wild notion and then turned away and scanned the sky as though looking for patterns in the clouds.

* * *

OH, IT WAS A STRANGE MIXTURE for me. I was bitter and I couldn't help it. Mr Dryer had turned away from me as a cully would his regular miss when a pretty new creature came to the convent; I was cast aside the moment Tom threw his fist at the fair. I'd been fighting for Mr Dryer for near my whole life, and now he didn't even feel the loss of me. My days, but I felt it. My hand was broke, and badly; if Mr Dryer hadn't taken a fancy to Tom, what should we have done? I couldn't fight for months, if ever again. I must be glad; I was glad. And here was the most bitter piece of it: Tom was to try for a dream so great I'd never have thought of wanting it for myself; it was impossible, of course, for a woman. But I'd done things most women couldn't do. I'd brought in the money, I'd stood upon the stage. Now here was Tom, taking all I'd done and doing it, and more. If he should succeed, we'd be risen further than we'd ever dared dream. I couldn't help but be proud—but what painful pride it was.

AND SO TOM'S TRAINING BEGAN. Mr Dryer came ever more often to the house, but now he came for Tom. Sometimes he had him thumping at the dummy in the yard, but most often he took Tom away with him, to run for miles beside the carriage or to fight. Sometimes, after a mill, Tom came home with his pockets jingling, and if Dora thought herself entitled to a cut of it, I never heard her ask. But then, Tom knew my sister well enough to keep her sweet; he brought home cider for all the house in jugs from The Hatchet, he brought in whole joints and gave them over to Dora without a blink, and watched her serve herself first when the meat was cooked.

"We should be saving, Tommy," I said. "Keep your coin. We should have something laid by."

"In case I lose? You'd have me jinx myself," Tom said, and wouldn't keep a penny back.

One afternoon he turned to me as I fumbled with my boots, and taking me by the wrists—to be sure he didn't hurt my injured mauler—he gently pulled me up to stand before him.

"Mr Dryer's waiting for you," I said.

"Let him wait, then," he said. "I've a present for you. I meant to wait till tonight, but I can't say how late I'll be. Besides, I'm bursting with it!"

"Do not you burst, my love," I said, "but you shouldn't spend your money on me."

"What else is there in the world to spend it on?"

"You're too good," I said. "Our dinner last night, and our bacon this morning, that was enough for me."

"It wasn't enough for me," Tom said, and he went to the trunk at the foot of our bed and fetched out a folded cloth. This he gave to me with such high pride I felt my chest tighten even before I saw what it was.

It was a dressing gown, pinkish, with white embroidery at the neck and cuffs. It was of softest damask, so soft that I couldn't stop stroking it. It ran through my hands like warm milk. I couldn't take my eyes from it.

When at last I looked up, he was looking at me with eyes as soft as the cloth between my fingers. I couldn't find words to thank him, but I knew my mug showed what I felt.

Tom said, "You've never had a dressing gown, all the time we've been married. I've always wished one for you. Lilac, the lady said the colour's named. Ain't that a pretty word?"

The unshed tears burned my throat like gin. Never mind that we'd not a stick of furniture besides our bed and our battered trunk. Never mind that I had only one dress to wear when I wasn't fighting, and that one ragged at the hem. My husband had bought me a dressing gown soft as a whisper, a dressing gown that a lady might wear. Somebody else's work-roughened hands had taken the needle to this lovely cloth. Somebody else's eyes had squinted by rushlight to work the neck so fine. And that it should be this, when a different dressing gown had brought me to Mr Dryer. But I never had told Tom about that.

* * *

THAT EVENING DORA AND I sat at the kitchen table, she in a waspish temper, Mr Dryer having got another baby on her and she unable to shift it.

"It'll be a monster when it comes," she said, drumming her fingers on her belly. "I've tried every cure on it."

"It's hardy, at least." I was gently rubbing lard into my hand, which had lately had the splints off it and was as twisted and ugly as a chicken's foot. "It may as well know the kind of mothering it can expect."

"Oh, it's strong. It'll be in your image: ugly and impossible to keep down."

I smiled a little at this, meant as insult but quite sweet to my puffed-up ear.

"Don't think that means I'll look after it," I said.

"You should indeed take it." Dora got up heavily and began to clank around in the larder. She had a bottle hidden in there, and she always did make a great deal of noise fetching it out. I think she was hitting the jars with a spoon so that I'd not hear where it was kept.

"I'm even less the little mother than you are," I said.

"You keep your belly flat enough." Dora returned with her bottle and held it up to the lamp. She shook it and peered at its dark blue glass like Ma peering at a shilling. She must've determined it was enough, for she poured some into my cup as well as her own and sat again.

"I take that many hits to the guts," I said. "Would you like me to do the same for you?"

"You, out-at-heels as you are? You couldn't thrash Jacky."

"I'd break my hand again for the pleasure of driving the breath and the babber out of you," I said.

Dora, seeing me grown gloomy, only laughed; it brought my sister up to see me brought down. I didn't think she'd thought much upon how far I'd rise, if Tom did become champion. Or perhaps she thought I'd bring her up with me. Perhaps I would.

Above us we could hear one of the girls giving it her all. Dora raised her eyebrows.

"That one shrieks near as shrill as you," I said.

"She's working well, I'll give her that credit. Go and see how the new lad does."

"Me? It takes me an age to go anywhere," I said. Though I was much better, I was still not able to move at much of a pace.

"I'm fat and my feet hurt," Dora said, "and you're bringing nothing into the house. That lad's wages are due to your husband leaving his post. Now go and see how he does, before I find it in me to shake you by the hand."

She meant my broken hand, of course. I stood, holding the table with my left, and went to the kitchen door. Opening it, I could see the front door half open, the dark shape of the new boy against the evening sky.

"Go out properly," Dora said, seeing I meant to just stand at the door and look.

"What do you want me gone for? You needn't hide to break wind. Or belch some of that gas out of you. You're just blown up with air; there's no infant on you."

"You're blown up full of something, and it ain't air." Dora tried to summon a belch but only made a face.

"Handsome, ain't you," I said.

There came the sound of voices on the step. Dora sat up straight and looked at me. I ignored her, though she wanted only a nod to tell her it was Mr Dryer and Tom come back, which I knew by then it was.

In they came, Tom helping Mr Dryer along. Mr Dryer's pale face had some colour in it and his hair had come down. His hat was too low, as though it'd been jammed upon his head. Tom had caught himself a mark across one cheek and I could smell the fight on him, salt and something else that I can't explain, but any pug knows about. I could smell the rum on both of them.

They saw me at the same time. Tom made gleeful eyes at me; he wanted to run to me and tell me all he'd been doing, but he'd not say a word of it while Mr Dryer stood there. Mr Dryer didn't greet me at all, only said, "Tell your sister I am arrived," and took himself off into the parlour. He walked carefully, as though he might at any moment tumble.

I turned and looked at Dora, who was already heaving herself up from the table. Then I turned back and straight into Tom's arms. He'd come upon me that quietly that I didn't hear him. My husband was beginning to learn how to carry his size. His neck was clammy where the night air had chilled the sweat on him.

"You have to towel off, Tommy," I said. "You'll catch cold, else."

Dora pushed past us where we stood in the doorway. We moved aside for her but didn't let go our hold on each other.

Tom said, "How d'you fare, Dore?"

She only huffed in reply. I didn't even look at her, only looked up at my good man.

"I'd have dried off, only Mr Dryer threw my coat to me and I didn't like to say. So I just put it on and then he was having me shake hands with swells and it was too late for it."

"I expect they liked that all right, shaking your sweaty mauler."

"Don't you want to know who won, Ruth?"

"I know who won, my love. And I can say that without even you telling me who you were against."

"You want to hear about this one, mind." Tom smiled wide at me, and I got a little shock.

"Oh, yes," he said, "I lost a tooth. But I wasn't using it much," and he laughed.

"Come on, then," I said, and took him into the warm kitchen. Dora had left her gin on the table. I poured the whole of it into two mugs. Then I wet a rag in cold water for his poor knuckles, which were already stiffening up. Then I let him tell me.

Those three gents had taken him to The Hole in the Wall, a tavern Tom and I didn't much visit. They took him there and he found the whole place filled with the fancy in tall hats and tailcoats, all waiting for him.

"I nearly piddled myself," he said. "There's something fearful about a gang of them like that."

I knew what he meant; just the thought made the back of my neck itch. They didn't mean him harm, though. What they did was, they took Tommy into a back room, and there they set him against a boy from Bath, an apprentice chandler.

"We were fighting so close I could barely swing. The room was packed with swells; I kept thinking I'd jab a gent with my elbows," Tom said. "When I knocked the lad down, they all leapt out of his way and still he fell against one gent's leg."

The fight was what the fancy term a trial, to see what a man's made of. They came out to see how Tom would fare, and they'd not been satisfied till he'd basted the chandler's boy so badly that they carried him off in a cart.

"Mr Dryer's that pleased," Tom said, then, "he says he wants to have us close by him. He says he'll give us a house to live in, on his land."

Tom shook his head, and I found myself shaking mine. The idea was too strange to credit. We'd neither of us had a house of our own, and for my part, I couldn't have told you where in the world Mr Dryer lived, though he'd been coming to the convent so long.

"He was pretty well in his cups," Tom said, taking his hand from the towel and flexing it gently. He winced to do it.

"I've never seen him fuddled before," I said.

"I had to help him along to his coach, he was that bad. He called me a soldier. He kept saying, 'You're a soldier, Tom'; I couldn't hush him."

"Look at you," I said. "He's never once called me anything. I couldn't swear he knows my name. I'd swear home he don't."

Tom laughed, and then cocked his head, listening.

"He's having trouble with the stairs," he said.

Dora's voice came, impatient and scolding.

Tom got up and looked out of the kitchen door.

"He's on his knees. Your sister's trying to lift him."

"Let me see." I went to the door.

Mr Dryer's hat had fallen off and he was indeed sagging upon the stair, both hands upon the rail. He wasn't quite on his knees, but more hovering himself just above. Dora had her hands upon his elbow and was trying to heave him up. I laughed aloud and she saw me, so I spoiled the game for myself. Tom got him into bed pretty quick after that, though his poor hands were so sore and stiff.

MR DRYER WENT HOME the next day, or perhaps that same night, before Tom and I laid eyes on him to see how his revels had left him. We'd a few days peace then; Tom and I thought him ashamed to show his mug and laughed over it. As the days went on and became a week and then two, we kept laughing, but I knew Tom was feared Mr Dryer never would come back. I knew the old goat would be back at the convent, for when had he ever stayed away? I expected him well enough. What I didn't expect was what came.

Tom and I were coming up from the cellar, he with his hand—fairly well healed up—under my elbow, though I was near mended again myself. When we crossed the last step, Tom gave a huff of surprise. Jacky stood pressed against the wall like a clammy grey serpent, as though he meant to leap out at us. His hair was as tangled as a beggar-boy's.

"Oh, my days," I said, "look at this creeping thing."

I always did say something like that when I came across Jacky. I liked him to know that I saw him and he only made himself a fool.

"I came to find you," Jacky said.

It was always queer to hear him speak because he did it so rarely. His voice was quite usual, just like any other boy's; you'd have expected him to hiss.

"You found us," I said. "What prize do you get by it?"

"There's a man outside on a cart says to fetch Tom," Jacky said, as though he was telling a juicy piece of gossip.

"Right, then," Tom said. "Let's go and see a man, shall we?"

There was a dogcart upon the street, just a one-horse rattler of the kind you might see anywhere. The sight that had brought Jacky out to gawp wasn't the cart, but the man driving the thing, all done up in livery with shiny buttons and a silver wig. This was novelty indeed; we had plenty of nobby footmen call, but they came as cullies and would leave off their livery so as their employers wouldn't discover where they took their leisure hours.

"Look at the shine on that coat," the new lad said, seeing me come to the door. He moved aside so that I could stand next to him.

"We'll have you dressed up like that, if Tom makes enough wins," I said.

"I'd not throw it back at you," he replied.

Tom went out there bold as anything, as though liveried footmen called for him every day. I stayed in the doorway, next to the new lad, feeling as much of a creeping sly-boots as Jacky. Jacky stood behind me and peeked out through the gap left between me and the bully.

The footman looked devilish queer up there in his shiny coat, on the dusty seat. I could see he fancied himself pious as a saint. Tom greeted the cull as friendly as he did everyone, and I saw well enough that this lay-preacher knew what kind of a house he'd come to and was all over sour about it. His mug was as pinched as a cat's backend. He shook Tom's hand as though he'd rather not and kept his hand curled when he pulled away. I could see him itching to wipe it off. I'd never much cared when folk were uppity at me, but I couldn't abide Tom being treated low. My fists clenched by my sides without my meaning to, and the pain that shot up my arm from my broken mauler made the sweat pop out on my neck.

When Tom came back inside, he was frowning. He didn't say a word about my black face, though I could feel the glower upon it like an iron hand about my brow. His worried mug smoothed out my own.

"What is it?" I asked.

Jacky came sidling up, and I turned and showed him my good fist. He started and moved back quick enough; he could see how much I'd have liked to fib him one.

Tom shook his head. "He's Mr Dryer's man," he said, "come to fetch us to our new house. He says he'll be back for us in an hour."

I didn't know what reply to make. I stood staring at him like a noddy.

"What'll we do?" I said, at last.

"What can we do? We must gather our things and go, mustn't we?"

And indeed, what else could we do, then? Back in the cellar, I stood still and couldn't think where to start. It was Tom who had to begin putting what few things we had into our trunk. It didn't take long, for the trunk was almost all we had and we already kept our clothes in it. All he had to put in were the small things: my hairbrush, Tom's razor, our mufflers. We didn't know what to do with the jug, the ewer, the thunder pot.

At last Tom said, "Leave them. Leave them, you haven't even a good hand to carry them."

Tom was half laughing as he said it, but I left them where they were. I was as dazed as if I'd taken a fib to the chops. I was moving as though I was pushing through treacle.

I couldn't help Tom much with the trunk; he insisted, in any case, that I shouldn't, and began dragging it up the stairs by its handle. I went up to see who might be about to help him and it struck me: I had to bid farewell to the folk in the house, to Dora and to Ma. I told the new bully on the door to help Tom, if he could do it without leaving the door too long.

I climbed the stairs. My belly shook. My ribs ached.

Dora's chamber door was shut. She answered my knock by calling out, "Hush up and go away."

"It's me," I called.

"Hush up, Ruth," she called back.

"Are you alone?"

"If I am, it's not your company I want."

I paid no heed and opened the door. My sister was lying on her back in bed, her belly making a little hill beneath the blankets. Her face was as free from paint as it ever was, the skin only a little streaked with white, the carmine caught in the lines on her lips. Even unkempt as she was, she wore a dressing gown laced up the front with scarlet ribbons. Her head lay propped on a bolster to keep her hair nice, pushing her chin down toward her chest.

"I knew you'd come in," she said.

"Then you should've just bid me enter," I said.

"I'd not rob you of your little joy in disobeying me," she said. Her voice was made soft by gin. She'd been left by Mr Dryer these last days, the same as Tom and I.

"Mr Dryer's sent a cart for us," I said. I came a little closer and stood near the end of the bed. Dora looked as weary as I'd ever seen her. That unshakeable babe was giving her a rough time.

"For us?" Dora struggled to sit up.

"For Tom and me."

"Oh." She slumped back down. "Climb on it, then."

"He's taking us to live in a cottage on his land."

"I know, he told me he would. You're luckier than you deserve to be."

"I'll come back," I said. I sounded quite usual. I might've been telling my sister I was going to The Hatchet, not leaving the only home I'd ever had.

"Do what you will," she said, and closed her eyes.

"He'll come back to you soon, mind, and he won't like to find you so bedraggled. I'll tell one of the girls to come and make your mug nice."

My sister neither moved nor spoke. I turned to leave, feeling as though I'd like to strike her or bring up the contents of my belly or both.

When I'd crossed the room and had my hand upon the door, she said, "Take the gown I took from Lizzy before she died; she pinched it, in any case. It's too dull for me, and Lord knows you've nothing respectable."

I turned around. Dora still had her eyes shut. She waved one arm toward her clothes press. I crossed to it.

"It's the blue muslin thing," she said, "and there's an apron for it. You may as well have the plain shift, as well. I never use it. Don't slam the door when you leave."

She turned over with a little breath of effort at moving her bulk and pulled the blankets over her head.

The press was full of Dora's silks, all of them bright, a rainbow of sliding cloth. Beneath them lay a gown I'd never seen before, in bluish-green silk and devilish old-fashioned. It wasn't the kind of gown I expected my sister to have, but I thought the cloth was good. I lifted it carefully, and there was the blue dress. It was a lovely thing, good muslin with green sprigs upon it. I picked it up as carefully as if it'd been glass. It was indeed respectable. No wonder it'd lain unused.

Dora didn't move as I crossed the room to go. I should've thanked her, but I found I couldn't, and in the end it was easier to just close the door soft, and let the quiet click speak for me.

The staircase up to the garret was beginning to sag. I climbed it as careful as I could, keeping my left hand upon the wall to stay steady.

However frail Ma grew, she never lost her hold over my nerve. I, who could stand up against a miller twice my weight and send him to the ground with one blow to the windpipe, now I knocked upon Ma's door—which had been my own—and felt as creeping as I had as a babe. A noise came from within which might, or might not, have been meant to bid me enter. I put my good hand upon the door and swung it wide.

The smell of the place was truly, cruelly foul. It was thick as flommery; night soil and medicines and Ma's own flesh rotting from her frame. It crept warm into your nose and throat. You could taste it; you could near enough see it. Tendrils of it came down into the rest of the house, but noth-ing could prepare you for the experience of opening that door and walking into it as though it were a bath. You might as well climb into the pit be-neath the privy—perhaps it was worse even than that. I stood for a mo-ment on the threshold, just to firm up my nerve.

The window didn't open, but we might've taken Ma out every month and cleaned all we could with lye or burned sweet herbs. Instead she lay up there and the most we did was send Jacky up with broth and medicine. I couldn't have said when last I'd climbed up there to see her; I wondered if Dora ever did. It was Jacky who brought the pot down in the mornings to empty. He lived up there in the stink, scuttling about the attic like a white rat.

He put his head up now from beneath the bed, and I thought again what a bird's nest his hair was. Mr Dryer being so occupied with Tom, he'd not called for Jacky as he would've in the usual course of things. No one in the convent would brush Jacky's hair without Mr Dryer to brush it for. Jacky gave me one of his queer, cutty-eyed looks and disappeared again. God alone knew how he fit under there, the bed was that low. He must've been flat on his belly.

Ma was shamming sleep, in case my footsteps should be Dora, coming to vex her. Her face, once handsome enough to earn her the name Twelve-penny Helen, was grown queerer than ever. She was lumpen as a potato, all curious bumps and sores. The quilt was wet with her spittle. Someone had left a filthy bucket beside the foot of the bed, filled with yellow water. A rag floated in it like a dead fish.

"Ma," I said, "I know you ain't sleeping. You never sleep."

"Indeed I never can"—her eyes cracked open—"or these girls would poison me in a moment. They're witches all."

The chamber was small and poky, filled too close with Ma's furniture. It was all old hulking stuff, dark and heavy, making the air more stifling still: a dresser, a clothes press, a chair with a high, curved back. The only thing that was missing was her bed; Dora had taken that. Ma slept in the straw-pallet bed that Dora and I had shared as girls. Perhaps Jacky curled up there too. There was nowhere else, unless he took the hearthrug.

I sat in the wooden chair beside the bed: near, but not too near. There was a book beside the chair, very much worn about the binding.

"Did you hear me, Ruthie?" Ma said. "They'll see me cold if I sleep for a moment. I'd let them too, if I didn't think they'd use me ill, afterward."

Her hands were in fists on the quilt. Her knuckles were so swollen as to look nearly as sore as my own.

I couldn't think how to make Ma a good-bye she'd understand. Instead I picked up the book. There was an engraving on the inside cover which showed a lady looking upward with a look of rapture, as an eagle swooped down upon her. The bird looked about to tear her heart from her breast, with its terrible beak open and its talons poised before it. The lady thrust her breast toward the bird as if offering a gift.

I turned the page and stared at the letters there. Dora, I knew, could read a little; Mr Dryer had taught her. Perhaps she'd left the book there? Did my sister climb that narrow stair and sit in the cloud of rotting flesh, reading to the woman she'd so gladly confined there? It was a strange notion. And surely, I thought, Dora couldn't read so well as this, all these words printed so small, and in such great numbers?

Dora had started, once, to teach me the letters of my name; I thought I knew them still. When I tried to pick them from that great block of ink, I found them jumbled up in my head and I couldn't be sure that I remembered rightly. Soon I grew vexed at my own stupidity and threw the book down. Ma had closed her eyes again. Her breathing rattled as wet as if she were drowning.

I could hear the sounds of the convent starting up: the cullies came in, the girls came down, they went up again together, the door closed, the creaking began. Ma must lie here night after night, listening to the play beneath.

At last I simply said it. "Tom and I are leaving. Mr Dryer's given us a house."

If I'd thought her asleep, I was mistaken.

"That man's a devil," Ma said. "He brings devils and surgeons. They'll sell me to the animists."

"Anatomists, not animists."

"They will, I tell you. They'll sell me before I'm dead, to be cut up and poked about."

"You're too raggedy for a surgeon, Ma. You'll turn to dust before you die, so slowly are you taking it."

"The man brings them in, to look at me," Ma insisted. "I'm too old for this work, I told them, but they take their pleasure on me, whether I gives them leave or no."

Her clawed hands began to twitch on the counterpane. It was a quilt that Dora and I had made by turns as girls, to a twelve-patch pattern. You could see the patches I'd made; I was always clumsy with a needle.

"No one's taken their pleasure on you in years," I said. "Who was this cull, a suicide?"

I began to tell her about Tom's being trained for champion of England. When next I said Mr Dryer's name, she shouted out, "I seen that gentleman! He meant to have taken us all," so loudly that I had to leave off my story.

"Hush, you know Mr Dryer. Hush, now."

Ma wouldn't quiet. She writhed about in the bed and drummed her painful fists upon the quilt in a spasm. Her face, always bulging now, seemed readying to scream. Her eyes were wide, and her breathing came quick. Her lips drew back to show gums black as a hound's, hung with cords of spittle that took light from the lamp like dew-dropped cobwebs.

Jacky's head poked back up beside the bed.

"God alive," I said. I'd forgotten he was there.

Jacky gave me a sidelong glance and then took up a bottle from beside the bed and filled a spoon. He fed Ma as gentle as if he were the mother and she the child. She took it, her lips covering his fingers as well as the spoon. Jacky prised his white fingers free and wiped them on the quilt's edge. Then he crawled back under the bed. I could hear him there, whispering to himself. Or perhaps it was Ma he whispered to. She'd not release the spoon long after it must've been empty, sucking on it as a babber will suck on your fingers if the breast is dry.

When she opened her mouth at last, the spoon fell onto the quilt trailing such a high quantity of drool that I determined I'd leave it where it fell. It formed a dark puddle across a patch that Dora had stitched, scarlet flannel with a border of white.

Ma's eyes had gone dull and dreaming.

"She'll sell me if she can," she said, slowly, "and so she should, she says, I sold her so many times over."

"Hush," I told her. I'd have patted her hands if I could've borne to.

"You tell your husband to take all he can from the gentry. They'll take all they can from him." Her head tipped back, while her mouth stayed open.

I was surprised to hear her say anything so sensible; I'd not thought her listening.

"I will," I said. "I know it well enough."

"Give them what you must and not more." She held out her hand, her face still turned to the eaves. If her eyes were open, I couldn't see them.

"Take it," she said, gesturing with her closed hand. "It's less than you're owed. Take it, and don't tell Dora."

At first I thought it was an empty fist, but when her swollen fingers uncurled there was a tooth lying on her palm, a pitiful blood-streaked thing. I didn't take it, but neither could I stop looking at it.

Her hand dropped back to the bed. The tooth rolled out and came to rest in the wet patch.

"They'll take all they can," Ma told the rafters. "Take it, and tear it, and get their fingers in it."

I rose then and closed the door upon the sour stink of her like someone escaping from a tomb.

Chapter 14

✦ ✦ ✦

The sour-faced old goat came back dead upon the hour. He looked as ill-tempered as before; it would've been comical if we'd not been to climb up beside him. Of course, as Ma always said, Christ himself came down amongst the whores and blessed them all; this fart-catcher wouldn't even step down from his cart to help us with the trunk. The trunk wasn't so heavy, in any case. I knew we'd not much, but when it was packed it seemed even less, and shameful. How easily our lives could be loaded into a dogcart. Tom carried the whole from door to cart in one journey.

I settled myself in the back, which smelled of dogs and straw, holding on tight to the basket I'd packed myself with the only things I called precious: the lilac dressing gown and the cigar box which held the feathers Tom had brought me, and one more thing—wrapped in the old, stained dressing gown was the little portrait of the girl in mourning. I wondered how long it would be before Dora noticed I'd whipped it from the parlour. She might even beat one of the misses as having stolen it. The blue muslin she'd given me I'd put in the trunk, so that I'd not dirty it on the road.

The convent stood above us, its eyes blank in its narrow face. Not a soul came to the window to see us leave, though the neighbours all came out and called, "Got yourself a coach and driver now, have you, Tom?" and the like. Of the convent folks, you'd never know they were there. I'd not been fashed to wake the misses to bid them farewell; let them find us gone.

They'd likely be relieved to hear it, Dora being fond of using me as her bullying arm. Only the new lad on the door was there to wave to us, and he'd known us least time of all.

Tom climbed in beside me, cheery and full of ginger, waving to all the folks watching from their doorways. He leaned back on the wooden trunk, his long legs bent up, looking as easy as a man resting under a tree under a blue sky. You'd never know he was going somewhere unfamiliar, to chance all he had against a dream. He looked as though we were going on a picnic. I couldn't play-act that I felt as merry as he, and Tom, seeing this, poked out his tongue at the liveried back of the old bastard driving us, and looked to see if he'd made me smile.

My belly had the shakes as we drove away; bile rose at the very notion of the road ahead. I found I couldn't look back. I'd been born in the convent, and I suppose I'd thought I'd die in that dark house, with its constant footfall. It wasn't that I wanted to stay, more that I couldn't imagine where we were going.

As we neared the end of the street, Tom said, "There's Jacky, look. I swear he's crying to see us leave. I never saw the whelp cry before, a day in his life."

I turned to see his slight frame standing at the convent door. Perhaps there were tears upon his mug, though more likely they were shadows. To my eye, his face was as blank as the windows.

As Tom raised a hand to him and cried out, "Be a good boy, now, Jacky," he stepped back into the dark of the hall and shut the door against Tom's good-bye. Tom laughed and dropped his hand.

"He can't have been crying much," was all he said.

The haughty jackanapes at the reins hardly said a word to us, and I couldn't have told you what position he held in Mr Dryer's house; I was as green to it all as that liveried smatchet would've been, had he been asked to give a sermon on the running of the convent. In any case, once we were away on the road he whipped up the horses and drove for a good two hours. Tom and I jolted around in the back, holding on to the wooden sides and trying to keep steady the trunk and basket. I could only hold the side with my one good hand, and had devilish work to keep the other hand steady—it jumped about with every hole in the road, and made the bones thrum wickedly.

When once the road began to unroll before us and we passed through streets we didn't often walk and then into countryside proper, Tom couldn't keep his face steady; so many feelings crossed it that it almost seemed to ripple. I could see how excited and fearful he was, and I couldn't say I felt differently. I'd barely been outside the city before in my life, except once to visit Tom's father and brothers at Coalpit Heath, and a few times to the prizefights at Lansdown. At Lansdown it was always dark when we arrived, and all I knew of the place was a vast crowd gathered and a quantity of gin in my hand. The small grey mining village of Coalpit Heath was the only picture of a place outside Bristol that I had clear in my mind, and it would keep popping up whenever I thought of the word "cottage"—a little house with coal-dust about it, and barefoot children coming to see us draw up.

There I was, travelling into the country, to be a wife in a cottage. It was so unlikely that I couldn't take hold of the idea; it slipped about in my mind like an eel in a bucket. I'd never been mistress of my own home, nor anything you could call respectable. The future was grown so queer that I felt as numb as in the moments between taking a fib and feeling the pain of it.

At last, when there wasn't a comfortable position I could sit in and my arse was grown as numb as my heart, we began upon a lane closed in by tall hedgerows that seemed to go on forever. Every now and then the hedgerow was broken by a gate leading into a field, and then I could see the countryside stretching away so far it took your breath, with never a house nor man. I preferred the blinkered lane, though it was a little like travelling a tunnel. When finally the cart drew to a halt, I thought it a mistake. We'd arrived beside a pair of towering gates, each one topped with a brass lantern. The road behind these gates stretched away, up a hill and out of sight. It was like the entrance to a kingdom, except that I could see nothing beyond the gates but road, and on either side of it, fields of stubbly yellow grass. The roof of the house that stood beside these gates didn't even reach the lantern's tops, but still I thought it so grand I hardly liked to look at it. This wasn't what I'd brought to mind at the word "cottage." It was as elegant as a Bristol merchant's house, only not so large, with its leaded arched windows and curly bits all about the roof. It was tiled with black slates, shining with recent rain. The walls were of pale yellow stone and smooth as butter, the front door painted blue. There were curtains at the windows. It was clean all over, as though someone had scrubbed the whole with a bucket and brush.

I only stared at the towering gates against the sky, and that hedge-tunnelled lane, and the golden stone of the cottage, which wasn't a cottage. Behind it lay that road, winding through the stubble of the fairy kingdom, and over the hill. It was all too strange; I couldn't believe we were meant to climb out here and go inside. I wasn't sure even that I wanted to.

"This is never the place," I said.

Tom looked worriedly at the golden walls of it and shook his head a little.

"Sir," he called to Old Pious, sitting straight-backed in front of us, "is this the place?"

Sour-face turned, nodded once, and turned back again. Tom shrugged and climbed down. He reached out for the trunk, and I laid down my basket and moved to help him. Once moving, it was easy enough to keep doing so. I pushed the trunk out, making sure he had hold of it, and then I climbed down myself, holding my basket close.

Old Pious didn't turn to look at us but stared down the lane as though he could see something interesting beyond the hedge. He must've been peeking though, for the moment my boots touched the ground he whipped up the horses and off he went, with only a raised hand for farewell.

"What, off so soon?" Tom called out after him, and to me, "There goes the most obliging cull I ever thought of throttling."

"He barely waited till I was down from the cart," I said. "He must've felt your hands a-twitching."

"A moment more and I'd not have been able to stay them," Tom said. "I'd have found his neck in my hands before I bid them go there. He did give me the key, mind," and here he reached into his pocket. "That's the only thing the piss-licker did for us."

I kept my eyes upon his dear face, but at his words I felt the scrubbed front of the cottage behind me and I'd never felt so filthy in my life. My skirts were dusty from the road, the hem turned quite black, though that was nothing new at all. The sole of one of my boots I'd mended myself with a nail, and wasn't quite straight.

"It's never the place," I said again.

"How come I to have the key, then?" Tom dangled it in front of me by a piece of string. It was just the key for that place, as curly as the roof-edge and shined up bright.

"I'd say you pinched it," I said, not in any seriousness.

"Then would that hedge-preacher have brought us here?" Tom was beginning to smile. "Come, my love. I should carry you across the threshold, by rights." He held his arms out to me.

"We've been wed six years," I said, but I could see I was spoiling his fun, so I shrugged and put my basket down with great care, and then reached out to be lifted.

"We'll have to come back for our trunk, now," I said, though I was glad of how strong he was just then. I could bear to be carried across that scrubbed step in my husband's arms, where perhaps my own dusty feet would've needed pushing.

"You're the best thing I own," Tom said, and made a great fuss of fitting the key into the lock whilst keeping me steady. It turned as smooth as anything, as newly oiled as you would expect of a door so shining as that one.

He pushed the door open with one great fist.

How to describe what scene met me then, without running on into raptures? For a girl not raised as I'd been, no doubt it was a common enough house, but to me everything in the place seemed too good, too clean to touch. There was a good-sized grate, all swept out, and a fire laid ready. There were two three-legged stools beside the hearth, where we might sit and warm ourselves. The mantel held a teapot and two mugs, all in tin, and with the dents beaten out near perfect, so that only where the light caught them could they be seen at all. Above this was hung a picture prettier to my eye than anything Dora had at home, all in needlework, of a boy and a girl holding hands beside a stream. There was no hearthrug, but that was the only thing wanting, I thought, in the whole of the house. Beside the window was placed a round table with curved legs, and two chairs, not matching, but quite as pretty. One, that had a heart-shape about the back of it, I thought especially nice. The other, more sturdy, I thought Tom could sit upon without fear of snapping it beneath him. Everything in the place was nicely done. It was respectable, that was the word. The floor was of grey flags, as clean as anyone could wish. The curtains had a pattern of yellow leaves upon a blue ground, and only when I examined them close could I see that they were faded; the inside of the folds was a deeper hue than the outside, which always had the light upon it. The curtains were lined with something soft, in cream. A bracketed shelf was upon the wall for what few things we had.

Tom set me on my feet, as quiet as I; it was a powerful thing, to be in that place and try to imagine it ours. I walked around careful as a priest in a bawdy house, my hands behind my back so that I'd not be tempted to touch. I could barely breathe with the particular niceness of it. Even things that might've seemed quite ordinary in the convent, an iron boot-scraper beside the door, a basket of kindling beside the hearth, here seemed neater, more special, than anything I'd laid eyes on before. True, Dora had silken gowns in the brightest shades imaginable, and oil lamps, and lace. But those things were coloured by the house that held them, and here—I'd not have been surprised to find that the furniture wouldn't cast shadows.

"You look like a straw man in a forge," Tom said, "afraid to touch anything. Look, this is all ours, Ruthie. Ours for a good while, at least. We'll starve if you're too afraid to bring your hands from behind your back."

I drew my hands out, and looked at them. They were lumpen claws. The house wouldn't like to have such hands upon it.

Tom came and took them in his own pug's hands. His knuckles were near as bad as mine now and like to get worse, big hands being injured more often, as a rule, than small. His rough thumbs stroked my palm.

"Here, I know what we should do now—let's find the pantry," he said. "Mr Dryer talks all the time of how I'm to build my strength and how he's to have sole charge of my diet; I'll wager he's left us something. Are you hungry, Ruthie?"

"I'm always hungry," I said, suddenly so happy that I began nearly to laugh, "and I've always wished to be fed up strong by some rich swell." I felt as though we'd fooled him, right and true. Look at this house he'd given us! Tom would've fought for pennies a day, and here we were to be fed and coddled. It was beyond anything.

"Come, then, let's see what we've got," Tom said, and kissed me, and I kissed him back, quite as firmly.

I began to laugh in earnest when once I saw the pantry. It was one thing to be awed silent by the polish of a table, but meat—meat was too real to be taken for a dream, and here it was. There must have been nearly half a side of bacon hanging on a hook, and cold mutton under a cloth. There was a cheese, also wrapped in cloth, a jug of milk, an earthenware jar of oats, another of flour, and little lidded jars of sugar and tea. Two loaves of bread—and the price of flour what it was—bread baked by someone else, and brought here for us to eat. Besides that were four eggs in a dish, a good bit of butter, and a basket of potatoes, carrots, and turnips. I'd never seen the like. Tom and I stood and laughed at that pantry like madmen. And then we took down the cold mutton and the bread and Tom hunted out a knife and two plates, calling out all the while, "Where's a knife? Here it is, look! Here's plates, for me and my wife"—he span around as though he were dancing—"here's a roast mutton dinner, here's a big bit of pig," and he slapped the bacon.

"Here's the champion of England," I said, and kissed him, and Tom turned pink with the pleasure of it, for I'd never said such a thing before.

"You light the fire, then," I said, and took the knife from his big mauler.

The meat was lovely stuff, marbled with thick fat and seasoned with something—I knew not what—by some unseen cook's hands in Mr Dryer's kitchen. I cut careful slices, far neater than I'd have carved had I been in the convent—and carried them through to where Tom knelt beside the grate.

Once he had it going, I drew the stools up and we sat, our plates upon our knees, both of us turning to marvel at the rest of the room and then turning back to each other, and then again, we'd turn to look about ourselves. Neither of us thought to sup at the little table. Perhaps that was too great an act of ownership.

The stools beneath us were so newly carved and pegged together that they smelled still of green sap. Beside the fire, a brass bowl was filled with coal so nicely that there wasn't a speck of black dust upon it. The convent could never have been so nice, not if an army of misses had scrubbed it from dawn to dusk. It was too old, the dirt become part of the beams and corners, the boards holding the memory of too many pairs of sailors' feet. No miss had ever lifted her skirt for a sailor in this cottage. Perhaps a pretty, unspoiled maid could kiss her sweetheart here. I wasn't pretty, I could never be called unspoiled, and nor did I feel clean. I felt as awkward as a maid that night and Tom wasn't much better. When at last we got up courage to find the bed and climb into it, we were too shy to do more than hold on to each other.

THAT FIRST MORNING, Mr Dryer came with the dawn while we still lay in bed, too full of the strangeness of the house to rise. He came and sent a boy to knock upon the door, and what else could Tom do but go, and leave me there alone? I spent the day pacing about the house, still too afraid to touch anything, my hand too sore to sew. It was one of the longest days of my life.

When at last Tom came back he was in a queer humour and I was no better; I felt weak, suddenly, as though the dress I wore, the blue sprigged that Dora had given me, had turned my heart womanish. I wanted to run to him and have him hold me, but I'd not let myself. He came in and stamped his boots harder than he need.

"What do you think he had me do today, Ruth?"

"I'm sure I don't know."

"You don't, indeed. He had me stand before his friends so that they might squeeze my arm and say how thick it was."

I put my hands before my mouth, but looking at Tom's face, I began to laugh into them. After a moment he joined in laughing, and then he did come to me. I sank into his arms like a weary man to a bed. I put my hand upon his arm where it came across my body.

"How thick your arm is," I said, in the best swell's voice I could.

"Oh, God, Ruthie, they had me standing there like a noddy."

"A fine kind of training I call it, posing you like a bitch before a cully." I meant it as a joke, but somehow it stopped us laughing. We were both thinking the same thing: we'd come to Mr Dryer's house and now we were in service to him. I'd not seen it so before. I was cursing myself for a fool, I couldn't say if Tom was. His disposition was so much the sunnier, he mayn't have felt it cut him as it did me.

We were indeed in service. Our days became odd ones, even less our own to shape than if Ma had had the running of them. Our food came on a cart, carried into the pantry by a boy in livery, quantities of beefsteak and fresh milk. This boy goggle-eyed Tom like he thought him a hero, and every word from Tom's mouth put him to the blush. Blushing Henry was far more welcome to me than Old Pious of the dogcart, but still I found it strange to be served so, and hear Tom's voice grow ever heartier, at seeing how the lad panted after him.

Tom was under orders to eat meat at every meal, and train hard all the while that he wasn't pushing beef over his tongue. Each morning began with the yolk of an egg mixed with a spoonful of rum, and his face as he swallowed the mixture made me laugh aloud. I took to swilling it with him, so that we could laugh at each other. I made a good play of hating it, but really, it wasn't so very nasty. I came to look forward to it, when once I'd grown used to the feel of the yolk.

Mr Dryer sent a leather dummy, just like the one in the convent yard, and had him set up on a pole behind the cottage. It pained me that my mauler wasn't healed enough that I could spar, but I trained beside Tom in all I could do, bouncing up and down upon bent legs and fibbing at the air, first left, then right, to keep balance. I couldn't join him in the press-ups— my hand wouldn't take my weight so long—but I sometimes sat upon his back to give him a load to push against, patting him and calling him my mule. We practised sparring, our fists stopping in the air, so that Tom might practise attack and riposte. Beside the fire, in the evenings, we pickled his knuckles in brine, till the skin was like leather.

I grew near as lean as Tom. I tried not to dwell upon how useless it was to be training myself up, with no fight to be had. It wasn't in my nature to sit quietly, watching my husband. I'd even have taken a beating, just to set my blood pumping again. I tried to be cheerful, but I could feel the low spirits, always on the edge of my mind, waiting. At night I dreamt of walking up to scratch, the crowd howling.

Every day Mr Dryer came and took Tom away. He was kept nervous by never knowing what use Mr Dryer would put him to; sometimes he only wanted to take Tom around to taverns and gentlemen's clubs to show him off. On other days Mr Dryer had him run beside his horse for miles at a time, and on still others carried him off in the carriage, to pit him against some young bully he fancied as likely. I couldn't swallow my envy on those days, but neither could I admit to its taste in my mouth. I wished it was I sweating there with my fives up; I wished my own knuckles filthy with blood instead of grease from the pans in the scullery. More, I must wave Tom off and wait to hear all he'd done when at last he came home. This I found most trying of all; I'd always been scornful of those wives who did no more than wait for their cullies, and jumped at every sound of boots on the road. Now I found myself straining my ears for Tom's homecoming worse than any soaker's wife—I was a lapdog, with nothing else to hang my day upon. Besides this, I longed to watch, to learn what I could from standing beside the ring. I wanted to hold the bottle and sponge Tom's brow. I wanted to see the maulers flying. By all accounts, the training Tom was receiving was nothing more than sparring for the pleasure of the swell and his friends, but I'd have done it gladly. Mr Dryer had promised my husband a man of experience to have the training of him, and daily Tom expected this prize to appear. I doubted it. Mr Dryer seemed only playing at training; how could he expect to make a champion, the way he was going on? It was only the happiness in Tom's voice that held my tongue still; I couldn't stand to sour him.

Mr Dryer came at all hours, just as he had at the convent; we could be taking breakfast, or readying ourselves for sleep, and here would come the sound of horses, and "Ho, Tom!" and Tom's head would pop up as quick as an old goat called up the convent stairs. His tongue would near hang out with eagerness, on would go his boots, and I'd be suddenly alone.

We'd been made animals in a cage, fed by Mr Dryer's hand and Tom borne off whenever the fancy struck him. I was left useless, slowly turning in an empty room. I knew I should be seeing to my wifely duties, and I could see that the cottage wasn't kept as nice as it had been when first we came there, but I'd never had the running of a nice home before. I'd decide upon a task, some simple thing that I was used to doing at the convent, the scrubbing of the flags, perhaps, and then become distracted in the kitchen, and begin instead scouring a pan to scald the milk, only to forget what I'd meant to do after the pan was cleaned and begin blacking the grate. On other days I'd wash the floor all right, but spend the whole day at it, which might've been done in an hour, for fear of stopping and having to find out what else might be done. I crawled about on knees grown numb, scrubbing over and over ground that had already been scrubbed.

I didn't cook much; the meat and bread being brought to us, I preferred to serve up cold rather than cook up a dinner for which Tom might never arrive. I've never been one to court disappointment, and there was no telling how late Mr Dryer might keep him.

Tom, being an obliging fellow always, never complained but only ate his cold meat and through every mouthful told me of the hits he'd made, and the promises of glory Mr Dryer had repaid him with. For the most part, he'd come back in only because the cull was grown weary of his toy.

"Oh, he's tired of me for today," he'd say, "unless he rolls back up to the door at midnight."

Tom thought as I did, that we must take what we could and be done when once we'd taken it. Where our thoughts ran different was that Tom was sure that this moment would come when he raised his arm as England's champion, where I didn't trust Mr Dryer had a serious intention that way, or that his ideas of training were good enough.

One night Tom didn't come home for supper, nor after that. I spent a lonely evening, my hand still too clumsy to make good work of my mending, and nothing else to do but watch the fire, my cloak about my shoulders for comfort, and whittle a stick. I didn't carve anything of it, only shaved it to a sharp point and then kept the knife at it, peeling it ever sharper, round and round, till it was little more than a pointed stub. Then I swept the sawdust up with my hands as best I could and threw both that and the tiny spear I'd made onto the fire. The sawdust caught while it was still in the air and became a shower of sparks. Then I took up another stick and began again, and thus passed the dullest night imaginable. I could feel the emptiness beyond the cottage walls, and I didn't like it at all. I didn't like to sit there and feel all that countryside pressing in, but neither could I bear to leave the hearth and go up the little staircase to that cold bed.

When at last Tom came in, so late it might best be called early, he looked as merry round the gills as if he'd just gone for a swill of ale an hour before. He saw me standing and put his arms out, smiling, before he saw how sullen I was. His smile dropped, but his arms stayed out.

"What's this?" he said. "Who took my wife and left this sour mopsey?"

"You were gone so long," I said, in a sniveller's voice so unlike my own that it surprised me into silence.

Tom didn't seem to know how to take me either. He dropped his arms and looked hard at me.

"I had to stay, while Mr Dryer would have me there," he said. "You needn't be out of temper; you must know I'd never stay away unless I must. You'll be so glad when I tell you all I've been doing, Ruthie."

I couldn't speak, but only shook my head. Tom stepped across the room and drew me into his arms. I struggled only a little.

"What ails you?" he said, into my hair. "This ain't like you, my fighting wife. When came you to be so weepish?"

I pushed away from him like a ship from dock, feeling the pain travel up my arms as I did. He let me go quick enough, and I saw that he recognised me now, all right.

"Since my husband turned into the quality's cully. When came you to be so cheap?" The spite in my own voice was like a surge of black liquor; my eyes turned from water to fire and seemed to burn in my head.

"Your mind is filth." Tom rubbed at his eyes. "You've no idea what I've been doing."

"I know what things gentlemen do to those they have in their pockets, and I know what men do when they don't come home to their wives."

"Noddy," Tom said, and turned his back on me.

I hated to be brushed off, as Tom well knew. He might've turned his back on purpose to make me leap upon him, which I did, for how could I have done differently? He turned back as he heard me move—my husband was far too fast these days to be taken unawares. He went to seize my wrist as I swung at him, and it was natural to me to use the move we called the Jew's stop: as Tom made to grab my wrist, I chopped his arm with the side of a flat hand, using all the power I had, careless of my own pain. His arm dropped, his eyes tightened, and I knew I'd hit him well. When the Jew's stop is done right, the chopping hand turns with all speed from the arm to strike at the enemy's throat. His neck was unguarded; I could've dealt it a good fib and had him gasping, but some tenderness stayed my hand. Instead of chopping his windpipe closed, I found myself fibbing Tom's chest closed-fisted, which never would hurt a cull as solid with beef as my Tom. We both of us knew then that I'd forgive him, and all the fight went out of us.

Tom reached out for my wrists again, and this time I let him take them. He held me there, my chest to his chest, and looked down into my face.

"Mr Dryer would throw me off my training, Ruthie. No skirt, no drink, no nothing, almost, but beefsteak and sparring. Think you on that, even if you will take me for a cod's-head. He's got me tied up stricter than a monk."

"What does he have you at, then, that keeps you away all night?"

"He took me to Bath, that I'd mill for some swells there. They stayed at their cards and dice, and left me to sleep in a chair by the fire. There was nothing you need feel ill over."

"I know it," I said, "I knew it really."

"I'll not leave you so long again, Ruthie. I'll tell him we can't be parted."

"You needn't," I said, against his chest.

"I'll always come home, Ruthie."

"This ain't home. Tell me we'll not stay here, Tommy."

"Here! Of course we won't. We'll go anywhere we please, when once I'm champion. You and I together."

I tilted up my face to him, and he bent to kiss me.

"And no man the master of us?" I said, against his lips.

"Nor woman neither," he said, and the kiss was a promise.

* * *

A FEW DAYS LATER, as I knelt sweeping out the grate so that I might have a fire when Tom came home, the hooves sounded on the lane and my husband burst into the room even as I was still getting to my feet, brushing the dust off my apron. His face was as flushed as if he'd been at the wet all day.

"He's taking me to London, to begin my training proper, at Fives Court," he cried, looking wildly all about him.

I said only, "What do you look for?"

"Mr Dryer said I'm to fetch what things I need, but I can't think what that might mean."

"Take your coat," I said. "Take your other shirt, take some bread."

"He'll give me bread. My clothes, yes—"

Tom thundered up the stairs to fetch them and came straight down again, bringing only his coat and his razor.

"The shirt's stained," he said.

"I could clean it—" I began.

"Ho, Tom!" came the cry from outside.

Tom jerked as though pulled on a string. "I must go, kiss me, quickly."

I kissed him and he rushed from the cottage, slamming the door in his haste. I went to the window to see him run to a grand carriage pulled by four horses. A gloved hand opened the door; a slice of Mr Dryer's thin face showed itself. My husband's broad back, in its well-worn shirt, disappeared inside that glossy coach, and then the groom flicked the reins and they were gone.

I'd not told him to take care, nor wished him good luck. I didn't know when he'd come back. I stood at the window a long time, looking out at the blank hedge of the lane, the feel of Tom's rough cheek still upon my lips.

Chapter 15

✦ ✦ ✦

No one had been near me for weeks, not a soul since Tom left. The pantry, so well stocked to begin, was dwindling to nothing, its shelves as bare and cold as the trees outside. Why hadn't we guessed that I'd be left thus? We'd had our heads turned by the food and been kept nervous by Mr Dryer's coming whenever the fancy took him. As soon as Tom was gone, so was the liveried footboy. Who'd bring beefsteak to a wife? Mr Dryer always had dropped me from his mind, whenever he'd no use for me. *But oh, Tom, how could you not have thought of it?* We'd neither of us thought of it, or Tom would've asked for a few shillings for me against future earnings, or asked that the pantry be filled, even just a little, till he came home. He might've asked when he'd be home. I'd no notion of when he might come.

Now I stood in the pantry and looked over what was left. The flags were cold on my bare feet, but I'd not fashed myself with stockings. I'd not changed from my gown for a good while, even to sleep, and my nice sprigged dress didn't look so pretty anymore. I didn't like to wear the lilac dressing gown. I wasn't sure how long it was, because all days had grown the same. It had been long enough.

I had a crust of bread, grown hard, which I kept because somehow matters would seem the worse if there were no bread at all. Better to keep this drying crust as a charm, that might in time call other bread to its side.

I had enough oats for three good bowls of porridge, or perhaps seven or eight bowls of gruel. I had no milk, no eggs, but a little cheese left. I had some butter, turning rancid now. I had three turnips, one gone a little soft about the tip, and four small potatoes, and a bowl of fat saved from the last of the bacon, which I was eking out as long as I could stand. I had a jar of preserves, half empty, and a handful of flour, but nothing else to make bread with. And I didn't know when I might get hold of anything else at all. I stood before the shelves and looked over this sorry collection again and again. Each time I broke down and ate something was a defeat, and all I had left must be counted again. Hunger, that wasn't much to me, but I was used to stepping out of my door into streets filled with people I knew and folks selling foodstuffs from carts and trays. If I'd been in Bristol, I'd have had no trouble making a few pennies by my fists, or even by my cunny, if driven to it. Instead I was trapped in the middle of flat fields and grey sky and not a soul around, either to buy or sell.

I went out walking, though I hated to. Inside the cottage, I could almost make believe that I wasn't alone and miles from the places I knew. Outside on the lane, hemmed in by those tall hedgerows of bare and tangled sticks, I could see nothing but what was ahead and behind me, which was to say, only more lane, stretching away till it turned, to wind off to God knew where. When once I wound with it, and the cottage went from view, the sameness of it made me feel trapped, and as blind as your arsehole. The lane was a devilish place, a gaol roofed by blank grey sky. Here and there I came to the gaps in the hedge, crossed by wooden gates, where the wind roared through the gap to bite my face, and dull earthen fields stretched away with only a few scrubby trees to break the view. I felt adrift in an endless and empty world. I could almost have believed that I'd died and been left in limbo as the Papists believed, neither Heaven nor Hell but a blasted, lonely waiting. I'd never in my life been so much alone. I'd never been alone even for a day before Mr Dryer took us.

This, then, was the countryside. These, then, were fields and farms. But where was all the food? Where was the wheat, the cows fat with milk, the chickens, the women with baskets of eggs? I'd not a penny about me, but I'd have worked, or bargained for a supper, if only a farmer could be found. I couldn't imagine that here was the land from which all food sprung. If it was, it was whipped away before ever I saw it, and by invisible hands. I saw nothing I could eat at all, bar nettles, which I gathered and cooked just as I had in Bristol, and once a flock of distant sheep.

I went out walking each day that I could stomach it. I walked in either direction along the lane, but I never chose the road behind the cottage, through the tall gates. I knew that Mr Dryer's house must lie up there, though he himself, I thought, must be in London with my husband. I knew that someone must be there, to keep house for him, Old Pious and the liveried boy, but I couldn't go a-begging. I was saving that road. If I came to walk it, I'd know I'd lost my pride. I walked the lane and went as far as I could stand, though I came to understand later that by the terms of the countryside I walked no distance at all. I'd grow disheartened and turn back, taking with me what damp twigs I could to make the coal go further. The coal was dwindling faster than the food, and the days growing frosty with it.

Back at the cottage, I took a knife from the kitchen and went back out to hack what I could from the hedge, though I scratched my hands and arms cruelly. What I did gather was too green to burn well and smoked miserably.

I let the cottage grow filthy. I didn't comb my hair, or brush down my skirts. I couldn't sleep at night, with the world outside the window filled with animal rustling, and the dark as deep and black as Hell. I slept sometimes in the daytime, as the misses were doing at home. I slept in front of the hearth, with my old cloak spread beneath me to keep the worst of the cold from the flags and my good cloak acting the part of a blanket. Sometimes I was fashed enough to go up and fetch the blankets off the bed, but still every night I took them back upstairs, to lie sleepless in that beamed attic.

One day, fetching water from the well, my eye fell on the dummy hanging in the yard. I left the bucket and stood before it, letting all my rage rise up to my fists. I fibbed it hard enough to knock the straw from it, and oh, my stars, I wished I'd not. The hit set the bones of my hand aflame. I sagged to my knees, holding my hand in front of me, curled over it. Water came to my eyes, not just for the pain. I wasn't built to be a wife, in a cottage, with my husband gone, I was born to stand before a crowd and hear them scream as blood hit the sawdust. Weeping a little, I got back to my feet and beat the dummy with my good left hand till that one sang out too. I didn't care a fig; it was better to break both hands than be brought down to nothing but wife. I beat the leather dummy till I knew I was only beating myself—my good hand was near as sorry as the bad by then. Having injured myself enough, I crept back inside, to sit and stare at walls.

And so I went on. I ate almost nothing but nettles, preferring to watch the turnips grow soft rather than strike them from my list. I believe I may've been taken mad by loneliness. I began to be sure that Tom was gone forever, and that I was left to die, but I think now that I didn't believe it in truth. If I had, I hope I'd have gone out and taken Mr Dryer's road. If I couldn't stand to do that, I could've caught a sheep with my bare hands, or walked till I found a living soul. I'd like to think I'd have walked till I came to Bristol, as I often thought of doing. The one great fear I had in that direction wasn't that I shouldn't find the city, or die before I reached it, though I did think of those things. My fear was that once I walked too far, when once I'd gone past too many crossroads, I'd never again find the cottage. I'd not an idea in the world where I was, nor even what was the nearest town or village. I had to wait for Tom. It didn't occur to me that if he found me gone, he'd surely think to look for me at the convent. I felt as though, in losing the cottage, I'd lose him forever. I didn't know if he'd ever return but I had to do my part. I had to wait for Tom.

DAYS PASSED. At last the coal was gone, but for a couple of handfuls of small coal of the kind normally used to set a fire going, nothing that would keep warm my bones. I sat in the window of the bedroom, wrapped in all the blankets we had—I had, the cottage had—gazing at the drear laid out before me. It was raining, and had been for days. The inside of the window had its own coat of drops, from which I tried to hold back the blankets. Tucked up there as I was, I couldn't stop them getting a little wet. I was miserable cold. I'd eaten nothing at all that day. There was nothing left save oats and a turnip, and what could I do with that, with no fire to cook on? I was trying to stir myself to go down and eat cold oats and water, but I was so devilish cold I couldn't move. I'd have to go out into the rain, mind, to fetch the water from the well. The hunger gnawed at me with the teeth of a rat, then it would hide awhile and sleep, only to come back again.

The drops raced one another down the pane. All was murk and mist outside, though I knew well enough by now what view there was to be had: the lane with its walls of hedge, and the fields stretching away. In the distance, the dark spread of woods began, like black clouds fallen to earth. And that was all.

I thought over again what choices lay before me; they were as dismal as the fields. I could wait there for Tom's return, perhaps to die in the waiting. I could take my handful of oats and turnip, and set out to walk to Bristol, though I'd no idea which way to take. Surely I'd find a soul along the way who might help me, at least in the direction, if not with food. If I met no one, I'd likely croak it on the road. I'd prefer to die by the roadside than here, like a bunny forgotten in a hutch. How far could I go on foot, with a turnip and a handful of oats? What if I took the wrong road and walked into the wilderness, never to come out of it? I felt that I'd landed there already. I could take the last choice and walk Mr Dryer's road behind the house. This last made me feel as though I might as well die. It made my insides crawl, as I must surely crawl before Old Pious when once I got there, and I couldn't be sure that he'd help me. I thought that it would be worse, perhaps, to be turned from Mr Dryer's house by Old Pious to starve, than to stay where I was and choose starvation by my own hand.

I named the raindrops "waiting," "Bristol," and "Old Pious," after the roads I might take, and watched them race. The drop that first reached the bottom of the pane was the path I'd choose. The first time I did this, the droplet named for waiting alone came out the victor. The drops I named for walking got lost and ran into other drops. I began again; this time "waiting" came to a halt halfway down the pane, whereas "Bristol" ran into "Old Pious," ate him and sped toward the finish. I liked that, for Bristol could eat that shit-sack, I thought. Bristol was bigger and more teeming than any cull alive. I missed the city near as much as I did Tom. I won't say that the race of drops made my decision, but instead showed me a new road, a road I might take more safely. "Bristol" should eat "Old Pious"; the two paths together to make one more sure. I'd walk Mr Dryer's road first, go to Old Pious, and ask which was the road to Bristol. I'd have to beg for food for the journey, but I thought that even if he turned me away without, he'd surely tell me the road. And I'd ask him to take word to Tom on his return and tell him where I'd gone. The rain was beginning to ease; I'd leave as soon as it let up.

I rose and began to search out what things I'd need; there wasn't much. I had my two cloaks, of course, and I'd take Tom's old coat, for extra warmth. I longed to take one of the blankets from the bed, but couldn't risk being named a thief. The oats I put into the small jar that'd held preserves, now scraped quite clean. My precious things, the dressing gown and the box of feathers, I folded and put into the basket that'd brought them there. The portrait of the little girl was still inside. I'd never brought it out. The oats and the turnip I put on top. I stood for a moment, considering my padded mufflers. They were heavy, but I thought I'd best bring them. It wasn't just that they were my own, and few enough things could be called so, it was also that I thought I might use them, if ever I found a town or village, to put on a display of sparring and science in exchange for a few pennies. At last I tied them to the basket by their laces and let them dangle, even though I knew they'd swing and hit against my legs as I walked.

This done, I sat at the table, in the chair I'd called Tom's, and waited for the rain to lift. My belly shuddered and clenched and grew quiet again. After a time I grew cold enough to put Tom's old coat on and my cloak on top of that.

I sat and imagined Tom hearing where I'd gone to, and coming back to find how I'd been left. His rage would be something fearful, and I only hoped he'd keep sense enough to hold his temper toward Mr Dryer. I wanted Mr Dryer to die, I wanted him locked in a room to starve, I wanted to hear him beg me for food, for company, for any piece of hope—but I didn't want Tom's hand to serve the devil his due. My husband I wanted safe, not thrown into a gaol, not sent to swing. I'd have to leave word, along with my direction in Bristol. I'd have to leave a message with Old Pious that Tom would understand.

I looked about me. The cottage wasn't clean; it was worse than not clean, it was shameful. I didn't care for Mr Dryer's sake, I'd have burned it down, if it were only he to find it. It was the thought of Tom, finding out what low state I'd been brought to, that I couldn't bear. I rose and began making things, not nice, mind, but a little less ugsome. The grate I swept out and put the ashes out of the door. The rain was so light now that it was more a wetness in the air than anything you could call falling. I made the bed. I swept the flags. I put my dirty dishes in the scullery, and though I couldn't heat water to wash them, I stacked them neatly beside the sink and called it good enough. The thunder pot beneath the bed I'd not emptied for days and it was too full to carry easily. I realised how weak I was grown; my arms trembled and set up aching the minute I lifted it. I carried it down the stairs as slowly as I could, holding it away from my body, but still a little of the mess slipped over the rim to foul my skirts. I had to put it on the floor so that I could free my hands to open the door, and when I did I near fainted away, for there was Old Pious upon the step, his fist raised to knock. He startled me so that I stepped back in surprise and bumped against the pot. More filth slopped out and wet the flags.

We only stared at each other. The rain had stopped, bringing a clean, grassy air that chilled the face. Behind him, I could see his horse, nosing through the drifts of leaves along the hedge. It was one of the queerest moments of my life. I'd been alone so long I'd near stopped believing other folk real. Then I'd thought to call upon Old Pious and there he was, brought to my door as if called by my mind, his thin cheeks reddened by cold. I stood and gazed at him like a noddy. I had half an urge to simply shut the door again and make as though he wasn't there.

His look as he got over his surprise and let his eyes drift over me brought me back to myself. I saw him take in my uncombed hair, Tom's old coat—which I still wore, though I'd taken off my cloak—the pot of night-soil at my feet. I've always been stirred up by haughtiness, and when he looked at me it was as if I came back into my own head, from somewhere else entire. I glared at him.

"Yes?"

"Good afternoon." He tipped his head in the smallest way. His voice was thin and a little from the nose. He was all dressed up stiff in his coat with polished buttons.

I tilted my head back at him.

"Move aside," I said, "if you'd not like piss upon your breeches."

I bent and picked up the thunder pot and made to move past him. I was watching my hands, the yellow liquid licking the rim and sending trickles over the edge, so I didn't see his mug. The shape of him blocking the door-way dithered and then leapt back as I moved toward him, as if I meant to heave it at him. I'd have liked to, but I only kept walking steadily, staring into the foul mess as if it could tell my fortune. I poured it against the hedge. His horse looked up, flared its nostrils, and bent its head again to the leaves.

I'd forgotten entirely that I'd meant to beg this man for help. Even out-at-heels as I was, the moment he stood before me with that frost in his eye, my head lowered to charge and I couldn't have spoken a nice word for a cartload of bread.

He stood beside the door, straight as a post. When I drew near him, he did his little head tilt again and said, "Good afternoon," quite as if he'd not already seen me with a full piss-pot in my hands.

"Good afternoon," I said, as haughtily as I could. I carried the thunder pot before me like a shield. Once I reached the step, I turned and stood upon it as though I'd just opened the door. I bent to place the pot upon the flags beside my feet, and when I came back up I felt light-headed.

"Mrs Webber, I must confess myself surprised to find you returned. It was only when I received a letter, from your husband—"

Little stars seemed to pop in my sight like black snow.

"My husband can't write a line," I said.

"Nevertheless, I have word here"—he reached inside his jacket—"directed to Mrs Webber, at the gatehouse. My master wrote to me himself and included a letter from Mr Webber, addressed to you."

I reached out to clutch at the door frame.

"Mrs Webber? Are you unwell?"

"It's only the surprise of it," I said, so soft I wasn't sure he heard.

Then his hand was under my elbow and he was saying something I didn't follow. My eyes were quite swimming with dark specks, soot upon the wind. He set me in Tom's chair, and I bent over my own knees, sure for a moment that I'd empty my guts. I could hear Dora in my mind saying, "Have you a padlock on your arse, that you've to shit through your teeth?" which was what she always did say, when any miss lost her dinner.

At last I felt clearer and lifted my head.

Old Pious was standing beside the chair I'd called mine, straight as ever, with as much of the cold fish about him as before, but his voice was kind when he asked me if I felt recovered.

I said I thought I did.

"I hadn't realised the news would shock you," he said, "or I should have been more gentle in delivering it."

I just shook my head. I tried to sit up as straight as I could, but my body was grown limp and useless. I couldn't help but sit wilted, soft as my last turnip.

Old Pious held a paper in his hand. Now he stepped forward and placed it in mine. I held it in my lap and looked at it stupidly. It was folded in three and had writing upon it. Had they taught Tom to write? I couldn't stomach it; would he come home so changed, or not come home at all? The curls of ink were blue and the paper so clean that my fingers upon it looked black. I suddenly feared I'd make fingerprints and drew my hands away quickly. The paper lay in my lap, looking at me with its tightly curled ink.

"Will you read it?" Old Pious said.

I didn't reply.

"Should you like me to read it to you?"

My belly clenched. I didn't want to know what the paper said. Good news never was delivered in a paper to people like me. Still I watched my dirty hand pick it up and hold it out to him. His face was grown quite soft and unlike itself.

This is Christian charity, I thought, and tried to make the thought hard. I felt like a child. There was much rustling. I stared at my hands and my spotted apron.

"My Ruth," he read, *"Mr Bowden has joined us here and has kindly agreed to write a word to you. He tells me it will reach you in two days, by which time I will have fought again. I wish you to know that I am well. I have been beating every man they bring me and eating beef for near every meal"*—here I felt myself bite my lip—*"and every drop of blood I spill here is in your name, my wife. Mr Dryer is best pleased and says he will make me champion yet. You would be amazed at the places I have been and the number of fine gentlemen who wish to shake my hand. I am sending you a piece of fine muslin I have chosen for you with all affection. I hope you will fashion a gown, to wear when you come to London to see me fight for my title, which I have reason to hope will happen soon enough. They tell me I must best six of London's heavyweights, and I have taken three. Be well and remember me fondly as I think of you, your Tom."*

I could feel myself shaking my head, though I couldn't have said what I meant. Old Pious stepped forward again and put a parcel wrapped in paper into my hands. It was soft. How like Tom to send me muslin when I'd no bread to eat.

"Shall you like to keep the letter, Mrs Webber?"

I was still struck dumb.

Old Pious placed it on the table. He looked cold again; he'd determined me run mad, or simple. He inclined his head again.

"Good day, then. I shall inform Mrs Bell of your return," he said, and stepped toward the door.

"Wait," I cried, and stood so quickly that I grew faint again, "please."

He turned and regarded me with a look that said he'd indeed decided me simple.

"Please," I said, holding the chair to keep my feet. "I ain't returned. I've been left. I've not had a crumb to eat for days. They've left me here." Hearing the words out loud brought me to weeping. The shame of it, begging and weepish in front of a starched bastard like him, only made me cry the harder.

"Please," I said again.

I sat carefully, feeling the muscles of the horse's broad back moving beneath my legs. I held on with both hands. The saddle was of the wrong kind for sitting side-saddle, but Old Pious had fussed when I went to throw my leg over, and I was too weary and brought down to argue. I held on and felt every moment that I'd tumble to the ground. Old Pious and the horse plodded together up the lane, he holding its bridle in his gloved hand.

We were walking up Mr Dryer's road, bare winter fields on either side of us, and beyond, a stream. A bird on a stump, a spreading tree, a herd of sheep with dirty wool. We began to ascend a hill. The journey took longer than I ever would've credited it. If I'd been on foot I'd have been disheartened and turned back, or fallen by the roadside in despair. The movement of the horse made me feel sickly, and the sweat was like ice on my skin. I badly wished to lie down.

◆ ◆ ◆

THE HOUSE WAS THE GRANDEST thing I'd ever seen. I'd not known that buildings came so large; in Bristol there were fine houses enough, but they were neat, standing in fancy rows up Park Street, or the busy halls, with columns and curly bits, all along Corn Street. This house was a monster. It looked as though it'd eaten a street of houses and grown fat upon them. It had wings, stretching out to catch me up. I had plenty of time to take this in, for we rode around the whole of it. I'd never have approached it, had I taken Mr Dryer's road on foot. I'd have turned and run. I'd have had no idea where to knock. At last we came to a part of the house that seemed less grand and awful, a cobbled yard with a good layer of mud across it and enough boot prints that I knew this was a well-used place. A door stood open here, steam wisping from within. As we approached, a dumpy maid came out of this door and stood still to see us, a copper pot in her hands. It looked to be heavy from the way she held it. A voice behind her cried out something, scolding her to move, I'd warrant, for she started then and came outside, carrying her pot across the yard a little way to another building, smaller and with sheets hung on lines outside it, high up to keep them from the mud. She kept turning to watch us as she walked. She looked simple enough to begin drooling.

I shouldn't be here, I thought, *I should never have let Old Pious put me on this horse, I should've run from him.* I didn't know what I was doing there. Everything about that place was unfamiliar and wrong. It wasn't a place for me.

The Henry boy who'd brought our food turned up, and took the horse's bridle from Old Pious. Old Pious came as if to help me down, and seeing this, I slid as quick as I could to the ground. I didn't want to take his hand. My pins could barely hold me when I landed on them; my knees sagged, and I thought, *I couldn't have run from him. I can't now run anywhere.* The horror of that thought bolstered me up and made it a lie; I felt my knees grow firmer. I'd always run if I needed.

Old Pious took my elbow firmly.

"Come, now, let us get you some soup."

I let him lead me toward the open door. Even with the promise of soup, I felt as if I were being led off to be shot. The pain in my belly had returned like a sharp-nailed hand squeezing me inside.

The moment we stepped into that steaming room I grew so dizzy that I could barely see. Firm hands led me to a seat; it was hot as Old Nick himself would have it. The air sat upon my chest like a solid thing, and from somewhere a steady clopping sound beat upon my ears. I shut my eyes; I could feel the seat sturdy beneath me, but I was pitching and rolling like a ship.

"But we thought her in London! You can't mean to say, Mr Horton, that all this time . . . ?" a woman's voice from somewhere.

Old Pious I could hear muttering urgently, and the woman's replies, softer now.

Another voice, a girl, cried out, "Oh, for shame," and was shushed.

I opened my eyes a slit and peeked out. My head was tipped back upon the chair, devilish uncomfortable upon my neck. At first all I could see were winking lights and sparks, but as my vision cleared I saw that the walls were hung with brass and copper pans, all of them reflecting the light from the great hearth. Against this glittering wall I could see Old Pious and a woman, thin as a cane and wearing a cook's apron.

Never trust a thin cook came into my head, unbidden.

The two of them were talking together at the other end of a long table, at which I now saw I sat. It was bigger even than our table in the convent kitchen. Old Pious leaned close to the cook's ear, she all the time chopping something, her arms moving so fast they seemed separate from her body. This was the clopping sound, the knife upon the wood. Behind them was the fireplace, taking up most of the wall. Iron spits ran across it, and a huge pan on three legs sat upon the flames and sent up clouds of steam. The whole room was copper pans, table, hearth, and steam.

Old Pious looked over and saw my eyes upon him. I thought of closing them again, lest he think me spying, but he still looked quite soft and called out, "Wait only a moment, Mrs Webber, and I will bring you soup."

"I don't have soup I can spare, Mr Horton," the thin cook said. "Don't promise the poor mite things we can't deliver. I've porridge here and an egg, perhaps. Shall you like an egg, my dear?"

She raised her voice to speak to me as though I were old.

"Thank you," I said, though I found my voice too soft again.

The porridge arrived in front of me. It was far better than the pitiful gruel I'd been feeding myself on, swimming in milk and with a spoon of preserves atop it. The scent of it made my belly cry out and grit itself together like teeth. I grew dizzy again and the blob of red jam spread and swirled in my vision.

"Why, you haven't given the girl a spoon," the cook said.

A spoon was put in my hand, and gripping the warm wood of its handle, I grew calm. I watched my hand move and dip and bring porridge to my lips. The sweetness of it swept over me as though I'd dropped my face into the bowl. My throat could barely close over it; I'd forgotten, somehow, how eating was to be done. Slowly I spooned and swallowed. I couldn't eat half what I'd have liked to before I began to sweat and grow sick. I laid the spoon down and closed my eyes. The steam and the food together were suffocating. I felt as though I'd sleep sitting there, and in sleeping slip into death. Time went by; I couldn't say how long. I kept my eyes closed.

Another woman was in the room. I could hear Old Pious muttering once more, joined this time by the thin cook, who cried out, "She's half starved, look at her," though she looked near enough starved herself, to my eyes.

I must've been falling asleep, because when the other woman spoke, close to my face, I'd no notion that anyone had come near. Even so, I was so dozy then that my surprise was a far-off thing, dulled by steam.

"Mrs Webber," the voice said, and it wasn't soft, "open your eyes, if you please."

She was crouching in front of me but that was the only thing gentle about her. She was all in black and bracket-faced. Her voice could've sawed logs in two.

"Mr Horton says you have told him a sorry tale," she said. She didn't sound as though she was sorry at all.

"I don't tell tales," I said. I began to struggle to sit up. She was far too near to me for my comfort and looking at me devilish mean.

"Our master never would leave a body to starve," the old baggage said. "He's famous for his good treatment of his servants."

"He ain't my master," I said.

She stood and turned her back upon me.

"I won't credit it. More likely she's run away from her husband," she said, to Old Pious and the thin cook.

The dough-faced girl had sprung from somewhere with water splashed across the front of her apron and her sleeves rolled up to the elbow. She stood in the doorway and stared.

"Has Mrs Bell guessed it? Did he beat you?" asked the cook.

"I'd have his head off if he tried it." The words came out slower than I meant them. I knew that in any usual case I'd be spitting, but now I couldn't seem to rise to it.

Old Pious looked sad and shook his head. "I must disagree, Mrs Bell. I read Mr Webber's letter aloud. There was no mention of her having run away. In fact"—he put his hand to his forehead and rubbed at it as hard as if he were trying to rub out a stain—"there was no mention of Mrs Webber having been in London at all."

"I'll not credit it," she said again. "I won't have Mr Dryer accused of cruelty."

I knew I could tell them things about their Mr Dryer that would shrivel the words upon her tongue. *Mind, Ruth, if you do that,* I told myself, *they'll know what kind of house you come from.*

"I ain't accused no one," I said, "only told the truth. I've been left with no food, nor money to buy any."

"This is your husband's responsibility," Mrs Bell turned about. "Let no one say that this household would fail its Christian duty. We will certainly see you well fed. But I won't hear you talk against Mr Dryer. I warn you, I shan't stand to hear it. It is your own husband at fault."

"Well might it be." I stood and stayed standing by holding on to the back of the chair. "I don't care a speck for blame. I didn't ask to be brought here, that man there insisted. I only want to know the road to Bristol. I'd rather die on the road than stay another minute here, in your scaly old master's house. He's not my master, nor ever will be. He can have his bleeding arse fucked by the devil."

I scandalised the place; every person in the room gasped aloud. Old Bracket-Face looked as though I'd handed her a bounty; her mug drew itself in at the brow, her lips pressed so thin as to be white, but her eyes were gleeful. It would've been comical if it weren't for my shaking legs and cramping belly.

I'd not give her the pleasure of turning me out; pride alone drove my legs onward.

The cold of the air outside was like a backhand to the face; I near fell over with the shock of it. When once I breathed it in a few times, it had the opposite effect and pressed me on, across the yard, to where I knew the road began that would take me back toward the cottage. I'd not stop when once I reached it. I'd never set foot in that stinking coffin again. Raised voices behind me seemed to be shouting at each other; I felt a dull gladness at that.

"Miss," came from behind me, and I turned to find the thin cook coming quickly across the yard, a cloth bag in one hand. She stopped and held it out. I took it. She wrapped her arms around herself against the chill. For a moment, she only stood and looked at me, and then she shook her head sorrowfully.

"It's not right to turn you out," she said, "though I call your language shocking. You should pray forgiveness."

"Please," I said, "which is the road to Bristol?"

"You cannot mean to walk so far."

"Which road?"

"Take the drive back to the gatehouse and turn left," she said. "Saltford is three miles on. Someone may take you, if you speak sweetly and mind your tongue."

I was already walking away. I should've thanked her for the bag, but somehow I'd already forgotten it. *Turn left,* I thought only, *three miles.*

"You'll not get far, ill-mannered as you are," she called to my back, but I didn't turn.

I FOUND I COULD WALK only by watching my feet. If I looked up, the world became wavy and I knew I'd fall. If I watched my shoes, the ragged hem of my dress, I could see the solid road and know it was as firm as it should be. I could be sure I was going in the right direction because there was only one direction to travel, down the hill, toward the cottage. I kept moving in my circle, road, shoes, muddy dress.

When at last I came near to the cottage, I'd not look up at it. I kept on trudging slowly, watching the foot of its walls slide past till I was well beyond it. I walked around it and turned left onto the hedged lane. *Now,* I thought. *Now I'm on the Bristol road.*

Only when I'd gone too far did I think of the basket with my dressing gown, my feathers, the portrait of the girl, the turnip and oats. I remembered too the muslin Tom had sent. *I'd have sold that,* I thought, *for a place in a cart.* I'd not turn back, mind. I'd not stop moving till I reached the docks, the masts of ships, the damp bed in the convent cellar.

When I did fall, I was so deep inside my thoughts that I didn't feel it. I was thinking of the convent's front door, when I felt a pain in my hip and found that I was lying on the ground. The hunger was back, but not like a rat now, more a gentle ache. I remembered the bag that the thin cook had given me. I'd not looked inside it; it must be food. I sat up in my mind, but not my body. I couldn't even twitch my fingers. I watched the sky for a while, till it grew dark or my eyes closed. I didn't know which, and didn't find I cared.

PART 6

Charlotte

✦ ✦ ✦

Chapter 16

✦ ✦ ✦

My eyes had been forced open by all I had seen at the fair; I could not close them, but neither could I act. The house seemed to shrink about me, more gloomy than ever. I saw anew how old and heavy was the furniture, how dark the rooms. Whenever Granville was from home I had been in the habit of sitting only in my dressing room, making believe that the whole of the house was pretty and papered in elegant colours. Now my sanctuary seemed too poky to bear. I had changed, but the world had not, and I could not shift from my narrow place in it.

I do not remember ever being told directly of Granville's plan to make that chivalrous brute into a champion of England. I picked the knowledge up piecemeal, in his conversations with my brother and Mr Bowden. When once I did understand, it seemed something bright to hope for. I found myself imagining that tree-trunk of a man raising his arms before a crowd that stretched on to the horizon, perhaps to the King himself. If that were to happen, where would my husband be? Where would I be? Surely, then, we might go sometimes to London. We might have gentlemen visit and bring their wives. I might make a circle of acquaintance; I might be allowed another horse so that I could take the carriage out when Granville was from home. I might call upon my aunt. It was easier, always, to be bold in my imaginings. If my husband trained a fighting champion, perhaps I would be a little braver myself.

The sight of that lady boxer had sparked a longing for boldness in my own breast. On one of those mornings soon after the fair, as Mrs Bell served me my chocolate, I found myself gazing at the keys at her waist and finding it unbearable. I was alone—I had been at breakfast in just that way on countless occasions, and yet this day I sat up very straight.

Without determining whether or not I meant my words, I said, "I have decided it is time I learn the running of the house, Mrs Bell; you will show me the accounts and turn the keys over to me."

My legs set up trembling. I was glad of the tablecloth. I chided myself, *Why, in the name of all that can be called good, are you afraid?* I could not be afraid of Mrs Bell. Perhaps it was the idea of change itself. And yet I longed for it. My feelings churned so that I could not meet her eyes, but I would not be cowed before her. I brought my gaze as close as I could and found myself taking in the details of her ear, the wispy hairs escaping from her cap. There seemed to me a long silence before she said, "Yes, madam. When should you like to be taught?"

I did not object to the word "taught," although I might have done.

"Come to me as soon as you have done with your tasks for the morning, Mrs Bell."

"My tasks are never done, madam, but I shall come as soon as ever I can."

I nodded and began to eat. My hands were not quite steady. Inside my heart I responded, *Well, then, soon you shall have one less task to plague you,* but I did not rebuke her out loud.

Mrs Bell did not make me wait overlong, but even so, by the time she came to me in the parlour, her arms weighed down by a huge ledger, I was regretting my impulsiveness. I should never be able to do it, I had never before dealt with columns of figures; Mama had only just begun to talk of teaching me to manage accounts when she grew sick. I could not look glad to see Mrs Bell then. My legs again wished to tremble; this time I forbade them sternly and they kept still. I could not speak, however.

Mrs Bell placed the book before me upon the table and stood at my shoulder just as a governess would. She opened the ledger. Great columns, just as I had feared, with neat and incomprehensible numbers inside them.

"You can see I have kept them nice, madam," she said, as though warning me not to spot the pages. "What do you wish to be shown?"

I did not know what to say. I could not say "You will have to teach me everything." I looked down at the book again. Here were columns: glover, haberdasher, lace maker, breech maker. I saw more than a guinea paid out for "linen and muslin," though what use this cloth had been put to I could not have said, nor guessed whether the price had been dear or cheap.

"These are my accounts, by which I mean the housekeeping books," Mrs Bell said at last, when still I kept silent. "Mr Dryer holds accounts for the stable bills, the saddle maker, and the like."

"Yes, I see," I said.

Mrs Bell turned the page. Here were columns for lamp-oil, coal, meat, milk, and all sorts besides. Here was the column for servants' wages. I did not wish to learn after all. I wanted only to hold the keys—but perhaps I did not even wish for that. Mrs Bell would be always coming to me. I felt strange, peevish and sick, my baby turning in my stomach as though disgusted with its mama's weakness.

"The running of a household is quite a task, madam," Mrs Bell said, "and Mr Dryer, as you know, can be quite particular. Shall you like me to sit beside you and guide you through the ordering of goods?"

The very idea of her sitting beside me, of our heads together like schoolchildren over a primer! But then, Mama had managed her own house; she had taken charge of everything.

"No," I said, despising myself. "No, take them away. I am tired. You may send me wine."

The keys clinked at her waist as she left.

Alone in my dressing room, I took up my tambour hoop and pulled free the unfinished cloth, with the lady upon her donkey. In its place I laid a new piece, not large, but just enough to screw into place. I took up my pencil and made soft lines to show where I would place her. Her skirts would be pinned up and her head high. She was to stand in a ring of silken cord. I thought I could knot the silks to make them stand out from the screen. I had never seen this done, but I thought I knew now how I might do it, six silks, twisted about each other, as I imagined one might make rope. I would not depict blood upon her. She was to stand ready and proud, with her hands raised before her.

GRANVILLE WAS FROM HOME even more often than he had used to be. I found myself restless. For the first time in our marriage, I felt a little flutter at the sound of his boots in the hall and was glad to have my husband home. Even more of a novelty was my new forbearance for my brother. It was not that I enjoyed his company any better or that he was grown less boorish, but that I found myself listening to their talk with something like interest. When they spoke of boxing now, I could imagine the scent and the atmosphere. When they spoke of one fighter's victory over another, I knew now that a real man had spilled the hot blood of a fellow and that real hearts beat the harder for seeing it.

Mrs Bell came and knocked upon the door of my dressing room, and I threw a shawl over the hoop of my tambour, where the lady boxer's raised arms were slowly growing pink beneath my needle.

"I have had word, madam, that Mr Dryer will be at home to dine and will be bringing some gentlemen in company with him."

I thought her eyes touched upon my shawl-covered screen. I thought, *I will not leave it where she might see, when once I put it away.*

"Do we know the names of these gentlemen?" I asked her.

"Mr Dryer did not say, madam. Only that we must make table for four persons."

I said only, "Then it could be anyone at all. Make sure the dinner is a good one."

I left her to decipher what might be best pleasing to the gentlemen.

When once she had closed the door again, I found I could not settle but rose and paced about. I looked at my own face in the glass; I thought my complexion more sallow than usual.

Granville would not like me to make myself too fine—I had Lucy dress me in a grey crepe gown and a cap with silver beads about its edge. The gown had sleeves, so my arms were well hidden. When Lucy was gone, leaving only the lingering scent of lye soap and mutton fat, I drew the paint all the way down my throat. I had time to paint the backs of my hands so that I might leave off my gloves at dinner. I would keep them on until the introductions had been made, of course. I could not give my scarred palm to gentlemen. When once this poor effort was complete, I had to be satisfied.

I stood in front of the looking-glass. The dress, at least, was pretty. I picked up my skirts and held them as though they were pinned at the knee. *How brave she is,* I thought, *to stand so exposed before a crowd. How brave and how brazen.* Through my thin stockings my scarred legs showed mottled, like a fresh-plucked goose.

I dropped the silk from my hands and tried a boxing stance, holding my fists before me as she had done. It felt surprisingly natural, being not so different from the en garde stance one adopts before fencing. Perry had used to have me fence with him whenever he came home from school for the summer. We held sticks, and I would do anything I could to hold him off; it was not really fencing. I would wave my stick at him and he would drive me backward until I turned and ran, or fell over my skirts. When once I became really frightened and thrust my stick toward him he was too surprised to stop me, and I struck him a good poke in the stomach. He played not so often with me after that, but said that I was too dull to make a good match with. I had learnt to stand en garde, however. And I had learnt that my brother could be driven off, if I struck him where it hurt.

Now I stood en garde, with my head up and my fists before me, and thrust them at the mirror. I drew on my dinner gloves—a very pretty dove grey, almost silver—and pretended that they were the padded ones the pugilists wore. I tried to make my eyes fierce.

I hopped from foot to foot, as the lady boxer did. Immediately my feet caught my petticoats and I stumbled and stopped. I could not risk a tear to my gown. In any case, I did not look fierce, I looked only ridiculous. My skirts were not pinned up, my gloves were not padded, and I was not free to do anything. In a moment, the bell would ring and I would walk down the stairs and talk politely with gentlemen.

After all that, the gentlemen were only my brother, Perry, and Mr George Bowden.

Mrs Bell had defined a good dinner as mutton-ham, asparagus, and force-meat balls. Perry, I was sure, had been enjoying his wine before he arrived. His face was flushed and his brow shone.

I was seated beside Mr Bowden, which meant I need not look at him. He could not catch my eye unless I turned my head. I was glad; his conversation seemed always to be teasing, or to have layers of meaning. That evening I did not want to be bothered with the unravelling of them.

"This night will be a high treat for the fancy," Perry was saying. "A real set-to, as it should be done. If your man stands up well this night, we shall all be able to back him with the greatest confidence."

"You, back my man?" my husband said. "You may lay down your guinea, and welcome, but I shan't look for it."

"What do you think of this, Mrs Dryer?" Mr Bowden said. "Your husband is as set on this fellow as a man might be on a maid."

"With very different intentions," Granville said.

"Not so different," Perry said, "pounding, sweating, and the exchange of money!" He thought himself the highest wit.

"Please, Mr Sinclair, my wife is present," Granville said. I knew he was displeased, because in every usual case he called Perry by his Christian name.

"Charlotte is a barbarian," Perry said. "We all took note of her, screaming out for blood."

Mr Bowden turned to me, obliging me to turn toward him also. I kept my eyes upon his hand, tapping his wineglass with one finger.

"Were you much shocked, Mrs Dryer?"

"I was." The image of those terrible, meaty hands rose before me. Mr Bowden's fingers on the wineglass were not meaty. They were the hands of a violinist. I shook both thoughts from my mind. "Would you care for more wine, Mr Bowden?"

"I have wine aplenty, Mrs Dryer," he said. His finger stilled. "You, however, have none. Should you like some?"

I was trying, at that time, to resist temptation in company.

"Let us all have wine," Perry said. "More wine, Bell!"

I watched Mrs Bell's face as she poured, to see how she liked being addressed thus. I thought the very placidity of her face betrayed her. She hesitated over my cup.

"For everyone, Bell! Pour it out and let's have done," my brother cried.

She filled my glass. No one could tell me I might not drink when it was pushed upon me thus. I took a long swallow and felt its warm fingers stroke my throat. Even as I did so, I looked at my brother and wondered if I might not come to resemble him, if I did not stem my appetites for wine and liquor. I should hate to be in company and have all about me think me foolish and a bore. To quell the thought, I took another deep draught of my wine.

"But dear Mrs Dryer, you do confess to being a little thrilled, despite yourself?" Mr Bowden's voice had dropped and become intimate.

"It is thrilling," Perry boomed. "Of course it is. Charlotte need not confess—you need only look at her. She was like a hound after a fox."

I felt my face grow hot and begin to tingle as it had at the fair. I dropped my eyes to my lap. All of the gentlemen had turned to look at me; I could feel their eyes upon me even with my head bowed. I did not like to be examined.

The gentlemen grew tired of me and began to talk amongst themselves. I looked up at last, toward my husband. I could look at him most easily of all the gentlemen. He saw my eyes upon him.

"No harm has been done you, has it?"

"None," I said. My smile was stiffer than I would have liked it.

"And you think the fellow a fine one? You approve of my choice?"

"I am glad it is he you favour and not the other," I said.

Granville nodded at me seriously.

"The other man has clumsy form," he said, as if I knew about such things. I blinked and looked back toward my plate. I had not thought the fellow clumsy—although, now I thought of it, he was like a battering ram, bludgeoning all he could reach. Perhaps it was the same thing.

"But my dear Mrs Dryer," Mr Bowden said, "what would you say if I told you that your brother and I thought him not clumsy, but a fine pugilist? Where would you lay your coin then?"

"My wife does not gamble, Mr Bowden," Granville said. "I thank you not to entice her to begin."

"I speak only in jest, my good sir," Mr Bowden said.

I watched my hands, clasping each other below the line of the tablecloth. Where I gripped them, the skin grew white and the scars seemed almost to disappear.

I KNEW BY THE SETTLED MANNER in which they called for their pipes, even as I rose from the table, that the gentlemen would not be joining me in the drawing room before I wished for my bed. Still I went there, not to wait for them, but because I could not stand to be in my dressing room at that moment. As pretty as I had made it, it was filled with my own loneliness. I preferred the dark and cavernous space of the drawing room at night. The fire was a low and glowering red. Beyond the hearth, the room stretched off into lumpen shadows. I did not call for a lamp, and Mrs Bell, when she brought me my glass of ratafia, did not offer to bring one. Perhaps she knew I preferred the darkness at that moment. Perhaps she did not think me worth the oil. I sat and stared into the embers. The ratafia spread its warmth like a hot poultice inside my chest. The bleakness I felt then was so familiar as to be almost comforting. *The only thing in the world that could shed any light upon my life would be this child,* I thought.

The door opened behind me with a creak and a swish as it brushed the carpet. I straightened and turned as quickly, as if I expected an intruder, and was only marginally less shocked to see George Bowden silhouetted there.

"I thought you might be here still," he said. "I came to find some sweeter company than that in the dining room."

He was in his cups, I could see. He leant against the door frame and puffed upon his pipe as though it were quite common for a man to seek out a lady not his wife and smoke at her.

"Well," he said, "will you not speak? Do you not invite me to sit?"

"Please, sit," I said.

"I will take that whisper as an invitation, madam, though I heard not a word of it."

"Please do sit," I said, though he was already crossing the carpet. He seated himself on the chair closest to the end of the sofa where I sat, the nearest he could put himself without sitting directly next to me. His closeness and the darkness combined to make me feel a little drunk myself. The fire threw black shapes across his face, sinking his eyes into dark holes.

"Why do you sit in darkness, Mrs Dryer?" Mr Bowden's pipe was a floating orb of red that waxed and waned with each puff upon it.

"I must say I am not sure. I had the inclination, tonight."

"I cannot blame you. Darkness is soft and forgiving. Like a lady."

My face grew hot. He meant that he could not see my scars.

"Is it not, Mrs Dryer? As forgiving as a lady?"

"I am not sure."

"You are not sure? Perhaps it is my fancy, only. I have always thought forgiveness a most ladylike quality. You, of course, will know better than I."

"I know very little about darkness, Mr Bowden, except that we cannot stop its coming."

"Oh, my dear lady, how similar must be our hearts. I do believe the season is changing, however. I do believe we shall feel the sun warm us soon, Mrs Dryer."

"That would be lovely, of course," I said. He was drunker than I had thought him. "Although I cannot expect it. Surely only God himself could prevent winter coming as it always does."

"You are right, of course. You are always right. Only I wish I could ask you to trust in me, Mrs Dryer. May I ask you to do that? Is it devilish presumptuous?"

"Goodness," I said. I did not know what reply to make.

"If your husband's man should win his fight . . ."

"Do you think he will succeed?"

"By God, I hope so. I will make my fortune upon him if he does. Your brother's stubbornness will set me free, Mrs Dryer. I will be a man of standing."

"I don't understand you," I said.

"A man of standing," he said again. "It will be a greater win even than the house at Queen Square."

"We always wintered at Queen Square," I said. I knew it was a senseless thing to say, but somehow I could not help it. It was as though we were having two different conversations at once.

"I remember it well. You shall again, if Granville's man wins. Although, no, more likely he will sell it, I should think."

"Whatever can you mean?"

"Those houses are not worth what they were, you see."

"But why should my husband have one to sell?"

"If he wins it," Mr Bowden said, "from your brother. That is the wager that they have made. If Mr Dryer wins, he takes the house. If Perry wins, it is Granville's plantation."

"My husband, win my mama's house? But this is too . . . Mr Bowden, you cannot know how often I think of that house. I dream of just walking there and looking over it."

"Go, then, and look upon it all you like."

"Go? I have not a means of getting there."

"Have not the means? What can you be saying? You have a carriage, do not you?"

"We have only two horses at present. Granville rides one, and the carriage cannot be pulled by one horse alone."

"This is not to be borne. I shall lend you the use of my phaeton. It needs only one horse to pull it. It is far superior to the machine I was used to drive you about in."

Did he refer to our kiss? I did not know what my response should be, but my face grew hot in the darkness. At the last I only thanked him.

"Nonsense, it is my greatest pleasure. Perhaps one day, perhaps . . . but I cannot think you would like to drive with me again."

I began to speak, but Mr Bowden waved me quiet with a wagging finger. I could see his hand clearly; my eyes had grown used to the dark. His pipe looked to have gone out, but he puffed upon it quite heedless.

"But I! I, Mrs Dryer, will be a man to be reckoned with. What will you say to me then?"

"I am sure I don't know," I said. I could not stop thinking, *My husband, win Mama's house!* I wondered, suddenly, how many of her things were left in it.

"You speak too low. But I cannot expect you to answer me now, in any case. I don't suppose that you might . . . that is, perhaps, you might just allow me to kiss your hand?"

I could not refuse him. His lips brushed the rough surface of my bare hand. He held it too long; he seemed to breathe over it. I thought then of the paint I had put on my hand; it would mark his lips. I pulled away. For a moment, he clung to my fingers even as I pulled, and then he released them so suddenly that my hand was near flung back to me.

"Just give me reason to hope," he said. "If your husband's man should come out victorious, Mrs Dryer, tell me that then I might be allowed to hope?"

"Mr Bowden—"

"No, you are right. Of course. Forgive me."

He raised himself with both hands on the arms of the chair and walked to the door. As he opened it, the sounds from the dining room floated in to greet him, the murmur of male voices and my brother's laughter. It was extinguished with the soft click of the door.

I did not expect Mr Bowden to remember, but in the morning I found he had left his phaeton in the yard, with a note expressing his wish that I should find pleasure in the use of it.

It being Stephens' half-day, Henry had to be entrusted with the phaeton. When first he understood he was to take the reins, his eyes grew wide and he looked half excited and half fearful.

"You must go slowly," I said. "I understand that a careless driver can turn a phaeton on its side before he knows it."

"Yes, Mrs Dryer. You needn't fear."

Indeed, once we set off and he had the feel of the thing, Henry seemed perfectly at his ease, whistling as he drove. The air was chill, but I had dressed warmly enough and I had remembered to wear a veil this time. I had Henry keep the top down so we might look about us. This was enjoyable whilst we travelled country lanes, but when we entered the city I felt as though dust and grime were hanging about me in a fog, and the people upon the streets gazed too openly at my cloak, my bonnet and veil. Bristol seemed even rougher than I recalled it. Perhaps I was grown more sensitive through being so long in the countryside, or perhaps the child I carried did not care for the scent of the docks; by the time we entered the leafy quiet of Queen Square, I felt as tremulous as if we drove toward a terrifying un-known, rather than a house holding the happiest memories of my girlhood.

The square itself was just as tranquil as I remembered it, made more so by being surrounded by the bustle of the city. I had Henry drive around it so that I might calm myself before we stopped. I knew, of course, that all the fashionable people of quality had abandoned the square for the heights of Clifton and the King's Down. The houses of the square were filled now with the wives and children of the better class of traders, yet I could not have told it from the outside. The railings were as highly glossed, the grass as neat. The curtains in the windows looked to be of good quality, more handsome indeed than anything Granville would allow me without trembling at the expense.

I could not stop the thought, rising like a bubble. *I must live here again, I must. I cannot keep at The Ridings all year long.* The houses slid past, stirringly familiar. At the corner beside the Hole in the Wall tavern, I bid Henry halt.

I looked upon it all and it seemed very simple, suddenly. I wished to live there, and Granville must be persuaded of it. There was no disguising the pleasing elegance of the houses. It was not just the pleasant associations; the square was very nicely made. Even without the best people living in it, I should be happy there. I myself was become the wife of a trader. It was better, thus, to accept my new place and make a home of it. I gazed upon the closed door of Mama's old house. I thought my husband might be pleased, to hear me ask to live humbly.

The house looked entirely unchanged. We had spent so many winters there; it was fitting that I should be seeing it now, with a chill in the air and the leaves drifting from the trees. The curtains at the drawing room window were the same ones Mama had chosen so carefully, of yellow damask with a white silk trim. Of course no one would have changed them, for who was there to do it? Perry had shut up the house almost as soon as Mama and Papa were buried. Still, the sight brought a strange sensation to my chest, as though my child had reached up and pulled painfully upon my heart with his tiny hands.

Caught as I was by the curtains, it was only then that I realised that the reason I could see them at all was that the shutters were drawn back. The house was not blank-faced and closed, as it should have been. The windows were dark, but surely Perry had not left the house unprotected? Could it be that he was airing it out in the event that he must turn it over to Granville?

As though called by my thoughts, I saw the front door of the house open and the familiar figure of Bede, the retainer. I felt a rush of pleasure at the sight of him. He had been our butler when I was a girl; his presence drew the past closer. A second figure came out past Bede, inclining her head to him as he held open the door. In that moment, the world seemed to sharpen and swoop, for there was my mama, absolutely my own mama, in a gown of teal silk that I remembered perfectly. She looked to be with child, just as she had been when she died. I can say with confidence that in that moment I came to understand how it is that people die of fright. The breath in my lungs seemed to freeze.

In the next moment, she turned, and was not my mama after all. Her face was too rounded, too young. Before I could begin to wonder who she was, a third form appeared beside her upon the step and offered her his arm.

It could be nobody but my husband. Even from so far away as that, there was no mistaking his particular, neat way of holding himself or the brown upon brown of his coat and breeches.

Henry, too, had noticed Granville and had turned to look at me enquiringly. I opened my lips, but I had no words at all. Then came the worst thing: standing on the step of my childhood home, right in front of Bede, a woman wearing my lost mama's gown kissed my husband. He took her by the shoulders and moved his face from her lips, shaking his head—Granville was never a man to kiss in public—but it did not look like a first kiss, not at all. My mind was wiped blank with the shock of it; the knowledge that I recognised her came as though it were something I had always known. It was the lady from the fair, though "lady" was too nice a word for her. It was the strumpet in the bright pink gown, who had touched my husband's arm and spoken to him as he stood upon the stage. The trollop whose bosoms had looked ready to fall from her bodice now turned to let my husband help her on with her cloak. Bede looked past her, directly at me, but I could not tell if he marked me, veiled as I was. At last he simply closed the door.

ALL THE JOURNEY BACK I felt nothing at all. I went quietly home and sat in my chair. I called for brandy, and when Lucy brought me a modest amount, I chided her for presumptuousness and sent her for the decanter. I drank. I sat very still, the only movement my hand, bringing the glass to my mouth.

I could not begin to examine the day's events; my heart had tucked itself up and gone quietly to sleep. When Lucy arrived to dress me for dinner, I allowed her to push me into a gown and went down the stairs like a somnambulist. I did not even insist that I dine in my room.

Granville had returned in time for dinner, bringing Perry and Mr Bowden with him. The gentlemen were all in high spirits, and even Perry greeted me with smiles and courtesy. I felt the smile on my own face a falsified thing, painted on along with the Pear's Almond Bloom. Granville did not look changed; he was not changed, indeed. My knowledge of him was changed. I had always thought him gentle, for all that he was dull and tight-fisted—I did not know what he was, now.

We sat and I drank a glass of wine rather too quickly; all the edges of the world were blurred.

The rabbit was brought out. I was toying with the meat, which was very soft, separating the flesh into clumps of damp threads, when I felt the warm rush of blood. There was no pain, just a release of some secret dam inside myself, and all at once my petticoats were sodden; I was sitting in a puddle. Despite how numb I had grown, I heard myself gasp aloud.

"By God, that was a thing to see. I have never been so close to a fighting man in action," Perry had just been saying. "I was quite sprayed with his perspiration and his blood."

At my gasp, the gentlemen turned to look at me, and of course all assumed it was the subject matter which had brought a breath to my lips. Perry considered shocking me the highest pleasure.

"Oh, yes, Charlotte," he said. "My white sporting jacket was thoroughly bespattered. I cannot decide whether to have it cleaned or framed as a memento." He ate a piece of rabbit with the greatest gusto.

I felt extremely odd, as though I were standing beside the table, watching us all.

"What sport, to be bathed in a man's fluids," I said. It was the kind of thought I often had, but did not dare speak aloud. I was bathing in fluids of my own.

Perry glared at me, and Mr Bowden was startled enough that he had to cough his wine into his napkin.

"Now, my dear," said Granville, "perhaps our talk has been too rough for table. Forgive us. Let you not grow rough in response. We will talk of pleasanter matters." He waved for more wine.

I was still clasping my knife as though it would steady me, and forced myself to put it down.

"Nonsense," Perry said. "Charlotte is well enough used to sporting conversation. If she forgets her manners, let us not reward her."

"Mrs Dryer's sensitivities are no doubt too fine to grow used to the brutal art, no matter how often she may hear of it," Mr Bowden said. He regarded me thoughtfully; I wished that he wouldn't. "She shows a delicacy of spirit very becoming to a lady."

"She shows a vulgarity of manner becoming to no one," Perry said.

I shifted a little in my seat. It was even more terrible than I had feared. It was just as though I had relieved myself; worse, perhaps, since my gown was of white muslin. I imagined that I had ruined the embroidered seat of the chair.

"You should not mock," Perry said to me then, "what you cannot understand."

I was silent, only sat and felt the warmth beneath me cool. I tasted blood in my mouth and realised that I had been biting my own lip.

Perry turned to Granville. "That young fellow of yours has bottom, I will grant you."

"And a fist like a horse's hoof!" broke in Mr Bowden.

"Certainly, he has that to boast of. But I maintain, sir"—Perry drew himself up like a cockerel—"that we shall have him call out, 'enough,' when he and the Bath Bully meet this Saturday next."

I found myself staring at the piece of rabbit on my plate. The gravy was congealing into a cold and clinging jelly. In a moment, Mrs Bell would remove my uneaten rabbit and we would have the sweet, the same Neapolitan cakes and syllabub we were served every Wednesday. Then I would be expected to withdraw, with my skirts turned scarlet and cleaving to my thighs.

"The Bath fellow shall see the same end as the chandler's boy," Granville said. "Did you not see they carried him off in a cart? How come you to be so confident?"

"You are short-sighted," Perry said. "The room was too close; the boy could not display the science of defence. An unbalanced contest is no contest at all. He was trapped within range of those hooves."

Perhaps I might begin to weep; it could hardly have reduced my dignity any further than I would shortly reveal myself to have sunk. I could see no course of action that would safely keep my secret. Perhaps I would sweep out of the room, carrying that spreading stain of claret as though it were the latest innovation in evening dress. Perhaps I should faint. The pond I had released from within myself was my dream of a child dissolved. My hopes were saturating the seat beneath me. I expected that I was at fault; what tiny spirit, waiting to be born, would choose so dreary a host? It was not unexpected. It was only so very ridiculous. That exaggerated monthly course that came upon the second course. It could not wait for the sweet. I believed I should faint, after all. The world was swooping. The rabbit had been removed and I never saw it hop away.

Chapter 17

❋ ❋ ❋

I awoke into the scent of pastilles burning, like rising into the past. I was very miserable indeed, although I could not remember the cause. I was very hot, and it took me some time to remember that I should push away the eiderdown.

Someone had put me into my plainest chemise. I lifted myself tentatively and felt the cloth stuck fast to my thighs. I was lying upon layers of linens, put down to protect the sheets. I had ruined them disgracefully. I began to weep. My thoughts were muddled, still; my first thought was that Mama would be furious. Then I recalled that she was dead, which thought, instead of bringing me to despair, sobered me somewhat. I remembered then what had come to pass and felt the weight of it land upon my breast like a great ugly bird.

The bed was an old-fashioned thing of oak, so high that I must climb three steps to reach it. Mrs Bell must have had quite a job to put me in it; perhaps the gentlemen assisted her. I dearly hoped that they had not—although, what difference could it make now? My humiliation was complete, whether Mrs Bell had carried me or Mr Bowden.

Perhaps, oh, good Lord, perhaps Mr Bowden offered me the use of his phaeton knowing what I would see at Queen Square. That thought brought a stab of shame so sharp that I pushed it away and determined not to consider it.

There was a bottle of tincture upon the nightstand. Perhaps the doctor had visited. I could remember nothing of it, if he had. I could not see a spoon. My mouth tasted foully bitter.

I tried to lift myself and found that my head swam horribly. I fell back against the pillows, and there I lay, thinking that if I lay long enough, I might bleed to death. No one would be sorry.

I DID NOTHING SO DRAMATIC but only lay for days, calling for brandy, heedless of what the servants or my inconstant husband might think of me. When I thought of the house at Queen Square, I could not help but moan aloud, which brought Mrs Bell and the threat of the doctor. I did not want to see the doctor; I could scarce imagine what state I had been in when he last came upon me. Granville did not come to enquire after me, as I had known he would not. I had always considered him made awkward by painful emotion, but now I considered that perhaps he was only unfeeling.

At last—after a number of days, I could not say how long—Mrs Bell said, "Well, madam, shall you get up today, or shall I call the doctor? I must call him, if you're determined to stay abed."

I surprised us both by shivering myself out of the bedclothes unaided and standing meekly to be bathed and dressed.

The greatest shock awaited me; I came downstairs to find the hulking figure of Tom Webber standing in the hall. The sight of him gave me such a surprise that I stopped on the stairs and put my hand to my throat. I thought I felt the child inside me sense the presence of the man and shudder, and then I remembered that there was no child, any longer. If I shuddered, it was on my own account, then.

He really was an enormous fellow. He looked deeply uncomfortable at the sight of me and tugged at his forelock like a farmer. He did not look as though he knew what he was doing there.

I found Granville at table. He stood when I entered and held his hands out to me. His tone was entirely usual when he said how pleased he was that I was recovered and rang the bell for service.

I only thanked him and sat. I felt as though I looked upon him from a great distance.

Granville called Mr Webber in and had him sit at table with us. Mr Webber looked quite as uncomfortable as I felt. He sat as though he were afraid he might break the chair, and when Mrs Bell poured him a cup of coffee, I would swear that he cringed.

"Is not Mr Webber the finest example of a man you have ever seen, Lottie? Look at the size of his arms. He is built like a tree."

"I am glad you are pleased with him," I said.

"Good Lord, yes," Granville said. "Lord Denheim has his pug set to go against Webber this very week. What did we think, Webber? Was his arm so thick as yours?"

"No, sir." Webber's voice was softer than I would have expected it.

"It is quite the thing amongst the London fancy, to have the training of a prize-fighter," Granville went on. "I have earned a welcome into London's first circle."

"I am glad," I said again.

"Are you? I hope so, although I can never tell, somehow."

He was absurd. I did not know how to talk to him.

"Lottie, look at me. Look at me, for goodness' sake. I must tell you something else, and I hate to talk to your bowed head in this way. Please, my dear, must you be such a nun?"

It was difficult indeed to hold his gaze. I could feel my eyes twitching with the desire to look away. Granville had a crumb of some foodstuff beside his mouth.

"I have renovated the gatehouse," he said. "What do you think of that?"

"It is admirable," I said.

"Is it?"

"Yes, it has been needed for a long while. I am glad to hear of it."

"Will you be glad to hear that I have moved Mr Webber there, with his wife? I could not house them here, you know. Mrs Bell would not hear of it."

I could not help but twitch my eyes toward Mrs Bell. She was standing perfectly still beside the door, holding the silver coffeepot. My head throbbed just to look at her. I felt very strange; perhaps I should not have risen. I looked then toward Mr Webber, but could not meet his eye. His hands were furred. My husband's hands, which I had once thought so hairy, were as a baby's by comparison.

"Webber does not mind my speaking so," Granville said. "He knows what a rough creature he is. It is why I prize him."

I could not hold my husband's gaze any more than I could Mr Webber's. I let my eyes settle on my lap and felt the kind of relief one feels in taking off a pair of tight boots.

"You must not walk down the drive any longer, Lottie," Granville said, "unless accompanied. I know you are accustomed to so doing, but it will not be fitting now. It is growing chill, in any case. I should think you will not venture out much now. Lottie, you must answer me, if you will not look at me. Have you understood?"

Mrs Webber, in the gatehouse. I found myself shaking my head at the thought. It was so odd.

"You do not understand?" Granville said.

He thought I was shaking my head at him.

"Of course I understand," I said.

We did not speak another word.

As soon as breakfast was concluded, I fled to my chamber and made the door fast.

I could not begin to order my thoughts. My husband so changed in my eyes—Mr Webber—Mrs Webber, so close—and yet I was forbidden to walk to see her, forbidden to walk at all—would I really obey an order so unreasonable as that one? I pulled the bolster from the bed and set it on its end upon the chair. A very little work with the cushions held it firm. I regarded it there, embroidered so many years ago by Miss Gale's hands in a pattern of autumn leaves. She had used to pinch my legs if I did not sit still and the back of my neck to force me up straight. Now I drew off my glove and drew back my arm. For just a moment, I felt foolish and weak—then I knocked the teeth from the bolster's mouth.

The rough fabric grazed my knuckles as though it bit me. I drew back my fist again and again; I pounded the leaves from those needlework branches. I heard my breath come as heavy as a horse's. I felt the pins working loose from my hair, the stray locks clinging to my dampened brow. I was made pure, I was cleansed of fear. Every moment of my life that I had spent without pounding my fist into something seemed to have been wasted time. I kept on until my legs trembled and the autumn leaves had tasted my blood.

I kept my gloves on all the evening. That was not unusual, and Granville made no comment. We sat together in the parlour, and I took a glass of warm wine and water, and then another, and dared him to question it. He did not. He barely spoke at all, only wrote in his ledger and smoked his pipe. I worked on my tambour. I was sewing the maid upon a donkey again. Granville should never see the other one. I sewed daisies for the donkey to walk upon, and with the movement of each stitch my glove rubbed against my raw right hand.

I MIGHT HAVE EXPECTED, after such a blow as I had felt, that I would fall into the arms of the liquor, perhaps never to rise again. I was surprised to find that I did not, doubly surprised that it was an action as simple as the beating of a bolster that made the difference. Almost every evening I locked myself away to grow as wild as a savage and pummel the autumn leaves into dust. I would sit at dinner, facing Granville's blank-faced deceit, and feel the desire to strike out at something humming through my limbs. I made that bolster wear my husband's likeness in my mind, I made it his strumpet's swelling stomach. I became a fury, a tempest, a swarm of bees.

◆ ◆ ◆

NOT LONG AFTERWARD Granville left for London, taking Mr and Mrs Webber with him. I bid him good-bye with never a blink and did not trouble myself to ask when he might return. His absence was like the opening of a door; I might do anything. I cared nothing, any longer, for his wishes.

Although I felt a great and fearsome freedom, I did not yet know how I might use it. I had never been at liberty before. Perhaps more than this, I was afraid that nothing would change, that even without the influence of my husband or brother, the world would reveal itself to be quite dull and ordinary.

I began stealing into Granville's library. He had a collection of sporting pages cut from newspapers large enough to fill almost an entire cabinet, all mounted upon stiff card and slotted into the drawers. The card exactly fitted the drawers; my husband was always a precise man. It was thrilling to go where I knew I should not. I took a book of Mr Douglas' sermons. I thought, *It is perfectly respectable for me to borrow this.* The sporting papers sat inside it almost as neatly as they did the cabinet. I took them back to my dressing room, and there I burned an extravagant amount of lamp-oil, sitting up to read of the ferocious battle between Mr Mendoza and Gentleman Jackson. The words themselves were often dry—*Mr Mendoza gave a fine display of science, but could present no match for the stalwart champion of the ring. The bout lasted only twelve minutes, with Jackson declared undisputed victor*—they mentioned nothing of fear, or sweat. Of course they made me think of Mrs Webber, who knew everything of fear, sweat, and a thousand other things I could only imagine. She had been living so very near, I could scarce believe I had not been brave enough to go out and find her. Now she had been carried off to London, before I could make her acquaintance. I thought, *If ever I am given the chance, I must summon the courage to talk to her.* I sat at the window of my dressing room, picking at the bumps upon my arms and sometimes, now, my breast. I did not care if

I bled or made myself ugly. I barely painted up anymore. I did not walk out; I had grown used to sitting within doors, and it was a grim, dreary kind of winter. There was nothing pretty to see.

I WAS SITTING in the window when I spied the old manservant, Horton, leading the brown mare around from the front of the house, with a sorry-looking figure upon it. I could see it was a woman, slumped and huddled in her cloak. I watched as Horton helped her dismount and handed the horse to Henry, the footboy. Horton took the cloaked woman by the elbow and both disappeared toward the kitchen door. I watched her as she passed beneath my window but saw only her bowed head, unkempt and beggarly. I took her for a poor woman from the village. I was not sure that it was proper that she should be brought to the house.

I did not call for a maid to enquire about the beggar, I called for wine. Lucy, the chambermaid, answered my bell.

"Who is it that Horton has brought to the kitchen?" I asked her, when once my glass was poured.

Lucy looked as stolid as she always did.

"It is Mrs Webber, madam. From the gatehouse."

My interest roused itself like an old dog beside the fire, slowly and shaking its head.

"Mrs Webber? It cannot be. Mrs Webber is in London."

"That's what we all thought, madam, but here she is, plain enough."

"What can you mean, Lucy? How did she get here? Why on earth did she look so ragged?"

"I couldn't say, madam. You called so quick I hadn't time to hear."

I looked at her, but she looked blank. I did not think she meant to be impertinent.

"Go, then, and enquire. You may tell Mrs Bell that I asked most particularly. And Lucy"—I could feel my own heart quickening—"tell Mrs Bell that Mrs Webber is to be given whatever assistance she requires."

I had been so much alone and confined to the house. I knew that some emotion rose within me, but I could not name it, nor hold it still. I felt myself grow impatient as Lucy's slow steps descended, and I waited to hear them come again upon the stairs.

It seemed I waited a long time, and when the sound of footsteps came at last, they belonged not to Lucy, but to Mrs Bell. She knocked upon the door, though it stood open.

"Come," I said.

"Lucy said you wished for news of Mrs Webber, madam."

"Yes, what news have you? Is it really Mrs Webber I saw from the window?"

"Yes, madam. It seems she decided not to travel to London. She has a touch of the ague, madam. Nothing as to require a doctor. Horton says he will take her home again when once she has eaten and rested. I ordered that she be given some arrowroot."

"But why did he bring her here? Why did he not bring the arrowroot to the gatehouse? A sick woman should not be riding up and down the drive."

"Perhaps you are right, madam. I will speak with Mr Horton about it directly."

"You may send him to me. Let Mrs Webber rest here. Make up a room for her and let us send for the doctor. It is always better to err on the side of caution."

"I am not sure that a doctor is required, madam," Mrs Bell began.

"I did not ask you for your thoughts, Mrs Bell."

My tone was sharp, and she looked as though I had reached out and slapped her cheek. When once the door closed upon her resentful back, I rose and began to pace about. I went to the window, expecting any moment to see Henry set out to fetch the doctor. The yard remained empty. I paced the room again. One turn of the room, two. In what room would they place her? Three turns, four. There were the two empty servant's rooms at the top of the house. Should I order her put there?

I went back to the window. There was a figure in the yard, trudging slowly away from the house. The steps were unsteady, the hooded cloak pulled quite over the head. A cloth bag dangled from one hand. A few sorry strands of hair waved in the breeze. I strode back to the bell and pulled it as hard as I could. It rang just as it always did, faint and musical, in the depths of the kitchen. It did not sound at all as I felt.

At length, Mrs Bell appeared.

"I have seen Mrs Webber walk away from this house," I said.

"She would not stay, madam, she is as wild as a heathen. You would not wish for her here, if you had heard the way she carried on."

"I made my wishes clear!"

"Madam, she would not stay. We could not keep her if she did not wish to be kept. She ate porridge and then she would not stay for anything."

I sat, heavily. I should never see her.

"Send the doctor to the gatehouse, then. I will do that much."

At least I will have news of her, I thought. It was a sorry compensation.

If I had not insisted then and seen Henry sent out for the doctor, she might never have been found until it was perhaps too late. As the case stood, it was not the doctor but Henry himself who found her, slumped in the hedgerow. He behaved admirably; he made Mrs Webber comfortable on the grass verge and covered her with his own coat, before running back to the house to raise the alarm.

When I bid Mrs Bell make ready a room, she looked thunderous.

"Madam," she said, "consider. She's a savage; the language she used, you've never heard the like. She should be brought to the gatehouse, surely. She cannot be part of a Christian household."

I could do nothing more than repeat myself: "Get ready a room for Mrs Webber, Mrs Bell."

Her mouth opened as though she would retort, but I kept her gaze until my eyes began to water. When she turned and left to do as I bid her, I felt suddenly exhausted.

I saw Henry still watching me and said, "What do you wait for? Go, take the dogcart and fetch her! And when you have brought her here, go back out for the doctor."

He blinked and made haste from the room.

I watched Henry come into the yard and lift Mrs Webber gently from the gig. She was awake; I thought she protested. I could not see her face, but her hands waved about his neck and would not settle. He turned his face away as though she would scratch him and carried her inside and out of my view. There came the sound of his feet upon the back stairs. I could not decide if I should go to look. Would it be proper? I could not tell. I had the strangest urge to check my face and hair in the glass, as though Mrs Webber were a lady visitor. At last my legs decided for me; as I heard Henry's steps reach the garret above me, I hurried from my room and up the servants' staircase.

As I reached the room, I heard Mrs Bell's voice.

"There, you bad thing, lie still and be thankful Mrs Dryer has a soft heart."

Then came some indistinct cursing; the words were lost, but the venom in the tone caused me to pause at the threshold. She sounded like a savage indeed.

"You may say so," Mrs Bell said, "but it is she who feeds you now, and you will learn gratitude or be left to starve once more."

Again the vehement muttering that I could not decipher.

When Mrs Bell cried out, "For shame," I suddenly knew that I had stood too long to raise my fist to knock. I could only steal back down the stairs, my heart thudding painfully. I had no sooner reached my own landing than Lucy appeared at the top of the main staircase. I could not tell if she had seen me appear through the servants' door.

"The doctor is come, Mrs Dryer," she said.

I made my back straight.

"Send him up to Mrs Webber, and when he has done, extend my invitation to take tea in the parlour," I said. My voice was more anxious than I would have liked it.

"THE FOOTBOY IS TO BE COMMENDED," the doctor said, accepting another glass of brandy from the butler's proffered decanter.

I nodded and smiled. I had been nervous before the doctor was shown in; I spent an age painting my face and neck. I did not know what humiliations he had seen when last he came upon me, bloodied and in a faint. I felt so flustered that I had taken up my embroidery just so that I would not pick at my scars. Once he was there, however, playing the dandy in his white waistcoat and carefully arranged cravat, I felt fairly well capable. I had only to do as I knew Mama would have done.

I smiled. "I am sure we will find reward for his heroism. Tell me again, Doctor, you say Mrs Webber has no fever?"

"She is only weak. It is nothing a few hot meals will not cure," he said, taking out his snuffbox and then, perhaps thinking better of it, returning it to his pocket. "She has been refusing to eat, in a fit of nerves over her husband's absence."

"Heavens," I said. "I never imagined Mrs Webber to be prone to nervous fits."

"I am afraid all creatures of your sex are vulnerable to attacks of nerves, my dear Mrs Dryer."

"I see. May I be assured that with a little care and nourishment she will be perfectly recovered?"

"You may be easy that you have done all you can, Mrs Dryer. A woman does not let herself starve without being sinfully willful. I understand that she grievously abused your staff when they attempted to extend a charitable hand."

"Yes," I said, "I understand that she did."

"Do not feel, in this case, that you need be too gentle. In fact, Mrs Dryer, I recommend that she be given nothing too fine to eat and be left quite alone, to think upon what she has done. You might consider that she be whipped."

An image rose up before me of Mrs Webber in the prize-ring, blood-soaked and swaying on her knees.

"I am not sure," I said. "My husband may be home soon, you know. I should prefer that all was tranquillity for his return. He thinks so highly of Mr Webber, you see. I am sure he would want Mrs Webber made calm and well."

Now the doctor looked thoughtful. "Of course, of course, there is Mr Webber's training to think of. I have been following it with great interest myself. Perhaps in this one case sportsmanship must take precedence over the moral lesson. Tell me, Mrs Dryer, have you news of your husband's progress?"

"He does not write to me of sporting matters."

Granville's infrequent letters were as stiff as his conversation—*The weather continues cold. I do hope you are not idle, &c.* My replies to him were not much better.

"No, no. I can imagine not. Well, then"—the doctor's eye had taken on quite a different light—"if she will not recover herself willingly, we may be forced to step in."

"I do hope that won't be necessary, Doctor. Do you think I might visit her myself and attempt to bring her to reason?"

"If you feel comfortable in doing so, you may be the person best fitted, Mrs Dryer. Speak to her of a woman's place, of acceptance and duty. You are too good, Mrs Dryer. Too good indeed."

I was too good, then.

WHEN NEXT I CLIMBED the servants' stairs, I walked with a surer step, for this time I went on the advice of the doctor. Before me, the ribbon at the base of Henry's neck quivered with each step that he took. He was carrying a laden tray and went slowly.

The tray held bismuth salts for Mrs Webber's stomach and a tincture of valerian for her nerves. There was also a good bowl of the white cullis I had ordered for my own supper and a slice of the plum cake I was so fond of eating when I felt melancholy. Mrs Bell could not stop her mouth twitching when I ordered this, but neither could she disobey me. I thought even the most willful woman could not deny herself such a treat.

I was exceedingly nervous. The very word "willful" had set my heart to fluttering.

When I declared my intention that morning, Mrs Bell had protested again, "Oh, madam, she's a heathen. It couldn't be proper."

"The doctor himself advised that I visit her and talk to her of duty," I said. "I shall take Henry with me; Mrs Webber owes him her thanks, and perhaps her life."

In Granville's absence, I was daily becoming more mistress of my household. I had never thought it was he that kept me so meek.

Henry knocked upon the door. There was no reply. He turned to look at me.

"Go on," I said, "call out."

"Mrs Webber," he called, through the wood. "We're come to bring you food. Your mistress, Mrs Dryer, is here."

He opened the door as cautiously as if he thought she might fly at him.

The first thing I noticed was the smell of her: damp cloth, stable cats, and sour milk. She lay on her side with her back toward us, very still under the grey blankets.

Henry put the tray upon the floor, there being nowhere else to put it. The only other furniture in the room was a stool and a washstand. The walls were bare but for a cross made of woven straw, held up by a nail. I wondered if all the garret rooms were so sparse. How strange it was never to have been here before. The dust made fairies in the light from the narrow window. Even beneath the blankets I could see that Mrs Webber's shoulder-blades were sharp as twin axes. I recalled her being stocky and as solid as a wooden doll. I was suddenly seized with the idea that this was not her. I had not seen her face from the window. Perhaps she was a beggar girl, only calling herself by Mrs Webber's name.

Henry was again looking at me for instruction.

"Wake her," I said.

Henry looked surprised, but moved toward the thin, still figure on the cot-bed. As he did so, the figure spoke.

"I ain't sleeping, but I would be left alone." The accent was as thick as fur.

She did not turn to look at us. I knew then it was she, and as uncivilised as Mrs Bell had painted her.

"Your mistress says you're to talk to her," Henry said.

"I ain't got no mistress."

Now she turned over and sat up as though it pained her to do it. She was terribly thin, but somehow more fearsome than she had been when she stood upon a stage with blood spattered across her dress. The skin beneath her eyes and in the hollows of her cheeks was as dark as a bruise. There was as much hair escaping her cap as kept in it, and it hung about her face in lank strings. I had not known before that her nose had been knocked off to the side. I wondered if I had witnessed the hit that set it so, that day at the fair.

"How can you say such a thing?" Henry said, fetching the stool for me and placing it a good distance from her bed. I sat gratefully enough; my legs were weak.

She made no reply, so he said, "Look here, what good Mrs Dryer's brought you."

Now she dropped her eyes.

"I never asked for charity."

"I'm sure Mrs Dryer didn't ask for a filthy wretch to come begging at her door, but there you came. Now, you speak nicely."

"I didn't beg! I came to ask the way to Bristol. If I was only stronger I'd be on my way there now."

When she spoke that little speech, she raised her head and I saw what a puzzle were her teeth; they seemed to gather into clumps, with great gaps between. She looked straight at me, with a hopeless defiance. She knew nothing about me. She could not know that I had seen her at the fair, that I had stood before the glass and pretended to stand as she had stood. I could say nothing of this, of course.

Instead I said, "If you wish to go to Bristol, I will have you brought there, as soon as I know you are made well. Now please, eat, I beg of you."

She eyed me then with even greater distrust. I thought, *She is like a neglected dog, or an unbroken horse. I must be gentle and slow.*

As if sharing my thought, Henry picked up the tray and hesitantly put it upon Mrs Webber's lap, all the time watching to see if she would knock it from his hands. The moment it was before her, however, she seemed to lose her fire. She closed her eyes, and I saw her sigh and her nostrils flare. A good steam rose from the bowl; the scent of white cullis will always speak straight to the stomach. She picked up her spoon and began to eat with hands that shook a little so that drops fell all the way from bowl to mouth. She did not even look to see if she spotted herself.

"Leave us, Henry," I said.

"Are you sure, madam?"

"Mrs Webber will be quite safe with me, Henry," I said, though it was the other way about that I thought he was uncertain of.

Henry had no choice but to leave, though he seemed to wish to say something. I had forgotten that Mrs Webber owed him her thanks. When once the door was closed behind him, I grew quiet and still. I had grown used to the scent of her. The only sound was the drip and splash of Mrs Webber spooning her supper. Her face was covered with a ghastly sheen, and she seemed to be breathing raggedly. She was racing to eat as though she feared that I might snatch the bowl from her.

At last she slumped back upon the pillows and closed her eyes. She had eaten only half of the cullis but looked sicker than she had before she began.

I did not know whether she was sleeping, nor even if she knew I was still there. Since she took up her spoon she had not once looked at me, nor thanked me. She had not touched the cake.

Without opening her eyes, she said, "That's the best thing I ever ate."

"It is a particular favourite of mine," I said.

"What is it?" She had her eyes closed still.

"It is white cullis: bread soaked soft in veal broth, cream, and I don't know what besides. Have you never had it?"

"Never."

It was curious to be conducting a conversation with someone who looked like a perspiring corpse.

"Have you had done with it?" I asked. "Shall I have Henry fetch the tray?"

Her misshapen pugilist's hands stole back to the edges of the tray and gripped it tightly.

"No," she said. "I can finish it. I only need a moment's rest, look."

"It is very rich," I said.

There was a silence so long I thought she must have fallen asleep in truth. At last she said, "If I was a proper lady, I'd eat white cullis every day." She spoke dreamily.

"While you are under my care, you shall," I said.

She opened her eyes a little and turned her head to look at me.

"Why d'you say that?"

"Because it is true. If you like it so much, I will order white cullis every day, until you are strong again."

"You're different to your husband, Mrs Dryer." She closed her eyes again.

I did not know what reply to make. I wondered how much she knew of Granville that she would say so. Before long her breathing slowed, and I knew that this time sleep had come upon her. I stood and came quietly toward her. Her face was softened in slumber. I thought of taking the tray from her, but I thought she might wake when she felt the weight of it leave her, and in the end I just stole from the room and instructed that she not be disturbed.

I WENT AGAIN the next morning, accompanied by Henry and the tray. I should have been far more nervous without him there.

She did not seem surprised to see me, but neither did she seem glad. She was glad to have the tray, however; she closed her eyes and breathed in the scent of the cullis, and then seemed almost ashamed to have done so. She ate quickly, turning her shoulder to hide the food as though she did not like us to look at it. That morning she cleaned the bowl without any of the terrible effort it had seemed to cost her the day before. Her face was already pinker about the cheeks. I sat again on the little stool and watched her.

"I am glad to see your appetite returned, Mrs Webber," I said.

Her lip curled as though she might snarl. Even thin as she was and lying abed in my own house, her pride was so solid a thing that it seemed to rise up and wave its fists at me.

"Returned?" she said. "It's only now I'm hushing it. You'd know nothing of that, though, would you? Being a lady."

I did not know how to take her; she cared nothing for propriety, or my sensibilities.

Henry stepped forward from his post beside the door. "For shame, Mrs Webber! You speak properly to Mrs Dryer, or she'd be right to turn you out."

I did not look at him when he spoke; I was watching Mrs Webber. She barely blinked—she cared nothing for Henry either.

"You say I know nothing," I said, at last. "I've certainly felt too anxious to eat, before now."

"That ain't quite the same now, is it?" She sat up very straight upon the bed, but I thought it cost her to do it. She was as rigid as a wax doll, the cords standing out upon her neck, her hands gripping the blanket.

I shied away from her gaze.

"The doctor told me you had suffered an attack of nerves and had been unwilling to eat," I said, my gaze upon my lap.

"Unwilling? Unable!"

"What can you mean?"

I looked at her then. She swung her legs so that she sat upon the edge of the bed, as though she meant to stand. For a moment, I thought she meant to charge at me.

"Can you not know?" She leant forward and hissed the words. "It was low, very low, to leave me so. I won't say it wasn't, no matter if you do bring me this white cully." She nodded to the empty bowl, on the floor beside the bed.

My face set up its queer tingling. "Henry, what's this? Do you understand?"

Henry looked as though he should like to run away. His cheeks, usually so rosy, were pale as plaster. "We thought she was in London, madam."

"I've never been to London a day in my life," she said. She looked, for a moment, as though she meant to spit upon the floor, but checked herself. Instead she gave a snort quite as scornful as spitting would have been.

Henry bit his lip like a child. "We'd no idea she was there, madam, or we'd have sent food."

I looked from one to the other, and I am ashamed to admit that my clearest thought was, *Now she will never like me.*

"I had not thought . . . I did not realise. I was told you had starved yourself, Mrs Webber, quite willfully."

"That bracket-faced bitch," Mrs Webber said, softly.

Henry and I both jumped with the surprise of it. Neither of us knew what to do, except to pretend that she had not said it.

"I expect Mrs Bell was afraid you'd lay the blame on her shoulders, madam," Henry said, to me.

The fury, which had been hanging about me in a cloud, now gathered in my breast and quivered like the needle of a compass.

"Not Mrs Bell," I said, as the needle swung. "No, the blame for this must be laid entirely at my husband's door."

My head, my very eyes, ached with rage. I could not even be glad that Mrs Webber gave me her first, faint smile.

I went to find Mrs Bell. I could not sit still to ring for her. I walked about the corridors as fast as if there were a hand in the small of my back, pushing. At last, when I had looked into almost every room in the main of the house, I came upon her standing at the open door of the downstairs linen cupboard, checking over the tablecloths and napkins.

"Mrs Bell, I would speak with you."

She turned immediately, closing the cupboard and smoothing her apron. Henry was right; she was anxious, indeed. Well might she be.

"Mrs Bell, you are to see that white cullis is sent to Mrs Webber every day. Every meal, if she wishes it. She may order any little thing she likes, and it must be brought."

"Yes, madam," she said, as meek as a wet kitten.

I felt my vexation curdle and sour; I should have preferred her to be defiant.

"I am quite serious, Mrs Bell. If Mrs Webber has a fancy for a roasted goose, you will find one and have it plucked. She is not to be denied a single thing."

"Madam, I hardly think—"

"You need not think, Mrs Bell. You have shown an aptitude, thus far, for an absence of thought."

Mrs Webber never did ask for any such thing as a roasted goose, so far as I could tell. She asked only for very ordinary things: soups, porridges, bread, and bacon. I went to see her every morning. Slowly she grew used to me, though she never said much. I would sit and ask her how she did. She would say that she did a little better. Then I would ask her if there was any little thing she might need. She always said no, thank you. After that I would not know what to say and she would seem to be waiting for me to leave her. I did not know what I wanted from her, but it was not this. Perhaps I wanted for her to like me, nothing more than that. I wanted her to tell me again how different I was to my husband, but she did not.

SHE LEFT, as I should have guessed she might, the moment she was strong enough. By Lucy's account, she had risen and packed her few things and was preparing to "run off without a by-your-leave." When I heard this, I ordered that she be taken by cart back to the gatehouse, if she would consent to it, and that she be given everything she might require to be comfortable. I sent this message by Henry. I could not trust anyone else to deliver it kindly.

"She looked black about it," he reported back to me, "and said she'd prefer to go to Bristol. I said, 'The mistress said you were to go to the gatehouse, not Bristol,' and she did let me take her down there at last, madam. She cursed a bit, though. She said she didn't go for you, but so that her husband might find her. I said he could have her and welcome." He blushed, but I could see that he felt pleased with himself.

"Thank you, Henry," I said. "I will pay her a visit soon."

"Madam, I know it ain't my place to say, but if I was you I'd make it very soon. She's like to bolt off at any time, that's what I think. If you want to catch her, you'd best not wait too long."

"Then I shall not. Thank you for your advice, Henry."

"You're most welcome, madam." He coloured again. He was a sweet boy.

I WENT THAT VERY DAY. I had Henry carry a basket of good things: eggs and ham, seed cake, bread, and a jar of white cullis sauce. Mrs Webber need only heat it through and soak her bread in it. In the other hand he carried a jug of fresh milk. He walked a little way behind me and whistled as we went.

I had not realised how much I had missed walking to the gatehouse. My spirits lifted with each turn of the drive. My legs seemed to wake and shake themselves after too long a spell of stillness. In my own hands I carried the book of sermons with one of Granville's card-mounted sporting papers hidden inside and, wrapped in a shawl, the piece of muslin on which I had begun embroidering the image of Mrs Webber so many weeks ago. It was a heavy load for me, but I would not give it up, and I was weary by the time we reached the gatehouse; I had grown unused to walking so far.

"Well, Henry," I said, "we are arrived."

"Am I to knock, madam?"

"Yes, carry on." I could not have said why I felt so nervous.

Henry smiled and stepped up to the door. He put his burdens down and raised his fist. As soon as he had knocked he stepped back, as quickly as though he expected the door to fly open and Mrs Webber to strike him from within. The door remained shut.

"Knock again," I bid him.

Still nothing happened.

"Likely she's gone out, madam."

I felt exhausted. I should have to turn and walk straight back. I would not be able to show her my sewing or the pictures in the sporting paper.

"Shall I leave the basket on the step, madam?"

"Yes," I said, my voice dull. "Yes, let us leave it there."

I turned and began to walk back up the drive. Now I could feel the ache in my legs. My ears were burning painfully with cold. My fingers were growing numb inside my muff.

Behind me, I heard Henry leave the step and his footsteps follow me. I felt as grey as the bare fields. I should have to trudge all the way back up the hill and spend the day alone, again. The only occurrences in my life seemed to be the expectation of events that never happened, which were not occurrences at all. I stopped walking.

"Madam?" Henry said, behind me.

I turned. "Suppose," I said, "that she is collapsed again, as you found her? Are we not bound by duty to be sure?"

"I'm sure we are, madam," Henry said, so quickly that I thought he might have been expecting it. "Shall I see if the door's unlocked?"

"Yes, Henry, check the door." My breast had set up fluttering again.

We retraced our steps. The basket was gone.

Chapter 18

✤ ✤ ✤

Henry and I looked at each other.

"This is exactly like feeding a hedgehog," I said, though I could see that Henry did not know what I meant. I was turned silly by the surprise of the basket's disappearance.

"Knock again," I said.

He did. Again, nothing at all.

"Will you have me call out, madam?" he asked.

"Yes, do," I said.

Henry put both hands to the door and called through them, "Mrs Webber, your mistress is here. You must open the door or we'll come in whether you bid us or no."

There was no response at all. Could we really go inside? Was that not trespass, although my husband owned the gatehouse? At least I knew that she had been fed; perhaps that was all that I could do.

Before I had decided, there came a shuffling from within. Henry and I looked at each other with wide eyes. In that moment, she had become a mythical beast, a troll, perhaps. When the handle of the door began to turn, I felt I might scream.

Of course, it was only Mrs Webber, looking just as she had when last I saw her, except that she had a fierceness about her that I had not been expecting. She did not bid us enter, but stepped aside wordlessly, holding open the door. Henry and I took this as a welcome and walked in past her. She did not curtsey, and I said nothing about it.

The gatehouse was filthy and cheerless, and smelt quite as badly as Mrs Webber had when first Henry brought her to us. There was a pile of soiled bedding in front of the hearth, which was out.

I turned and looked at her. She stood beside the door, but as I watched she closed it and stood still, head bowed slightly but her eyes fixed upon me, quite as oppositional as before. She looked as though she expected me to chide her for untidiness. Perhaps I should have.

"My days, haven't you made a mess," Henry said.

"I've been working at it," she said, twitching at her apron. I saw now that it was smudged with something black, coal dust perhaps. "I didn't know you was coming so soon." She spoke to me, rather than Henry.

I did not know what to do, then. I did not like to embarrass her.

At last I said, "I should have sent word, of course. If I might rest a moment, we'll leave you to keep house."

She did not answer.

"Ain't you going to invite Mrs Dryer to sit, Mrs Webber?" Henry said. "She's come all this way to bring you charity, look."

Mrs Webber looked at him as though she might leap at him and bite, or turn and run; she did not look usual. At last she seemed to compose her features.

"Please sit," she said.

I sat upon a little chair. My eye fell upon a picture above the mantel, of a boy and girl holding hands beside a stream. It was one I had done myself, in needlework, when first we were married. I had given it to Granville, to hang in his dressing room. Evidently my husband had not admired it.

Henry took the food we had brought into the larder and came back soon enough. Mrs Webber and I were as awkward as if we had never been in company before. All my manners had left me and she had never had any to begin; we did not speak, and neither of us knew where to look. Henry was the only easy person in the house.

"Shall I bring you in some wood, Mrs Webber? Or draw you some water?"

"Oh, yes," I said, "do let Henry help you."

Mrs Webber shrugged. "There's water to be fetched, I won't say there ain't. The wood and coal ran out, though."

"I'll fetch you in some water, and I'll get you some coal down from the big house before tonight," Henry said.

He went out of the back door and set himself to work. We could hear him whistling.

I could not bear to sit without speaking any longer.

"Please carry on with whatever you were doing, Mrs Webber," I said.

"What's that?" She pointed to the book and the shawl-wrapped picture.

I had used to have my fingers slapped by Miss Gale if I forgot my manners long enough to point.

"Some things I thought might interest you."

I opened the book and pulled out the sporting paper. She wiped her hands on her apron before she took it, although the apron was as black as her fingers. She looked at it for a long while, handling it as carefully as Granville would have.

"I never knew there were such things," she said at last.

"I hoped you would enjoy it. Some of the descriptions are quite exciting. You may borrow it to read, if you are careful with it. It is my husband's and I must put it back exactly as I found it."

She looked at me with an expression that said that she knew I had taken it without permission, but she made no comment. What she said was, "I can't read."

"Look at the pictures, then," I said. "And if you will allow me to visit you when you are settled, I will read you whichever parts of it you like."

"If my Tom wins his fight, perhaps he'll be drawn in a paper."

"He certainly will! I should be surprised if he were not."

She seemed suddenly shy and looked about for somewhere to lay the card. The tabletop was covered in crumbs and dust; she laid it at last on the seat of the other chair.

"Here is another picture," I said. I could scarcely stop my hand from shaking as I handed it to her.

She took it and held it up, drawing the muslin out tight between her hands so that she could see the figure there. I could not read her expression.

"This is like me," she said.

"It is supposed to be you, indeed."

"Did you make this?"

"Yes. It is not as like as I had hoped."

Her eyes squinted like an art collector surveying a new piece.

"My face ain't so square, and I'd be knocked out straight with a pose like that; my face is open."

"I thought the pose must be wrong, once I looked at the pictures in the paper."

"And my costume ain't like that, it's got less sleeve to it and a strip of blue about the skirt where it's sewed up."

"I knew I had remembered it wrongly."

She stopped and looked at me.

"You seen me fight?"

"At the fair," I said.

She only nodded, as though ladies came to watch her box every day of the week. Perhaps they did.

"Hark at this," she said, looking over her shoulder for Henry, "I got an idea for you. I'll put my costume on and my mufflers, and I'll stand for you so you can draw me."

"Would you? That would be so kind of you."

"It ain't kind," she said. "I'll want paying. Shall we say, two shillings a time?"

I had never in my life been propositioned in such a way. I was too startled to do more than nod. I had a few pounds of my own.

◆ ◆ ◆

I STOPPED BRINGING FOOD to her after that. I sent it instead by Henry in the morning and walked down alone to call at the gatehouse in the afternoons. I took care over my face and dress, although Mrs Webber did not seem to think about such things.

She never mentioned it, nor offered me so much as a glass of water, but I could see by her face that she was eating. She lost the pinched look, and her eyes grew brighter.

Once, when Henry passed by me as he went about his duties, I stopped him to ask how he thought she got on. Was she recovering well, did he think?

"I'll say she is, madam, with the care you've given her."

I said I was glad and nodded for him to leave me.

He stopped, however, long enough to say, "She's interesting, ain't she? She's not like anyone else you're like to meet, madam."

I could hardly have agreed more. The more I came to know her, the more fascinating I found her. She never behaved as though I was a guest in her home, but neither did she have the air of a guest in mine. Her head would come up, and she would regard me with the air of a dog that has decided not to bite, but has not entirely discounted the idea either. She would usually put her occupation aside, her mending or sweeping, but it seemed she did so not for politeness, but because my visit was a greater diversion than keeping house. She never offered me a seat, nor did she stand to greet me. She had no manners about her at all; she never once called me madam. No matter how often I was in her company, she never became forthcoming with conversation. She replied politely and sometimes even asked questions of me, but if a silence settled over us, I must always be the one to break it.

For all this she was ready and obliging to pose for me. If she saw that I brought my drawing-things, she would rise and go upstairs to change into her boxing costume without a word. If I came without charcoal and pad, she only sat and waited to see what I came for.

I laboured hard over those sketches. I wanted to translate her very spirit onto paper. I was trying, in one image, to bring to mind that tooth, flying through the air with its train of blood. I sat and fretted, adding strokes here and there, until often I would add too many and think the picture ruined. She stood very patiently, and when at last I grew tired and thanked her she would reply, "You're welcome; 'tis your coin to spend."

She said this as though it were a very commonplace thing. She never seemed in the least to be mocking me.

Then I would fetch out my drawstring reticule and dig in it for my purse.

BACK IN MY DRESSING ROOM, I pored over the pictures. None of them captured her quite as I wished. If I could only find one that suited me I could begin to render her image in needlework; I was always most comfortable sewing. I cursed myself for a poor artist. Sometimes I would feel the old urge to claw at my skin come creeping upon me, but I stayed my hand.

I was still nightly beating the bolster. Sometimes I grabbed it near to the top—where I imagined its collar to be—and, holding it there, struck it until I could see teeth fly, with their tails of blood.

The servants had begun to look at me queerly. They had always thought me odd, I knew that much, since I did not pay visits or go to plays, and drank more than a lady should. Now I thought Lucy handed me my powder box or glass of wine as though I might at any moment fall down raving. Horton, too, looked at me as though I had turned out not as dull as he had thought me.

I wrote to Granville, telling him that Mrs Webber had been anxious, and that the doctor had recommended that I visit her. I could not help but be nervous, for if I did not tell him, he could not object. *It is all for you, of course, that I do it,* I wrote. *I should hate Mrs Webber to make herself ill and disrupt Mr Webber's training, through his concern for her.*

Mrs Bell brought his reply a few days later, along with the sweet course. I read it with a growing sense of relief.

"Listen here, Mrs Bell," I said, when once she returned with my Madeira, "I have had word from Mr Dryer: *Keep visiting Mrs Webber as often as you can,* this part is to me, you see—*and speak to her of wifely obedience. As for the servants*—here he speaks to you, Mrs Bell, take note—*bid Mrs Bell to send her wholesome but modest dishes, to keep her in best health and humble spirits. Charge her to look after the needs of Mrs Webber as carefully as she would my own, for my happiness is tied as firmly to Mr Webber's serenity as if we were one person. He swears he must have his wife by him at his championship fight, and if she is to come to London she must be fit to be seen in company. You do great work toward a great cause, my dear. You have pleased me greatly this day.* Is not that wonderful? I have been wondering all this time if I was right to scheme to improve Mrs Webber."

Mrs Bell's lips twitched in a way that warmed my heart. *There,* I thought, *now whisper against me. I have my husband's express wish that I should continue as I am.*

I WAS STILL SNEAKING into Granville's library. Sometimes, although not often enough, I came across a line in the sporting papers I thought like poetry:

He stops as regularly as the swordsman and carries his blows truly in the line. He steps not back, distrusting of himself, to stop a blow and puddle in the return with an arm unaided by his body, producing fly-trap blows such as pastry-cooks use to beat those insects from their tarts and cheese-cakes.

I read those papers as I had used to read novels, with my heart rising up in my breast and with every sketch or engraving of a fighter I stopped and looked hard at the face, the position of the arms, the tilt of the head. I was coming to understand why it was called "the noble sport." I wished they would write about lady pugilists, but they did not. It was curious to think that Granville and I now had a shared interest and he did not know it. I practised standing as the pugilists in the sporting papers did, one foot behind the other and both fists raised, and I had Mrs Webber stand in the same way.

I HAD BEEN SO ABSORBED in my drawing—I was gazing at it very hard, for it seemed so nearly right, and yet, in some indecipherable way, all wrong—that I had not noticed Mrs Webber move from her pose and come around behind me. When her shadow fell across the page, I looked up, but by then she had already marked how my knuckles were crosshatched with grazes. She looked at my hand and her eyes grew knowing.

I expected her to laugh, but she did not. She regarded me frankly, and then furrowed her brow. I sat silently, as if waiting for judgement.

"You ain't fibbing right," she said at last. "You'll hurt yourself, going on like that."

She took my hand from me. I was excruciatingly conscious of the scars that dappled them, back and palm.

"What've you been hitting at? You want to practise on something soft and smooth. What was it, a flour-sack?"

"A bolster."

"A rough one, then. You'd do better to keep your gloves on."

"I cannot make a good fist in my gloves; they are too tight." This was one of the queerest conversations I had ever had.

"You can't make a good fist anyhow. Here, it should be done like this." She pushed my fingers with her own to curl them. Her fingertips were rough as sand. "The thumb outside, tucked here, and not so tight. There, now if your hand twists you won't be so like to break it. Squeeze the knuckles together, not the fingertips. There, now."

I took my hand back, but kept its fist.

"Now mind you throw it straight," she said, "from the shoulder."

I nodded.

"Do you know what I mean by that?"

"I am not sure."

"Would you like to know? You can go on drawing, if you'd prefer. It don't signify."

"I should like to know," I said.

I noted with a kind of satisfaction the sheer brazen cheek of her, giving me permission to go on drawing. I could not imagine what Granville would think, or Mrs Bell, or anyone at all. She was so far beyond the bounds of convention as to be almost other-worldly. I might do anything, I might take off all my clothes and run about screaming and scarred and Mrs Webber would not blink at it. Suddenly I was seized with a wish to test it.

"Dumb-glutton scut," I said out loud. It was the closest I could come to running about unclothed.

She had begun to move, but now she stopped and looked at me strangely.

"Do you call me that?"

"No. I only say it because I can."

She laughed. "Cursing for its own sake? You're not anything like I fancied a lady would be."

"I only thought I might be able to say those words here. I thought you would not mind it."

"And so I don't. Come on, then, and I'll show you how to throw a straight fib."

"Do you know what the words mean?" I stood to follow her.

"Don't you?"

"No. I am not sure. I think they must be something very bad. Will you tell me?"

We were walking toward the scullery. The back door was open, and through it I could see the leather man, hanging from his frame. She did not stop when she replied.

"If you can throw a good fib, I'll curse at you till the air's blue and teach you all the meanings besides. You're to work for it."

I found myself laughing aloud. The light in the yard was very bright, but the hedge was high and there was no one around to see us.

SHE HAD ME STRAP her own leather mufflers to my wrists. First she made me show her the fist I would make and pressed upon my fingers until she was satisfied. Then she held them out and I pushed my hands inside. I had expected them to be warm, but they were chilled and slightly damp. I could not help but think of all the sweat and blood that must have soaked the cloth that lined the leather. They smelt like an old, well-worn saddle. My arms immediately wanted to drop with the weight of them.

She laughed to see me.

"My stars, don't that look a treat. You with them frills and mufflers on your hands."

I could not stop gazing at my own arms: my sleeve ending at the elbow with a fine lace trim, my white, pox-speckled arms, painted with Pear's Almond Bloom. She was right; the brown leather mufflers looked absurd, like a fawn with the hooves of a cart-horse.

"Here," she said, and without asking whether she might, she picked up my kid gloves from where she had laid them on the windowsill and pulled them over her own, large-knuckled hands.

"Now we're both wrong-handed." She held her hands up.

I laughed to see it. The gloves were so very neat and strained at the wrist. The buttons would not meet. Her arms were brown and her apron coarse and spotted.

She pulled them off quickly enough, saying, "Ain't they little? I'll say they are."

She said I need not pin my skirts up just yet, since she only meant to have me stand and hit. Then she stood me in front of the leather man.

Suddenly it was as though I saw how foolish I must appear. I could not hit the leather man. Even lifting the mufflers made my arms ache. I felt as though I might run away, or perhaps weep.

"Come on," she said.

I only stood, feeling more ridiculous than before.

"Give him a blow, he's called you a dumb-glutton."

"Has he?" I smiled, but I could feel my eyes grow wet.

"Have at him, come on."

I hit him.

"Not like that, fib him like you mean it. Take him down. Say he's a lover has jilted you. Say he's your friend, that's bilked you. Hit him!"

"I don't know that I can."

"You can, you can. Say he's told foul stories about your husband."

"I should not care."

"Say he is your husband, then!"

But I could not rise, just then, to rage against Granville. "Perhaps he is my brother," I said, instead.

"He is, he's your brother. Look at him, he's mocking you."

I hit him then, and she cheered so that I hit him again. Mrs Webber was dancing around me. The sweat ran paint into my eyes and made them sting. I felt my hair come down around my face, and still I beat Perry's pink cheeks until his head rang. I beat him until he caught pox and was scarred.

THAT NIGHT I COULD NOT even put my gloves on, my skin had grown so tender. Mrs Webber said I was not to mind it. She said that true fighters pickled their knuckles in brine or liquor, to harden the skin. She said I had better not, being a lady, but would have to be brave if my knuckles stung. I sat in my dressing room and flexed my hand again. Each squeeze of the fingers was a dull, pink ache. I could not sew and so did not know what I might do with myself. At last I called for my supper on a tray, and with it, a glass of brandy, and then I dabbed my hand with it. It stung murderously everywhere that the skin was broken.

"Dumb-glutton," I whispered to my hand. I had wondered, once, whether the word might not lose its power once I knew the meaning, but instead I savoured it. Dumb-glutton: the private parts of a whore—a scut— the part that is always hungry but cannot speak. I thought of Perry, calling me that name so long ago. I thought that if I hit the leather man well enough I might ask Mrs Webber for a filthy name for a gentleman. I thought of Perry's face, were I to call him so.

I TOOK UP THE HEM of one of my old gowns to make a boxing costume. I wore my stockings, but even so I felt the strangeness of the breeze. Mrs Webber laughed to see me. The more unladylike I showed myself, the easier she was with me. It drove me on to new measures to please her. I tucked all my hair up underneath a cap. I brought brandy. I even, once, brought a cigar I found in Granville's library, but I could not like it, and even Mrs Webber declared it tasted like straw bonnets and wood chips.

I learnt that I had been standing in the wrong posture, after all; Mrs Webber made me lean at an unnatural angle, to keep my middle from harm's way. My knees she said I must keep bent, my left leg advanced a little, and both arms directly before my chin. I felt foolish.

"You look less a fool than if you stand open, for another cull to strike you," she said, and bid me practise my posture until I found it as natural as walking.

I practised hard, and she began to greet me with something approaching eagerness.

One afternoon, as I prepared to leave, she finally said, "I reckon you'll be ready to learn a bit of science soon. It's no good throwing a fib if you can't get shy of someone else's maulers. And now you've that frock you'll be able to dance about a bit."

I nodded. I had been wondering all that time, *How far will she let me go? Will she stop at my hitting a leather man? Will she let me hit her one day? Will she hit me?*

I might have just gone on beating the leather man until the day she grew bored of me. I was not sure I would ever have asked to do more, but I could not stop thinking of it. In bed at night I wondered how it would feel to be struck in the face. I found I hungered for it and dreaded it equally.

THE NEXT DAY the doctor called again.

"I have had word from Mr Dryer asking that I look in on the patient," he said. "I thought I would give myself the pleasure of your company first."

Why had I not expected this? Of course Granville would want her progress—our progress—reported upon. I smiled and bid him sit and pulled the bell for service. Thankfully it was Henry who answered my bell. I blessed Lucy for her idleness.

"Bring us tea and something sweet," I said, "and then run down to the gatehouse and bid Mrs Webber make herself nice for the doctor."

Henry's eyes widened just enough that I thought he understood.

"Oh, no, Mrs Dryer, I think it better if I come upon her unexpectedly. A more complete picture of how she does," the doctor said.

I smiled again. "You know best, doctor, of course. It is only that I wished you to see how obedient she is grown. If I send word by Henry that she is to make herself pleasing, you may have it on my honour that you will find her neat and ready to receive visitors just as I have been teaching her. It is the sweetest thing."

This was enormously risky, for of course I had taught her nothing. Even if Henry were to give her the message as I meant him to, she still did not know how to be sweet. But she must be forewarned. He could not come upon her if she was working the leather man, her hair sticking to her sweating face, cursing under her breath.

The doctor rubbed his chin. Henry bobbed slightly on the balls of his feet as if he were about to run. I kept my smile.

At last the doctor said, "Yes, perhaps you are right. You have made her obedient, you say, Mrs Dryer?"

"She is still a little rough, but I believe she progresses well. I do hope you will be pleased," I said. "You may go, Henry. Have Lucy send up the refreshments. And shall we have wine, Doctor? Or a glass of rum-and-water?"

"Yes, perhaps a strengthener would be wise at this time of day, Mrs Dryer."

"Of course. See to it, Henry."

THE DOCTOR DID NOT RETURN to see me after he visited the gatehouse, and I could not be sure how long he was there. I sat in my window and looked for Henry, but I did not see him. At last, though I knew that it would only fuel the servants' talk, I rang for Lucy and bid her send Henry to me. He arrived looking perfectly cheerful.

"I helped her tidy up a bit. She changed her dress and agreed to curtsey and call the doctor 'sir.' Wasn't much else I could do, madam."

"She agreed to call him sir! I am amazed, and, if she did it, I am relieved indeed."

"I told her to do it for your sake, so that you'd not have trouble from Mr Dryer. I knew she'd have to if I told her that."

"Did you? Does she like me, then?"

"I should say she does, madam. She said she hasn't had you spar with her yet. She said she can't let you go before she's felt a real lady's hand hit her chops."

I know my face showed my shock, because Henry looked anxious and said, "Please, Mrs Dryer, I'll never breathe a word. I've known of it a good while and I've never let slip to anyone."

I could only nod, so breathless did I feel.

I brought it up, stammering over my words, the moment I was through the gatehouse door.

"He's a good boy, though, Henry," she said. "He's got a good hit on him, as well. I've been teaching him a bit in the mornings and we sit together, sometimes, and look at the pictures in the papers you bring me."

"My goodness," was all I could say. "I did not know."

"You'll have to look about you more, won't you? Else you won't know what's coming at you. We'll begin today with that."

Chapter 19

❖ ❖ ❖

The air on my legs had begun to be familiar, but I was acutely aware of it now. I felt aware of everything: not only Mrs Webber standing before me, the leather man visible over her left shoulder, but the curls escaping my cap and tickling my forehead, the packed earth beneath my half-boots, the wall of the gatehouse a little distance behind me, the sunlight bright against my eyes.

"Now, Mrs Dryer, what disadvantage have I put you to?" she said.

"You know everything, and I nothing. The advantage is all yours."

She waved a hand. "You've the sun in your eyes. You put yourself there, all lit up and half blind. Come, move about. Let's both stand sideways to the sun. Now"—she scuffed two parallel lines across the yard with the toe of her boot—"let this be scratch. Stand ready, put your fives up."

I did so, but not to her liking, for she stepped forward and, taking my wrists, moved them into a position she thought better.

"Now you fib me," she said, "just as you would the dummy." In the sunlight, her eyes were lit the golden brown of a cat's.

"I cannot."

"You'd better, or I'll fib you."

I threw my fist, and she hit my arm away with a force that I had not expected. I stumbled, and she moved with me. Her own hand she stopped just inches from my cheek.

"There, you see? You were too slow and left your face open. Now try again, and quicker."

Again I hit out at her. Again she hit my arm away, in the same spot, so that I felt a dull pain. Again her fist stopped just before it struck me.

"You ain't trying! Will you leave your head there for me to fib it? You can't stand so still. Keep your hand here"—she grabbed my left wrist, roughly—"and cover your face. Now think, Mrs Dryer. I've shown you what I'll do. I'll not change it, this time. But will you let me?"

"I do not know! Cannot you show me what to do?"

"I'm showing you. I'm also bidding you think. Get those tears from your eyes. Don't you weaken now. Strike me!"

I threw my fist again, and again she hit my arm. I should have a bruise there later. As she did, however, I threw my other hand, wildly and with desperation. It struck not her face but her wrist, as she moved toward my cheek. It was not a strong hit, being knocked sideways by her own strike upon my arm, but it was enough to prevent her blow reaching me. She dropped her hands and I dropped mine. She smiled so that all her odd teeth were displayed.

"There! That's thinking. Now I'll hit you, and you try to stop me."

And so we went, turn and turn about, until I was quite ragged with exhaustion. Still neither of us had struck a true blow upon the other, I because I could not, and Mrs Webber because she would not. It did not matter; my heart beat with a wild joy that sometimes swooped toward despair. I could not do it, I could not do it, but here, I was doing it! It was harder than I'd thought, but I was more capable than I had thought myself. Both were true at once. When at last we stopped, I was trembling all over with the exertion and the thrill.

Of the doctor's visit, Mrs Webber said only, "He just wanted a bit of sweetness. I told him he was all kinds of hero. He's just like any gent I ever met, in that regard."

"And you did not mind it?"

"I never do mind it, if it's sham. And I thought, if I did it right, he might never come back."

"Unless you were too sweet, Mrs Webber."

"I didn't give him any, if you mean that," she said. "Though he would've took it if it was offered. He had the eye on him."

She flexed her hands, grimacing with satisfaction as the joints cracked. I only stood, looking at my own as though I had never seen them before.

I slept that night without strong drink and without dreams.

WE HAD ENTIRELY GIVEN UP the posing and the drawing. Instead I paid her two shillings daily to strap gloves onto my arms and have me dance about the yard. I began to learn to watch her movements, and what those movements meant. Once she saw that I was watching, she began to play tricks on me, twitching her left shoulder so that I thought she would move from that side and then striking from the right. I learnt that it is better to dodge than to block a blow when you are smaller than your opponent. I studied hard, and still she avoided my every attempt to strike her. In return, she defended herself and stopped her fist as she had that first day, to show me where my own defence should have been. She would not strike me. After a week of this, I grew peevish.

"Are you truly fretting that I won't fib you?" she said. "If you must fret, let it be because you can't land a hit."

"I wish to know what it feels like! I have never been struck. Even when I was a girl, my nurse would not spank me."

"I reckon you were a good little girl, who didn't need spanking." Mrs Webber looked at me sideways.

I laughed. "I was not! I was punished in other ways."

"I was funning with you," she said. "I know you were bad. No good girl would've come here to me begging to be struck about the chops."

"Will you, then?"

"I'll spar with you in earnest, if you mean it. If I hurt your looks, you mustn't cry over it."

"My looks were spoiled long ago."

"You've all your teeth, which is more than I have."

I thought of that tooth flying through the air, but it was not enough, any longer, to give me pause.

I STOOD BEFORE HER with my fists raised. I felt my own eyes narrow.

"Good," she said, seeing this. "We ain't playing now."

"We are not," I said, and stepped forward.

I hardly knew what happened next. I had scarce begun before my head was driven sideways. *Why, it does not hurt at all,* I thought. It was only so surprising, and so powerful. I barely kept my feet. It was like being swept away by a stream.

Mrs Webber had stopped and was regarding me anxiously, her arms dangling by her sides. I put my hand to my cheek and straightened myself. Now I could feel the pain begin, muted and irritating, like a fly droning in my ear.

She opened her mouth to speak, but before she could I rushed at her, hitting every part of her that I could reach, all ideas of science and defence gone from my mind, as wild as a hoyden. The sheer surprise of it drove her backward, and she stumbled for a moment. Then she began to defend herself, as I was forgetting to do. Later I realised that she could have struck me many times, but she let me whirl about like a windmill and only protected herself. At last she grabbed my wrists and twisted me so that she was behind me and holding me by my arms.

"Now will you be still, you cat?"

In answer I bucked as hard as I could and felt the back of my head crack painfully against her own. She cursed aloud—"Hell!"—and let me go. I turned to face her, feeling a terrible mixture of anxiety and excitement that I had hurt her in earnest, for I had not meant to strike her with my head at all—I turned, and turned straight into her fist, which struck me squarely on the chin and knocked me to the ground. I crouched in the mud, my hands to my face. My eyes were running with water.

She helped me up, and we went slowly inside together, her hand upon my elbow. She put me in a chair and went to make tea while I sat and touched my chin, the tender and marvellous softness of a new-born bruise.

THE NEXT DAY MRS WEBBER had me back in gloves and working at the leather man—for she said we would not spar again until my head was healed, "lest it turn you queer; too many knocks on the crown will do that, you know."

I was thrashing at the leather man, and, whilst each hit seemed to jar the insides of my head, I felt differently now that I had struck a real person and been struck myself in return. Each pain only drove me on to hit, as though it were the leather man that injured me. Mrs Webber stood by and watched.

"Don't drop that hand. Bring it back up, cover your face. Good! Now, what's he imagining you'll do?"

"I cannot say. Hit him again?"

"Yes, and in the same way you've been doing, for it's all you've done. Do it again, and now, quick—poke him in the belly. Turn that elbow out. Now if he comes up you'll fetch him a jab with its point."

"I don't understand."

Mrs Webber looked over my shoulder. "Henry, come and show Mrs Dryer what I mean."

I span about; I had not known he was there. It was one thing for him to know my secret, but it seemed another to have his eyes upon me while I hit out at the leather man. I felt clumsy and foolish and haughty, all at once. Henry walked over to us and shrugged his coat off.

"Now, Mrs Dryer, you give him a blow to the guts. Not a real one, mind."

I did so.

"More real than that, just don't hurt him! There. Now, Henry, if that were a real blow, what'd you do?"

"I'd block a blow like that quick as anything."

Mrs Webber clipped him about the head. I jumped a little, so unexpected was it, but Henry seemed not at all surprised.

"I meant you'd fold up," she said.

Henry obediently bent over as though winded.

"Now, Mrs Dryer, instead of bringing your arm back here, bring it round, like this, and when he starts to stand—come up, Henry, slowly, mind—you're to dart him in the peeper with your funny bone. Like that, good. You'd have his eye ruby, then."

WHEN WE HAD DONE and were sitting beside the fire, feeling our chilled skin thaw so fast that we courted chilblains, then Henry told us why he had come.

"I heard from the coalman, who heard from a fellow in Keynsham, that two ladies are set to fight tomorrow night, in a field at Lansdown."

"Ladies?" I said.

"Females, then." Henry blushed. "Will you come?"

"I should think we will!" Mrs Webber said.

"I? How can I go to see ladies—females—fighting in a field?" I said.

"How can you not?" Mrs Webber asked.

"It would not be proper. People would talk."

"I promise you, you shan't meet your quality folks there. We'll give you a plain cloak and a scarf about your head and no one will blink at you."

"But at night! Where would I say I went? Who will take me? Henry? Mrs Bell already thinks I favour him."

"And so you should. He's the only one of your servants worth ha'penny."

"I cannot think of a place I would go, at night, with Henry. They already say that I am queer."

"I should think they say you're lovers, more like."

"They do not!"

"Look you at Henry's face and tell me they ain't whispering something like that. What do you care?"

Henry blushed. "They don't say anything so wicked. They do tease me that I'm your particular favourite, madam. They call me a catch-fart, they say I follow so close behind you. I tell them to still their tongues. I say they're run mad."

"I expect that makes it the worse," Mrs Webber said.

I could feel my breath begin to come quickly. Mrs Webber softened.

"You may not credit it," she said, "but I know what it is to feel your name made dirt. But they—people of all kinds, I mean—they'll say whatever they will to please themselves, and you'll not stop them. But you can stop them from stopping you, Mrs Dryer."

"I am not sure," I said, "I am not sure."

"Well, we won't judge you. Henry and I'll go, and he'll tell you all he learned."

"But already he knows so much more than I do."

"Well, he ain't waiting home so that you can catch him up. Either come along or hold your peace."

"I will come," I said.

"Of course you will. Henry'll help you."

HENRY, IT TRANSPIRED, had thought of something so simple that I could hardly believe that I had not thought of it myself two years before; he fetched Granville's old one-horse cart out and made it clean. I had seen the servants drive it so often that I had quite forgotten that once it had been a respectable gig. He scrubbed it down and put a blanket over the seat. He told Mr Horton that I had asked that it be made nice and the old man had not blinked at it. Nor did Mrs Bell, when I said that I went to see my brother and that she need not expect me home that night. I could not believe that I had been so much confined when liberty came so easily.

For his part, Henry solved the problem of how he was to join us and gave the servants something to talk about at the same time.

"I told Mr Horton there's a kitchen maid I've a fancy for, up at Aubyn Hall," he said, as we set off. "I asked if I might be allowed to drive you, so as to see her. He didn't want to come out on such a cold night as this in any case, and gave up the reins almost before I finished. Mr Horton hates to play the groom."

"And is there? A kitchen maid?"

Henry smiled.

"There is!" I said.

"She don't like me, I don't think," he said, "but I keep hoping, if I'm sweet enough, she might look kindly on me."

"She is a fool if she does not," I said.

Mrs Webber was waiting outside the gatehouse, carrying a bundle. I leant over and put out my hand. She took it, and I felt the full weight of her as she scrambled up. Once safely aboard, she thrust the bundle at me by way of greeting.

It was a black homespun cloak, old and smelling somehow of rabbits. There was a scarf, plain wool, in a greyish blue. The scarf smelt as rabbity as the cloak, but they had been bundled up together, so perhaps it only borrowed the scent. I dared not comment upon it, but put them on and raised the hood.

"There," Mrs Webber said, "no one will tell you ain't a common Judy. It's luck I'd another cloak. I've given you the nicest one."

How glad I was that I had not spoken. I looked at the cloak Mrs Webber wore, but the sky was darkening so that I could not make out much of it; perhaps it was thinner, a little more frayed.

Henry started the cart moving. The sunset was turning the sky to autumn shades of gold and bronze. I had never before been so utterly without chaperone. Oh, I had been out with only a servant, but Henry and Mrs Webber were not servants, they were conspirators. I thought, *I am out at dusk, in unsavoury company,* and felt the joy of it bubble in my throat. Henry whistled a tune that caught my rising excitement so exactly that I felt as though he read my thoughts; Mrs Webber was looking upon me with a smile somehow doting and roguish together. I felt absolutely wild.

The journey lasted long enough that I began to feel nothing but tired and half frozen. The roads wound on, the cold crept in. I clutched the rabbit cloak about my throat. The only merry thing then was Henry's whistle, which never lost its gaiety. Now the very jollity of the tune made the darkening skies seem the darker and the cold that much more biting. By the time we rattled into the cobbled yard of an inn, I was aching with the jolting of the cart and sitting so long in the wind. The place smelt as though they had not cleaned out the stables for weeks.

"We walk from here," Mrs Webber said.

"Is it far?" I did not like to let go my close embrace about myself and admit the cold.

"It's a fair walk, I'll not say it ain't. But someone must keep the horse."

A man with a lantern in his hand—a groom, I supposed him—waved us toward the stables and walked beside the cart until we stopped where he directed. Then he reached up and took the reins from Henry. They spoke to each other, but I did not attend to what they said; I was looking about myself at the shadows across the cobbles—which could have been any kind of filth—the utter blackness inside the stables where the light from the lantern did not reach. The man's face was lit from below, throwing his eyes into shadow.

Mrs Webber's hand pulled at my elbow, and I made myself stand and scramble from the cart. I made a fumbling business of it, unable to keep my skirts straight and hitting my leg against the wheel.

"Wake up, now, missy," the groom said.

I had forgotten until then that I was dressed so common. The inn itself looked low and mean. No one would know how I was to be treated.

He turned his back upon us and began unhitching our mare.

"Come." Mrs Webber took my elbow and started my sleepy legs moving toward Henry. She set a quick pace, and soon enough my blood warmed, though my feet stayed numb.

Once out of the yard, in the pitch-black lane, my spirits roused. The light of the inn was lost with the winding of the roads; I could barely see. The sky was a spangled dark grey above the black hedgerows; Henry and Mrs Webber were hooded silhouettes. Henry had fallen silent, and the only sounds were our own breaths and the rustling of nocturnal creatures. I had never been so much part of the night. I felt like a bat, a spirit, a rogue. I understood what it might be, to be a witch.

We climbed over a stile, Henry giving me his hand, and crossed a field, my boots growing heavy with mud. Before we were halfway across, I realised that the pale orange glow I had taken for a remnant of the sunset was flickers of firelight and flitting shadows. As we grew nearer, the shadows turned to a mass of people, like dark trees swaying in the wind. Here and there a brazier was burning, and then they became people again, grotesque in the firelight, all shadows and crimson skin. Pieces of conversation drifted out to our ears and were sucked back into the drone. Then we climbed over one more stile and became part of the crowd ourselves, a great gathering of savages. It seemed fantastical that a field should be transformed into this coven of cloaked figures. The link-torches and lanterns bobbing about the crowd made green spots come before my eyes when I looked away. I knew that if I lost sight of Henry and Mrs Webber, I would be lost forever. I stayed so close behind Mrs Webber that her cloak wound about my legs and when a man stepped between us, moving in the other direction, I reached out a panicked hand and grasped the cloth of it. She kept moving, and I jerked her back. She turned in surprise and said, "All right, I won't lose you."

Henry behind me was jostled so that he had to take hold of my shoulders in order to avoid being pressed too tightly against me. The people around us were hardly people at all. If I was knocked down, none of them would notice; they would trample me where I lay. But of course, Henry and Mrs Webber would not let that happen.

Then we came to the heart of the crowd, where a string had been tied to stakes pushed into the earth. The people came right up to the string like sheep jostling a fence. It was not strung tightly and undulated against the legs of those at the front, as those behind pushed forward. There were lanterns hung on iron poles and more braziers, each with a knot of people gathered close enough almost to burn.

Mrs Webber led us so close that we could not help but sway and shuffle as others pushed past us. I found I could see again; we had entered a circle of yellow lantern-light. My view of the ring—the space that was to be the ring—opened and closed with the movements of the crowd.

Henry was grinning like a boy at the circus.

Mrs Webber jabbed her elbow into my side and said, "Give us a six-pence."

I dug about in my reticule and found a shilling. She disappeared into the crowd, but now, with Henry beside me and in the circle of light, I let her go. *Henry,* I thought, *will keep me safe, and in any case, she is sure to come back.* I remembered that I had not trusted him to look after me at the fair. I had been so ignorant then.

Mrs Webber did return to us, coming from the opposite direction to the one I had expected and holding a small bottle. She pushed it into my hands and I put it to my lips obediently. It was sharp as sucking on a lemon and burned like lit coals. Tears sprang to my eyes, and I buried my face in my shoulder to cough; I could not help it. I felt Mrs Webber lift the bottle from my fingers. My throat felt as though I had hung my head over the fireplace.

"Rag-water," Mrs Webber said. "Warms the blood."

She took a long swallow, gasped aloud, and handed Henry the bottle. He coughed almost as badly as I had done.

A hot fist had clenched in my stomach and now spread rays of heat out to touch my limbs. I began to look about myself with great interest, and well I might have, for it was then that four women came into the ring; the two fighters and their seconds.

The first woman—built like a washerwoman, with thick arms and wrists—shrugged off her cloak. I felt a shock go through me like a dash of cold water. She was bare to the waist. Her bosom hung like ripe pears, catching in the yellow light. The other woman was as bare as the first. Hers were smaller and more like my own, but closer together. *Are mine far apart,* I found myself thinking, *or are hers near?* They must have been unbearably chilled; I felt my own bosom shrivel in sympathy. I had never seen another woman stripped bare before. I forgot, in the shock of it, that they were to fight.

I saw how Mrs Webber and Henry were watching me: he apprehensively and she with a look of great amusement.

"I give you my word, Mrs Dryer, I'd no notion they'd be like this," Henry said.

"Well, no more did I," Mrs Webber said, "but you mustn't mind it. Girls do fight with their dugs out, sometimes."

"Do you?" I could not help but ask.

"No, not I," she said. "Not unless the pay's handsomer than what these wretches will have." She laughed so that I could not tell if she were speaking truthfully.

The women closed in on each other and the crowd hushed. I was watching the smaller of the two. Her shoulders were tensed, but at the call of "time" she seemed to drop them in a sigh before she leapt upon her opponent. *Here we are, then,* her face seemed to say, *and I had better get on with it.* They fell upon each other in a grappling, clawing manner much different to the strike-and-defence that Mrs Webber practised. The larger woman would not let the smaller go, and the crowd was not pleased; she seemed to want to crush her, rather than exchange earnest blows. They swung together in a desperate dance while all about us the cries rose.

"Have at it honest!"

"Ah, you big fussock! Give the girl her arms!"

The larger woman threw the smaller to the floor with a force that I thought would break her neck; the crowd screamed in savage joy. The smaller one scrambled to her feet as though she expected to be kicked while she lay upon the floor. The large woman's breast heaved and her bosoms swung like bags of meat.

The next round began; now the smaller knew what the other might try and would not get close enough to allow it. They began to circle each other with their fists raised. I felt myself raise up onto my toes as though I were with them. When at last they began to swing at each other, I moved and gasped with every blow.

Watching that fight was an entirely different experience to the fair. I was not afraid, or at least not much, of the crowd about me. I did not imagine that one woman would kill another. The most marked change was that I could see, now, what each fighter did. Not all the time—they moved so quickly—but here and there, I thought, *Yes, she moves to block,* or, *Now she will go for the left side.*

The smaller woman was too slow. It infuriated me.

I believe I called aloud, "Be quick! Oh, be quick!"

She dealt the large woman a blow and then waited too long before skipping away. She would be caught any moment, I knew. As soon as she made a skewed blow, missing her opponent's face and striking her shoulder, the other woman grabbed her as a hawk grabs a mouse, and they were back to their grappling embrace.

I looked to Mrs Webber, but she was looking past me at a girl of about my own size, wearing a brown wool cloak and with a harelip like a knife-slash from lip to nose.

"I seen you, you nibblish bitch," Mrs Webber said. "You were like to foist my cousin here." Her voice was harsher than I had ever heard it.

"I'll say you never." The harelip twisted further into a snarl.

I looked from one to the other and put my hand to my throat.

"I tell you I seen you, witch." Mrs Webber put a hand on my arm, protectively.

"What?" I said. "What was she doing?"

"She was readying to pick your pocket, except I saw her first."

"Oh, muddy slander," the harelipped girl said. "I should give you a slap."

Another girl, with great dark circles around her eyes, appeared beside her. I felt Mrs Webber's shoulder come against mine.

Henry was smiling to see us quarrelling. All about us, in fact, people were turning to watch as though our disagreement were as exciting as the action in the ring.

"Don't you call my chum a prig," the sickly-looking girl said directly to me.

"I've not called either one of you anything at all," I said.

"Hark how she talks!" the sickly girl said. "Like a lady. You've come down a way, ain't you?"

Both girls laughed.

"It'll be you down if you don't hush your lip," Mrs Webber said. She nudged me. "Fib her one."

"What?" My voice was weak.

"Slap her," Mrs Webber said. "I'll be with you."

"Set-to," someone behind me called out, and the cry was taken up by other voices all about us.

"Set-to, then!"

"Let's see you go at it!"

"Go on, Mrs D," Henry called out.

I began to say I cannot, but the sickly girl shot her hand out as fast as a snake and grabbed me by my hair. It was astonishingly painful; my body shrivelled and pulled upward, as though all of my limbs hung on puppet strings from the roots of my hair. More surprising than this was that even while part of my mind cried out—*Stop, stop!*—another part whispered,

Move into her hand. I thrust my head up into her fingers and the pull loosened. Then I thought, *If I hit her now, while she has hold of my hair, she will pull me down.* I could not think what to do, so desperate was I then to make her let go. I chopped my hand at her arm with all my might. Pure luck—for I had not the foresight to aim for it—drove my blow into the inside of her elbow, forcing her arm to jerk closed. Her grip stayed strong enough that, although she let go, some of my hair went with her. It was a hot pain entirely unlike being struck. I felt myself filled with outrage, laid over with fear. I hit her as hard as I could, and felt my knuckles jar against her cheek. Then my eye exploded in white light.

AT THE TIME, it seemed to me that I should never be allowed to stop fighting, although Henry said afterward that it lasted only moments. It had been the harelipped girl whose fist had given my eye such a blow, after which Mrs Webber had struck her so hard as to knock her quite dazed, and had pulled me away from my sickly assailant.

"You weren't doing badly," she said, "but I didn't like to leave it too long."

I had been quite giddy from the excitement whilst the quarrel lasted, but huddled in the back of the dogcart travelling home, I was only injured, exhausted, and terribly cold. I managed to smile, but even moving my lips hurt.

"I think you did right." My voice was cracked as though it, too, had taken a beating.

"Next time you'll hit her before she gets hold of your head," Mrs Webber said.

"Don't," I said, for laughing was like sharp fingers in my ribs.

"Well, then, next time, shall I find you a smaller one? Only I thought you were well matched, there."

I stared at her.

"You didn't think I caught her with her hand in your purse, did you?"

she said. "My days, Mrs Dryer, the sharpers there are like rats: too quick to catch, and as common. No, I just thought, it ain't really a mill till it's a mill, if you catch my meaning. Thought you'd be getting sick of the dummy."

"I might have been hurt," I said.

"I was there, wasn't I? Did I let you come to harm? Besides a bit of your hair being out, I mean."

"I suppose not." Most ladies would be hard put to think of something worse than losing a handful of their hair.

"There we are, then."

Ahead of us, on the cart-seat, Henry began to whistle a tune so pretty, and so strangely sad, that we both fell silent to listen.

I COULD NOT STOP TOUCHING the tender part of my scalp. In one patch, my hair was half pulled out, and where it remained, it looked as ragged and sorry for itself as an invalid's. I could not smooth it, the roots seemed to cry out. I was glad that I had taken to wearing my hair inside a cap instead of having it dressed. Glad, too, that I was so proficient in the use of paint. There was a small purple-grey patch upon my cheekbone and a long scratch along my jaw, but they disappeared well enough under the layer of white. I kept my gloves on, but there was nothing unusual in that. I painted up so convincingly that, surveying myself in the long glass, I felt a little disconsolate that I did not appear more changed. I was changed; I felt it in every ache of my limbs.

I felt it all the more when I came downstairs. The breakfast table was as it always was, with my plum cake, my chocolate, the boiled meats I rarely touched but which were always brought. The clock ticked upon the mantel, the unknown portraits frowned down from their frames. Lucy stood as silently as always, waiting to step forward and serve me. I sat, for what else was I to do? I picked up the cup of chocolate. My swollen hand moaned in protest as my fingers curled about it. It was this, I think, that moved me to speak.

"Today I would like these portraits removed, Lucy. Have Mr Horton put them somewhere safe. I will leave it to his judgement as to where."

"Yes, madam," she said.

And that was all. When I thought of it, what else was she to say?

ONCE I HAD BEGUN, I found I must carry on. If I had to quarrel over it with Granville, let it be a larger matter than a small. I had Horton and Henry work together to take down the portraits from all about the house. I had them take the heavy candlesticks to Granville's study. I had the stuffed fish removed from the hallway.

I was alive with excitement, pointing at everything about me, saying, "And this, and this! Remove this! And the sword, take that away. Keep it safe, but take it away. What else, what else?"

The menservants did exactly as I told them. Horton seemed a little dazed by the sudden activity; I suppose he did nothing much in our house but polish the banister and see to the silver. Henry could scarcely conceal his smile.

Mrs Bell came into the hall at full speed, as though she expected to find burglars there. We heard her coming up the back stairs, heavy as a country hobnail. When she burst through the servants' door and saw us she stopped short. I was directing the removal of a painting depicting a bewigged gentleman with forbidding eyes. It was high enough that Horton had been obliged to fetch the step-ladder, which Henry had climbed. Now he was trying to unhook the painting safely from the wall, while Horton craned up to support the heavy frame. The whole procedure was ungraceful, with cries of "Steady there!" and "Hold her, Mr Horton!" while I waited impatiently for it to come down, so that I might direct them to the next. I could not help holding my gloved hands before me as though I myself held an invisible painting. This was the scene Mrs Bell came upon. Her mouth opened and then quickly closed itself and squeezed tight.

I saw her face and felt glee rise up in me.

I could not help but say, "Yes, Mrs Bell?"

She drew herself up and said, "I came to see what the noise was about. I'm sure I was not expecting this."

"You need not have expected it, we have it perfectly under control."

Just then the painting came away from the last hook and fell. Horton stopped its collision with the stone floor by falling to his knees and giving a terrific grunt as he caught it. Mrs Bell looked at him coldly.

"I would have liked to be given notice of anything irregular, madam," she said to me. "I am in charge of the household, after all. I cannot run the staff if I don't know what they are doing."

"I am mistress of the house, Mrs Bell." My heart was thumping in my chest. I could feel my scalp prickle against the tender, half-pulled-out roots beneath my cap.

"Yes, madam. Mr Dryer—"

"Is not here. And is in any case not your concern. Now, I do not wish to keep you from your duties. As you say, you have a staff to run."

The menservants had grown still. I could see by the set of Henry's shoulders, the careful bow of Horton's head, how intently they were listening.

"Yes, madam." She said nothing more, only turned and went through the door to the back stairs.

After that I lost my enthusiasm. I started to see how the bare patches, where the paintings had hung for so long, stood out brighter and cleaner than the rest of the wall. It showed how dark the house was. I had nothing to hang in the place of the paintings. I had no money of my own to buy anything like a painting. I ordered the men to wrap everything they had removed and went up to my dressing room. My fists itched inside my gloves, where scabs were forming across the knuckles.

THE LETTER ARRIVED at breakfast the next day, and it was all I could do to finish my chocolate before I threw on my cloak and hurried down the drive. I was out of breath when I reached the gatehouse, the cold burning in my breast. Henry was beating at the leather man with both fists, so close that his brow almost touched the leather. Mrs Webber stood behind it and held it still, her legs braced.

"Is that all you have?" she was saying. "Why, a bantling has more hit than you."

Henry let out a shout and redoubled his effort. His bare back ran with perspiration, and I knew that his fists would be raw when he stopped. Mrs Webber saw me and winked over Henry's shoulder.

"Here's Mrs Dryer, come to look at you. What think you, Mrs Dryer? Got a fib on him like a feather's touch, don't he?"

"I have a letter," I said, "from my husband."

Mrs Webber laid a hand on Henry's arm to still him. He stopped his milling and straightened up, blinking the perspiration from his eyes. Mrs Webber passed him a rag.

"Do you, now," she said.

"He writes that he has found Tom a mentor, a Mr Mendoza. I see by your face that you have heard his name before."

"I should think I've heard his name. He was champion of England in his time. I'd guess near anyone would know it. Henry will, I warrant you."

"Mr Mendoza, the Jew." Henry nodded. "He came up with the Jew's stop. Named after him, it is."

"He'll teach Tom some good science," Mrs Webber said, half to herself.

"There is more," I said. "We are to go to London. We are to go before the week is out. My husband has taken a house for us. He is sending Stephens back, with the carriage. Your husband is to try for it. Oh, goodness, Ruth," I had never called her so before, "he is to try for champion of England, just as your Mr Mendoza was."

I realised, suddenly, that I had read Mr Mendoza's name myself, in one of Granville's sporting papers. I had not thought of it before. It seemed almost fantastical, that Granville should hire a man famous enough to be written about in a paper. I grew quiet.

Mrs Webber only nodded. Henry stood and looked between the two of us. His chest was chill now, and pimpled.

"What's this?" he said. "Ain't this good news?"

"Course it is," Mrs Webber said.

"Of course," I agreed.

We went inside and Henry dressed, and we sat by the fire and drank to it, just what beer Mrs Webber had in the house, and tried to talk merrily of all we would need for London. Mrs Webber was cheerful enough while we spoke of dresses and hats, but I thought, whenever the conversation paused, that I could see my own thoughts in her eyes.

What now? After all that has gone before, what is to come to us now?

PART 7

Ruth

* * *

Chapter 20

* * *

We were two days on the road to London. We went in Mr Dryer's coach, sent back specially for us, with a cull I'd never clapped eyes on before at the reins. Henry wept like a babe when Mrs Dryer said he'd to stay behind, and I saw it near broke her heart to leave him, though she acted careless. She couldn't help it, though, for what reason had she to bring him? Mr Dryer had sent this cull, Stephens, on purpose to fetch us.

The coach was so grand I could scarce make myself step inside. It had seats of shining wood with velvet cushions, and brass brackets for the lamps, shined up gold. The windows had curtains at them, tied back with braid. Even the floor and ceiling were shiny as a conker. I sat as careful as I could, afraid of spoiling the seat, though I didn't know how I might spoil it. I couldn't stop stroking the velvet, one way smooth, the other rough. Mrs Dryer sat beside me.

I was wearing my new dress, made of the muslin Tom had chosen me, a cream ground with thin blue stripes. I knew I'd dirty it in no time, but my days, wasn't it pretty. Mrs Dryer had it made up for me by a proper needlewoman, in the new style. I thought it a marvel. Besides it being the finest thing I'd ever put on—so fine I felt an ox in it—on top of that, it was the most comfortable thing I'd ever worn. The waist was so high I need only have the shortest stays, which Mrs Dryer also had made for me, as a gift. I was of half a mind not to take them, but I could hardly wear long stays with a gown that fell from just under my dugs, so I gave her the last lessons without charge, to make us even. Those short stays left my waist free, and if you never wore short stays I couldn't explain how it felt to be so much unlaced. I could run, or fight, or anything.

Now we jolted along, talking in fits and starts, our moods as uneven as the road. Mrs Dryer clenched and unclenched her hands in her lap for a time, but the journey unwound and neither of us could keep nervous for two whole days. Dullness always will creep in after so long as that, whatever waits at the road's end. I spent hours thinking over Tom's fight to come, and wishing I'd been there to see him ready. He was to stand up against a lad by the name of Jem Belcher, a Bristol boy himself. I'd heard the cull's name more often than I could count, called "Bristol's great hope," and the like. I wished I'd seen the boy fight, but I never had. Near as soon as he'd shown his talents some London swell had whipped Belcher off to teach him. Since then, he'd been working his way through the London rings and showing himself quite the pug, by all accounts. I comforted myself that whatever help Belcher had been given, he'd not have had so fine a trainer as Mr Mendoza.

We stayed the night at an inn. I'd never done such a thing before. Mrs Dryer called me her maid, and the innkeeper called me miss, and goggle-eyed my gown. Mrs Dryer asked that he find me a bed near her own room but what he gave us was a bed for me directly next to hers, a little cot-bed with a straw mattress, placed behind a screen, for the sake of her modesty.

Stephens slept out with the horses and took his supper there too. I envied him the ease of it; bread, cheese, ale, and a pile of straw. He could do exactly as he pleased and no one would look twice.

Mrs Dryer and I ate a supper of venison pasties in a parlour that smelled of damp leaves, though we'd a good fire. Mrs Dryer said she thought the pasties were beef, and only called venison. I couldn't have told you, but it could've been the innkeeper's puppy sliced up and roasted and I'd not have cared. We drank a good deal of wine, not speaking much, and then we went up to that odd little room and looked at each other as awkward as newlyweds. I went behind the screen and began to undress.

"Mrs Webber," her voice came, all blurry. "I find myself stuck."

"Stuck!" I said, and went around the screen, in my shift.

She'd tried to pull her dress off without the buttons all the way undone and got herself tangled in it. We laughed then, and I felt less queer. I pulled her gown back down and spent an age getting the little buttons unfastened. My fingers are clumsy with small things.

"My days," I said, "who'd want to be a lady?"

"Indeed, no one should," she said. "It is a hateful thing to be. We are bound in every direction."

"What'd you rather be, a gent?" I looked away as the gown came off at last, but not quick enough that I didn't get a little shock. I'd known she was scarred, but somehow I'd never thought of it as being all over her. She was scattered with lumps, seeds sown under the skin.

"Gentlemen are worse," she said. "No. I would be something wild and free. A deer, perhaps. Will you unlace me?"

She didn't make it easy, hunched over as if she expected a fib in the belly, though I stood at her back.

I had, then, to fumble my fingers over the knots. Her skin was so pitiful it tugged at my heart. I thought of how her ma must've wept over it. Between the seeds there were pits, as if birds had pecked some of the seeds out. I'd seen a vast deal of poxed misses come to the convent, but Mrs Dryer's case was the worst I'd laid eyes on. *She must've near enough died,* I thought.

"If you were a deer, a gent would come and shoot you and have you on his table," I said.

"Then I would be a boxer," she said. "Like you."

"I've never been free a day. You can't imagine how tight I've been bound, and to what."

We both got quiet then and went to our beds.

I lay behind the screen and listened to Mrs Dryer sigh and turn in her own bed. After I was sure she must be asleep, her voice floated out of the darkness.

"I don't know that I can bear to see him."

It was so low that I wasn't sure she meant the words for me. At last I replied, equally soft, "Who do you mean?"

A sigh. "My husband, of course. I could hardly mean yours."

I couldn't blame her; Mr Dryer had in him everything that was blackest about the quality, as I saw it.

"Do you not love him?" I asked, at last.

"Love him? No. I don't believe he has a single soft feeling for me. He has betrayed me worse than I could have dreamt."

"Took a lover, has he?" I thought, *Now, does she mean Dora, or ain't she the only mistress he keeps?*

A silence. Then, "You must think me a fool."

"Never that, Mrs Dryer. Not unless you forget to block when I swing at you."

She laughed a little then, a sad laugh, but better than none.

"I saw him," she said. "I saw him take her into my own poor mama's house. I think, I have begun to believe"—her voice caught—"I have begun to believe that if he wins the house from my brother—as he means to do—I think perhaps he will set her up in it, to live. In the only house I've ever felt truly happy, with my mama's things about her. Sometimes, Mrs Webber, when I think of that, I find myself imagining terrible things. I don't expect you can know what I mean."

"Not know? Don't forget, he left me without food."

"I never forget. It was the greatest sin."

"So we're both sinned against by the same gent, ain't we?"

"We begin to sound like conspirators. But I will not lower myself, just because he does. I have thought it over so often that my head aches."

"You're too good, that I know," I said.

"But oh, Mrs Webber, this woman, in my mama's house. She is so cheap. She wears the most violent shades of pink and red. She is vile! I find I hate her." Her voice grew thick once more.

"Hush, now," I said. "Try to sleep. This helps nothing."

"You are right, of course," she said, meek as a child, and I heard her turn over and sigh and grow still. Sometimes there came a sniff, but she didn't speak again.

I lay and thought of Dora, and the bright pinks she always favoured. Likely, I thought, Mrs Dryer would hate me if she knew that Dora was my sister, and who'd blame her? I'd been trying not to think of it for weeks, truth be told.

Mrs Dryer's ma's house, I thought, and couldn't tell how I felt to think it. How far for my sister to rise; poor, good Mrs Dryer. If I had the choice, would I let Dora take that house? Perhaps I would. I didn't envy Mrs Dryer, married to that unfeeling cully, dry in name and nature. I swear home I did feel for her, but that house was something Dora would never have another chance at . . . Like the championship of all England. I tried to picture my Tom's face. I could see him as he was when first we met, awkward and bashful. I couldn't conjure his face as he'd been when last I saw him, only his broad back, disappearing into Mr Dryer's carriage. The carriage we'd travelled in, I realised then. My Tom had sat upon that velvet. I wondered if he'd stroked the seats.

LONDON PUT ME IN MIND of Bristol, so that my heart ached to see the wide streets filled with carts and folks going about their business, everything dusted with soot. It wasn't much different that I could see, except that it took us so long to go through it, and, I suppose, so much longer to go from shabby to grand.

The house Mr Dryer had taken was in the grand part, and was smaller than the one he'd had with Mrs Dryer, but that ain't to say it wasn't a palace to my eye. The door was opened by a footman I'd never seen, and like the innkeeper, he saw my gown and called me miss. I near laughed, being then so devilish nervous.

"I will see you later, Mrs Webber," Mrs Dryer said. Then to the footman, "Will you show Mrs Webber to her room?"

He said he would, and she went off, led to her own room by a maid, another one I'd never clapped eyes on before.

I followed the cull down the stairs to a room beside the kitchens, and he opened the door for me, just like a butler opening the door for a lady. He didn't try to step inside.

"Mr Webber's quite the man," he said, and I nodded. "He's with Mr Dryer and some other gentlemen, but as soon as he's free, I'll tell him you're here."

I don't know if I replied, because that moment I stepped inside the room and first thing I saw was Tom's razor beside the ewer and his old, familiar hat upon a chair. I felt as if I'd had a poke in the eye. As soon as the cull shut the door, I went to the chair to put my hand to the hat, but before I could reach it I spied Tom's shirt, left on the bed in an uneven fold, and so picked up that. It smelled so familiar that I had to put it from me and sit on the bed's edge. My husband was that moment making conversation with a bunch of swells—on the eve of his fight for all England. Here I sat, in this strange London room, in a dress too fine for me. I thought of how much had changed since Mr Dryer sent me to fight at the fair. I was rageful then and my hands curled into fists, but I couldn't have said who I clenched them for.

I waited like that all evening, it seemed like. I opened the door and listened out for voices, but I got nothing at all. I paced about that room, picking up all Tom's things in turn and then placing them back, as careful as a sneak-thief, though he'd never have minded. At last I washed my face, my arms, my legs, and dried myself on a rag, all of it quick, in fear that Tom's first sight of me would be my bare arse crouching over the basin. I put my fine gown back on and spent an age fussing with it, to get the skirts to sit straight. Then I had nothing to do but stare out the narrow window at the view, which was only a slice of a bare courtyard, a brick wall and the corner of what might've been the privy. My thoughts went around like pugs circling each other; he'd never come, he must come, he'd come every minute, oh, he'd never come!

Then the step on the stair, and my heart squeezed itself almost shut; I'd never have mistaken it. I heard him cough halfway down and it was my own Tom's cough. I couldn't have said how it differed to any other cull's, but it did. I heard him hesitate outside the door, and I didn't know what to do with myself. Should I stand, or sit? My face wouldn't settle.

Then he was there, bigger and more real and exactly the same as I remembered him, all at once. He crossed the room in two steps and swept me into his arms before I could turn queer. He smelt of sweat and sawdust and beer. His jaw bumped against mine as though we'd forgotten how kisses were to be done.

He held me tight and then put his hands on my shoulders and pushed me out a little to look at me.

"That dress looks well on you." He went as pink as he'd done as a lad.

"Thank you for it," I said.

"You're welcome. I wanted to send you more. After tomorrow I'll buy you anything you can think of. You're thinner, Ruthie. I hope you've been eating well."

I could feel my smile grow tight. Tom let my shoulders go, sat, and pulled me onto his lap. I let him tell me all about his training and the bouts he'd fought, the swells who'd shaken his hand. I couldn't be as easy as he wished me, nor as I wished I could. At last I stood and walked about while he talked. He talked on, only leaning forward in his chair and following me with his head. He scarce noticed I didn't reply. The beef he'd eaten, the places he'd seen, the hits he'd taken and dealt out to others. And oh, Mr Mendoza, he had to tell me all about that. The fellow was so small, you'd never guess he'd been champion in his time, and he'd had the grace to tell

Tom all kinds of tricks. He'd been his trainer for all of a week and then he'd gone back to prison, or some such. I barely listened, only looked at how Tom's face was lit with it.

At last he grew weary of my pacing and tried to pull me back to him. I let him take my wrist and stood before him, but I didn't sit on his knee again.

"What ails you, Ruthie? I've been waiting to tell you all this! You hardly heed me."

How could I say that I hated to hear Tom sing the praises of that useless clotpole, Mendoza, who'd let himself be carted off to prison when Tom needed him the most. Again, my husband was bending to kiss the boots of cullies who weren't worth half what he was, cullies who'd kept me away from his side and filled his head so full of puff that he forgot to think of me. The very sound of Mendoza's name made my stomach drop. Mr Dryer's name was worse; my stomach felt the same, and my fists itched with it.

"I'm only weary," I said.

He took me to bed then, and I tried to be soft when he put his hands to me. It was a strange, faraway kind of love, as though my heart was fallen down a well. He couldn't reach me, or perhaps I'd not let him. He only kissed me and sighed and murmured as he always did. I wanted to weep that he'd not noticed, but the weeping piece of me was as far off as the loving piece.

Afterward I turned away, but Tom only moved close behind me and wrapped me in his arms.

"I've missed that," he said, "and I've missed this. I've been picturing you, all alone in that big bed and wondering if you slept sweetly, and how you did."

"You've no notion how I've done, for you ain't asked," I said.

Tom's hold on me tightened.

"Tell me all you've done," he said, warm in my ear.

"You won't believe me," I said. I felt queer, hateful and weepy together.

I didn't know if I should keep silent, I didn't know if I could bear him to touch me, and yet I wanted to turn into his arms and cling to him like ivy.

"I've been teaching Henry to fight," I said, at last.

"Blushing Henry? Have you, then? Is he good?"

"He's fair."

"I'm glad you've had diversion, Ruthie."

"I've been teaching Mrs Dryer, the same." My heart began beating hard; I was surprised he didn't feel it thumping against his bare arm.

"Mrs Dryer? I don't follow. D'you mean she shows you, how to be a lady?"

"I teach her to be less of a lady."

"I don't follow you," he said again.

"I've taught her to box."

"You have taught her . . . !"

"She pays me two shillings a time."

"Have you run mad?" Tom released me and rolled onto his back. "Mr Dryer won't like this."

"Mr Dryer needn't know. Mr Dryer left me to starve."

"He'll be hopping when he hears of it. Why've you done this, Ruth? You'll spoil everything. We've only to bow to him one more day and we'll be rich and free. I can't fathom you."

"I can't fathom you! Did you not hear me? He left me there to starve."

"He brought us more than we could eat."

"He brought *you* food! You! That was gone as soon as you were. I'd nothing, Tom. You can't imagine."

"Mr Dryer won't have meant you to be hungry. I'd warrant his servants were to blame, through pure idleness."

"What, do you worship him so?"

Tom only made a sorry noise and got out of bed. I didn't try to hold him. I lay and stared evils at the wall. I heard the creak of the chair as he settled into it.

Neither of us spoke for a long while.

At last I said to the wall, "You should be glad I've saved a purse for us. Unless you like being beholden to Mr Dryer so much."

"I won't be beholden after the morrow," he said, "and all you've shown me is that you're faithless. You've saved against my losing! You shouldn't have even come here. I wish you hadn't, I swear home."

What could I say, after that? I only lay and felt my eyes burn. At long last, Tom rose from the chair and I felt the bed buck and settle as he got into it beside me. I felt myself stiffen, and he must've felt it too.

"Don't fret—I ain't about to touch you. I'm only in bed because tomorrow signifies too high that I'd lose sleep for you."

He seemed to sleep straightaway. I lay wakeful for what felt the whole night long. It can't have been, mind, for then it was morning and I was waking.

I COUNT THAT MORNING as one of the worst I've spent my life long. I woke to find Tom lying beside me, staring up at the ceiling, where a spider of cracks danced across the plaster. He'd not smile, and, for my own part, I found I couldn't make my hand reach for him.

He swung out of bed without a kiss for me—he'd never risen without one, in all our marriage. If I were sleeping, I'd still feel his lips upon my cheek before he heaved himself up, and if I were the one to rise first, I'd do the same, and lay a kiss on his sleeping face. A small thing, the lack of a kiss, but it felt like a fib to my stomach. I raised my head as he began to move, and when he didn't turn to place his lips on mine, but swung his legs from beneath the blankets, showing me his broad back, I caught my breath with the surprise of it.

I lay and watched him stretch out, grimacing as his muscles crackled with stiffness, a feeling I knew so well that I near felt it in my own limbs. The ceiling was too low for him to stretch fully upright, but he did the best he could in the space, pushing his palms against the cracked plaster and arching his back. He didn't once look at me.

I held the covers tight under my chin, and when he did turn, I couldn't speak. The worst of it was that I could see how I'd hurt him, but I couldn't show him my own raw heart. I could only give him a tight little smile and curse myself. Tom looked at me sadly.

"You can't help your own feelings, Ruth," he said, as though I'd spoken. "I can only try now to prove you wrong."

If I'd been a different woman, I'd have clutched at him and wept. Instead I could only say, "Can it ever be wrong to take care of what may come?" with an ache in my guts.

So the morning went on, in a kind of dull agony. Tom and I'd never had such ill-feeling between us. I didn't know how to begin to mend it.

When I slipped off my dressing gown, my first gift from Tom's success, I felt as though it was our luck that I took from my body and left crumpled on the blankets.

We breakfasted in our room and in silence. A maid with red hair and freckles so close they'd formed blotches brought us a tray of victuals and didn't know whether to curtsey. She'd likely never served a breakfast in servants' quarters before. In the end she bobbed a little on her pins and looked so fuddled that I did the same, which made her shake her head, as though she'd water in her ears. I was devilish glad when the door shut behind her.

I took the tray and put it on the chair, there being no table, and then I took a bowl of porridge from it and a cup of small ale and handed them to my husband. I didn't know if I offered them in penance or not; I only felt heavy. Tom took them and thanked me in a quiet voice but then spooned his porridge so slow that I couldn't bear it. He kept his eyes on his bowl. I thought he'd a nervous stomach, and that here was a place we could understand one another, but no matter how I looked at him, his eyes wouldn't raise to mine.

At last the maid came back and said, "You're to go upstairs, the master says."

You could see she'd thought it over and wished she'd not bent her knees to us.

"Right, then. Best we get on," Tom said, standing as slow as he'd spooned his breakfast.

The coach was standing in the yard. Tom and I looked at each other then, because we didn't know what to do with ourselves. We were so evenly matched for nerves—I could see it in his eyes—that I felt a wash of calm. Then he turned away and only stood, shifting from foot to foot, and the calm drained away. I felt a great despair come over my head like a hangman's hood. We stood there, Tom shifting, and I blind with misery, for Lord knows how long, till at last Mr and Mrs Dryer stepped out into the yard.

If I'd thought myself twisted up before, now my heart turned into a churning thing I had no hold on, like a river in flood. Mrs Dryer met my eyes and the gladness in her own at seeing me was so clear, I suddenly felt all the tears I'd held come rushing to my throat in a straining fist. Then I saw how Mr Dryer's eyes flickered past me without even a nod and how he looked Tom over, like a horse-dealer checking a nag, and I felt hatred strong enough to fold my knees. This got all tangled with the weeping, and for one moment I thought I'd fall down in a faint. Then the hate came to the fore and I clung to it like a branch, and was glad of it. I stared at the side of Mr Dryer's face and wished him dead. He was lucky indeed I'd not the power to grant it.

WE WERE ALL TO RIDE in the same carriage. Mr Dryer held the door open for his wife and they stepped inside. Then he leaned out and called, "Come, Webber," like a cully calling a dog.

Tom didn't even look shamed to follow. He held the door open for me, and I might then have looked him in the eye, but I was riding the fury and couldn't think of anything else.

We sat opposite the Dryers, them facing forward and Tom and I travelling backward. I didn't stroke the seat this time. I barely looked at them at all. I'd no room left in me for thinking of trifling things. I could feel fear start up and try to take down my rage, but I'd not give it up. I dug my nails into my palms and stared at Mr Dryer's legs and hated him as hard as ever I could. When at last the sight of his legs made me feel queasy, I looked instead at Mrs Dryer's feet, almost touching my own. At last I raised my eyes quickly to her face, just to make sure of her. I was glad that I couldn't speak to her. I'd never have known what to say. It was a comfort, though, to have her there and know she'd kept an even greater secret from her husband than ever I'd done.

She held her head very high and looked about herself, out of the window and upon us all, devilish bold. She'd covered the last of her bruises with her paint, but they were there if you knew where to look, swimming faint beneath the surface like fish in a duckpond. She wore gloves, but I thought from the careful way she held her hands that they were tender, and I wondered if she'd been fibbing at a bolster again. She'd covered her poor hair with a bonnet.

Tom's shoulder shrank away from mine, and he kept his eyes shut fast. Every so often Mr Dryer made some half-witted comment, on the rain being likely to hold off, or my husband's bloom of health, each time bringing fresh hatred, like bile, to my mouth. Tom stayed silent. Each time Mr Dryer spoke, my husband winced and his eyes squeezed even tighter, forming wrinkles across his cheeks that I'd been more used to seeing in mirth. His mouth was so tight that he'd lost his lips.

I might've expected Mr Dryer to be vexed at being so unheeded, but instead he grew ever more cheerful; he'd not be quiet a moment. I'd never seen him like it. It was dreadful to be shut up with this babbling fool, my husband sitting rigid, and I quivering with words unspoken. I had to wind my fingers tight together to prevent them flying out to touch Tom's arm, the veins that coiled like ropes. He was as far from me as if he'd taken his corner already; I could do nothing but watch. The fear was gaining ground over the hatred, made all the worse through Mr Dryer's flapping chops. He was cheering from the ringside, as useless as I, and Tom was left to do what he could by his fists. None of us would be able to stand beside him when it signified. Though I'd barely eaten, my stomach rolled like a sailor's walk.

Too soon, and after an age, we reached Wimbledon Common. It was said afterward that the crowd that day numbered twenty-five thousand. I didn't stop to count, and so must believe it. I know that when I first saw the fancy gathered there, the great number of horses bearing gents in tall hats, I felt as though I'd any moment see what little breakfast I'd eaten drop onto the turf.

I'd not known anything, I'd had no notion of what a mill this was to be. There were reporters there from the London newspapers, ready to write down each fib and poke. There were any number of swells, as I've said. Worst of all, most of all, there was the Duke of Clarence in a seat at the ringside, with his men gathered round him. I didn't know who he was then, thanks be. I'd have dropped, to know that royalty had turned out to watch my Tom fight.

Through the carriage window the press of people seemed a cauldron at the simmer: thousands of shifting, bobbing heads packed tight under the grey sky. I thought they'd the air of a crowd before a hanging. At a very little distance, stark against the sky, the gibbet stood clear to see; a last skeleton left forever hanging in his chains. He swung in the winter wind, rags a-fluttering, as though he, too, was fretting after the championship.

"Well," Mr Dryer said, "here we are, eh, Webber?"

No one said a word.

No sooner were we climbed down, than we found ourselves encircled by culls, sent there by Mr Dryer to meet us. They all hailed Tom and to my surprise he greeted them in his usual easy way. Only his tight shoulders showed his nerves. He didn't introduce me.

Within this circle we were hurried through the crowd, the men call-ing, "Tom Webber, coming this way! Make way for the next champion of England!"

The crowd craned to look. The boos and cheers turned into one great sound that beat at my ears like wings.

I was beginning to feel a strange calm, not unlike the hush that came over me in the ring when I knew myself about to take a basting. I looked at Tom's back as he walked, his head a little bowed, and wished him strength. I wished he might know how much I loved him. The crowd were nothing, hooting beasts, they might all rot, they didn't signify. Their noise ebbed from my ears till I felt I could hear my husband's every step crunch upon the frosty grass, his breaths ragged in his throat.

We passed men and women, quality and common. We passed folks selling ale and hot potatoes, and braziers ringed with people warming their hands. There were voices, lifted in song. And through them all we walked, in our circle of guards, and me in my bubble of quiet and fright.

We walked to the ring, and it wasn't till we reached it that I remem-bered what we came for. I saw the ring, and something in me woke up and shook itself. *Why,* I thought, *Tom will win it, surely. Tom's scarce lost a fight his whole life long.*

I could see Tom thought the same. He straightened up and began to look about him and flex his fists.

The ropes marked out a square of the frozen turf, not raised at all. Most of this vast crowd never would see a moment of the goings-on, except those who'd pushed to the front, and the gents on their raised benches and on horseback.

The beefy culls around Mrs Dryer and me ushered us toward a row of wooden stools, against one side of the ring. I looked once at the stools and when I looked back Tom had been parted from us, swept to his corner and over the ropes, like a lone sailor in a life raft.

"Shall we sit?" Mrs Dryer asked me.

I shrugged, but did as she said; there was nothing else to do but sit.

Some of the culls who'd swept us there stood behind us, to keep the crowd from falling on our necks.

I was glad to be out of the press of the crowd, but now it seemed that everyone towered over us. The noise had begun to pound against my ears again and no one had even started to cheer yet.

Tom had been joined in the ring by Mr Dryer and two other culls, his second and his bottle-holder, I knew they must be. I didn't know either one of them and it seemed devilish queer that it should be they, who could've been anyone, rather than me there beside him. All four of them came toward us, sitting as we were by Tom's corner. We were separated then only by the ropes; I could've stood from my seat and touched Tom's arm, if I'd a mind to. I looked up at my husband's face, which was grown boyish and wide-eyed, like a child told a moral tale meant to give fright. I wondered then what those culls were whispering, to make him look so.

"Who're they?" I asked Mrs Dryer, but she only shook her head.

One of them, a wiry long-shanks with something of the snarl about him, now spoke to Tom in a manner that looked to be cheering. He smiled his alley-cat smile and touched Tom's arm. Tom made his replies with earnest face. The other cull, shorter but broader, bound Tom's hands round with cloth, though leaving the knuckles bare. Tom's eyes caught mine over the cull's shoulder. I wasn't ready for it; my face stayed stiff as a poker. Next second he'd looked away.

"Mrs Dryer, Mrs Webber, what a pleasure," a gent's voice said, and I turned to see the handsome gent that Dora was always sweet for take a seat by Mrs Dryer's side.

I nodded at him and turned back to the ring without waiting to see if he took offence.

That day it was as though the moment I took my eyes from something, other things appeared, or disappeared. Now a small group of culls had appeared in the ring in the opposite corner, in the time it'd taken me to nod to Dora's handsome gent. One of them, I knew, must be my Tom's opponent.

"That's the cove, there," Dora's chum said, pointing a gloved hand.

I'd already guessed it; this cully was built small, but he had a pug's air about him and was beginning to bob on his toes in the bitter air. He had a longish nose and a point to his chin; I thought Tom might get a good fib in, on either of those. That jaw was ripe for the breaking. The culls about him talked excitedly and waved their hands.

"He's a formidable fighter, I hear," the fellow went on, "but I hold out great hope for Tom. Mr Belcher shall not best him. He must not—I have laid too great a sum upon it!" He laughed aloud.

Mr Dryer leaned over the ropes and addressed himself entirely to the gent.

"The betting is five to four on Belcher, though I think nothing of that. I've laid down five hundred guineas on Tom."

I blinked. Five hundred guineas. That was a sum so great as to be ridiculous. And, I realised, the betting was against my Tom, then. Just an arm's length away from me, he took off his shirt and handed it to the alley-cat cully. Straight off, I saw his flesh pimple in the cold.

Beside me, Mrs Dryer fetched out her own little purse and leaned forward to bid her husband put ten guineas on Tom, for herself. Mr Dryer looked at her sharply. Then he seemed to think better of it and took her coin. He climbed over the ropes and pushed off through the crowd.

"It is Mr Dryer's own money," she said, leaning in to whisper to me. "It was hidden in his dressing room; my husband is not as ingenious as he likes to think himself. I shall return it, when once Tom wins."

Even sick with nerves as I was, I had to smile to hear that.

As the squire took the ring, to call the pugs to scratch, Tom looked over at me again. This time I stood up just as though he'd called to me, and so quickly that my head span.

Tom came to the ropes and leaned toward me. I came close—I wanted to fly to him, but some foolish pride kept me back a little.

Looking up at him to read his face, I saw a vast distance in his eyes and knew he'd gone already to that place inside his head, that well-known spot

I curled myself in whenever I took the ring. Nothing signified now but the bout to come.

"You'll slaughter him," I said. "You'll have him spitting teeth. You'll splinter him like kindling."

"I will," Tom said. "When his jaw breaks, that'll be all for you," and I smiled in sheer relief.

The squire now called the crowd to attention, lifting his arms above his head.

"Go." I put my hand on his arm and felt how chill was his skin. "I'll see you when you're champion of England."

"A kiss for luck," he said, and I obliged, while all about us the crowd screamed.

Then he nodded once, turned to the ring, and was not my husband, but a pug to his core.

"Splinter him like kindling," Mrs Dryer said. "You are a poetess, Ruth."

The pugs stood at scratch, their fives at the ready before their chests. Their breath steamed in plumes from their noses, like bulls. The crowd hushed; there's something terrible about so many men, making not a sound. Even those who couldn't see were quiet as corpses.

Suddenly Belcher struck out—oh, he was quick! Tom wasn't ready for it, and Belcher's dart caught my husband's left eye, snapping his head back upon his thick neck. I found I was on my feet, howling already. Tom didn't fall; he could take any number of fibs and stay standing. It was a solid facer, mind; in an instant the eye began to swell.

I sat, then stood, then sat again. Mrs Dryer put her hand on my arm.

"He took that blow well," she said. "We will see Belcher's jaw break yet."

I nodded so firmly, I felt my neck twang.

Now Tom seemed to wake up. He vastly outweighed the cull, but he'd sparred often enough with me that he knew well how speed could outclass size. He couldn't afford Belcher time to think, but grabbed him now in his two thick arms and threw him to the ground. I saw Belcher's head bounce upon the frozen earth like an apple shaken from a tree. Mrs Dryer and I screamed in victory together. The first round was ours.

Tom came back to his corner. His skin glistened as though it were frosted. He sat upon his second's knee and took the bottle offered him.

"Towel him off!" I shouted, even as the bottle-holder handed him a cloth.

Tom looked at me, and I thought, *Steady yourself, Ruth,* and tried to smile.

"The betting has evened," Mr Dryer reported to us. He was sitting now beside Mrs Dryer, the handsome cull having moved aside for him. I felt a flush of pride; my husband had shown them already. Even bets; the fight was anyone's. The fight was Tom's, I knew it.

They came back up to scratch. The worst of sitting in Tom's corner was that we could see only his back and Belcher's face, his narrowed eyes on my Tom.

The call of time sounded. Now Belcher took the method I should've in his place, and dove and ducked so fast that Tom just stood foxed and watched him. From the whirling dance, Belcher fetched Tom up a flush right to the left side of his face.

Damn! The cull can mill, I thought, and I screamed aloud, "Catch him, oh, catch him!"

Tom began to swing at Belcher as he danced about. He landed a couple of left-handed punishers that must've been felt, but for the most part his mighty arms missed time and again. I began to see what I couldn't bear to; my husband looked like a man outclassed. Belcher was too quick on his pins.

Tom's fives were groping the air like a blind man. I pulled myself up and made ready to scream to him—*Grab the cull and wrestle!*—but just as I opened my mouth, one of those flailing fibs landed: Tom's fist slammed into Belcher's windpipe. It was a blow such as only Tom could give, like the kick of a cart-horse. The boy went down, crumpling like a scarecrow come off his post. He looked to be dead, he lay so queerly.

"He's done!" Mr Dryer cried. "He's caught him in the jugular!"

Tom came back to his corner, where Mr Dryer leaned over the ropes to him and talked very fast in his ear. Tom looked very calm, but I knew he was glad. Alley-cat rubbed the sweat from his bare back before it could freeze his skin.

Belcher's seconds had come and pulled him upright, looping one of the cull's slack arms around each of their necks and dragging him back to his side. The cull lay back in the arms of one of them, his face dead-white, his eyes glazed.

"He's beaten, he's beaten," the crowd screamed.

Belcher's seconds had only a half-minute to return him to the scratch; surely he'd not breathe again that quick, not enough to stand. Belcher's second was frantic, pummelling his chest, rubbing him down with a towel. He looked to be trying to force water down his throat enough to drown.

The squire looked at his pocket-watch and opened his mouth; Belcher's second lifted him to his feet, and at the call of "Time!" he stumbled up to scratch and stood, swaying like a drunkard. It would take little to have him down again. One hit and Tom would have it.

"Charge him!" I screamed, but I needn't. Tom ran at Belcher like a heated ram, even as the cull shook his head, dazed.

Belcher didn't try to fight, but only covered his head with his arms and veered, almost fell, to one side. Tom, too eager, now foundered past, missing his man.

Belcher straightened up, and I could see that his head had cleared. If only Tom hadn't missed him! That one moment had been enough for Belcher to regain his wits; the fight was again a fight in earnest.

Now Tom felt the sting of a hundred blows to the head, till he bellowed as though he'd stepped on a hornet's nest. His face was wild and savage. I hoped dearly he was keeping his wits about him—if he got hot he sometimes grew reckless. His left eye was near shut, so quick was it swelling.

Both men stood fearless in the ring's centre, exchanging blows—this was a high treat for the fancy and they cheered the pugs as loud as ever they could. There's nothing the fancy likes to see more than two culls slugging at each other without dodging, each taking the hits and landing his own. Tom landed fewer, but his fibs had more force and he could take whatever Belcher threw without flinching.

Mr Dryer said, "That is real pugilism, dogged and determined."

This old-fashioned bout was ended only when Belcher closed Tom's eye completely, provoking my husband to seize him in his arms once more and hurl him to the ground.

With his eye swollen tight-shut, Tom would have a hard time judging his distances. I knew from experience what a feeling it was to have your eye swelled so—the pressure of the blood building fogs your mind and makes your thoughts run slow.

They came up to scratch, my husband now the one staggering as if drunk. The round lasted only a moment. At the call of time, Belcher threw his fist straight into my husband's swollen eye, and down Tom went.

"Five to one on Belcher," the call went out.

Tom's nose was bleeding, his eye was closed. I thought he'd banged his head something terrible when he fell. I couldn't breathe. As he went back to scratch, I felt Mrs Dryer take my hand and I couldn't help but squeeze her fingers, hard. She didn't take her hand away.

Tom now took a battering made the worse by his refusal to fall. My husband had bottom like no other cull, he'd not give over. Now he stood and let Belcher drive again and again at his face. He swung of course, but he didn't defend himself. Where was his training? Mr Dryer had stood and was screaming at him, to put his hands up, to cover his face. Blood from his nose coated his lips, bubbled with his breath. He looked to be out upon his feet; any other pug would've fallen. By the time Tom went down, it was to fall to one knee, from exhaustion and blindness and blood in his good eye. Belcher didn't knock my Tom down; the bottom simply fell out of him. He'd taken everything he could.

The cheers were mixed with hisses as Tom sagged to his knees and his seconds came hurrying over. The crowd would've liked a straight knock-down, but I knew Tom well enough; if he sagged, he couldn't stand.

Tom's seconds near dragged him back to his corner, where they bathed the worst of the blood from his face.

I stared at his bare back, almost near enough to touch. If I could I'd have helped him back over the ropes and taken his place. I'd have stood in front of him and broken Belcher's jaw myself. A half-minute was likely not enough, this time. It had to be enough.

They left Tom at the scratch hardly able to raise his fives, blood pouring afresh from his nose. He stood slumped, as though draped over an invisible pole.

The book-men were calling out odds of twenty-to-one on Belcher's victory. I wanted to pray, but my mind was empty of words. My teeth were clenched so tight that my jaw ached. I felt my heart calling out to him as he stood there, blood running claret streams down his bare chest. He didn't need to do this, I should never have loved him the less. I'd have done anything to take his place, or to pick him up, had I the strength, and run. I'd never in my life felt more powerless. I couldn't even blink, I was so tense and stiff. My eyes were devilish cold and dry in the winter air.

The crowd grew silent again as Belcher came toward my husband. Belcher eyed Tom for a moment, his fist feinting in the air, as one practises an axe-blow when splitting logs, and then the blow came down, right on my husband's swollen left eye, and Tom screamed, and fell, and didn't get up.

A cloud of pigeons took to the air to carry the news; my Tom was brought down, and Belcher was England's champion.

I WAS UNDER THE ROPES and at Tom's side before I knew I was moving. Both eyes were closed and swelling faster than I'd ever seen before. *They'll need lancing,* I thought, *just to open.* I took his hand, though it being in a muffler, I couldn't hold it, only lifted it and felt its weight. He was in a dead faint. His chest rose and fell, but I could hear blood in his breath, bubbling in his pipes. I was afraid he'd drown.

"Help me turn him," I cried out to the nearest cull to me, a stranger in a homespun jacket.

Now I saw that there were folks all about us, as many hands helped me turn Tom onto his side. He went over heavy, his arm slapping against his chest like dead meat. His skin was growing chill, but before I could ask, someone laid a coat over him. His face was grown shiny and tight about that eye; I could see it more clear, now that he lay on his side. I touched it very gently, and I couldn't help but cry out as a drop of blood seeped from under the lid like a scarlet tear.

"Dear God," someone said.

I couldn't speak, but all around me the cry went up, "Fetch a doctor, a surgeon!"

There were people crowded about, all too close. They towered over Tom and me like trees that might at any moment fall, and all of them speaking at once.

"Move back," a voice shrieked. "Move back, lest he be crushed!"

I felt an arm about my shoulder and turned to find Mrs Dryer crouching next to me. It was she who'd shouted; tears made lines through the paint on her cheeks. It was only now she held me that I felt how hard I trembled; my shoulder-blades shook against her arm.

Tom made a sound then, the most pitiful mew, pained and surprised. I broke away from Mrs Dryer and bent over him; the right eye was open a crack and looked at me blankly. The swelling about the left twitched as though he'd open it if he could. Blood had begun to clot about its lid. He mewed again.

"Stay still, my love," I said, very low.

"Can we not put something on his eye," Mrs Dryer said, beside me. "A wet rag? The air is cold enough. It might help the swelling."

Straight off someone put a wet rag into my hands. The crowd were keeping back now and a hush had fallen, which was worse than the noise. I laid the rag upon Tom's eye.

"There, my love." I felt better now that the horror of that blood was hidden. "You be still. You've had worse than this." I didn't know if he had.

I could do nothing then but put my hands on his arm and shoulder—the unbruised parts of him—and try to love him so hard that I could lift his pain. So fixed was I on this that all the crowd seemed to fall back, and when the doctor came, bustling through the crowd with cries of "Make way, make way there," I started in surprise. Behind him came Mr Dryer, and I felt hatred well up in me at the sight of him, more rage than I'd ever known a heart could hold. It came up into my face and drew my lips back from my teeth as though I were about to rip out his throat. I'd have done it in that moment and never wept a tear for him.

"Ruth!" Mrs Dryer said. "He is the doctor."

She thought it was the doctor I snarled at. Now I looked at him and saw he was exactly as stern and self-important as every doctor who ever came to the convent to dose one miss and take pleasure on another. He paid me no heed but crouched beside me too close, so that I had to draw back or be pressed against him. It was Mrs Dryer's hands that lifted mine from Tom's arm. She did it gently enough that I let go my hold and stood up. I was unsteady on my pins, and Mrs Dryer again put her arm about me.

The doctor busied himself touching my poor husband's face; he lifted the cloth and put his fingers on my husband's puffed-shut eye. Tom had grown very still. I thought he must be afraid.

Mr Dryer said, "Will he fight again?"

And the doctor only shook his head and said, "Hmmmm," sadly.

"God be damned!" Mr Dryer walked away from us.

I wasn't fashed, I wanted him away. Mrs Dryer felt different—she took her arm from about my shoulders and went after him like the devil in a high wind. The doctor kept on with his poking.

I was so weak with the waiting of it that when Mrs Dryer came back I found myself reaching out for her of my own choice. The doctor had found a litter and a great number of folk were now involved in lifting my Tom onto it. They weren't taking care enough; I couldn't bear it.

"Come," Mrs Dryer said, trying to lead me off. When I pulled away, she added, "I am taking you to the doctor's house, Ruth. Tom will be borne there. Come."

I didn't want to leave, but by then I couldn't see him, so close was the press of folk about him. I let Mrs Dryer take me to the carriage and sit me in it. The screams I never would let out were tangling my thoughts and blurring my eyes.

I remember hardly anything about that journey except that it took too long, and when we got there, the doctor had a manservant who'd not let us near the room where they had Tom lying. They'd called in a barber-surgeon. I tried not to think of it. The room we sat in was all brown walls with brown pictures upon them. Mrs Dryer found brandy from somewhere—the manservant, I suppose—and we sat and drank till I felt my nerves steady. My fear was coiled in my stomach; I wanted to be very still and I wanted to run and kick and find Belcher and swell his eye and then take Mr Dryer and do the same. I believe I did moan aloud then, and Mrs Dryer looked at me.

I said, "Your husband's fit for the devil; I'd like to put him to bed with a spade."

"At this moment, I should not blame you for it."

"He's monstrous wicked. He's the devil's bastard." I'd risen and was pacing about the room, my fists tight. The pain from my ill-mended mauler was the only thing keeping me steady and I clenched it till I felt the knuckles shift in their sockets.

"He is Hell-bound," she said. "That is certain enough."

After that I think we kept silent and I retook my seat.

At length Mr Dryer appeared and sat in the corner, as far from me and Mrs Dryer as he could place himself, sipping at a glass of his own. I tried not to look at him.

At last the doctor entered, smelling of something bitter and pungent.

He held his hands out to us as though in pity but his face was as empty as a statue. He'd got flecks of blood on his cuffs, but he'd changed his gloves; they were of clean buff kid. I was sure that my husband was dead.

"I am sorry," he said.

His words cramped my bowels. I bent over in my seat, and once again thought I'd lose my breakfast in one way or another. I'd not have given a fig. I was sweating cold.

"I could not save the eye," the doctor said, then, "but if he does not take infection, I believe he will live."

"You could not save the eye," Mr Dryer said.

At the same moment his wife cried out, "He will live!"

"He will never fight again with one eye," Mr Dryer said.

"Ruth"—Mrs Dryer had her hand upon my shoulder and bent down to speak into my ear—"he will live. He shall not take infection. We will nurse him together, if you wish it."

I kept my eyes closed for a moment. Hot tears spilled from under the lids, and I couldn't halt them. Mrs Dryer's hand was patting my back. She took me into her arms, and I let her hold me, rocking me like no one ever had, not even as a babber, not like that. Her cheek pressed against the top of my head, her breath stirred my hair. She smelt nice; flowery, but dry. Powdered flowers.

I heard Mr Dryer and the doctor leave the room together. Mrs Dryer only held me the tighter.

After a long while, I felt words burning in my throat with the tears, and I let them spill and didn't care.

"Your husband's mistress is my sister," I said, very low and choked. I was likely wrong to tell her, and yet perhaps I'd meant to all day. At any rate, I couldn't have stopped it then, for anything.

Mrs Dryer's hand stilled itself for a moment, and then, very gently, the patting resumed.

"Tom will live," she whispered. "He will have white cullis."

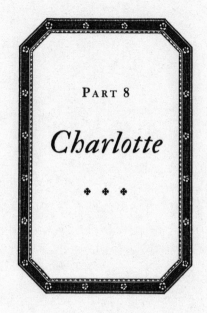

PART 8

Charlotte

❖ ❖ ❖

Chapter 21

* * *

When poor Mr Webber was defeated so badly, Granville stood by and watched without a thought for the man's injuries, so disappointed was he for himself. When the doctor looked up and showed by his face that Mr Webber's outlook was bleak, my husband walked away as though he were a dog that he was obliged to have shot. I chased after him, pushing through the crowd; I did not care who saw me do it. In that moment, I thought my husband capable of leaving us on the common to find our own way, distraught and blood bespattered, and even now I cannot think I was far mistaken. I caught his arm and he turned with eyes that did not see me.

"You cannot leave us," I said.

Now he saw me and clearly thought me irksome.

"I will leave the carriage for you if you must stay," he said. "I will take a chair, or walk. I do not care."

"You will not come to the doctor's house?"

"I have lost grievously, Lottie."

"You have lost money, nothing more. Mr Webber is left injured! You cannot abandon him."

"Whatever I lost, he lost it for me. I will leave you the carriage."

"Will you pay the doctor? Granville, at least tell me that you will pay for that."

My husband waved a dismissive hand as he walked away. I did not know what it meant. I was left to stumble back through the crowd to Mrs Webber's side.

IT WAS ONLY LATER that I realised that carriage or no, Granville had indeed left me without any escort besides an unconscious man and a wife too distressed to look about her. Anything could have happened to me at that moment, in a crowd of strangers and with the carriage a good walk across the common. I had not even any money about my person. I did not think of danger at the time—the lack of money was the only concern I had, besides the safety of Mr Webber. I still did not know if Granville had agreed to pay the doctor's fee. Privately I decided to assure the doctor that he might send my husband the bill with all confidence. *Let us concern ourselves with it later,* I thought, *when Mr Webber is made safe.*

When Granville at last crept into the doctor's waiting room, looking as miserable as if he were the one who had lost an eye, I found that my heart had shut him out entirely and made him a stranger—and not a pleasant one.

I WOULD NOT LOOK at Granville throughout the time we travelled back with poor Mr and Mrs Webber, feeling each bump of the carriage. Perhaps he thought me ashamed, I was not sure. I was not ashamed, but disgusted with him. It coursed through my veins and set my hands and feet to tingling. On top of the anxiety and dismay of Mr Webber's injury, there was Mrs Webber's revelation; it sat in my throat like bile. I did not know that I could swallow it.

We regained our lodgings, Mr Webber managing to walk with the support of two footmen. The bandage across his face was a terrible sight, blood blossoming through it, although it was newly applied. His face was so swollen that the bandage did not sink where the eye was gone, but even so, I knew that it was missing and shuddered to think of it. I was bitterly glad that Granville had bestowed a comfortable room upon Mr Webber when he had had such high hopes for him and could not take it from him now that he was so gravely ill. It was good luck that it was beside the kitchens; Mr Webber could not have climbed easily to a garret room.

Mrs Webber was instructed to dose her husband with laudanum till he slept and to keep him sleeping, letting him wake only for food. She would only promise to find a supper for herself when I scolded her.

"You are not long made strong," I told her, "and you will not help your husband by growing weak again. I will not have the two of you bedridden."

We watched them walk off around the back of the house to the service entrance, Mr Webber as slow as an old man, sandwiched between the footmen, Mrs Webber hovering behind, carrying the bottle of laudanum.

At our door, Granville fumbled with the key.

"The servants will be abed," he said. He had forgotten the footmen, who must surely be inside now, helping Mr Webber to bed.

I did not say any of this, only listened to the clink as his clumsy hand struggled with the lock. At last we were admitted. He stalked ahead of me, and rather than stand in the dark hall, I followed him into the parlour, where the light from the dying fire made a vague silhouette of him.

I heard him fuss with the spills upon the mantel, meaning to take one to a candle.

"Do not you make a light on my account. I am for my bed." I turned, meaning to go away from him and up the stairs. The rage was fading a little and all I knew was that I did not want to be near him.

"Do not be foolish, take a candle," was all his reply.

"Very well," I said, for I thought, after all, that it would be unpleasant to stumble about in the dark in that strange house.

I stood while he fussed about and when at last he straightened up, his face lit by the flickering flame, I took the candle from him without a word. I could not even thank him.

As I turned to leave, he said, "Do not linger in the morning, Charlotte. The journey is long enough without delays."

"Journey? You cannot mean to leave!"

"For what purpose would I stay?"

"For Mr Webber. He is gravely injured."

"You understand very little, my wife. You speak as though Mr Webber were my brother or my bosom companion. He is neither of those; he is an investment gone to the bad."

"He is a man!"

"A man who is no longer of use. A one-eyed man cannot fight, and I do not make it my habit to support fellows who cannot be of use."

"It is your duty to make him well."

"I have paid the doctor. I have business in Bristol. I cannot wait for Mr Webber's eye to reattach itself."

"You have more than business waiting for you in Bristol! Mrs Webber is right, you are monstrous."

"You are run mad."

"I am seeing you more clearly than ever I have. Will you throw over Mrs Webber's sister when you tire of her? You are not faithful to your duty to me or to poor Mr Webber; you are in every way inconstant."

Granville took in a sharp breath. I could not see his eyes, but I knew well enough that he had not expected me to say such a thing. I thought he might speak, but instead he darted toward me and gripped my wrist. I was still holding the candle and my arm jerked with the surprise of it; hot wax splashed upon my hand.

"Let me go, this instant."

"You will make me an apology." His face was lit strangely, so close to the candle. He looked like nothing so much as a demon.

The candle's flame wavered with my trembling. With my free hand, I took it and put it carefully onto the mantelpiece. Then I turned to face him.

"You took her to my mama's house," I said. "I am glad you lost. There."

Now I began to tremble so violently that his grip was all that kept me standing; when he released me, I had to put out my hand to the mantel to keep from falling. He stood and put his hands behind his back, as though we stood in polite conversation beside the fire.

"What would you have me do, barren as you are?" he said.

I felt as though he struck me; I am sure I gasped aloud.

He leant toward me. "She has borne me a son and will give me another any day."

I recoiled back from his poisonous face, and as I did, it was as though the spirit of Mrs Webber stole from where she wept over her husband, flowed through my limbs, and drew back my arm. Granville was so unprepared for anything of the kind that he did not evade the blow and I felt the most ringing pain shoot through my arm as my fist made contact with his nose. He fell back into the dark, making a tremendous noise as he landed against some piece of furniture. He cried out in surprise and pain.

I stood, panting, my hand still humming from the impact. I could feel the enquiry—*Are you hurt?*—in my throat, and I would not release it.

Slowly the black shape of my husband stumbled to his feet and regained the candlelight. His face was a terrible thing of shifting shadows, his hands to his nose. Above us I heard the shuffle of feet and the opening of a door. We stood in the dark, facing each other like boxers at scratch, waiting for the call of time.

The feet came halfway down the stairs and then stopped.

"Who's there?" came the housekeeper's voice. "I warn you, my master has left us the use of his gun!"

"Get you back to bed, Mrs Dawson," Granville called, through his hands.

"Sir?" she said. "Are you quite all right? Are you hurt?"

We heard her steps begin to hurry down.

"Get you back to bed!" Granville shouted, in a voice I had never heard from him before. "If you want to have a place in the morning, you will not open this door!"

The steps stopped. I thought I heard her say, "My stars, the things that . . ." although the rest was lost. Her footsteps began to ascend again.

Now Granville shot out his hand and gripped me again by the wrist, bringing it up to my chest and pulling me so that I was captured against him. His other hand still covered his nose; a warm drop fell upon my lip. I put my tongue to it without thinking and tasted the warm tang of his blood.

"Curse you, witch." His face was so close that I could not see him properly.

"You, curse me!" My voice was breathy with hysteria. "You, who will make your heir on a whore? I have always known I married beneath myself, but you, sir, are lower than a worm. You are lower than ever I thought you."

"I am low? I have a drunkard for a wife."

I could feel his fingers digging deep into the flesh of my arm. His breath was wet upon my face. I thought, very clearly, *If I do not stop you now, you will have the mastery of me*—and I raised my free hand and gripped him by the throat, pushing with all my might. He did not let go my arm, but the shock of it made him step backward, pulling me with him. He fell over some small piece of furniture there and we both tumbled to the floor. One of my legs twisted underneath me, and I cried out. I landed atop him, his breath puffing out in a rush. For a moment we lay, shocked in the darkness, and then I sat up astride him. My twisted leg sent a bolt of agony through me as I moved.

Out of nowhere, Granville's open hand met my cheek. My head snapped to the side with the force of the slap, jerking my neck painfully, my teeth clacking together. I shook my head, as Mr Belcher had shaken his when Mr Webber struck him; I could not help it, though it hurt my neck.

I was filled with a desperate fury. I could not see, but that did not prevent me from throwing my fist downward, into the black shape of him. I struck some part of his skull—the impact travelled up my arm in a terrible vibration. I heard the thud as his head hit the floorboards.

His flailing hands found my throat and squeezed. I felt no pain, only fear jolting through me like an ice-bath. *He must not conquer me, he must not*—I thrust out my hands as blindly as he had done and felt the horrible bounce of my finger against his eye. He cried out again and his hands fell. I scrambled off him, feeling my leg scream with the effort of it. Like an animal, I backed away from the light and stood panting in the corner, watching him. My pulse beat hard in my aching throat.

Granville sat up and again put his hands to his face. He did not try to rise.

The candle was still sitting upon the mantelpiece exactly as I had left it. I went to it and took it up, keeping as far away from him as I could. I had a thought that he might reach out and grab my ankle, but he did not.

"Good night, then," I said, without meaning to.

He made a noise into his hands, something between a snort and a sob.

I left him there. What else was there to do? I walked up the unfamiliar stairs, hearing the wakeful servants creak the floor above. It was only once I found my bed and started to feel how injured I was—my hands sore, my arms bruised, my throat as tight as though he squeezed it still—it was only then that I thought, *I won a fight. I shall have to tell Mrs Webber.* Then I recalled the whole of that awful day. My tears burned my throat, and I hardly knew any longer which of us I wept for.

I slept and my dreams were full of water, and when I woke, the darkness was very deep. I heard the sound of my own sobs as though I had been crying without pause. After a moment my mind cleared and I realised it was not myself I heard weeping but Granville, beside me.

WHEN I AWOKE, Granville was gone and I could not be sure that he had been there at all. When the maid, Brown, came to fetch me up, she stared at my face quite openly before she remembered herself and dropped her eyes. She had come, she said, to tell me that Mr Dryer had asked her to say that he wished us on the road by nine.

She continued, "Mr Dryer bid me tell you he very much wants you with him and that if you come now, he'll see that Mr Webber is looked after here and carried to Bristol when he's stronger. I am to tell you that if you must stay, madam, then the Webbers will stay with you and he won't foot the bill for it." She blushed, but I thought she was enjoying being the bearer of such an uncommon message. "And then he used language, madam, that I don't like to repeat."

He was holding Mr Webber to ransom, then. I was too exhausted to debate it. If my husband wanted my company so badly, then I would travel with him. He was my burden, and I his.

I sank back upon the pillow.

"Then you may tell your master that I will be quite ready by nine o'clock, Brown."

"Yes, madam." Her voice was sweet as honey.

I sent her away as soon as she had helped me into my gown. My hair I secured in a knot beneath my cap. I had a little shock when I looked into the dressing glass, and knew then what had made Brown stare so; I had the beginnings of a bruise upon my cheek where Granville had slapped me, and upon my throat there were faint finger-marks, like the ghost of a broken necklace. I thought of painting them over, but I had not time—I wanted to see Mrs Webber before I left.

I hurried down the stairs and asked another parlour maid where I might find Mrs Webber. She led me to a room beside the kitchens, glancing all the time at me from the corner of her eye. No one answered her knock.

"Mrs Webber?" she called, and opened the door a little way.

They were still abed, though it was almost nine. Mr Webber's mouth hung open, the bandage askew upon his swollen face. His battered hands he held to his chest. His breath came as loud as a man gasping for air. Mrs Webber, small as she was, had curled herself about him, her arm hooked over his enormous rib cage. Her face was obscured by his shoulder but I thought, from the stillness of her, that she slept as deeply as he. All this I saw in just a moment, and then I whispered, "Leave them," and the maid closed the door.

I came up the kitchen stairs just in time to see Granville descending the main staircase, calling for the butler in a furious tone. Immediately I saw what a feast of gossip we had brought that household—both his eyes were blacked and his nose had swollen ridiculously, like the nose of Mr Punch in a puppet show. He held in his hand the purse from which I had liberated ten guineas the day before. I had forgotten all about it, in the anguish of Mr Webber's defeat.

"Granville," I called out.

"Not now, Charlotte! We have a thief amongst us." His voice was changed, made high and strange by his swollen nose.

The butler, appearing at the drawing room door, now drew himself up very straight and looked grave.

"A thief, sir?"

"Granville, you must listen. I took ten guineas from your purse."

Granville stopped still and turned to face me. "May I ask you to repeat yourself?" he asked, as though he meant to frighten me.

I felt only weary. "I believe you heard me. I laid it upon poor Mr Webber's victory. Now it is lost, along with everything else."

I had thought he would berate me, but his shoulders slumped and he only sighed and turned to the butler.

"We will leave immediately. Ready the carriage," he said.

I followed him out obediently enough, though I was dreading his company. I did not know that I could bear to be shut up with him for two whole days. The servants, I could see, were watching us from the windows of the house.

I sat opposite him and tried not to look at his bruises. The shame of it all kept us silent; I recalled sitting quietly beside Perry, when we had been punished together by Nurse. The stillness of my body and the movement of the carriage caused all my tender limbs to ache.

Once we were on our way, Granville said, "I have had them pack us a basket of food. We won't stop, except to change the horses. You must say, Lottie, if you need to stop the carriage for any other purpose."

I only looked at him.

"What," he said, "will you not speak to me, all the journey?"

"You have forced me to return with you; will you make me speak? Will you send word to have Mr Webber harmed, if I do not?"

"You treat me harshly," he said.

"I, treat you!"

"Why should I not have my wife with me? Even after all." He gestured to his grotesque face. "Have I not forgiven you your thievery? Have I not done what you asked of me, and seen Mr Webber made safe?"

"You brought him to danger," I said.

Granville sighed. "You would not understand, Lottie. It is a matter for men."

"It is a matter for morals," I said. "You would not understand that."

I would not speak to him further. I spent much of the journey pretending to sleep. When I heard Granville's breath slow, I allowed myself to open my eyes and look at the passing scenery until it grew dark. The carriage rattled on, through the night.

EVEN AFTER A JOURNEY such as that I could not be glad to see The Ridings, rising out of the morning fog like a clumsy sea-monster. All was dreary and we had lost. I followed Granville into the house only because there was nowhere else to go. The servants looked at our bruised countenances quite as avidly as the London maids.

Granville halted in the hall and stared at the bare patches upon the walls.

"What is the meaning of this? What in God's name have you done with the portraits?"

"I ordered them taken down," I said.

"Indeed?" He glared at me. His eyebrow twitched strangely. After a moment I realised that he was attempting to raise it but was prevented by his bruises.

"Yes. They are quite safe. If you like them so much, you may put them in your dressing room." I went quickly to the stairs, so that he would be forced to speak to my back or say nothing. He kept his silence.

WHAT RELIEF TO GET BACK to my own dressing room, and yet how queer. It seemed the room of another woman—seemed, perhaps, like the untouched chambers of the house at Queen Square, where everything was arranged according to the needs of a life now passed. I lay on my daybed like a woman in a faint. Nothing mattered. Nothing, except the fate of Mr Webber. I was in a frenzy of guilt that I had abandoned him. I had not left instructions that he was to be given white cullis, I had not bid either of the Webbers farewell. I vowed to myself that the moment they were back, I would find a way to repair my husband's wrongs. That thought recovered me somewhat, but even so, it was cruel and strange to be returned so, to this penitential drudgery.

Then, a thought, like a gentle tapping at a windowpane, *Henry*. The one person who could be relied upon to feel some of my own anguish.

I called for Lucy. Her eyes, usually so dull, regarded me brightly. I could not begin to guess what they were saying downstairs, to see us arrive home so bruised and Granville's man defeated.

"Have Henry sent to me at once."

Lucy bit her lip, and I thought she fought not to smile.

"I can't rightly do that, madam—he's been sent to his ma's house. He ain't well."

"Not well?" My disappointment was more bitter than ever I would have thought.

"No, madam. He came over queer when he heard of Mr Webber's being defeated." She gave me a sideways glance to see how I received this news. She must have seen what she wanted for she continued, "Mr Horton sent him home, till he can keep a grip on himself, he said. Like a baby, he was, and him a big boy of fourteen."

I drew myself up.

393

"Henry has shown a loyalty to Mr Dryer's interests that other members of this household would do well to remember. Would that all of you were so moved by your master's success or failure. Have Mr Horton send a message to that effect immediately. He's to tell Henry that we look forward to having him back whenever he feels himself ready and that he shall find his tenderness rewarded, not punished."

There, I thought, *now take your sly looks back to the kitchen and tell them all I said so.*

Dear Henry, I had known he would feel it as I did. It did not make me any the less alone, however.

GRANVILLE SEEMED NOT TO KNOW how to occupy himself, now that his boxing scheme was ended. He did not seem angry, any longer, that I had blacked his eyes, quite the contrary. He sought me out and called for wine in the evenings, to please me. He was often near me, enquiring if I might like his company, like a dog seeking a pat. I kept away from him as far as was possible and thought bitterly over all those days I had spent alone, waiting for his notice. I had another reason to find his attentions irksome; I wished for an opportunity of going alone to the gatehouse to pack up any belongings that the Webbers might have left behind. I could not imagine that they would travel back to fetch them, and it gave me good reason to visit them in Bristol and enquire how they did. I would not let Granville follow me to the gatehouse. I might want to sit and remember, I might wish to swing at the leather man.

It was not until perhaps a fortnight after we arrived home, that Granville finally took his gun out to the woods and left me alone. The moment he was gone I hurried upstairs and began to look out a walking gown, but no sooner had I opened the press than I heard the knocker on the front door, and then Mr Bowden's voice in the hall below.

This was most unwelcome. *Do not ask if I am at home,* I wished, silently. *Go away, go away.* I did not come down. I stood at the top of the stairs and heard his enquiry and Horton's response. Thankfully, Mr Bowden said he would go out and catch Granville, and had Horton point him the direction.

I went to my window and watched him walk from the yard. I told Lucy that I was going to take a turn about the lawn, and without even changing from my morning gown, only calling for a cloak—I slipped away.

It was glorious to walk down the drive alone. The air upon my face and the sense of solitude chosen quietly lifted my heart.

The key to the front door of the gatehouse was just where it should have been, tucked out of sight upon the lintel. I had never before made use of a key to open the front door of any kind of dwelling. Keys had been things to secure the doors of bedrooms, or music boxes. I felt like a house-breaker, and somehow like a grown woman—or perhaps I felt like a man. How odd to see my own hand turn the key and push open the door. Then I felt strange all over again as I stepped inside.

The chairs and tables were where I was used to seeing them, the stools drawn up to the hearth, as had been our habit. These things remained, as of course they must, but the air of the place was changed. It smelt cold and damp, with something of rot, like a country lane turned rancid. Looking about me, I saw what else was changed: the whole house was too clean. The hearth was swept, the floor was scrubbed, the curtains arranged and tied. I could see nothing of Mrs Webber's left at all, nothing that I might take to her. The scullery was tidied. Pans hung neatly, earthenware jars arranged in a line. The larder had a few things left upon its shelves, made into cheesecloth bundles that might have held anything. These, too, were lined up neatly, like a row of cocoons.

The staircase had been polished and smelled of beeswax. I felt a sneaking excitement as I climbed; I had never been up there before. Surely, here was where Mrs Webber's possessions would be stored. Here, where she had laid her head as I lay in my own bed, feeling my swollen knuckles throb in time with my pulse. I opened the plain wooden door as quietly as if she might be sleeping there still, but the room was empty and so unremarkable as to have been any room, anywhere. The coverlet was smoothed and tucked, the boards swept clean, the ewer emptied and set neatly beside the jug. There was nothing that could be considered a personal effect in the whole of the house. Had they come and fetched away their things, and never called to see me, nor sent a word?

I descended the staircase feeling I might weep, as though the days spent there had been taken from me and even my memories spoiled.

I went out into the yard and felt somewhat soothed. Here nothing could much be changed. The leather man hung from his chain just as he always had. The grass around his pole had grown to brush his underside, but he was the same. I had struck at him till I trembled. I had leant against him, exhausted, and marked him with damp from my brow.

"We have been abandoned," I said to him, and felt surprised to hear my own voice in the quiet.

I pushed him, to make him swing, and heard the creak of the chain. Mrs Webber had never allowed me to strike at him without mufflers on my hands. I wished she had left me those, at least. The chain made such a mournful sound that I steadied him with my hands to stop it. Then I leant forward and put my mouth close to the leather.

"I shall get some mufflers, from somewhere," I whispered, "and Henry and I will be back here to see you made use of."

Then I turned and made to go back inside.

"Mrs Dryer," came a voice.

I started and whirled around as though I expected to be attacked. When I saw it was George Bowden come upon me alone, I was almost as flustered as if it had indeed been an assailant. I put my hand to my breast to feel my heart racing as fast as a bird's.

"Mrs Dryer, I came to find you."

He looked queer, his eyes shining as though with fever.

"Are you ill?" I asked.

"No, quite well, quite well, I assure you."

He came suddenly toward me and took my hand and drew me back into the gatehouse. I let him, and stumbled a little as he pulled me across the step. His other hand found my elbow to steady me, and once we were inside he stepped forward, so that I found myself pressed against him. His eyes searched my own as though trying to read my thoughts. I gazed back at him. His eyes were as wide and as long-lashed as ever, their colour as rich. Did they move me? I could not tell. My thoughts were as hidden from me as they seemed to be from Mr Bowden.

"What is it, Mr Bowden? Why should you look for me?" I did not ask him to release me.

His mouth was so close to my own that I could feel his breath upon my face. His perfume was exactly as it always had been. It spoke straight to my memory of his holding me, beside the stream. I had been so hopeful, and hopeless, of all the wrong things.

"I have always looked for you," he said.

I felt, suddenly, how alone we were, how far from any other soul. I felt a thrill much like the one I had felt when Mrs Webber, Henry, and I had set off in the dogcart, under cover of darkness. *I am alone, in an isolated place, with a man not my husband. Not a soul knows where I am.*

"Please, you need not compose pleasantries for me."

"Does the way I speak displease you? Only tell me what to alter and I will change it."

He still had one hand upon my elbow; now it moved to my waist. My other hand he held clasped against his chest. His fingers were stroking at my palm. I did not like it, my palm being so scarred. He was breathing heavily; one might almost say, panting. I twisted my hand and wrest it from his grip, pushing at his shoulder with my free hand. I did not push him hard. He released me and stepped back, putting up his hands and running them through his hair.

I walked from him and sat upon a chair, beside the little table.

"What is it you look for, Mr Bowden?"

He followed me and stood again, very near. Only one step would have him standing over me. I did not look up at him. I found my gaze drawn to the places it should not be: his waistcoat, his trousers, his violinist's hands.

He knelt in front of me and again took my hand.

"I wish that you would call me George."

I watched him lift my hand to his lips with a sensation most strange; perhaps a kind of satisfaction. His eyes seemed pleading over it.

"If I call you George, will you explain, or let me go?" I said, at last.

"You have my word."

"Well, then. Why have you come to find me, George?" I blushed, and wished I did not.

"Oh, dear Charlotte. Lottie. I have come to . . . oh, by God, I am a fool."

He sat back, fetched a hip flask from his jacket pocket, and drank from it.

"What have you there?" I asked, though I could smell the rum plainly.

"Rum, only. I beg your pardon. My nerves, you see."

"May I?"

His eyes widened, but he passed the flask to me. I put it to my lips, and then, when I felt the good heat of it, I put it to my lips once more.

"Please," I said, "only say what you have come to say so that we might both be freed from suspense." I let my voice grow light and teasing, most unlike myself.

"I am leaving here, Charlotte. I am going away. I wish you to come with me. There, it is said."

He took my hand once more and looked up at me like a puppy. Again, I took my hand from his, although this time I did it slowly, sliding my own fingers over his palm as I went.

"I, go away with you! You have run mad," I said. I was enjoying myself scandalously. I felt as though we were reading lines from a book.

"I have not, indeed I have not." He really was most appealing when he looked so.

"Then you are come to tease me."

"Never." His cheeks grew pink. "I have always loved you, Lottie. You should have been Mrs Bowden instead of Mrs Dryer—it was only your brother that prevented it."

"Oh! Why tell me such things? It is too late, too late." I pressed the back of one hand to my brow—it seemed the correct thing to do at such a moment.

He took the flask from my fingers, drank from it, coughed, and passed it once more to me. I took it gladly and drank until it was empty and my throat aflame.

"I am going away," he said, again.

I looked at him, sitting at my feet, his hair disordered, nervously wetting his lips with the tip of a very pink tongue. He was a fool, but he was still the most handsome man I had ever known. My husband was not handsome, nor kind, nor constant. Both my husband and my brother would curse to see me now.

I looked at Mr Bowden for one long, delicious moment.

"Let me make you a farewell," I said.

He shook his head to protest, but I put out my hand.

"Come, George."

He took it. I stood and led him up the stairs. He followed me so quickly that he trod upon my skirts and had to catch me when I stumbled.

How can I explain what that afternoon meant to me, having known only Granville? At first Mr Bowden—George—was fearful that I might change my mind and begin to scream. Once he understood that I would not—well, I can only say that I had never known that the whole business could be so joyous, so absolutely free from all the usual tethers of propriety. I felt myself grow animal, unthinking. It was nearly as exciting as boxing.

Once it was done, I lay on that bare straw mattress and watched him dress. I felt like a contented farmer's wife, watching him button his shirt under those beamed eaves. I felt like stretching, like a cat. I did not even mind my scars. There was nothing left to blush at, after what he had shown me. I had never been so exposed and so comfortable, at once. He had touched parts of me that no other hands had found before; I felt like treasure unburied. He had lightly touched the fading bruises at my throat and said not a word, only quivered with feeling and kissed me the more ardently.

"You must come with me," he said now. "I have a plantation in the sugar islands. It will be all mine—ours—you would be my wife. They will none of them know who we were before we came."

I could only laugh. "Mr Bowden, George, that is a very great sin."

"Misery is the greatest sin! I have condemned us both, but I will free us now. Come with me, Charlotte, I beg you. Think of it, only—we shall both be set free."

He came to my side and leant over me, his breath tickling my ear.

"I have a grand house there," he whispered, "and I shall get us a carriage and horses—you shall have a horse like the mare I bought you once."

"Locket." I found myself whispering too.

"Yes, Locket, I had forgot that was her name. I will get you so many things, Lottie—"

"George, I cannot."

"You shall be mistress of a fine house in glorious sunshine. I have taken it from your husband."

"From my husband?" I felt myself grow still.

"I won it, rather, when his boxer failed."

It was as though he had opened a window in winter; all the warmth and softness was snatched away. I sat up so quickly that he was forced to draw back or be struck by my head as I rose.

"You wagered against poor Mr Webber?" I had not known I could sound so forbidding.

"It is the sport, Lottie. Of course, I pity the fellow now. But I have taken a fine house! We shall be so happy."

"No," I said.

"You do not mean it, you are only surprised. I cannot blame you."

"No, Mr Bowden."

"Please, I know you do not love Mr Dryer." He reached out his hand and let it hover, quivering, in the air between us. I would not take it.

"I wish you would leave," I said.

"I will not believe you! You must come."

"I tell you I will not! Do not ask me again."

Now I got up and pulled my petticoats down. I found my gown and stepped into it, despite my untied stays.

I turned my back to him. "Assist me, please."

I felt his fingers come upon the laces of my stays and pull. He did not pull them as tightly as he should, but I said nothing. Next he began, fumbling, to work upon the buttons of my gown. I was glad to have my back to him. I thought that if I looked at him, I might strike him.

"Very well," he said behind me, "I will go from you. You may never lay eyes upon me again, you know."

"Then I wish you a safe journey and a happy life, Mr Bowden." I did not turn, although he had finished with the buttons.

"You are cruel! Can you really send me from you?"

I would not reply, but only picked up my shoes and, carrying them, walked to the door.

"Then promise me one thing, Charlotte, Mrs Dryer. As a parting gift. If ever you loved me, grant me one favour."

I turned and regarded him with a gaze I knew to be hard. He stood with his hat in his hand, his eyes as wide as he could make them. I only waited. At last he sighed and seemed to give up.

"Take care of your brother," he said. "He is lost, and will be even more so when he finds me gone. Please, promise me only that. Watch over him as I have done."

I had expected something else, I knew not what.

"If he will allow me, I will do it," I said.

"You are too good."

He rushed to me again and put his hands about my waist. He drew me to him so firmly that I could only allow it or cry out. I stayed silent, but I felt how unyielding was my body.

"Please," he said, "only one kiss, upon your lips? For a farewell."

His kisses had been delicious an hour before. Now he pressed me against him too feverishly; I could not breathe. I was dizzy when at last he released me.

"You will not change your mind?" he said.

"Good-bye, Mr Bowden."

I opened the door and left him there. I did not look back at all. My lips tasted sour, no matter how I rubbed at them.

I DID NOT GO to visit the Webbers at Bristol; I was grieved that they had been to the gatehouse and come away without seeing me. However much I had hoped to see them, I was also afraid to go to their house, in what I thought must be a disreputable part of Bristol. I did not know what I should do, were I to come upon Mrs Webber's sister there. I was afraid, too, that Mrs Webber would be angry with me, or that I would find our friendship changed. I was a coward and had forgotten how bravery was to be done. To make up for failing in my promise to help nurse Mr Webber, I honoured the promise I had made to Mr Bowden.

I was by then desperate to escape Granville's company. He was still following me about the house, asking me to ride or walk out with him. I refused it all, and still he would not give it up.

"I will go to visit Perry," I told him, at last. "You need not accompany me."

His mouth twitched, but he did not stop me, nor claim greater need of the carriage.

"I hope it will make you happy," he said. His tone was piteous.

My feeling as the carriage began to move was one of glorious release. I watched all that passed outside the window as avidly as though it were a play.

I realised as we began the familiar, curving approach to Aubyn Hall that I had not been there in an age. When I had seen my brother in recent months he had been a guest at our table, and even those visits had fallen away considerably. I felt a great affection for the place, coming to it now. Whatever it had taken from me, it would always remain my childhood home. Louisa's feet had walked these garden paths; Arthur had run across the lawns. My papa's touch was here, where he had ordered the extension of the yew alley, grown faster now than I suspected he could have dreamt. Here, where the carriage drew up, was Mama's taste, the cheerful yellow curtains at the breakfast room window. Had I visited Aubyn without Granville, in all our marriage? I could not think I had.

Fisher greeted me with as warm an expression as a butler ever allows himself, and showed me into the parlour.

My good feeling vanished entirely the moment I stepped inside. The house was not changed in any perceptible way, and yet something was different. All was clean enough, all the furniture laid out the same as it had been when last I visited—but perhaps it was this very sameness that oppressed me. Perry could not fill such a house all by himself. Probably no feet but the maid's had been into the parlour in weeks.

At last, after what felt a long time, Fisher returned.

"He will see you, madam. I feel it my duty to say to you that Mr Sinclair is somewhat indisposed just at the moment."

"Is he ill, Fisher?"

"He is . . . not quite himself, madam. He is in the library."

"Thank you, Fisher. You may take me to him."

I followed his straight back out of the parlour and up the stairs to the library. Our steps sounded very loud. Fisher knocked once and swung open the library door.

"Mrs Dryer, sir," he said.

Perry was sitting beside the hearth, a rug over his knees like an invalid. He gave a weary nod upon sight of me, as though I came to pester him daily. He was clean-shaven, but his face had lost weight, making his eyes seem too big. His cheeks, always so quick to flush, were tinged with yellow. A spider's web of broken veins crawled across one side of his nose. I would not have believed, if I had not known, that here was a man not yet thirty. I looked at Fisher in surprise but he was as expressionless as ever.

"So you come to visit me, sister?" Perry smelt as though he had bathed in liquor.

"I wondered how you did," I said. "Fisher, I would like a drink. Ratafia, if you have it."

"Yes, madam. Anything for you, sir?"

Perry looked at the decanter at his elbow. It was half full.

"Not yet," he said.

I sat opposite Perry, in a winged chair that smelt unpleasantly of cigars.

"How do you do, Perry? Your colour is bad."

"Then I am in your likeness, my poxed sister."

I made no reply. At last he sighed and shuffled about in his chair as though he could not be comfortable.

"I do badly," he said. "I cannot find George. Is he with your husband, do you know?"

"No, not with Granville."

"Damn his eyes!" Perry jerked so suddenly that he soused himself with liquor from his glass. "He knows I cannot do without him! Rot him, I was sure he was with Granville. Perhaps, then, in Bristol, gambling away what remains of his sorry life, bastard that he is."

He tipped the dregs of the glass into his mouth and poured himself a generous replacement.

"What can you mean, to say you cannot do without him?" I did not mention Perry's foul language.

"Look at me," he held out a shaking hand. "I cannot be steady, I cannot sleep. I am alone here. He has left me."

He began to weep. I was frozen with the horror of seeing him reduced so terribly. At last, when he put his face into his shaking hands I stirred myself, crossed to him, and put my hand upon his shoulder. Immediately that he felt my touch he stiffened and then, in one jerky movement, threw his arms about my waist and began to cry in earnest. I stroked his hair. There was something encrusted in it. Behind me, I heard Fisher enter quietly and put a drink for me upon the small table. Before he could slide away, I turned my head.

"Fisher," I said, "my brother is not clean. His hair needs washing."

"Yes, madam."

"How can you leave him so?" I was growing angry with the sheer unexpectedness of the situation. Perry had grown still but would not loose his hold nor take his face from where it pressed against my waist. I could feel a dampness there, from his eyes and, perhaps, his nose.

"Mr Sinclair prefers not to be bathed, madam."

"He will be bathed now. Make the water hot and perfumed. Perry, you are to be washed. Do you understand? And then we will have something nourishing for dinner."

Perry looked up at me and wiped his eyes with his tremulous fingers.

"Will you stay with me?" he asked.

"I will."

"Until George comes home again?"

Ever since we had returned from London, I had wondered where on earth I could go besides my married home. What could be more proper than a sister caring for her invalid brother? My husband could not order me home from here. Surely he could not.

"I will not leave you while you need me," I said.

I SPENT MANY DAYS at Perry's side, though often he hardly noticed I was there. At other times he cried out for me and sobbed in my arms until my gown grew sodden with his tears. It was a welcome diversion to be of use to him, but oh, how strange and awful to be nursing my last surviving relative in the house where first Arthur and Louisa and then my parents were lost. Perry was not ill in the conventional sense, but I could not help but think that I was watching him slowly loosen his hold on the living world. He was awake only when he could not help it and all the time strove for unconsciousness.

I slept in my old bed and found the kind of comfort that is threaded with sorrow. I went often to Mama's room, just to sit. I had begun to find the dust-sheets soothing, the room turned to soft hillocks like the gardens after a snowfall. Sometimes I lifted the corner of a sheet and looked beneath, at the dresser or the chaise, but all was tidied away—there was no sense of Mama here as a real, breathing person. Besides, the furniture seemed sleeping; I could not help but feel that it would be kinder to let it all rest.

Granville came to visit me, as I should have guessed that he would, bearing tonics and sweetmeats. He did not seem to have wondered for one moment whether I would receive him. Though I had been gone some days, he had entirely lost his piteous air and was affecting a stern expression.

I took his basket. "Thank you. Your kindness is very much appreciated. You will understand that I cannot linger; my brother has need of me." I turned away, saying, "Pull the bell for Fisher and order anything you'd like," as though I were mistress of the house.

Granville caught my arm. I stopped, shook my arm as if he were a fly that had landed upon me. He removed his hand, both of us no doubt thinking of that other night, in darkness, in a different house.

"This cannot continue. When will you come home, Lottie?"

"I am at home," I said.

He did not stop me leaving the room.

TWO DAYS LATER he appeared again, with another basket and the same question.

"I will not leave Perry," I told him, then.

"What, is he so very ill?"

I looked at my husband. His face was exhausted, this time. His coat was dusty.

"Come and visit him."

Perry was sitting quite still before the fire, his chin drooping onto his breast. When Granville entered the library and spoke his name he looked up with a momentary expression of hope in his bloodshot eyes and then, on seeing my husband, dropped his head back down.

"Old friend." Granville went over and took his hand. "What ails you?"

Perry, I could see, was readying to weep.

I left them.

When Granville emerged, he came to find me. I was sitting in the parlour, embroidering, in dark silks of blue and grey, a scene depicting a country lane at night, where three hooded figures walked, the moon bright above them.

"May I sit with you awhile?"

I inclined my head and rang to have some refreshment brought. Granville sat opposite me. He looked wearier than ever.

"Your brother does badly," he said.

"I know it."

"I understand now why you stay here. But Lottie, you cannot mean to live here forever. You must come home and be my wife."

I only looked at him. I did not have any difficulty in meeting his eyes. He looked like a familiar stranger, if such a thing exists. His misery could not touch me. I was utterly indifferent to him.

"You have the right to force me there," I said.

He did not look as though he had the stomach for it.

"I wish you would come willingly."

"I don't believe that I will ever come willingly."

"Never?"

"I was unhappy in your house."

"Tell me how to make you happy, then. Tell me what you wish for."

"Do you want me home so badly?"

"I do. I need my wife beside me."

"You have never needed me there before."

He sighed. "So many things are different now."

"I will consider it," I said.

"I can see that you are changed as much as I am."

"I am. I am changed, and I believe that I am changing still. I will not leave Perry as he is, and alone. I will not leave him to die, Granville."

"Curses upon George! If anything happens to your brother, he will have it upon his conscience. He had better return soon."

I thought of Mr Bowden on his plantation in the sunshine while my brother crumbled.

"He may not," I said.

In thinking of the plantation, I realised that poor Mr Webber's defeat meant that Granville had not taken my mama's house. I thought of this while Granville sat opposite me, looking as though he feared I would at any moment kick him. I thought of it as I sat in my poor mama's room, amongst the gentle shapes of her things. I thought of it in the evening, while Perry sobbed in my arms.

"Where is he, curse him," he said, his voice full of tears and the cloth of my gown. "I swear, if only I knew when he would return, I could bear it. If only I knew what the devil he was doing."

I patted his back. He seemed not my brother at all. I imagined him an infant, or perhaps a kind of creature. I thought about hope and what a weight it could be. I could not say that I would ever love Granville, and yet I had allowed him to hope. For my part, I had begun to notice a familiar sensation in those most feminine parts of me and thought that perhaps I was once again carrying my own hopes, though of course it was George Bowden, not Granville, who had planted them there. I could not help thinking, *If I only live in Mama's house, I am sure my son will come safely.*

Here was Perry, soaking my waist with his own agonised hope and I knew well enough how to end his suspense. Was despair preferable to hope? Sometimes, I thought, it must be. He could not, at any rate, go on as he was.

"I may know where Mr Bowden is," I told him. "I will tell you all, if you will only sign over to me the house at Queen Square."

Perry grew very still. "You know where George is?"

"I do. You must sign the town house over to me, before I will tell you."

He sat up and seemed to see me for the first time. He looked upon me with an expression of distaste.

"Of course. You have never lifted a finger to further my happiness unless it held some benefit for you. You hold me while I grieve, you snake, and all the time you keep George's blasted secret behind your poison tongue."

Perry's lip curled and his nostrils shuddered. He drew himself up in his seat and wiped his eyes upon his sleeve so vigorously that the skin around them flushed pink. He rang the bell, pulling the cord as though he wished to do it an injury, and Fisher appeared.

I stood, my head held very high.

"Very well," I said, "I will leave. You need not have Fisher escort me out. And I will tell you where Mr Bowden has gone to. You are cruel to keep that house—you know that you do not want it—but I shall not be cruel, likewise."

Perry huffed out a scornful laugh and drained his cup of liquor. "You have laid out your demands, you she-devil, and I will meet them. You shall have your house, and then you will get gone from this one. Fisher will play the part of witness."

He slowly pulled himself to a stand, one hand on the back of the chair, and staggered across the room. He fetched the papers out of his desk without even troubling to conceal from me the secret drawer in his cabinet. The documents he slapped down upon the desk-top, and signed them so quickly, and so carelessly, that he spotted his breeches with the ink.

PART 9

George

* * *

Chapter 22

❖ ❖ ❖

I had gone to London to make my fortune, as so many young gentlemen
had before me, and I had lost everything. Following Tom Webber's defeat, I went back to Perry like a condemned man to the gallows. He greeted
me sullenly with "So you return, then. Let the bells ring out," and he pulled
the servants' bell for more brandy. He did not ask how Webber had fared.

I choked back a biting observation upon finding that he was not dead
by his own hand, as promised. I had not the heart to fight him. I felt like
taking myself to bed and staying there—I had never been disposed to melancholy before. Instead I took a seat by Perry and joined him in his cups.

Perhaps this will be my life, I thought. *I will become like Perry and we will
die of drink together, in a puddle of our own mess.*

That night we fell asleep in our chairs by the fire. I was woken by Perry's screams, as the night-fears came upon him.

"Arthur, no," he cried, again and again. His arms waved wildly, blindly,
like a man attacked by bees. He did not seem to see me, even when I caught
his wrists. Perhaps he thought his dead brother had returned to reclaim his
lost inheritance—if I had been Arthur's ghost I should have been unim-
pressed by the reputation my younger brother was bringing to the family.

In the morning—or perhaps it was the day after that—I sat down with
the books and looked over Perry's accounts. I recall that my head was

swimming with exhaustion and the lingering effects of liquor and depressed spirits. Perry, I could see, was doing well enough financially. We could indeed continue as we were until we drank ourselves into our graves. I would never be more than Perry's right hand and perhaps had always been destined to be so, since that day at school, when I put out my fleshly right hand to be joined to him in blood.

These thoughts were so bleak that I determined to crush them in any way that I could contrive. To this end I attempted to persuade Perry to accompany me to the inn in the village, to get out from the air of Aubyn.

"For what purpose? It is a God-awful hole filled with farmers and bad ale."

"For the change! To be somewhere other than here. I grow restless, Perry."

"Get you gone, then. I do not seek change. Get you gone, you weak-willed butterfly." He would not answer me more.

He would never seek change, but I must. I walked from the room and almost collided with Fisher, bearing two letters upon a tray.

The first of these was a note from Mr Tyne, the estate steward, informing me that in my absence he had taken the liberty of securing the rents from the estate in his own lock-box and would deliver them into my hands whenever I bid him do so. The second was a scrawl from Granville addressed to Perry, letting him know the sad outcome of the contest and inviting him to call when he pleased to collect his prize—the deed to the plantation in the sugar islands.

What man, just then, would not have had thoughts of betrayal? It was as though Old Nick himself had sent me the means to escape.

IT IS PERRY *who is weak-willed, not I,* I thought, as Blackbird's hooves clipped smartly along the lanes toward Granville's house. In my coat-pocket I carried the heavy purse containing the rents from Perry's estate. I had strapped a valise to Blackbird's saddle, containing a few other effects: my blue coat and a clean shirt, a cravat I was fond of, and a snuffbox I'd had from Perry a long time ago. This last was empty, save for the black dust of some ancient snuff collected in its corners. My own, more oft-used snuff-box was in my coat-pocket. I had brought the other as being a reminder of Perry that was small enough to carry.

Granville was not within doors when I called, but the butler directed me to the nearby wood, where I found him walking rather aimlessly with his gun, his face as serious as ever. I took care not to show my surprise at seeing that my old friend's eyes were ringed with the yellow-grey remains of a hefty pair of shiners. I could only assume that Webber had rebelled against his master, the faithful dog turned savage. Granville greeted me calmly enough, and I fell into step beside him.

"How do you fare, old friend?" I asked him.

"Well enough, though I am left the poorer. You have come to collect Perry's prize, I don't doubt."

So he had not heard from Perry. A little of the anxiety about my heart released itself.

"I have."

Granville looked older. Defeat had drawn lines across his brow. We returned to the house and he very obligingly gave over the deed to the plantation made out only "to the bearer."

"Do not you name it," I said. "I think to sell it on, and Perry is in agreement."

Granville only nodded and did as I asked. It was a sign of his low spirits that he did not even offer his opinion on the matter.

I rode away from Granville in a kind of numb fever. Emotions flitted across my mind, but I watched them pass through like the audience at a play; none of them landed for more than a moment. The trick, I thought, would be to get myself well away before the guilt descended.

I knew I could not go into my new life alone. I rode, therefore, toward the person I thought most likely to throw her lot in with a rogue. I rode toward Dora.

Upon passing the gatehouse at the bottom of Granville's drive, however, I spied Mrs Charlotte Dryer. It seemed that fate had placed her in my way. Perhaps I was meant to take Charlotte with me—Charlotte, who had once been a player in that earlier gamble for my freedom.

She would not even think of accompanying me, though I entreated most earnestly. Instead she made me the sweetest good-bye a lady can make to a gentleman, and I had to be satisfied.

I rode away with a churning sea within my breast. I had longed for her and finally had my way. I had given her up for love of Perry, and lost him to his own nature. Now I rode away from both, toward an unknown future. I told myself firmly that I must resolve not to think of the Sinclairs, or their violet eyes, ever again. It was for the best; I would need a hardy maid with me in my new life, not a delicate lady. I would think of Dora, and grand houses on tropical plantations.

THE BAWDY HOUSE was not as inviting as once it had been. The cove on the door was the same as ever, but within it seemed dirtier than I recalled, the young ladies more sour. There were only two of them there upon the bench. They looked up at me with that cold interest typical of whores.

"Where is your mistress?"

I shook the dust of the road from my coat; the floor needed sweeping, in any case.

"Up the stairs," one of them said, and then seemed to rally her spirits enough to add, "but you don't want her, sir. She's just dropped an infant, she's wide as a barrel." Both molls laughed.

I made them no reply, but I was disheartened to hear of it. She had been swollen with child when last I saw her, but she had declared with the greatest confidence that she would shake it from her. I could not feel easy about taking a nursing mother aboard ship. Perhaps she would pass more easily as my wife, but to what cost? I would be burdened before I had begun.

Dora had evidently heard my steps approach, but she still bid me enter as soon as my knuckles tapped the wood. The Dora I was used to would have made me wait until she had adorned herself with rouge and ribbons. This fact was sadly emphasised when once the door was opened; she was abed, with a babe at her bare breast. Her face was bare of paint and her hair needed reworking. The chamber was as unkempt as the rest of the house. Her expression upon seeing me went swiftly from ill-humour to surprise. She had not expected me, that much was clear.

"Mr George Bowden!"

I stood for a moment, assailed by the greatest doubts. She looked plain and brought down, like a housewife one might see on any street, lining up at the pump. Then I recovered myself. She could be made sweet again, away from this filthy house and the ugly creature at her breast. And I could not go alone. I was not sure I wished to go, if I must be entirely alone.

In the event she proved even easier to persuade than I had hoped. When once I had answered her questions enough, she swung herself out of bed.

"Here's what I've been looking for, Mr George Bowden," she said, and called for one of the girls to take the babe from her. She never even asked to bring it. Best of all, she had the acquaintance of a captain due to set sail within days.

I HAD PLAYED all I had in my hand, and come out the victor. This thought beat a tattoo in my breast as the ship gained speed and the high cliffs of the Avon Gorge began to slide by. I stood at the ship's rail and laughed as we passed the Hot Well, and then the houses of Clifton, shining pale in the sunlight atop the cliffs. I would never walk there again and I did not care a fig. Dora was warm in my arms and as she pressed against me I could feel the edges of the folded deed to the plantation, tucked inside my waistcoat. First Bristol, then the coast of England slipped behind us, and I stood at the rail for hours without tiring, my exultation only matched by the wind. I did not allow myself to think of the Sinclairs. I looked only toward the horizon, beyond which lay my future. We stood at that rail, heedless of the wind's teeth, until the sky grew dark. Then we went below to the captain's table and dined as well as one does on a ship just out of port, with the food still fresh and the rum dispensed as liberally as ale.

THE ELATION DID NOT LAST past that first evening. I awoke the next morning to the sound of Dora breathing heavily upon the bunk below and the guilt sharp as acid in my stomach. The weight of it advanced and retreated all day, in rhythm with the rolling of the waves and the nausea. I had never liked to feel confined, and a ship is one of the most limited places one can be. I felt trapped by the sea, and by Dora, and by my own actions. Now that I could not go back I was not sure, after all, that I wished to go forward. It was a miserable sensation.

I had never been so long in Dora's company before. She could not stop talking about what a lady she would be. This soon became tiresome; I grew short with her, and she grew sulkish. We were each of us only appeased when I desired her again and made her sweet by promising that she should have whatever she wished when we reached port. Then she would relent and remind me why I had brought her there to begin. When once I had done, however, she would begin again upon her imaginings of laces and jewels, and I would feel my irritation come stealing over me like a tremor.

Dora delighted in thinking of Granville's wrath upon discovering us gone, and the trick I had played upon him. She liked to have me fetch out the deed, so that she might cackle over it anew. I cursed myself for telling her of it; I despised her for her glee and myself for bringing it about. The taste of betrayal rose higher into my throat with every peal of her laughter.

For my part, I had begun to feel anxious at the thought of Granville's discovering us gone. Would he let us go? Would he remember the name of the island we sailed for, although he had always forgotten it before? Perry, I thought, would surely not stir from the bottle to chase me. Granville, I was less sure of. The plantation could not be called his, any longer. That I had stolen from Perry. But Dora—would Granville throw her off, or set out to bring us back? I could not help but wonder if my plan for escape had not, after all, been ill-thought-out.

I sought distraction and found that many of the sailors were pleased enough to game with me. By the second day I had several men already in my debt. I should have to wait, however, until the voyage ended and they received wages.

We dined again with the captain. I had known, of course, that Dora had his acquaintance from her time at the bawdy house, but I began to feel, as I sat in their company, that they were too well acquainted for my comfort. There were looks passed between them and an edge to their laughter. The captain told tales of his encounters with pirates and press gangs, which, by the way he looked hard at me, I thought were meant to frighten. Dora was amused by everything he said, and poured the rum into my cup as insistently as Perry once had. I retired to bed much fuddled with drink, and hardly sure whether the ship dipped and swayed or it was I who was unsteady.

On the third evening at sea I could not find Dora. It was the most infuriating thing—there were after all not many places to go, aboard ship. My urge to hunt her out made me feel as though I were become Perry, when he would call my name anxiously if I so much as stepped into the next room.

I did not say anything of Dora's absence to the captain at supper, and neither did he mention it to me. We sat opposite her empty chair and did not refer to it once. I could not have said why he kept silent, but for my own part, I had already grown to dislike him so much that I could not bring myself to admit that I could not say where the woman I was calling my wife might have hidden herself. The captain looked at me over the rim of the cup with an expression I thought might be mocking.

I spoke to him as pleasantly as I could. I had no other option; I was trapped until we made land on the Cape coast, in five or six weeks' time.

Then, of course, we would have another eight weeks at sea, before we reached the sugar islands. The journey ahead seemed a long one indeed. I had to hope that I could earn the captain's respect, or at the very least his forbearance, in order to make the time tolerable.

At length he suggested that we go up on deck and smoke under the stars, as the night was a still one.

"You'll not see a finer sight than the ocean in darkness, with the moon sparkling the waves," he said.

"I shall be delighted to see it," I said. "Lead on."

I found that I had to hold on to the wall as we went.

As soon as we ascended to the deck I saw Dora, huddled in a cloak, watching the sea. The night was not as still as I had thought it, and the ship rolled in great, lazy swells that made walking gracefully an impossibility. I excused myself from the captain and went to her as nicely as I could. She came toward me, and I grasped her by the arm.

"Where have you been? I have been looking for you an age."

"And so you've found me."

"I do not like you disappearing so, Dora. You must behave like a wife, though you have never been one."

"You've never been a husband, but you've the taste for ordering me."

"Don't be foolish. One of these coves will guess we are a sham and then where will we be?"

She laughed. "Do any of you boys believe this gent my husband?" she called.

There came quiet laughter from the darkness across the deck. I had not realised we were in company, and now it was I who felt a fool; I had slapped her before I knew what I was about. My hand flashed out like a white fish in black water and even above the roar of the waves the sound was sharp and loud. I should never have struck her, had I not felt humiliated.

"There!" I said. "You shall learn to keep by me, or I shall chain you up in the hold like a negro."

She said nothing, only put her hand to her face.

Now I saw dark shapes come toward us as the sailors crossed the deck. They moved all at once, as though called by my slap.

"It is not I who will be chained," Dora said, very low.

"What's this?" I said.

"All good parties come to an end sometime," the captain said, behind me. "It's time for you to be going."

"Going? We are at sea, man!"

"I've called you a carriage," he said. And here he laughed.

Dora reached out for me, and I pushed her away roughly. Immediately I felt strong hands grasp my arms, holding me still.

"Leave off me!" I cried.

Dora's hands slid into my waistcoat and though I bucked like a fury I could not stop her from taking the plantation deed. It barely had the sea air upon it, so quick did she take it and push it down into her bosom.

"Thief!" I cried.

"You know your own name, then," she said. She stepped toward me again, and I felt her lips brush my ear. "If ever they come after me, I'll see you swing as a thief. Be sure I'll see you roped beside me."

Her hand squeezed me through my breeches, and she laughed again.

"Reduced, ain't you?" she said.

I did the only thing I could, then. I threw myself forward within my constraints and struck her with my head. She fell back with a sharp cry. I did not see how much or how little she had felt it because a solid thing—a fist, I suppose—struck me in the stomach and all the breath was driven out of me. Held as I was my body could not fold itself up and I jerked and coughed, fitting about on my arms like a puppet on its strings.

Now the rough hands began to drag me forward, toward the ship's rail. Fear slid its gloved hands about my heart.

"You devils," I cried. "You mean to drown me!"

"Now, Mr Bowden," the captain said, "do you accuse me of murder?

ANNA FREEMAN

We mean to rob you only," and now they all laughed. There seemed a great
many of them; the whole crew was up on deck. I could hear Dora's shrill
cackle behind them.

"Damn you all!" I screamed, as a hundred pairs of hands clasped my
arms, my shoulders. My coat was ripped. I stumbled over my own feet and
was hoisted up again. Relentlessly, I was propelled to the ship's edge, to the
rail and the black water, so far below.

I screamed as we went.

"Don't drown me," I cried, "I beg you! Oh, God! Curses upon you all!
Rot you, rot you!"

We reached the rail, and my belly pressed against it. Any moment I
thought, they would topple me over it.

"Hush all that yammer," the captain said. "I told you I called you a
carriage. Can't you see it, there below?"

At first I was too wild to see anything but the rolling pitch of the dark
waves, but there, a life-boat, rolling alongside the ship. A tiny wooden
thing, and hanging from the rail, a rope-ladder, swinging and slapping
against the hull.

"Drown yourself, once you climb down," Dora said, from somewhere. I
could not see her. "Drown yourself, and welcome."

"You witch!" I cried, and had my head cuffed by some unseen hand.

"It's only for the sweet lady's sake that we don't see you drowned.
Now—climb down," the captain said, "or the boys'll heave you down."

I believe I began to cry, my tears like ice in the wind. It did me no good
at all.

MY MEMORY HERE GROWS HAZY. I recall being at sea, terribly cold and
very frightened. I was fixated on the idea of my bag of gold—a good
amount had been left even after I had paid the price of our passage—
which I had seen put into the captain's locker "for safety." The bitterness of

422

this thought was the hook that kept me from sinking into despair, the axle upon which my rage turned. I planned a million deaths for the captain and a million more for that thieving whore. I spent hours embroidering their torture in my mind. My fears were so numerous that they seemed like a wave that would any moment sweep me away. I was almost as afraid of meeting a ship as I was of starvation or drowning at the first; I could not stop thinking of the captain's tales of slavers going to disease-ridden islands, where they would as like leave me as not, or pirates, or navy ships one would be press-ganged onto. From all I had heard I thought it very unlikely that I should meet any ship that would not sell me, or kill me, or force me to work. At first this predicament seemed terrible indeed, though only a short time was to pass before I should have wept with joy and called out a halloo to even the most murderous-looking vessel rather than spend one more moment without water.

I recall dreadful, undignified things from this time, on which I should not dwell. I recall the salt, stinging my eyes and cracking my lips. I recall trying to fashion a fishing line from my stockings—a miserable endeavour. I trailed them hopefully through the water as a kind of net, catching nothing, of course, until a large wave slapped over the side of the boat and startled me, whereupon I dropped them. I recall wondering, as I added my fluids to the ocean, over the small boat's hull, whether I should be trying to drink them. I recall weeping, strange dry sobs, and wondering if I were too shrivelled inside even for tears. These memories are not lucid or continuous, but more like scenes from a picture book, with the crumpled pages torn out and put back in the wrong order.

This state of affairs must not have gone on long, for I survived it. I am told that I washed up on a dreary English beach, still in my boat, and was hauled ashore by a band of women gathering cockles there. We could not have been so very far out to sea when they put me over, so quickly did that whore and whoreson rob me.

I am told that I was taken away to be nursed by one of those women, and upon regaining consciousness, attacked her most ungallantly. I suppose I must have thought her Dora.

MY CELL WAS SO SMALL that I could have touched all four walls simultaneously, if I were to stretch out. A meaner, filthier place I had rarely seen, and certainly never been confined in.

I had arrived at the prison as weak as an infant, and was half dragged, half carried in. The doorways were so low that if I had not lost my hat at sea I should have lost it then. All the while, beneath the nausea of near-starvation and the foul unwashed odour of the prison, I felt the panic waiting. I have never liked small spaces. Now I was confined in one and not a window anywhere. I thought, *If I do not concentrate now, I shall go mad.* It seemed at that moment that to give in to fear would mean my death.

My body seemed to roil and wave constantly. I lay upon that straw pallet nearly delirious. Perhaps I was; it seems I accused my jailor of poisoning me, though I do not know if this is true. He said something later that made me conclude that I had been raving.

I do not know how soon I thought to look about me and wonder where I was. Oh, I knew I was imprisoned, I was not so weak as that. I mean that I gathered sufficient wits to wonder what city or town it was that held me, and how I had come to be there.

The little story of my rescue by the cockle-gatherers I did not learn until much later. In my cell, I could only ascertain from my rough jailor that I was held on a charge most heinous, and that I was at Plymouth. I learnt later that the cockle-woman had not been much hurt and that my charge consisted of nothing but vagrancy.

I should have been released, as like as not, and told to move on somewhere far away from cockle-women, had not the prison magistrates, in the course of their deciding what should be done with me, turned up a description of someone very like myself, wanted in Bristol for most serious debts.

Perry had not reported me a thief, only an absconding debtor. He saved my life, though he may not have meant to do it, for if he had named me a thief I should have hung quicker than gasping.

THE JOURNEY FROM PLYMOUTH TO BRISTOL was perhaps the closest I have ever come to Hell. I was carried in an open cart, facing backward upon a wooden bench, so narrow that I could scarce keep upon it and certainly could not find any comfort. My wrists and ankles were shackled to an iron ring set into the floor at my feet. Every time the cart jolted—and it jolted often—I was jerked about and could not steady myself; my bottom slid out from underneath me more times than I could count, striking my spine against the bench as I fell and almost wrenching my arms from the sockets. We did not stop, except to change the horses. There were three guards, and they took turns driving. Facing backward as I was, I could only hear them, laughing and calling to each other to pass the bottle. I could smell the smoke from their pipes. We went on this way, on the bumpiest roads they could find to travel, for perhaps three or four days. I could not be sure exactly how much time had passed; I was half in a daze of fear. When we stopped to change horses one of the oafs would come behind and open the back of the cart. I was unshackled then, just long enough to drink a tin cup of thin beer and eat some dry and greyish bread and do my business by the side of the road, leered over constantly. I learnt to sleep sitting up. When it rained, the guards drew on leather cloaks, while I grew damp. I was bitten about the face and hands by the wind; I was cold to my bones. I would feel my cheeks grow wet and find that I was weeping, without realising that I had begun.

Perhaps, I kept thinking, the roads unwinding behind us were my last view of the world. I would never be set free, for I could never hope to repay my debts. I could not pretend I would. My spirits were so low that sometimes it was all I could do to pull myself back onto the bench when I fell.

Where was Perry, now? How would he fare without me? I knew then, if I had never known it before, that you cannot break a promise made in blood. I had sworn to die rather than forsake him and God meant to make me keep my word. I would die in a prison cell, a death as slow as Perry's own by the bottle was sure to be. I felt it in every jolt of the road beneath the wheels.

PART 10

Ruth

✦ ✦ ✦

Chapter 23

❖ ❖ ❖

What a sorry pair we were, coming home defeated, and Tom with only one eye. He'd been mending well in London, but now he was beset by low spirits and he'd not talk much, nor look about him at the city streets. Mr Dryer had sent us a cull driving a cart filled with hay, and there were a couple of blankets to cover us. It was better than I'd hoped for, from that cold-hearted piss-licker. I made Tom as comfortable as I could and gave him my spare cloak rolled up for his pillow, though it was devilish cold.

"Can't he drive smooth? Every jolt's like a poke in the eye," Tom said, and after that I helped him to the laudanum and put him to sleep.

All the journey he slept, dosed high, twitching and moaning with his dreams. I sat watch over him in the back of the cart, to keep him well wrapped in the blankets and spoon him the medicine whenever he seemed to wake.

The big cull that Mr Dryer found to drive us knew enough to keep silent—I was sure he pitied us, ragged and low as we were. When night fell he stopped at an inn and looked over his shoulder at me, where I sat sunk in my thoughts. I'd propped my back against the side of the cart and had my knees bunched up about my ears, to give Tom the space to stretch out. He was sleeping so deep that it would've been murder to move him and the sky was clear, though chill. Mr Dryer had given me a very little money for the journey but I thought to keep it if I could, and so I begged the cull fetch bread, cheese, and ale from the inn and slept the night in the back of his cart. It was cold enough, I won't say it wasn't; my feet were numb the night through. I wrapped myself around Tom's slumbering form, tight as I could, tucked in the blankets and covered us with the hay. The cull helped me with that; he was obliging enough. Then he went off to find a bed with Mr Dryer's coin and I dosed myself along with Tom, so that sleep would find us both. On coming back to us next morning, the cully was gent enough to bring us a couple of pasties and wouldn't take a penny for them. He said then he'd been wondering all night if he'd find us froze to death.

Tom was awake, though bleary as a new-born calf. I'd let him wake to eat. He couldn't do much but he cracked his lips open and drank off all the ale. I'd not the heart to ask him to keep some back for me; he likely didn't realise we were meant to share. He drank it down and belched aloud.

"There's medicine," he said, and lay back again.

The driver broke into a smile at seeing this.

"Why, you ain't as far gone as I'd thought you," he said.

"I'm near enough mended," Tom said, though his voice was so weak as to make it out a sham.

I'd a lot of time to think on that journey, while Tom slept beside me. The country road unrolled behind us, and I was devilish glad to see it go. I hated the countryside with every inch of my heart. If it'd been a man, I'd have knocked his teeth down his neck. Someday, when Tom was strong again, I'd tell him what it'd been like, alone in that cottage.

Even low as we were coming home, home was where we were going. I was half desperate to arrive and half in dread of it. How sweet it'd be to stroll into The Hatchet, but how bitter it was that we came back beaten. The news would've travelled; how would they greet us, with pity or jeers? What should we do now? I couldn't imagine Mr Dryer would help us. And he'd be coming to see Dora, of course he'd come. How would it be to see his face? Could I clap eyes on the cull without spitting?

By the time we came into Bristol I was so weary that I could only look upon everything with a kind of dull relief; I'd been afraid for so long I'd never see it again. When we entered the city proper the rattling of the cart over the cobbles caused Tom to stir. I woke him gently.

"Look, Tom. Look where we are. We're almost at the Horse Fair."

Tom sat up and looked about him with a dazed air. I'd no idea if he was glad to be home. I fell silent as we passed St James' churchyard.

"Where we began," Tom said in a croak.

I didn't know if he meant Bristol or St James', where I'd been beat near as bad as he was now. I took his hand as gentle as I could and held it.

THERE WAS NO BULLY on the step; straight off I felt queer. The door was unlocked and even before we stepped foot inside I knew there was no one about the place. The hall was filled with dust and hush. Tom and I looked at each other. I could see him struggling to think through the laudanum fog about his mind. I'd made a racket dragging the trunk inside, but now I opened the door to the parlour as soft as if I thought someone might be sleeping there. There was no one inside, sleeping or otherwise. The lamps and the pictures had been whipped off by some sharper, but the settee and the occasional table stood there still. The stool was gone, and I thought perhaps there'd been a chair; there wasn't now.

"What's this?" I said, quiet.

Tom shook his head.

We went to the kitchen and found it just as empty and cold as the rest of the house. It seemed the colder, for always having been warm before. There was no food at all in the larder. There was a broken dish upon the table and some spillage upon the floor that had been mostly scraped up but no other sign of a fight, or of anybody being about. A few pans and plates were left, but the heavy copper kettle had been fleeced.

Now I called out, "Hi! Who's about?"

Tom lifted a hand to shush me, and then thought better of it and called out too.

Above us, I thought I heard a creaking. I waved Tom quiet. It came again. I could see Tom had the same thought I did; who'd try to stay silent, if he'd not ill-intentions? I took up the poker from the hearth.

We began up the stairs, as soft as I knew how, though every piece of that house creaked and Tom was a heavy cull. I went first and Tom followed and it was a measure of how out-at-heels he was that he let me lead. Just those few stairs and he was breathing as hard as an old man, clinging to the banister. Up we went, creak, creak. Above us, I could hear the floorboards make their own creak, as if answering the ones we trod. Was the cully up there hiding, or coming for us?

Then came a sound I'd not expected: an infant's cry. It was in Ma's garret, I could tell that clear as anything.

I couldn't still my heart. We went up past Dora's room, up the narrow stairs. The door of Ma's room was shut. Through the wood came the steady rise and fall of a new baby's wails and the soft sounds of shushing. I put my hand upon the knob and turned to look at Tom behind me. He looked as jumpy as I felt. I opened up the door.

The first thing I noticed was the smell. It was the same as it'd ever been—stronger if anything—and there was Ma upon the bed. For one moment I thought her sleeping, but then I saw how grey she was, the strange angle of her neck, and I knew her dead. The next thing I saw was Jacky, thin as a bird, tear-streaks on his dirty face, jogging a blanketed babe up and down. He was looking at us like he thought we'd come to murder him. I was still holding the poker.

WE SAT AND WATCHED JACKY picking every piece of flesh from the eel's bones. Tom and I'd been near as hungry as he was and I thanked God then that I'd kept Mr Dryer's inn-money. I'd run out into the street and found the first eel-man I could, and got us a pie and some goat's milk for the babber. I sat it on my knee and dipped my fingers into the milk, for it to suck them dry. Tom sat in Ma's old chair, looking weary enough to drop.

I'd tried to wrap him up in a blanket but he'd not have it. I let him be—I was glad to see him eating.

"When did that bitch flit?" I asked.

Jacky kept his head to his plate, but he cutty-eyed up at me. He put a needle-thin bone to his lips and sucked at it, though it was clean.

"Jacky, when did Dora go? You needn't look so. It's an easy enough question, ain't it?" I said.

Tom looked at me and frowned. "What does it signify, if he don't like to say? She's gone. She can rot."

"She can. She should, curse her. You keep your peace then, Jack. I'll not ask again."

Jacky had been looking from one of us to the other with his queer, sideways glance.

"She didn't leave me nothing," he said. "I don't know where she went."

Dora had left her two sons to starve together next to our own dead ma. I was filled, then, with the rage of it.

"Damn her stinking cunny-hole." I pushed myself up from the table with one hand, the other arm holding the babe.

Jacky cringed.

"Oh, stop," I told him. "No one will harm you now."

Now we'd to fathom what to do next, just when I'd thought all would be simple and clear. The only thing to do was to begin at the beginning, and have Ma put to rest.

Tom came over all weak, and finally he let me send him to bed. I found clean sheets and made him take Dora's bed. He lay down with the most grateful look upon his mug, even while he swore home that he'd be up in a minute to help me. The bandage over his eye had grown damp with something brownish that wasn't quite blood. I thought, *We'll have to see to that as soon as ever we can.*

Dora and the girls had fleeced the place of most of the good stuff. I bundled up what bits I could find quickly, some bed linen, a dressing glass, the lamps from Ma's room, and took them down to the bow-wow shop. I was so tired that just going into that close shop with its scent of musty things made my head swim, but I haggled as hard as I could and came out with ten shillings. I bought Ma enough of a burial to keep her from shame and what money I could keep over I gave to a woman down the street, to nurse Dora's infant every day—soft-hearted fool that I was.

I sent Jacky to fetch a doctor, a cull who'd been to see the misses often enough that I thought he'd not refuse to come. He was in a hurry to leave from the moment he stepped foot in the house and he'd not enter Ma's room. He stood in the doorway, his eyes squinting against the foulness, and pronounced her dead from long illness. Then he wrote out a paper ordering a salve for Tom's eye. I'd no money for his fee—I couldn't give him the burial money—but there was a carved wooden pipe left in the cabinet beside Dora's bed, some visitor's, perhaps Mr Dryer's—and he took that gladly enough and left as though the Hell-hounds were at his heels.

We none of us went to see Ma buried. I meant to, but when we saw the black cart arrive Jacky came over all queer, turned from his place at the window and hoofed it upstairs. When Tom and I led up the culls who'd come to carry her out, we found he'd shut himself in with her.

"Jacky." I pushed at the door. Something had been shoved up against it. "Jacky, don't be a goose."

No reply. The beefy culls made a face at Tom—not at me, mind—to say, shall we break down the door? Tom only shook his head.

"Jacky," he called, quietly, "we've to bury her, or she'll not be at peace. Do this last thing for Ma. Hasn't she been longing to be out of this room, and free? Don't keep her trussed up now."

Again, no reply. Tom sighed, and turned to me.

"All of us together?" he said, meaning, to push the door.

"Hold," I said, for I'd heard a scraping, scrabbling sound from within. I tried the door again. It wouldn't move.

"I can't shift it," came Jacky's voice.

"What can't you shift?" I said.

A pause. "I pushed it, but I can't pull it."

"Right," Tom said. "You pull all you can, and we'll push."

"Not you, Tommy," I said. "We'll all the rest of us push."

"Don't fuss, Ruthie." Tom put his hand to his bandaged peeper, as though to hide it.

One of the bull-beef boys said, "Now, don't take offence, lad, but your missus ain't wrong. You look all in."

Tom stepped aside and I was glad to see it, though I knew that his pride had been beaten along with his body, in London. I'd let him be the hero when once he was healed.

The door wouldn't budge. Jacky had managed to jam the bed right up against it, with Ma still in it. Lord knows how he did it. We had to take the door off at the hinges at the last, and didn't the cullies from the funeral shop look sour, when they smelled the full force of their load.

They wrapped her in a sheet and carried her down to the plain coffin waiting in the hall. Jacky hovered about them as though he thought to catch her if she fell.

When they laid her in the coffin and went to close the lid, Jacky went into a fit. He tore at their hands and knees, he screamed and wailed. He lost all his words and began to babble like a lunatic. It took all my strength to stop him following them out and climbing onto the cart, what with the babber in my other arm. I made to give Tom the babe, but instead of taking it, he only wrapped his arms around all three of us. We stood all hugged together, both brats screaming fit to bring down the sky, as they drove Ma away. It was a good enough display of grief for her.

WE BEGAN THE BUSINESS of settling in. Tom took to watching over the babber, when it wasn't getting its milk. I didn't feel easy looking after it—it ain't in my nature to mother things, which can hardly be surprising, given the examples I had about me as a child. Tom took care of it, and Jacky and I set about putting the house in order—I tried sending him off, but if he wasn't helping Tom then he must be helping me. It was easier to give him a brush and pan than to feel him standing behind me, waiting. Once the lad had a task he'd set himself at it and I could get on with my own work. And after all, it was company of a sort. I remembered how much I'd missed quarrelling with Dora when she was set to earn and I was left to be the maid to all the house. I remembered my desperate scrubbing of the cottage; keeping house is dull enough with company, but alone it's terrible. We took the broken crockery from the kitchen, we scrubbed the floors. We beat the mollies' mattresses to take the stink of years from them. We left the garret alone—I'd not quite the stomach for it yet.

One evening, as I laid out a supper of bread and dripping and Tom put the babber down upstairs, there came a knocking at the door. It was an ill-tempered, full-fisted knock, and it went on and on, as though the knocker would never tire. Well, anyone who's lived a low kind of life will tell you, you don't walk easy to answer a knock like that. I froze with a plate in my hand. Jacky looked cringing all over again, which he'd lately stopped doing so much.

"Go and peek out the window," I whispered. "Don't answer it, whatever you do. Just take a peek and run back to me."

He was back in a flash. "It's Mr Dryer," he said. He never did call him Father.

Mr Dryer. There was scarce a cull in all creation I cared for less. I should almost rather have had the magistrates. And for him to come and pound upon the door, it made the flesh on my shoulders squeeze into bars of iron. Of course, he never had found the convent locked against him before.

Jacky hoofed it into the scullery. I couldn't blame him; I'd have followed, if I could.

Mr Dryer's stiff mug seemed to stare straight past me, into the hallway.

I felt like a goose protecting her nest from a dog; I was ready to spring or spit even while I shrank from him. I wanted him away from us. The cull was poison, pure and simple.

I held the door open wordlessly. He walked in as though he were still lord of the manor.

"Tom," I called. "Here's Mr Dryer come to see how you do." I put my feelings into the name "Mr Dryer."

Tom's bandaged face appeared at the top of the stairs, with his ready smile. My good man was willing to smile upon even such a scaly runt as this cull.

"No," Mr Dryer said, "I come to see Dora. Kindly tell her that I am arrived."

Tom's look was cast down as fast as an axe blow falling. I'd not seen, till that moment, how much hope Tom had that Mr Dryer might yet turn out straight. After all that Mr Dryer had taken from us, that he should take this, my Tom's last shreds of hope, it was the puff that brought the roof down. I felt the fury lift me up and clench my fists.

I strode toward Mr Dryer. He knew something was up, mind. He held himself fearful stiff. Behind him, I saw Tom begin to come down the stairs. Mr Dryer glanced over his shoulder and I saw he'd marked it—he was caught between us.

I stopped before him and looked full into his goatish mug.

"That bitch has run off and she ain't coming back," I said.

Mr Dryer wouldn't flinch from me. He looked at me very level. Only the twitch of his eyelid showed I had him frit. I saw him take in the bare walls, where there used to hang the pictures and lamps that he'd paid for.

I said, "She's done a flit and I don't blame her for it. So you can forget that."

Tom had reached the bottom step, and now he stopped and looked at Mr Dryer and me as if he couldn't tell what I might do. I wasn't sure myself.

"Then I will take my leave," Mr Dryer said.

He made to walk past me and I stepped into his path.

"Move aside," he said.

Tom was at my side before I could speak, and putting a hand on my shoulder. "Now, Ruthie," he said, but that was all.

"No, Tom." My fury was a cold thing, not a hot. I was probably more alike to Mr Dryer in that moment than I'd ever been.

"No," I said, again. "This open-arse is going to give us what he owes."

"I owe you nothing."

I spat, then, upon his boots. It was too late to go back, after that.

"You owe us an eye," I said.

Mr Dryer did not even look to see where I'd spat. He kept his gaze on mine. It was like the moments before a mill when you stand at scratch, eye to eye with the other pug.

"What were you before I came? I lifted you from the dirt," Mr Dryer said, very calm.

"You kept us in dirt. You think all of us in this house are your play-things. You'll find out otherwise." My voice had a hiss in it.

"What will you do, then, you spitting cat? If you raise your hand against me I shall see you imprisoned faster than you can blink."

Tom held my arm fast.

"Be calm, Ruth. We'll not lose anything else."

"You've lost an eye, Tom. I swear home, I'll have one of his in return."

"This is nonsense. Step out of my path."

Was he quaking now? By God, I hoped so.

It was then that Jacky showed himself, carrying a tray as careful as a nest of eggs. It was the tray he'd always brought to Mr Dryer when he came to see Dora—the clod-head hadn't realised it couldn't be wanted now. Here he came, into the middle of this scene, his eyes on the tray, the scented water slopping about in its cut-glass bowl. He brought it to Mr Dryer's side and peeped up at him. I was growing used to Jacky now, and I thought that his look, which I might've once called sneaking, was only anxious and hopeful. Mr Dryer, mind, he thought Jacky brought the tray to make fun, now that my sister had run off and he'd never again need to wash his face in lavender-water.

"What the devil do you mean by this?" Mr Dryer said.

Jacky only bobbed a little on his toes, making the water jump in the bowl. He kept watching his father with that same sly face.

Mr Dryer's hand shot out as fast as a snake and cuffed Jacky on the side of his head, hard enough to send the boy sprawling, the tray and all it carried crashing to the ground. The bowl smashed upon the flags. The scent of the spilled lavender-water filled the hall.

Tom's shoulder knocked into mine as he charged at Mr Dryer. In the shock of it I grabbed for him to keep from tumbling; perhaps I meant to stop him, perhaps I wanted to fib Mr Dryer myself. There was no thought in it. Tom leapt forward and in grabbing at him, I went with him. So it was that we both struck Mr Dryer together, not with our fists, but with our bodies—Tom had been moving at speed and we went hard into him. We all three of us fell to the ground. Tom's skull knocked against mine. Some other piece of him—his knee, it could've been—smacked into my thigh, hard enough to leave it numb. Jacky screamed, and scrabbled to press against the wall. Upstairs, the babe woke and joined his screams to his brother's.

"Blasted hell!" Tom cried out, struggling to his knees, one hand to his bandaged eye.

I couldn't sit up straight off, my leg being numb. My only thought was for Tom's eye.

"Are you hurt? Tom, are you much hurt?"

He was rocking back and forth upon his knees but he still answered, "No."

I'd got myself up a bit and was reaching for Tom when Jacky screamed again. I'd forgotten, in my fear for Tom's eye, to see what had befallen Mr Dryer. He'd fallen to the ground with us, and now he was behind us, on hands and knees. He seemed not to be able to stand. In the dark of the hall he looked to be wearing a hood of tar, as though his head had been dipped and he waited for the feathers. Of course, it was not tar but blood that covered him.

"Oh, dear God, no," Tom said.

A piece of the cut-glass bowl stuck out from the back of Mr Dryer's head, catching what light there was like the shaft of a diamond dagger. I cried out to see it and Jacky screamed with me. The babber was still wailing upstairs, a rise-and-fall cry. We made a devilish harmony.

"Oh, blasted fuck. Oh! We've killed Mr Dryer," Tom moaned.

We were all of us still sitting on the floor, except Jacky, who'd pressed his back to the wall as though he might pass through it and run away. I could feel my hands waving in the air, unsure what to do.

"It is I who will kill you," Mr Dryer said, still on all fours. He did not raise his head. His voice was thick, perhaps with blood.

I came back to myself a little way. I got to my feet, though I seemed to feel my head swoop.

"There," I said. My voice was weaker than it should've been. "There, he ain't dead. And nor are any of us."

The glass poking from Mr Dryer's skull seemed to be looking at me. I couldn't stop looking at it, in any case.

"You will be," Mr Dryer said.

I thought then about kicking him. It would've been so easy and so foolish, both. Tom got to his feet and I turned to him instead.

"Tom, is your eye . . . ?"

"I jolted it only, I think."

"Thank God."

Tom went to Mr Dryer then, and knelt beside him.

"Sir, I'm going to help you up," he said.

My heart twisted to hear him say "sir."

Mr Dryer let Tom help him to his feet, though he swayed about and Tom had to hold him.

"Jacky," I said, "fetch the parlour chair."

"We ain't got a chair in the parlour."

I'd forgotten the chair had been whipped off.

In the end, Tom helped Mr Dryer into the parlour and sat him on the brocaded settee where he'd so often waited for Dora.

I sent Jacky for a lamp then, and for rum for all of us.

When the rushlight was brought, we were all of us struck silent by the sight of the blood. There was so much of it. Mr Dryer shuddered, and I think began quietly to weep. His shoulders were slumped; he wasn't so stiff now.

The light wavered violently as Jacky's hand shook. I took it from him gently.

"Go and see to the babber," I said.

It was easier to think without his goggling eyes upon me.

"What'll we do?" Tom said, as soon as the boy was gone. "Shall we pull the glass out?"

"Glass?" Mr Dryer said.

Tom and I looked at each other over his head.

"You've some glass sticking in you," I said, at last.

"No! Don't you touch it," Mr Dryer said. "Don't touch me. You must call a doctor. You must call a carriage to take me home."

I might've done it, but Tom said gently, "I can't, sir, can I? You'll see us snapped up if we let you out of here. You'll say it was assault, though it was an accident, pure and simple."

Oh, bloody damn, he might, I thought. *How can we let him go? But then, how can we keep him?*

Mr Dryer had the same thought. He tried to rise and only flopped in his seat like a fish. His head tipped back against the back of the settee, surely driving the glass in deeper. He didn't cry out, only gasped aloud and dropped his head forward. Blood dripped softly onto his lap, catching the lamplight like crimson sealing wax.

"Will you keep me prisoner, here, perhaps to die?" Mr Dryer spoke toward his lap. "You will certainly hang if you do."

Tom put his hand to his head as though he were stuck with glass himself, rumpling his bandage. "What in hell are we to do, Ruth?"

He sat down beside Mr Dryer, though there was hardly space for him to do it. I suppose he felt too weak to stand.

I stood before them both, shaking, making the lamplight wobble on my own account. I could only think, *If he dies, what do we do with him?* If I'd a good answer to that, I might've thought of helping it along. Mr Dryer was lucky, then, that I didn't. He was lucky, too, that he had his own answer.

"You must send for my wife," he said. "She is in Bristol, at Queen Square. Let her come and carry me away."

"I'll send for her," I said. "Though what we'll do when she comes I don't know. You'll have to give your word that you know we never meant to harm you."

"You threatened to take my eye."

"You still have it, don't you?"

I WENT TO FETCH HER MYSELF. Who else was to go? Tom must stay to watch Mr Dryer and I'd not send Jacky out, alone, to walk the streets at night. It was not so very far—it took me less than ten minutes, I swear home—and that was going round by the drawbridge over the river. Bristol's like that: the swells and the common folk pressed together, street by street.

I felt nervous to set foot on the paths of Queen Square, it being so grand. Probably they had servants or sentry men, whose job it was to keep my kind away. No one stopped me, mind. I didn't know that I'd ever walked there before. Even in the twilight it was so vast and clean you'd hardly know, once you were in it, that it was surrounded by the docks and dirt of the working streets. I wondered how it'd be to be a lady there, and have nowhere much respectable to go but around and around the square. I supposed they all had carriages and could drive away when they liked.

Mrs Dryer's house was at number thirty-six. It took an age for anyone to come to the door, and when they did I had to wait while what seemed like a hundred locks were turned, and bolts drawn back. At last an elderly cully opened the door just far enough to peer out.

"May I help you?" he said. I could see he was only a moment away from closing it in my face.

"Please, I must see Mrs Dryer. Mr Dryer's been taken ill. I'm Mrs Webber. Tom Webber's my husband. The prize-fighter. Please." I said this as fast as ever I could and with every word the frown on his mug grew looser. By the end of the speech he looked almost kind, and worried with it.

"Please wait here," he said, and then he did close the door, but gently.

I waited, shifting from foot to foot. I was beginning to feel how cold it was.

A carriage came around from the back of the square and drew up beside me. I watched it warily, half expecting some stiff to order me away. When I saw it was Henry at the reins, I felt almost like kissing him. He jumped down from the box and ran to shake me by the hand.

"I'm glad to see you, Mrs Webber. I'll say I am. But I was so sorry to hear. I expect I took it near as hard as you did. How does he fare, now?"

For a moment I thought he meant Mr Dryer, and looked at him queer. Then I realised he meant my Tom, and I clapped him on the shoulder.

"He's growing stronger all the time. You should come to see us."

The door opened again to show the old butler cully and, behind him, wrapped in a fur-lined cloak, Mrs Dryer. Her face was quite free of paint, and I could see just by looking that she'd been asleep when I knocked. I could smell drink on her. She didn't smile to see me; she looked fearful.

"Will you come, Mrs Dryer?" I said. I'd an urge to be gone. I was half froze and I didn't like to explain with the old cully there.

"Very well."

She followed me down to the carriage. Henry held the door and let her in first. I dithered, wondering if she'd rather I got up on the box beside

Henry. She'd still not smiled. Then I thought, *To hell with it, I'm freezing out here,* and climbed inside.

The ride was no time at all. I barely finished explaining what had gone on—sparing her the mention of Dora—before we were arrived at the convent. She'd scarce replied.

Henry came and opened the door of the carriage.

"You go in, Henry, and fetch him out," she said, in a queer voice. It was too dark to see her face much.

I thought, *Oh, bloody damn, she thinks I tried to kill him.*

"Go on, Henry," I said. "Tom will let you in."

He looked at us once and then nodded, and went to knock at the convent door. We watched Tom open it, the babe at his shoulder, and relief at clapping eyes on Henry writ all over his bandaged face.

"Do not you go inside?" Mrs Dryer asked.

"And leave you here, thinking ill of me?" I'd not realised till then that I'd missed her company. I knew I'd hate her to think me so vicious, even if I'd been ready to take his eye out an hour before.

"I, think ill of you! It is you who must think ill of me." She put her gloved hand to her breast.

That had me fuddled. "What can you mean, Mrs Dryer?"

"I left you behind, in London."

"We got home safe, didn't we?"

"Yes! That's just it, Mrs Webber. You must believe me; Mr Dryer threatened to leave us all if I stayed behind. I came on condition that he saw you carried home."

She leaned forward and spoke pleadingly. She didn't seem to feel the least hurry for the sake of her husband, bleeding himself to death in our parlour.

"Well, I hardly thought he'd done it on his own account. I knew you'd a hand in it, Mrs Dryer. I should've thanked you before now." I didn't know if that was the truth, or not. I'd been so upset over Tom's eye, I'd hardly given anything else a thought.

"Thank me? Forgive me, only."

"What can you mean? Forgive you what? Didn't you nurse me back to health? You've been as kind as anyone ever has." That, at least, was true.

"I abandoned you. I didn't give orders for white cullis. I thought, when you wouldn't call on me, you must be resentful indeed." She spoke to her clasped hands, her voice very low.

"Call on you? But Mrs Dryer, I didn't know you were in Bristol."

"Not at Bristol. At The Ridings. When you came to fetch your belongings. I went to the gatehouse and all was gone and you had not called."

"I can't say I know what you're running on about, Mrs Dryer. You took me to London, and the trunk came with me."

Now she gasped. "I did not know that was all you had."

I laughed, then. "Poor, ain't we? That was the whole of it."

"Can you really mean that you never came back to the gatehouse at all?"

"Mrs Dryer, I don't wish to give offence, but if any man tries to take me back there, I'll knock his head off."

"I share your feelings there." She gave a small smile.

"Now, are we friends enough that you'll come in? I didn't run to fetch you only for your husband to pass over into the afterlife while we sit here gabbing."

I thought that'd be it settled but she shook her head.

"I had better stay here. Your sister would not like to see me."

I gave a bitter laugh. "My sister! You'll not meet her. She's run off. She'll not be back in this lifetime."

"Was it not she, then, who attacked Mr Dryer?"

I thought then how brave she was to come at all, thinking Dora still here and murderous with it.

"Haven't I said? He fell and hit the glass of the bowl. I didn't tell you a lie."

Finally she smiled a true smile. "I could not have blamed her, you know, if she had."

"Come you inside."

Inside, Tom was pacing up and down the hall, jogging the babe against his shoulder to shush it. Without my asking he went to the door and stood on the front step, to watch over the carriage. Henry followed him. He was goggling Tom just as he had when he used to bring us food. I could tell he thought my husband the hero, eye or no eye.

Mr Dryer still sat in the parlour, his head bandaged and hung forward on his neck. He looked to be out for the count. Jacky sat next to him, murmuring, "There, there, there."

Seeing him, Mrs Dryer only said, "Henry and Tom can lift him between them, I'm sure."

"You took the glass out," I said to Jacky.

He held it up for me to see, like a conjurer pulling a silk hankie from your ear. After all that it was almost blunt, not a triangle but a ragged square. Here we were thinking Mr Dryer stabbed in the skull and it could only have stuck into the skin.

"Didn't he bleed a lot, for that little piece," I said.

I thought, *Perhaps enough to die of it,* but I didn't say so.

They'd bound the wound with paper and a pad of salt and ashes. All we could do then was hope.

We carried him out, and Tom, Jacky, and I watched the carriage drive away. All the night and the next morning we were in anxieties that Mr Dryer would die, or call us murderers. I wished we'd spoken more with Mrs Dryer when she'd come. All I could think of to do, while we waited for word, was finally to set about cleaning Ma's room. I didn't want Jacky with me for that work. I tasked Tom with keeping the lad busy and away from the garret.

"I'll think of some job for him," Tom said. "He wants to fetch for me all day. He puts me in mind of a goblin butler."

I laughed at that. "I'd warrant that he nursed Ma for that long, he doesn't know what else to be about."

"I don't need nursing; I lost an eye, not my legs."

"You play invalid for him, Tom. He needs to be useful." I didn't say, *and you need to rest,* but I was glad to see Tom sit back and how eagerly Jacky ran for him.

It was devilish foul in Ma's garret. Damp filth coated the underside of the mattress and all the corners were clogged with greasy, ashy dust. I kept a rag tied about my chops and went as quick as I could. I'd not let Tom inside, for fear of him taking an infection from the bad air. I burned sage. I scrubbed all I could reach with lye, till my hands cracked and bled.

I thought of Ma, holding out that tooth, saying, *It's less than you're owed.* I didn't know what I was owed, but I meant to have what there was and make the best of it.

Of Ma's things, I sold whatever I could. What I couldn't I burned in the yard in a damp, smouldering bonfire.

Jacky came out and stood beside me as her bedding went up slowly, in choking black smoke.

I was standing, watching the flames stubbornly eat at what was left of Ma's sickness, when a damp hand stole into mine. I let it stay. I didn't look at him, just held his paw, watched the fire, and thought about the foul marsh under Ma's bed. Jacky had been used to crawl under there.

"You'll be well with us," I said, as if to the air.

"Will you send me away?" he said.

I looked at him just as he stole a glance up at me. He wasn't as pale as he'd used to be. Tom was beginning to tease it out of him, and I was feeding him all I could afford. I'd been selling everything that was left in the house; only the Lord knew what we'd do when I'd cleaned the place out. But one thought had begun to snake about my mind as I'd sweated and scrubbed and it was this: if Ma was dead and Dora gone, was the convent mine?

"Jacky, as long as I've money enough to keep you, I will. There. It's all I can say."

"I know where money is."

"What can you mean?"

"I know where Ma hid it. She said she'd see me hung for a thief if ever I touched it, but I know where. But you have to swear home."

"Swear what?"

"You won't turn me out, nor hang me neither."

"I won't do either of those, money or no. I'd only see you turned out if Tom and I was forced out with you, you know."

He made me spit on my hand. Then he pointed at the fire.

"In the fire?"

Jacky got a stick and poked about the burning mattress till he turned up a cloth bag, just beginning to catch. It was lucky for us that it'd been so damp and never did do more than smoulder. There was enough to see us safe for a little while longer, at least.

THE NEXT DAY there came a knocking at the door. I went to answer it with a pressing in my chest like air that wouldn't breathe out. As soon as I saw Mrs Dryer upon the step, I knew he wasn't dead. Her face was too clear for bad news.

"Henry is driving the carriage around to the back," she said.

I called to Tom to open the gates to the yard.

She was shy, now it was daylight. I invited her in, shy myself when I realised truly what house she was come to. She'd thought of it too, I could see it in the secret way she tried to look over everything. *Go on,* I wanted to say to her, *look over the whole place if you will. Here's where your husband spent the days he wasn't with you.* I didn't want to say that to hurt her, only because I thought she wanted to do it and thought she'd better not, and I'd never have minded. Of course I said nothing. I'd learned enough manners for that, at least.

"He's alive, then," I said, as I led her to the kitchen.

"I'm afraid so," she said.

I laughed. "I never thought to find myself praying for Mr Dryer's health. Does he say we meant to hurt him?"

"No. He called it an accident when he spoke with the doctor. I will see that he does not change his mind."

Through the kitchen window I could see Tom, greeting Henry in the yard. They looked very alike just then, though they differed so in size. They both had such open faces. Before any time had passed at all, there came the muffled thud that meant they'd begun fibbing at the dummy.

"I hope they take it gentle," I said.

"How is Tom?" she asked. "I have had him in my prayers every night."

She looked so much like she meant it that I felt my eyes get hot.

"He does well enough," I said, and still afraid that I'd weep, I went and picked up the babber from his basket.

I brought him to her, wrapped up in his blanket. Mrs Dryer moved to take the corner of blanket away from his face, but I moved first and put his warm, sleeping body in her arms. Her arms tightened about him, natural as breathing.

"Oh, Ruth. What is his name?"

Just watching her soft mug it came to me, clear as day.

"My sister left him," I said. She looked up then and I nodded. "I can't expect she named him. No doubt someone will, when we know what's to be done with him."

"Why, what shall become of him?"

"There's a woman on the street's been nursing him when she can, and the rest of the time there's goat's milk."

"I am sure you will take good care of him," she said, in a quiet voice.

"If you won't have him, then I must." I couldn't stand to go softly.

She shook her head. "You know that I would like to." She didn't sound as though she meant to, though.

"Will you not, then?"

"How can I?"

"He's your husband's son."

She only shook her head again. She didn't lay him down, though, when we went out to the yard to watch Tom teaching Henry. She stood with him held against her, his little head on her shoulder, and she made sure she stood far enough from the action to keep him clear. She kept hold of him through the whole of Henry's lesson and afterward, when we sat at table. The babe stirred and woke and I silently blessed him that he didn't wail. I fetched him some goat's milk and showed Mrs Dryer how he'd take it dribbled down the handle of the spoon.

"What will you do now?" she asked us.

"We don't know as yet, Mrs Dryer," Tom said. "I think we'd all like to keep the house nice now. We'll know in time how it's to be done. There's a little money left to us by Ruth's ma, God rest her and keep her."

Mrs Dryer looked sorrowful. "I cannot help thinking that my husband owes you some assistance."

Tom shrugged. "It was never agreed that way."

"You must be compensated, at least, for the eye."

I could see Tom about to argue that she needn't fret, so I said, "We won't look for it, Mrs Dryer, but we'll not turn it away if it comes."

"I cannot help but feel it is owed," she said. "I cannot begin to pay Mrs Webber all that I think is due to her on my own account."

"I can think of one favour you can do me." I looked markedly at the babber on her knee. She didn't reply.

When it came time to leave, she was still holding him.

I said, "Jacky, go and say good-bye to the babber." I didn't say "your brother."

He went and stood near to Mrs Dryer's chair, looking at her with his queer eyes, till she held the baby out, and then he bent and put his lips quickly to its head. She looked almost as though she'd like to stop him.

"We will come again soon," she said, at the door. "Perhaps just Henry, the next time."

"You come whenever you like, Mrs Dryer, or send Henry alone," Tom said. "You're always welcome here, the pair of you."

"God bless you all," she said. She still held him pressed against her. I could see his little mouth open and working at the cloth of her gown.

"Go well, then, Mrs Dryer," I said, "and Henry. And little . . . ?"

"Arthur," she said. She was blushing but she didn't drop her eyes. "After my brother."

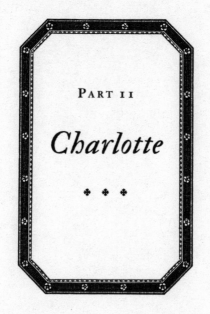

PART II

Charlotte

✤ ✤ ✤

Chapter 24

❈ ❈ ❈

I had Granville put to bed in Perry's old room, and dear Henry offered to sleep on the daybed in the dressing room, in case he should call out in the night.

I went to my own bed, full of conflicting feeling. How lucky it was for Granville that I had been already at Queen Square. I could not wish him to die, now that he was here; how might I have felt, however, had I been unable to come to his rescue? How would it have been to wake at Aubyn Hall to a note informing me that I need never see my husband again? In what measure would relief have weighed against sorrow? I could not know.

The next morning Granville was much recovered, although too weak to rise. I went to him and he looked at me with a wretched smile, like a little boy fallen from a tree he had been forbidden to climb.

"I am very grateful to you, Lottie," he said. "You are too good."

"I did only what anyone would. I would not leave any man to bleed if I might carry him to safety."

He looked even sorrier then, but I could not summon any softness for him. I called for the doctor, instead. Let him be soft in my place.

I stayed throughout the doctor's visit. There had been an accident, I explained, when my husband went to enquire how Mr Webber did. I looked hard at Granville when I said the word "accident," but he only nodded.

"I mean to visit them tomorrow, to express our thanks," I said.

Granville's face twitched, but he did not speak out against it.

"You should indeed," the doctor said. "The dressing they applied to the wound was most thoroughly done. It almost certainly saved Mr Dryer's life."

I noted the glower that crossed Granville's face.

"I will be sure to tell them so," I said.

THE NEXT AFTERNOON, I returned to Queen Square with Arthur warm in my arms, his fat hands tangling in the fringe of the shawl that I had pulled from my shoulders to wrap him in. I knocked upon the door of my own house, Henry beside me, and when Bede came to admit me, I pulled back a corner of the shawl to show Arthur's pink-cheeked face.

"I mean to keep him, Bede," I said. "He is the child of a friend fallen on hard times. We shall keep him and raise him a gentleman."

Bede, being a butler of the first class, did not even show surprise.

"It will be a great pleasure to serve the young master," he said.

If only Granville would be so easy! I knew I should have to fight him over it and I was ready to do so. I wanted Arthur as much as I had ever wanted anything. I did not care a bit who his mother had been; perhaps I should have, but I did not. I would be his mother now.

I could not help but be fearful, however. The house had been signed into my name, but it was Granville's money that we lived upon. My husband's recent attentions had not been entirely unwelcome—it was his good will that allowed me to live so freely in my mama's house. He could make matters very difficult for all of us, if he so chose.

I left Arthur kicking his little legs on the hearthrug, under Henry's watchful eye. Then I took a deep breath and went up to Granville. I stood for a moment to gather my courage. I made myself stand very straight. I knocked gently upon the bedroom door. There was no reply. Slowly, I turned the handle and opened the door a crack. Granville was sprawled across the bed as though he had tried to rise and fallen back. His face shone with perspiration, the skin a bloodless white. His mouth hung open and his breath came loudly.

It sounds foolish now, but for a moment I thought, *He has done this to punish me for bringing Arthur home.* Then I came to my senses and cried out for Bede, for Henry, for a doctor.

AND SO I HAVE MADE a new household and all in it is different, though many of the players stay the same. We are told that Granville has taken blood poisoning. He lies feverish in Perry's old room, and all of us about him wait for an improvement or a decline.

I could not think what else to do but have The Ridings shut up and summon Mrs Bell to play nurse. There is still no love lost between us, but I could not think of anyone preferable. She takes no interest in the running of the house, though we are not so organised yet as one might hope. When I told her that I have learnt the keeping of the accounts—which is not so very difficult, after all, with Bede beside me—she said only, "As I am sure you should, madam," and sounded sincere.

She stays always in Granville's room and treats him most tenderly; mopping his brow and trying everything she can to tempt him to drink broth. It is all he is allowed, of course, being taken with fever. The doctor comes almost daily to bleed the poison from him, and Mrs Bell engages him in conversation, as much as he will allow her. She will even talk to me, given the opportunity. She tells me of every rise or fall of Granville's appetite, every turn of his fever, every movement he passes, and all in hushed and serious tones. She has never spoken to me so much before. I think she is almost happy, now that she is nurse to him again.

Sometimes he seems to rally and we all think he will recover, and then he seems again to sink and will hardly wake for days. When he is strong enough I go to him, and sometimes take Arthur with me. I have explained to Granville, several times, that I mean to raise the child he got on his mistress. Sometimes I think he understands and sometimes I am not sure. He is not strong enough, in any case, to quarrel with me.

Henry, I have here as footman. I have told him that I would consider releasing him from service, setting myself up as guardian to him, perhaps. I offered him the opportunity to go to school, if he wished it, though he is fifteen already. He replied that he preferred to earn a wage, and to be his own man. He sees nothing to be ashamed of in the life of a footman. I suppose that when one comes from a family of farmhands, as Henry does, it is a rise in the world. I can see that he admires Bede; he watches him as carefully as he used to watch Ruth when she sparred. On his half-day he goes to visit the Webbers, so he has not given up his training entirely.

I have given up mine, however; I could not risk dashing my hopes of carrying this child. I am determined that no one, not even George Bowden, should ever know of its real begetting. I try not to think too much upon what to do, if Granville recovers and doubts my fidelity. Perhaps I might tell him that he lay with me in his fever. It is a revolting notion, but it is all I can think of. He can hardly disprove it; he does not know where he is, half the time.

I have been decorating the house. I had always imagined that if I had my own house I should want some of Mama's things, from Aubyn Hall. This house is so full of her already, however, that I haven't felt I need to. Instead I work to clean and brighten what is here. I think of what Mama would have liked, and, which is more delicious, what I should like.

I daily walk out into the wide lawns of Queen Square, and when Arthur is bigger he shall run under the trees there, perhaps with a little dog. We breathe the scent of working Bristol, though I still have fresh flowers brought into the house, for Mama. She would not have liked the smell of the river to be a welcome guest.

The other ladies of the square have begun to call upon me, although thankfully not too often. Granville serves as my excuse. I think, in time, I shall come to like one or two of them; one lady in particular, Mrs Grieves, very young and merry, despite her name. She came to call and found herself sitting beside the cushion I embroidered all that time ago, depicting Mrs Webber, standing ready at scratch. She picked it up and admired it.

"Oh, I do think this fine, Mrs Dryer. Is it your own work?"

"Why, yes," I said, "but I do not believe it very accomplished. The pose, you know, is all wrong. She has left her face quite unguarded."

At that Mrs Grieves laughed so heartily that I added, "Some brute will knock her teeth from her mouth, if she does not take care."

She shook her head and declared me great fun. I have not often been called fun. Perhaps, next time she calls, I will show her the piece depicting three hooded rogues, walking at night down a country lane. It is nearly completed.

I think, once my baby is safely arrived, I shall buy a horse and ask Mrs Grieves if she might care to ride out with me. I shall ride, with or without a companion. I will buy myself a soft-eyed mare and guard her with my life.

I have heard of a newly arrived family with six young daughters and two of them pox-marked. I think I shall call upon them as soon as they are settled. I hope I can be of service to those little girls.

Arthur is my joy. That woman is gone and she has left me a wondrous gift. I may have saved him from a life of the most terrible sin, and he, in turn, has rescued me from a slow and dreary death. Perhaps, in choosing him, I have made him more mine than anything has been my life long, though I did not bear him. I spend hours in his nursery, although I am sure that his nurse would rather I did not. I have found for him the plumpest, most kindly wet-nurse I could, but I am jealous of every moment that she has him. I cannot help it. I plan that if Granville recovers he should teach Arthur trade, and to be a good man. I hope he will be a good man, with none of his mother in him.

Perry has regained some of his strength. He is certainly drinking less liquor. I don't imagine that he will ever give it up entirely, but I have it on good authority—Granville's word, and Fisher's—that Perry has not been really drunk since I left Aubyn, after he learnt of George's betrayal. He is bent on finding him. I don't know what use it could be, nor how likely he is to succeed. He has ceased to suffer my company, in any case. I have called upon him once or twice and found him quite as determined to offend me as he ever was. Sometimes I have returned his insults, but he is still so diminished and his weaknesses so apparent that I feel cruel and leave off long before he would have had done, had our positions been reversed.

I put my hand upon my belly and feel the round push of it, firm and alive. I feel this one waiting to come home. I hope my child can feel my hand, this early caress. I hope she is a little girl, and that I can name her Louisa. I think perhaps Louisa Ruth. I hope so much to be delivered of her safely. Although it is still early, I imagine that I can feel her there, the secret curve of her body beneath my skin. I think, *She is not sleeping; she is waiting with her eyes open in the dark*. I think she will be a fighter, and never lie down for anyone else to tread upon her. I hope for so much for her. In so many ways now, I hope.

Chapter 25

✤ ✤ ✤

The house is changed. Sometimes one of the misses will come knocking in search of work, or one of the old cullies will come in search of a miss. It's as good as a play to see the look on their mugs when they spy how plain the place is done out now. We sold all that was left behind and bought instead the kind of solid, simple things we had at the cottage. There isn't a silk hanging or a fringed lamp in the whole of the house. The parlour has a rag-rug in front of the hearth and an old teakettle on the mantel, though I've put up the portrait of the little girl, and Mrs Dryer let me have the picture from the cottage, of the little boy and girl beside the stream. She sent for it to be brought, and when Old Pious—who I'd better call Mr Horton, now—when he brought it he came in and had a cup of beer, and said he was glad to see me made well.

The bench where the misses sat to be looked over has gone from the hall, and the walls are fresh whitewash. Callers can see they won't find what they look for without my saying a word. It ain't a convent any longer, but the Webber's Boxing Academy. I mean to have a brass plate made for the front door, spelling it out.

When the first of the little nobby lads came calling, I'd no idea where he'd sprung from. I opened the door to find a blubber-cheeked boy in a fine coat and good boots, asking me if he could come for lessons. I near sent him running before he showed me his shilling. Now it's plain enough—

Mrs Dryer's been talking us up all over Bristol. Prize-fighting is the height of fashion amongst the gentry, I'm told, and the sons of swells must study it along with their fencing and their Latin. I'd warrant we've boys from every family Mrs Dryer knows coming to us, and they tell their friends and so it goes. It's a sham of prize-fighting they come to learn, for they mustn't be injured much, but we show them the science of it and they pay good coin for the pleasure.

Even with the young gentry we've not as much money as we could wish, just yet. I think it may come in time and if it never does, well, we know well enough how to get by, Tom, Jacky, and I.

Jacky sleeps in the garret still, though we can't seem to scrub the stink from it, no matter what we use. There are plenty of other rooms now the misses are gone, but he's a queer little cull, and Tom and I don't argue it. He's still pale as death, still creeps about and peers around corners, but sometimes now he whistles as he goes. In any case, we've grown used to him. At first Tom and I thought to teach him to box, and he tried, poor lad, to please us. He stood at the dummy and fibbed at it with the same dogged little swing he'd shown his father, trying not to flinch when the dummy swung back at him. It wasn't till I marked how gratefully he came away afterward that I thought to ask him how he liked it. He just looked at me in his queer way and wouldn't reply.

"Tell you what, Jack," I said then, "there's pugs enough in this house, I'd warrant."

He looked frit then, so I added, "Far more welcome is a useful boy, who helps about the place in other ways."

He gave me one of his cutty-eyed glances. I nodded.

"I can be of use," he said. "I can help, if you'll keep me."

"I know it, you're a good lad," I said. "We're glad to have you, Tom and I."

Jacky came over all queer then, I thought he was like to weep. None of us were much used to praise, growing up in that house. I'd have patted his head, but he looked ready to piss his breeches already.

To calm him, I said, "Well then, get us the tea before we all starve," and set him to work.

As it happens, he's of more use than I'd ever have thought. He cleans the place and opens the door to the lads who come for lessons. He's learning how to cook and making a fair show of it. We feed the boys a tea when once they've had their lesson—we charge for it, of course. Jacky's learning to boil a good pudding, with raisins and sugar, when I can get them. We sit all together around the big kitchen table, just as we used to. The boys are near as noisy as the misses used to be, though their jokes ain't so bawdy.

Jacky doesn't seem to miss the babber. He likes to talk about what a gent it'll be when it gets big.

"He won't ever know he's my brother, will he?" he said, once.

I told him no, likely not.

He nodded as though he knew it.

Tom said, "He ain't your brother, Jack. He's Mrs Dryer's now, and you're ours."

I suppose he is ours now.

Tom never complains about his eye, but he carries himself carefully, and he'd always rather have me spar with the lads than do it himself. He'll set-to in play with Henry or me, because he can trust us not to swing wild and hit him in it. I think it still hurts him, though he won't say it. He has a leather patch and I'm used to the look of it now, even if he ain't.

He sets himself to teach the lads cheerfully and is as careful over them as an old hen, always fretting they'll injure themselves.

"Mind yourselves, boys, or you'll end up like me," he says, and lifts his patch to make them squeal.

I've begun sparring again, now my hand is healed. Not long ago a cull from The Hatchet came to ask when we'd be back in the ring. Tom swears home he never will, though I won't be surprised if he changes his mind someday. For myself, I expect I'll walk back up to scratch before too long. It's in the blood and in the fists. I can stand up against any man, but not against my own nature. Sparring in the yard won't do forever. I'll want to see blood spilled and feel the old fire in my limbs.

I never forget that though Dora's gone, she might still turn up and want her sons and her place here. I don't know what I'll do if that day comes. Today we're safe enough, and there's the smell of meat stewing—Jacky's work—and the sound of one of the lads fibbing at the dummy in the yard. We're as close to respectable as I ever hoped to get, perhaps as close as I'd like to be. I don't look to the future more than I can help. You never can be sure what will come, in a house like ours.

Epilogue: George

So low had I sunk when I arrived at the debtor's prison at Bristol, that the place seemed to me a veritable haven compared to the tiny cell at Plymouth and the jolting cart. More than anything, the cell I was put into reminded me of school: the iron bedstead, lime-washed walls, and narrow window, with the initials of departed tenants scratched into the sill, all of it might have come from Mr Allen's. It wanted only a couple of trunks at the foot of the bed and a house-master scolding me to wash my neck. I crawled into the bed and slept better than I had done even before leaving Aubyn. I had no dreams at all.

The novelty did not take long to fall away. The days were so dreary as to be unbearable. I was permitted to leave my cell, but there was nothing to do in that place, without money. Some of the men and women stumbling about the yard were so grey and thin that it frightened me to look at them. Worse was to look down and see my own dusty boots and know myself one of them. I found myself amongst the poorest of the prisoners, the ones who could not afford any type of luxury or diversion. For the right sum, the guards took pleasure in telling me, a prisoner could have all manner of things to increase his comfort: cushions, food, wine, a visit from his mistress. Of course, I tried to obtain a little credit that I might gamble with, from some of the prisoners with flush pockets. Their laughter drove me quite to fury. No one in that place would extend me a penny, or, at least, no one to whom I could bear to be indebted. I could not even afford a book to read, and all the while, every bite I ate was added to my bill and so increased my debt. I could not hope to get out. The rest of the time I was all alone, in that God-forsaken room.

At last I sold my clothes to the guard, every stitch I owned, and had him bring me a suit of homespun. With the money left over I bought paper, pen, and ink, and sent pitiful letters to my family, begging for assistance. I received not a word in reply. At last I gave up and took to writing out the story of my life. I found I could not keep to the truth, however, and instead my pen spilled out events as I wished they had been. Sometimes I had married Charlotte, sometimes won the country estate from Mr Dewsbury. Sometimes I had escaped to the sugar islands, strangled Dora with my bare hands, and buried her on my plantation. I never wrote of Perry. I tried not to think of him at all. I diluted the ink to make it go further and when I had filled a paper I turned it and wrote upon it cross-wise. At last, however, the ink was run out, and I could not pretend it was otherwise. I had nothing left to sell but the suit of homespun, and the nights were too cold for that.

I took to reading what I had written, although sometimes I found myself weeping as I read it. When I had read it all, I took it up and read it again, and again. I had nothing else. I began seriously to consider that it might be preferable to die, but I was too cowardly for it. I sometimes planned, at night, to starve myself to death, but could not last more than an hour when the breakfast tray was pushed through the door. I tried, once, to slice my wrists open with the nib of the pen, but it was far more painful than I had imagined it. I brought out only a bead of blood before I gasped and gave up. I sat and squeezed at my arm, and watched it trickle and run. I took up the pen and dipped the nib. I put it to the paper and wrote a single crimson word: *Perry*.

I did not know how many days later it was that the guard came at an unexpected hour. I did not know how long I had been imprisoned, only that it was long enough that my heart jolted when the bolts scraped back when they should not. I felt myself cower from the opening of the door.

"Well," a familiar voice said, "is this cringing thing what I have paid a fortune for?"

I looked up at Perry. He looked as weary as I felt. He was thinner than I'd ever seen him; his skin was ashen.

"Ain't you fortunate, Mr Bowden?" the guard said. "This gent's paid all your debts. You'll have a job to repay him. Be working your whole life over that, I'd wager."

Author's Note

The Fair Fight is a work of fiction, but female boxers certainly existed in the eighteenth and nineteenth centuries. They were often seen as a novelty act, as opposed to the serious sport between gentlemen. Women did fight men, just as Ruth does, although they more often fought each other. They fought doubles matches too—most famously, James and Elizabeth Stokes took on other male-female teams in the 1720s and 1730s. This was a brutal age when bear-baiting and cock-fighting were common forms of entertainment, and prizefighting went along with that.

Interestingly, as regards Charlotte, there was a woman, Lady Barrymore, nicknamed the "Boxing Baroness," who sparred and posed in boxing costume for the amusement of her husband in the 1820s.

Ruth's fight at the fair and Tom's championship fight are both composites, drawn from reports of several real eighteenth-century boxing matches.

Jem Belcher was a real man, who became champion of England in 1800, although his fight was against Jack Bartholomew. In 1803, after he lost an eye in a game of racquetball, Belcher was forced to retire from the ring.

Daniel Mendoza was also a real-life champion; he invented the move called the Jew's stop. He was jailed several times for debts and fraud.

I've tried to make the use of historical figures and the culture of prizefighting in The Fair Fight as accurate as possible, although I may have gotten things wrong here and there in my use of real-life boxing history.

The descriptions of Charlotte's sporting papers—and some aspects of Tom's prizefight—are drawn from the book *Strange Encounters: Tales of Famous Fights and Fighters* by James Brady (Hutchinson, 1946).

Broken entails like the one on Aubyn Hall were unusual, but they did happen. The legal breaking of an entail required that the owner and the next heir formally agree that it should be broken. In my head, I imagine that this took place between Perry's father and grandfather.

Aubyn Hall and The Ridings are both fictions, but the gatehouse at The Ridings and the long drive through fields are inspired by the gatehouse and drive at the Bath Spa University campus, at Newton Park in Wiltshire.

The Hatchet Inn still stands in Bristol city center, behind the Hippodrome; its boxing ring is now paved over.

Acknowledgments

I'd like to thank my wonderful agents at Tibor Jones, especially Sophie Hignett and James Pusey, for believing in the book and for their astute editing ideas.

I'm also grateful to Arzu Tahsin at Weidenfeld & Nicolson, and Sarah McGrath at Riverhead, for being such insightful and patient editors. You've made the book a stronger, sleeker beast.

I owe my parents eternal gratitude (yes, yes, and obedience) for their emotional and financial support, and for the interest they've taken in the development of the novel and the workings of my brain.

I wrote this novel as part of my MA at Manchester Metropolitan University. Thanks are due to everyone on the course, especially Jackie Roy, who supervised my dissertation, and my writing buddy Karin Hala, who, sadly, died last year. You are missed.

This novel came to be published largely because it was chosen as the winner of the Tibor Jones Pageturner Prize. Hence, I am hugely grateful to Kevin Conroy Scott and Landa Acevedo-Scott at Tibor Jones, and to the judges of the competition: Jasper Sutcliffe at Foyles, Roy Butlin at Herne Hill Books, Sophie Lambert at Conville & Walsh, and Evie Wyld.

I'd like to thank my sister Sarah for her thoughtful suggestions—especially for a major structural change—and her eagle-eyed proofreading, and my sister Debbie for her enthusiasm and support.

Acknowledgments

I owe thanks to Amy Underdown, for her suggestions, for all the time she spent listening to me, and for loving Ruth and Charlotte as much as I do.

Thanks to Jessica Winkler for always being sure that everything I do will be brilliant and never budging, no matter how much I argue that it might all go wrong.

Thanks also to James Davey, for helping me with some aspects of the experience of fighting that wouldn't have occurred to me.

I'd like to thank Ami-Jade McCarthy for her support during the novel's early stages, when my confidence needed careful handling.

I'd also like to thank all my creative writing colleagues at Bath Spa University for their teaching and continued support.

Thank you to Jamie Harrison, for being willing to discuss punctuation with me, over and over again.

Thanks to Ella Heeks, for listening, and all the animals.

I am also grateful to Jess Gulliver, Sophie Buchan, at Weidenfeld & Nicolson, and Sarah Stein at Riverhead.

Huge thanks to Sara Ford and all the management at The Hatchet Inn, where I worked for years, for their flexibility and support during the writing of the book.

Thanks are also due to all the helpful staff in the reference section at Bristol Library.